# Killing Shadows

## by

## Nikki Frank

## Dedication

For Richard, Brewer, and Briley
Thanks for being your own brand of weird.

Chapter 1

A steady drip followed by a moist spatter against brick raised the hair on the back of Greyson's neck. He stuffed the key to the pub in his pocket and kept his eyes off the shadows. The early October night, dry and clear, enveloped London. If he chose to squint between the buildings, he might even catch the singular wink of a star strong enough to battle London's light pollution. But he didn't. Greyson never glanced around once night closed in.

He stuck to the sidewalk and main street, even though the alleys would have been a faster way back to his flat. Thin though it was, the possibility the splattering came from a leaky pipe or something else mundane always existed, and Greyson clung to this. To his dismay, the dripping followed him. Crossing his fingers and hoping hadn't saved him.

Above him, some unseen thing squelched, slipped, and plopped. A moment later, an eyeball the size of a softball dangled in front of him. The pupil blurred in a frantic spin while the eye sagged on slippery ropes of tendon as thick as his arm. He gagged and flinched away from the gruesome sight.

Ducking around the eyeball, he kept his gaze forward and his steps purposeful. For the whole twenty years of his life, Greyson possessed the unwelcome gift of witnessing things other people couldn't perceive.

1

Every shadow potentially held some oozing monstrosity. Every door could open to the lair of a ghost.

The creatures had never attacked him, and it was the rare occasion when he witnessed the entities make contact with humans. Whether a blessing or a curse, the poor souls never noticed the organism they carried, sometimes on their heads, shoulders, or backs.

Greyson spent years honing the tactic of feigned ignorance. He acted like every other human—like he couldn't see the horrors inhabiting the shadows—a much easier task during the day. In daylight, shadows were thinner, and one had to go looking for dark places. But he couldn't both hold a job and attend university during the day.

So night became a routine plague, locking up when the pub closed and ignoring everything on the walk home. Decompressing involved a hot shower to scrub away the grimy sensation clinging to him and a stiff drink to dull the visions staining his brain. Tonight wasn't any different, and Greyson couldn't foresee any night in the future that would be.

Once he'd suitably relaxed, he climbed into bed, pulled up social media on his phone, and started scrolling through his friends' feeds. Two of his male friends were screwing around in the park tonight, posting pictures of their escapades. Part of him wanted to be there with them. They'd invited him, but he couldn't face the shadows and the creatures hidden within.

He'd been claiming a need to study or suggesting his friends hang out somewhere well-lit for years. Most of the time, they indulged him, but sometimes the night called. Oh, to be so unaware. They got on him for being a bore from time to time, but he could live with a bit of teasing because they meant nothing by it.

Better their good-natured ribbing than the label of "nutter" he wore all the way through secondary school. As if seeing this stuff wasn't bad enough, kids had to be cruel on top of everything. The worst part was that he'd only mentioned seeing the creatures once at school, way back when he was seven, but the label stuck for a decade. He'd met his current friends at university after choosing a school well away from where he grew up.

Greyson commented on a couple of their posts and then rechecked his feed. Whitley had added new pictures. His finger froze while a war raged in his brain. Why torture himself? They were ancient history.

He clicked the link anyway.

Whitley smiled at him, looking like a sun-kissed angel. Some tropical beach provided the backdrop for her bikini-clad picture, and frolicking in the background was the git she'd left him for.

Never mind. He tossed the phone to the other side of his bed and pulled his laptop off the night table. He'd watch a comedy before sleep. The nightmares that infected the dark spaces in his building seemed to stay farther away from his flat the happier he was. Thanks to some sketch comedy, he'd sleep all right tonight.

****

Fall wind blew Adriel's hair, tousling it and ruffling the feathers of his wings. Fanning their blinding-white expanses, he skimmed from stripe to stripe, treating the crosswalk like the stones in a stream, each foot brushing the paint.

Around him, Seattle went about its business, unaware of the angel in their midst. He'd worked unseen amongst humans for thousands of years, and such indifference wasn't new. Their inability to register his presence was a simple fact.

Other angels might find his choice to spend his vacation in the same place he worked odd, but humanity fascinated him, for example, the stripes on the crosswalk. Why make a space for the expedient and safe passage of foot traffic look like a game or challenge? Anything that invited dawdling in the road put people at risk, especially children. They seemed predisposed to distraction even when it imperiled them.

Not that he needed safe passage across traffic. Everything about human life slid past him, so he put nothing more than a ripple in their experience. He could throw himself on the windshield of a car like a splattered bug, and the driver would see nothing. He didn't, though. On occasion, a human would get a passing sensation of an angel the way a person might consider the air around them if a gust of wind caught their attention. In a car, that might be enough to cause a wreck. The last thing Adriel wanted was to cause unnecessary deaths.

Tires screeched, and Adriel peered up, expecting to witness a collision. Instead, he locked eyes with the driver of a car as he slid, untouched, along its side. Panic covered the driver's face, a young lady, perhaps in her late teens.

Strange, but he shrugged the anomaly off and landed on the sidewalk.

"What were you thinking?" A female voice snapped behind him.

He spun, wings splaying in alarm. Her glare stayed locked on Adriel. She was talking to *him*. He fell back a step, her gaze piercing him. "I…um…"

"I almost hit you. Why would you cross on my green

light?"

He scanned the traffic. "I think others are upset with you."

"Are you all right?" She eyed him, ignoring the blaring horns of disgruntled drivers. Despite the glare, her lips quivered, and her chin trembled.

This woman was concerned for *his* safety. He cocked his head, an idea forming. No laws said he couldn't interact with her.

The young woman crossed her arms over her chest and stepped backward toward her vehicle. "Um, okay, then. Right. If you're good." She scurried around to the driver's side and drove her car away, freeing the flow of traffic plugged behind her when she left.

Adriel's gaze stayed on her vehicle until she rounded a corner and disappeared. He hadn't managed to put his new idea into words and pose it to her. Now, both she and the moment were gone.

No matter. Divine knowledge told him he'd made contact with Felicity Landon. The same knowledge would allow him to find her again. If he wanted his idea to play out, he would need to approach her with respect and enough time to process.

He oriented himself according to the divine knowledge and disappeared, reappearing outside the building she lived in. From here, he would wait for her to return home. If she'd calmed down enough, he'd introduce himself.

Adriel's blaze of insight on the street stemmed from the unprecedented coincidence of a human seeing him while he was on vacation. He could amuse himself the way he always did. Or, if she were willing, he could experience something unique—a conversation with a human. If he got lucky, she might even spend a bit of time with him, explaining the subtleties of the human experience that eluded him. If all went well, this might turn out to be the best vacation ever.

After several hours, Adriel gave up for the night. She hadn't come to the front door of the building. Through the glass, he'd observed the elevator running without anyone entering from the street. The building must have an entrance from another location.

He toyed with the idea of waiting outside her apartment, but social conventions on lurking didn't seem all that different for humans and angels. He'd come off creepy if he hung around her personal spaces, and he didn't want to unsettle her any more than he already had.

One of the clubs downtown had standup comedy tonight. Adriel enjoyed such acts. Humans had amazing resilience, and laughing at issues in their lives was a brilliant coping skill. He learned so much about their lives by watching. Besides, a good laugh was difficult to come by in his line of work.

Adriel cast one last glance at Felicity's building, vowing to return the next morning and try again. If he got there before she went about her day, he could check for additional exits so he wouldn't miss her. Then he just had to wait for the right moment.

****

Felicity slapped her alarm, seeking the relief of the snooze button. She'd already shut off her phone. The clock was backup, motivating her to get out of bed when her cell wasn't persuasive enough, but it made her resent the hour even more. September and back to school were gone. The novelty had worn off, and almost two months stretched out before the reprieve of Thanksgiving weekend.

She hauled herself out from under her warm covers and groaned at the grogginess clinging to her like a weighted blanket. This morning sucked worse than usual due to the nightmares afflicting her all night long. Over and over, she failed to stop in time, hitting the young man who'd been acting like a complete dipwad, dinking around in the middle of the road. As her dad always said, he was a "Finalist for the Darwin Awards."

At least she managed to avoid him during the real incident. Though how remained vague in her memory. Fragmented pieces of stopping to get out and check on him remained, along with impressions of horns, swearing from other drivers, and the warm air swirling around them—something gross venting from below the street, most likely.

The man himself hadn't faded. He had silver hair, not white or old-people gray, but metallic silver. This drooped across his forehead toward teal eyes, making for a striking appearance that stuck out in her mind.

She hadn't mentioned the event when she told her parents how her afternoon in Seattle went. At the start of the school year, they'd been reluctant to let her drive in the congested city, but the car was a necessity for getting to her Running Start classes.

Today, her classes started at the high school. Felicity stuffed her lunch in her backpack, grabbed a banana for breakfast, and locked the apartment behind her. Four floors down, she headed for the bus stop, where she waited in the dark, peeling her fruit.

The hairs on the back of her neck prickled, standing up, followed by goosebumps all over. Felicity stared at the traffic passing her building. Somewhere behind her lurked something she did *not* want to witness. For her entire life, she'd seen things she couldn't define—ghosts, spirits—otherworldly entities. Some were no big deal. They looked like smokey, semi-transparent people. But others...

A huge shiver almost caused her to drop her banana. Horrifying things lurked in the darkest, dankest places. Searching for the source of her discomfort never ended well, so she stopped peeking years ago.

In opposition to the morning's otherwise stiff October breeze, a warm draft blew past her, shifting the nature of the sensations around her. A distinct feeling of being watched settled over her, very different from the crawly sensation the lurking creatures called up but unsettling all the same.

After the doors to the bus shut and her apartment grew distant, Felicity's muscles unclenched. With an eased mind, she focused on a benign subject—Homecoming. She still needed a date and didn't have anyone in mind. Her last relationship imploded at the start of the summer.

She could ask Jake if they could go as friends. No. Jake and Kristin were planning on going together. Now, there was a pair that raised her skepticism. But if it worked for them...

She drummed her fingers on her opposite arm so she wouldn't disturb the person in front of her by tapping the seat. This topic made a good distraction. Who should she take? Going by herself would suck because she wanted to dance. Wade, in her English Lit class at the college, had potential. She could get him a pass to go as her date if he was under twenty-one. Her nerves zipped. Did she even have the guts to ask a college guy to go back to high school for a dance? Judging by the squirming in her stomach at the thought, maybe not so much.

Reaching up, she yanked the cord for her stop. She had English Lit this afternoon. Wade was pretty damn cute. Maybe if she saw him, it would give her the courage.

The bus pulled to a stop, and she grabbed her bag, working her way off. Outside, the feeling of being watched, all warm and weird, persisted as potent as at home. Too bad she wasn't old enough to have hot flashes. Without a mundane explanation like women's issues, her imagination would cook up cringy images of what sort of creature brought in this new atmosphere.

"Flick."

At the call of her nickname, she spun. Flick's friends wove through the morning rush to greet her. Marisol waved. Jake followed along in her wake. Flick's pent-up tension melted away with the promise of company and distraction.

"You'll never guess what happened this weekend," Marisol gasped, reaching Flick.

"Is that an invitation to try?" Flick winked. "Your latest video went viral, but unfortunately, it features you running and screaming from a bug like a big dork."

Jake chuckled. "Let's see… You brought home a guy, but your parents refuse to let you date him because he's fourteen. We all know the best you can do is an eighth grader."

"Just stop, you two." Marisol made a face at her, then Jake. "I talked my parents into letting me have a Halloween party this year…mocktails, dancing, and everything." She beamed at Flick. "Next weekend, we're costume shopping."

"I'm not dressing up," Jake said.

"Who said you were invited?" Marisol teased. The joking dissolved, and she added, "You *are* dressing up. You can come with Flick and me. But you'll look dumb if everyone else is wearing a costume."

"*I'll* look dumb if *I'm* wearing a costume," he muttered.

Flick laced her arm through his. "Do something easy. Buy fangs or points for your ears and go as a vampire or an elf in normal clothes. But you know Marisol's going to make this harder on you if you resist. She's been trying to get her parents to say yes to this party since middle school." Flick cocked her head. "What made them change their mind after asking like seven years running?"

"College," Marisol answered. "Ever since Matt left for college last month and I started turning in applications, Mom and Dad have been freaking out. But I intend to cash in. If I can find a student DJ, they might even let me hire someone. They're determined to make the last year of the last child at home count."

Outside the school, an odd heat like she had experienced at the bus stop had replaced the usual eeriness of infested pre-dawn shadows. This warmth followed her inside, giving the transition an unsettling sameness. What the hell was going on?

This year, sensations of a deeper heat had occurred upon entering the building more than once—a first in her high school career. She'd assumed the HVAC system was cranked up on high for whatever reason. But today, everything was off.

Against her better judgment, she took a quick peek around. If ghosts now inhabited her school, she might have to take all her credits at the community college next term. She'd felt only the usual creepiness there. But nothing prepared her for the flash of a curious face, the owner of which sported silver hair and stared straight at her.

What was the guy from yesterday doing in her school? Was he new staff this year? Flick craned around Jake to get a better view, but the man had vanished.

"Looking for someone?" Jake asked her, extracting his arm from her grip.

"Have you seen a guy with silver hair and teal eyes this morning?"

"Outside an anime?" Marisol giggled. "No."

"I swear, a guy matching that description stood right over there, staring at me." Flick pointed. "The weirdest part is, driving around downtown yesterday, I came close to hitting that same guy."

"You're sure it's the *same* guy?" Marisol asked. "What are the odds you nearly hit a guy, and he ends up in your school twenty-four hours later?"

"How many guys with that description could be running around? Anyway, he was playing in the street like an idiot, and I had to slam on my breaks. And I have no idea how, but I managed to miss him. I even stopped to check if he was okay. He stared at me like I'd dropped out of space and started speaking Martian."

"PTDS," Jake proclaimed. "You were probably traumatized by the close call, and your mind is screwing with the details."

"It's PT*SD*, doofus," Marisol scolded. "But Jake might be half right. If you're still bothered by what happened yesterday, maybe your mind is playing tricks on you."

Flick sighed. "Maybe you're right. I did have nightmares last night."

Marisol patted her arm just as the bell rang. "We've got to get to class. Hang in there. I'll buy you a chocolate bar if you're still off your game at lunch."

****

Adriel studied students hurrying about their business. Going to school wasn't a pastime he'd ever considered. Sure, work took him onto a campus from time to time, but like playing in traffic, no one noticed him at school. He brushed past and skimmed over people the way a paper might slide through the crack in a door—there, but not substantial enough to matter.

But when Felicity stared straight at him in the hall before school, Adriel got the confirmation he needed. Yesterday wasn't a fluke or a one-off. She *saw* him. She'd been twitchy all morning, so he hung back, unsure how to start an interaction.

Felicity entered the bathroom between second and third periods—no need to follow her there. Adriel might lack finesse in communicating with humans, but even he knew you didn't corner strangers in the restroom.

The way the building was laid out, the ladies' room sat right on the edge of a corridor connecting the two main halls. Adriel tucked himself around the corner of this, where he could watch the ladies' room door but not be seen by Felicity when she came back out.

A hand came down on his shoulder, and Adriel spun, his wing feathers brushing the heads of two girls walking down the corridor. They glanced at him, but when they turned to look at one another, the recognition faded from their eyes, and the instance slipped their minds.

Adriel spun to stare at the owner of the hand and

found himself face-to-face with Felicity, hands on her hips, frown drawing her brows together.

"What the hell?" she snapped. "Are you stalking me? In the bathroom even?" Her eyes narrowed. "Who and what are you?"

"I'm not stalking." After pausing, he added, "I've been waiting for an opportunity to meet you." He glanced in confusion at the door to the ladies' room. "How did I miss you?"

"Not telling." Felicity crossed her arms. "You didn't answer the most important questions. Who and what are you?"

Adriel met her gaze while mulling over the best approach. He needed to find out how much she knew. "My name is Adriel. Why would you ask what I am?"

She held her silence a moment while a younger boy passed them, then hissed. "Because no one else sees you. You're not human, or at least not living. Though, I've never had any of the other spirits look so solid or act so alive, let alone talk to me."

Adriel's head twitched back. "Other spirits? Wait. What do you see when you look at me?"

She rolled her eyes. "You suck at answering questions." The warning bell rang. "Crap. I've gotta go."

"I'll come, too." Adriel followed her into the flow of student traffic. "I'd like to talk to you more."

"I'm not having conversations with invisible people," she murmured. "Everyone will think I'm nuts."

"Write your answers on paper then," Adriel suggested. "Or skip class. I have a feeling this is important."

"Right." She huffed.

Since she hadn't said no, he followed her into her

class. He might not have a physical form other humans noticed, but he still needed a chair if he wanted to sit. Felicity sat near the wall, making it easy to arrange himself beside her. Adriel found a chair and carried it over, the seat disappearing from human view once in contact with him. She didn't comment on this despite watching him. The methods Heaven used to conceal angelic activity on Earth from humans didn't affect her. Interesting.

Felicity must have been in a receptive mood because she laid a spiral notebook on her desk, open to a blank page. She held the end of a pen between her teeth.

A second later, she wrote, *I see a guy who ought to be in college, not high school. You've got silver hair and teal eyes. You're wearing fitted gray athletic pants and a mint green t-shirt with silver swirls. If you weren't dead, you'd be a normal-looking guy, aside from the hair and contacts.*

Adriel read the response a second, then a third time. "Seriously? That's all you see?" he asked.

*Were you hoping for more praise for your looks? I didn't know ghosts were vain.* She let out an audible gasp and covered her mouth with one hand. *Are you aware you're dead?*

Adriel laughed so hard the people near them scanned the room for the source. He smothered his mirth and whispered, "I'm well aware of my state of being, and I'm not dead. But thank you for the laugh. You mentioned earlier I might not be human. That's your answer."

Felicity shuddered, her expression tightening toward a frown. "What are you?" she whispered to her desk.

"An angel," he answered. "Speaking of other types of beings, what have you been seeing?"

*Disturbing things. Don't ask me here.* She drummed her pen against the pad of paper, then continued writing. *Are you really an angel? I thought they had wings. What if you're something else, and you're lying?*

"I have wings. Though, I'm not sure why you can't see them. I'll think on that. Do you mind if I stick around? I have a lot more I'd like to talk over with you."

She twisted her ponytail around her finger. *Most things I see don't go away because I wish they would.*

"Do you wish for me to go away?" he clarified.

*I guess it doesn't matter as long as you let me pay attention in class. Angel or not, at least you don't scare me the way some things I see do. But no more slinking around after me. That creeped me out.*

"You have my word," Adriel agreed.

Chapter 2

Kyrael hustled across an expanse of short grass, the warm blades caressing his bare feet. Above him soared the white marble walls of Gabriel's hall. Sun glinted off the polished stone, making him squint. Inside would be no better thanks to the seraph's own light. Gabriel's audience hours were over, but Kyrael's news couldn't wait.

After much reminding one another of favors owed, the task of interrupting a seraph fell to Kyrael. His nerves hummed, leaving him twitchy. None of the messengers wanted the unsavory job of delivering negative news. Angels who wasted the time of those in the highest choir often found themselves assigned unpleasant tasks. And no one ever knew which interruptions warranted such reassignments.

Kyrael pushed on the gleaming gate which led to Gabriel's courtyard. The messenger angel straightened his robe before entering the main building. He'd dressed in his heavenly best, hoping to appease the seraph.

Gabriel sat in the center of the expansive library filled with scrolls, books, tomes, pamphlets, and etchings, all six wings folded against his back in a feathery mass. Kyrael knocked at the doorframe, and Gabriel turned his gleaming face toward him.

The messenger fell to his knees, bowing his head to the floor in supplication. "I have a message from Earth,"

Kyrael said.

"I have audience hours again in three weeks." Gabriel's voice echoed off the marble walls. "If your message is urgent, please visit one of the other seraphim."

"I'm sorry. The consensus of the messengers was this news couldn't wait. And as the seraph most in touch with humanity and its events, they deemed you the appropriate one to receive the message." Kyrael let the cool of the marble floor take the heat from his head, built up by nerves.

"Present it."

Kyrael sighed onto the stone, keeping his face down to speak. "The death angel, Adriel, ran across a human capable of seeing angels while on his scheduled break. For some unknown reason, he engaged with this human. They are keeping company together. The human has been told of his true nature and…" His voice trailed away, replaced by tremors.

Gabriel wouldn't literally kill the messenger, but this wasn't good news, and the fallout could be unpleasant. Too bad he had traded duties with one of the guardian angels a decade ago. Angels were assigned a specific job for a reason, and if the seraphim caught wind of the trade, he might get punished. The other messengers held this over his head too often for his liking. One simple lapse in judgment left him in situations like this.

A rustle of robes and feathers preceded soft footfalls across stone. "Is this message complete?"

Kyrael shuddered. Gabriel had spoken from above him. "It's all the information we have at the moment."

Gabriel made a noise of impatience. "Stop quivering

like a lesser being. Occasional deviations from standard procedure, yours and now Adriel's, are natural."

Kyrael let out a groan, and Gabriel chuckled. The laugh rolled around the room, bouncing back at them. "Yes, Kyrael. I know about your trade in duties. Now stand and face me so we might converse on this matter."

Kyrael pushed himself to his feet, drawing courage before looking up at Gabriel's gleaming face. "Am I to be punished?"

Gabriel shook his head, eyes twinkling. "I believe your fellow messengers have punished you plenty. Or did you think it escaped the notice of the seraphim that the same angel has been delivering all the bad news for over a decade?"

"I didn't mean to question your knowledge." Kyrael bowed his head. "The seraphim are wise and just."

Gabriel waved at him to stop. "I don't need flattery. No one crossed boundaries in their conduct. But I have a question, and I want your honest answer, not the one you think I should hear."

Kyrael drew a deep breath. "All right."

"Are you still curious about work outside your duties as a messenger?" Gabriel asked.

"Yes." Kyrael's focus stayed glued to the floor. God had bestowed a task on him. Saying he wished for something different sounded ungrateful, or insubordinate, or disrespectful.

Gabriel sighed. "Sometimes angels outgrow their original assignment. If this is the case, I can find a more fitting job for you. Don't berate yourself for personal change."

"How did you know?" Kyrael chanced a peek at the seraph.

"You learn things after a few eons. Do you know where you'd like to be reassigned, or do you wish me to choose for you?"

"You'd let *me* choose?"

"Within reason."

Kyrael quivered. "I've never thought about what I would do if I weren't a messenger. I'm not that bold."

Gabriel placed a hand on Kyrael's bowed head. "How about this? I'd like you to work for me for a bit."

"I'd do anything you asked." His jitters amplified under the weight of a Seraph's hand, and the monumental honor and responsibility.

"What I ask is for information about the situation unfolding on Earth. I'd like answers to the following questions as soon as you get the information. Are there other humans who can perceive angels? Why did Adriel feel the need to make contact? And do the humans in question witness anything else otherworldly? Once I have the answers, I'll either suggest reassignment positions or send you out for further research. While you work, consider other assignments you would be interested in, and I will evaluate what I believe you are suited for. Perhaps when we compare, an ideal assignment will present itself."

"I'm already on it."

Kyrael scrambled from the room before Gabriel could change his mind. Outside, he spread his wings and shot across the garden and over the marble courtyard walls, heading straight for the path to Earth. Heaven's escalator of light drained travelers less than teleporting. But it took a while since the shaft of light traveled at the speed of light.

He touched down on the beam, which moved him in

an Earth-bound direction. Kyrael took the time to steady his breathing and change his clothes. He couldn't meet humans in his robes. They had worn nothing of the sort on Earth for a long time. Instead, he dressed himself in chino pants and a short-sleeve button-up with a tiny palm tree print. Fall still produced warm days in the northern hemisphere. Since the largest population centers were located there, the northern hemisphere was the logical place to look.

A touch on his shoulders sent his wings splaying in surprise. Kyrael spun to find Niciel grinning behind him.

"You're headed for Earth in a hurry. Word around the Earth-stationed neighborhood is you gave Gabriel the piece of news about Adriel breaking standard procedure and interacting with a human. Off to face your divine punishment?"

Kyrael grabbed Niciel's shoulders, face shining. "Gabriel's not mad about Adriel."

Niciel frowned. "Shouldn't you look less thrilled about punishment?"

"I'm not being punished for any of it," Kyrael trilled. "Gabriel even knew about my job trade. So the rest of the messengers can't hold it over my head anymore. No more delivering the bad news. Gabriel said reassignments happen from time to time. He's asked me to gather information on the human incident and report to him. Then he's going to pick me a new job, or—" A shiver rippled through him. "—maybe even let me pick my own."

Niciel shook his head. "You can't be serious."

Kyrael flicked his wings. "Why does no one trust the messenger today? Of course I'm giving you the most accurate account of what happened. It's what we do."

"I know. Gabriel's response is just so unlike the seraphim's usual rulings."

Kyrael folded his arms across his chest. "I'm not going to speculate what Gabriel wants to do with the situation. The seraphim will do as they wish, or rather, as God wishes. But after this, I won't have to be a messenger."

"I never understood your itchiness to leave your assignment." Niciel peeked over the edge of the escalator of light and changed his clothing. "I have no problem with my job of remala extermination. And I've been doing the same thing for how many years?"

Kyrael hopped off the light, spreading his wings and gliding to the ground. "Yeah, but you're centuries younger than me. Five hundred years from now, tell me if you've still never had a flash of boredom." His toe touched a cobbled street, and he took his weight on both feet, ignoring the car sliding along his body as if he were a slipstream.

Niciel came to rest beside him. "All right. I'm not going to argue with Gabriel's edict. The order surprised me, that's all."

"Hey, you work on Earth way more than I do. Have you ever seen anyone take notice of you?"

Niciel shook his head. "Not for more than a second or two."

Kyrael's wings drooped. "Me neither, but maybe someone else has." He turned and followed a woman with a baby in a sling, peering into the face of the child. "Can you imagine starting so small and ending so large? Do you think they remember any of the transitions?"

"Can't say the thought ever occurred to me." Niciel drifted along behind Kyrael. "Why did you pick Rome?"

Kyrael shrugged. "One of the holy cities seemed as good a place to start as any." He bent, sniffing a piece of pizza on its way to a diner's mouth. "I already summoned Mumiah."

Kyrael left the sidewalk café, heading toward the entrance to a church. Carved icons glared at passersby. Meant to inspire the faithful and ward off evil, they made him chuckle. People could be so creative. But the builders gave angels their due. Paintings of the saints and the hosts watched over the worship of those within. Kyrael could respect such reverence.

Leaning against an aged door, carved and studded with iron, lounged an angel with bright eyes and gleaming hair. Kyrael raised a hand in greeting. He gave Mumiah a report of Gabriel's order, then got to the question burning his tongue.

"Have you gotten any reports of humans noticing your angels?"

Mumiah pressed his lips together. "One of the guardians I oversee had an incident in London. A young child stared at him, turning in the stroller to keep looking. But children do the same for squirrels, so whatever called his attention might not have been the angel." He paused, eyes closed, thinking. "I made a note at the time. The child's name was Greyson Wheatley. Though, I doubt you'll find much. The incident happened almost seventeen years ago. The boy will be grown, and I haven't received any other reports. I doubt he saw my angel."

Kyrael nodded. "I'll try anyway. If you could put the European angels on alert and report any findings, I would be grateful."

Mumiah began to fade. "If that's all, I have an infant

about to be in a car wreck to protect."

Kyrael waved him away and turned to Niciel. "Will you pass the word amongst the extermination angels, then report to me?"

"If you wish."

"Yes, please. I'm leaving to track down this Greyson Wheatley."

\*\*\*\*

Having a so-called angel following her wasn't quite the disruption Flick expected. Adriel stayed to the side and waited through her third-period class, not making a sound. When the class ended, he slunk up beside her. His brush against her shoulder sent a shudder through her. She loathed even considering the possibility the things she saw might touch *her*.

"Where can we talk?" Adriel asked.

"Not here," she murmured.

She took a route against the main flow of students on their way to the cafeteria. Classrooms facing small plantings of bushes and such comprised the inner courtyard. Along the paths, several benches offered students a safe place to get some fresh air. A cool, damp marine layer coated the city today, leaving the courtyard deserted aside from those entering the classrooms.

Adriel sat beside her on one of the benches. "Now, please tell me about the other things you see."

Flick paused, waiting until after the final bell and the classroom doors shut before speaking. "I see ghosts, sometimes. They look like regular people but semi-transparent."

"Those are what frighten you?"

She closed her eyes and shook her head. Drawing a deep breath, she prepared to lay out the darkness no one else would believe. But Adriel existed on the other side of life, so at least he would believe her. Maybe, like telling her parents about a nightmare as a child, getting the horror off her chest would be a relief.

"There are things lurking in the shadows." Without meaning to, her voice dropped to a whisper. "They look like monsters or sometimes half-decayed corpses. The worst appear like drawings of demons. They have horns, tails, extra body parts, animal parts." Her voice shook. "I sense when they're near, and I try hard not to look. Then, today, you touched me. What if they can, too? I mean, I've seen them touch other people, but not me, so far."

Flick rubbed her face with both hands, trying to scrub away the memories of those awful apparitions.

"Remalas."

Adriel's voice clenched around the word. Flick glanced at him, stunned when his entire demeanor changed. Instead of looking like her initial impression of him, a combined clubbing jock muddled with a bespoke hipster, he sent her shrinking back toward the very shadows she feared.

"I'm sorry," she squeaked.

He startled, dropping the upsetting expression. "For what?"

"For making you mad." She cowered farther down the bench.

Adriel sighed and ran a hand through his silver hair. "You've done nothing wrong, and I'm in no way upset with you. On the contrary, I'm sorry you've suffered because of their presence. Remalas aren't meant to be seen by human eyes. No wonder you're scared."

"What are these remalas?" Curiosity halted her retreat.

Adriel crossed his arms and leaned back against the bench. His gaze drifted off, and his words trickled across the back of measured thought. "Remalas are not something I've ever had to try explaining. And since you don't understand the plane they originate from, I'll need a moment to find the words."

He fell silent, and Flick let him think. She used the silence to open her lunch and take out the dish of quinoa salad. She still wasn't convinced the whole "angel" story was the truth, but the unsettling feeling from Adriel's watching had long since disappeared. He didn't have the same aura as those dark things, so his presence didn't bother her.

"I guess the best way to describe a remala is a being of concentrated wickedness. Humans ooze both positive and negative energy. Earth is designed to absorb and redistribute the positive. That's why humans find such joy in connecting with nature. The negative is a bit like dust bunnies. It collects in unseen places, balling together until a unique creature is formed. Heaven deploys extermination angels to rid the world of those."

"Are none of the angels deployed to Seattle? Because I see a lot of the nasty things, but I've never seen an angel."

"I wonder about that." Adriel scrutinized her. "Do you still not see my wings?"

"You've never had wings."

He shifted, angling toward her. "Do you believe in God?"

"That's a little personal," she griped. When he continued to stare, she gave in. "No. For obvious reasons, I believe in things not of this world. But I can't believe in a God who lets so much bad inhabit the earth."

Adriel nodded. "I thought as much. You can't see the divine part of me because you don't believe in the divine. Maybe someday."

Flick swallowed a bite of apple. "Ah. Then goodbye, I guess."

Adriel frowned. "Was I going somewhere?"

"Um, you said you wanted to know what I saw. I told you. Beyond that, I assumed angels had things to do. You know, besides following high school seniors to class."

He chuckled. "I just started my vacation. You caught me amusing myself in downtown Seattle yesterday. So no, I don't have anywhere else to be. And if you don't mind, I'd like to stay in your company. I could visit other angels. But you are the first live human I've ever been able to converse with, and it's an unexpected pleasure."

"You talk to dead humans?" Skepticism laced Flick's question.

"Kind of. But let's not spoil your lunch with further unpleasantness. There's an added benefit for you. By letting me stay, none of the remalas will come around. They'll smell me from quite a distance and steer clear. They don't want to be exterminated."

"Are you one of the exterminators, then?" Flick opened a packet of multigrain crackers, nibbling one.

Adriel's teal eyes shifted sideways, avoiding her. "No. But I can kill them. Any angel could if need be."

"What aren't you telling me?"

He stared up at the sky, shoulders stiffening. "Another time, okay? There's a reason I'm on vacation, and it's to leave my job behind."

"What could an angel have to do that's so bad?

Don't tell me you hunt demons or something."

Adriel let out a hiss. "Don't tempt evil by opening your curiosity to it. Demons, true demons, are the devil's creation and inhabit Hell with their master. And while the devil and his demons can't leave Hell, the demons can contract with the most powerful remalas to do evil work on Earth in their stead. Exterminators hunt and slay the largest remalas before they contract with Hell."

"Then the worst things I've seen are the big ones?"

"Not a chance. Trust me. You'd know if you'd seen a remala powerful enough to contract with Hell. You'd probably be incapacitated with fear."

"One more reason to let you stick around, huh?"

He smiled. "You could say that."

"If they can smell you a mile away and flee, doesn't that make them hard to kill?" She snapped the lids back on her containers and zipped her lunch bag shut. Somehow, he sucked her into the conversation despite half believing the subject matter.

"Yes. Being detected is the biggest obstacle to getting rid of remalas."

"Do angels stink or something? You said they smell you."

A huff of laughter escaped. "Smell was the closest sense I could come up with for you to understand. Rather than smell, remalas sense our divine presence, in other words, the power that makes us divine. In the crassest human terms, I'd guess you'd call it our magic."

"And you seriously have no way of masking your power? I'd feel much better knowing angels were making headway in killing those creatures."

Adriel's expression slid from intrigued to delighted, and he sat bolt upright. "Maybe there is a way."

Chapter 3

Centuries had passed since such fresh inspiration jolted through Adriel. The girl stumbled across what might be a perfect solution to a dilemma facing angels for as long as humans had emitted negative energy. If an angel wished to conceal their divinity from remalas, they could, theoretically, merge with a mortal, using their body as a damper. No one in heaven tried this since forcible possession would result in an instant fall from grace. Heaven never envisioned a loophole, yet one stared him in the face. Humans had never been capable of speaking with angels, yet now one could, so if he asked her permission...

Felicity drew back, her nose wrinkled. "I'm not sure I like the look on your face."

"I have an idea, but I'll need your permission to test a theory."

"Permission for what?"

"I'd like to hide inside your body and try getting close to some remalas."

She jumped half out of her seat. "Like possess me?"

He held out a hand, begging her to stay. "No, no. You'd be hosting me. My control over your body would be bound to the functions you allow. I wouldn't have access to any of your memories. And you may kick me out whenever you want."

She frowned. "That still sounds weird."

He drew a deep breath and eased it out. "I'm asking for a lot of faith in me, which you don't have to begin with. And as yet, I haven't done anything to earn your trust. If it helps, you should know this experiment carries a huge risk for me."

"Oh?" The tension in her lips eased.

"If I in any way compromise your free will, I'll be banished from Heaven, fallen for crimes against humanity. This isn't a favor I ask lightly." He raised a hand, palm flat in her direction. "If you place your hand against mine, you'll host me for thirty seconds, then I'll leave, so you feel what I mean. If you dislike hosting, I'll never ask this of you again."

Nerves hammered the back of Adriel's ribs. Felicity hadn't moved. After long moments, her hand twitched, raising. Just before touching him, she pulled back.

"You're sure this will help get rid of those creatures? I'm not going to have to go near them, will I?"

He gave her a reassuring smile. "If merging works as I hope it will, we can identify humans capable of interacting with us. Some may volunteer to help us hunt, but you don't have to do anything you don't want, like touching me right now. The choice is yours. But if angels can get closer, the effectiveness of our hunts should increase, and perhaps we can start slaying some of the smaller remalas plaguing you."

With hesitation, Felicity's hand came toward his. The first contact of their fingertips made her flinch. Adriel stayed still, letting her approach him. When the warmth of her palm contacted his, he closed his eyes and let himself dissolve into his essence. Her palm absorbed him, and he unfolded inside her flesh.

Like a lining inside a garment, several connection

points kept them joined and in the same shape but separate. That was her wish. He could feel the desire for separation as clearly as if she spoke the words to his face.

Being inside someone invoked strange sensations. They shared the same sight, though Adriel had zero control over his movements without her permission. He didn't like the claustrophobic conditions, so he jumped free when the thirty seconds were up.

Felicity gasped and clutched the back of the bench for support. Adriel slumped, needing time to sort himself out.

"Well?" he asked.

She pressed a hand to her chest. "You were warm, like drinking hot coffee too fast. And everything still feels tingly."

"May I ask you for a second trial?" Adriel sat back up once the gelatinous feeling wore off. "I want to go for a walk and see if having you host me gives me the cover needed to get close to a remala. If we get close enough, I'll destroy it. If they still run from me, then my idea won't play out. Either way, this will be the last time you need to host me because I'll have the information I need."

Felicity didn't say no right away, so hope swelled in Adriel's chest. She rubbed her arms, thinking. Several times she started to speak, then fell silent again.

"If I do this, may I ask a favor in return?"

"Of course."

"There's a guy in my college classes I want to ask to the Homecoming dance. But asking is weird for so many reasons. I've never invited an older guy out. And what would he even think of attending a high school dance after graduating? On my own, I've got a week to get up the nerve, and I doubt I'd manage. But if you took over and did the talking, I couldn't chicken out, right?"

"I'll counter your offer. I'm not going to do the asking for you. But what if I were to set up the perfect scenario so you could?"

"Set up the perfect scenario? Like how?"

"I won't know until I see the situation, but I have my ways."

"I guess that could work."

Her expression said she wasn't convinced, but he'd take it. Adriel beamed a smile. "You'll get to ask out your man this afternoon. And this evening, I'll get to test out my idea. I guess we both have much to hope for."

\*\*\*\*

Kyrael faded from Rome the same way Mumiah had, reappearing on a London street the next second. People bustled around him, going about their business as if he didn't exist. Typical treatment. Whatever his reason, Adriel's contact with a human promised to set the status quo on its head. The prospect of something different tantalized Kyrael, tingling at the core of his being.

He stretched out a hand, running his fingers across the surface of a laptop in the arms of a passerby. The single touch allowed him access to all data therein, as well as everything on the web. Humans made the study of themselves so easy. Not only had they collected massive quantities of information in one place, but they unwittingly shared numerous details of their lives. For those connected, the thoughts they kept inside their heads were all that remained private. According to online records, Greyson should be at his part-time job, busing tables.

Reappearing outside the pub where Greyson worked, Kyrael drew in a deep breath to control the impulses that threatened to burst free. His blood fizzed beneath his skin. So much change in a single day was intoxicating.

Kyrael pushed open the door and peered inside. People packed the tables, eating and chatting, yet not a single face turned in his direction. His heart sank, but he stepped inside anyway. He shouldn't expect this man to come running straight for him. This individual might have a hard time coping with seeing an angel, period. He'd need to remove Greyson from the view of others, so if he did panic, he could do so in private.

No. Kyrael scolded himself. Gabriel trusted him with such an important task. He wouldn't screw this up by rushing or making assumptions. If he did, Gabriel might take everything back and leave him as a messenger. That would be infinitely more humiliating than getting caught trading jobs in the first place.

In front of Kyrael, a hostess tapped a stack of menus straight, then walked behind the bar, speaking to the bartender. She failed to acknowledge him in any way. A young man in an apron started to brush past, stopped, and frowned, glancing between Kyrael and the hostess.

"I'm sorry. Have you been helped?"

The question rendered Kyrael speechless for a moment. "Are you Greyson Wheatley?"

"Yes… Do I know you?"

Kyrael worked to restrain himself. He'd been seen. He wanted to hug Greyson or something equally enthusiastic. "Not yet. I'm Kyrael. It's nice to meet you."

"Would you prefer a booth or a seat at the bar?"

"I'd like the chance to speak with you about

significant matters." Kyrael stared at Greyson. Greyson hadn't reacted in any way to his wings. But many different kinds of angels worked on Earth. Perhaps Greyson saw enough of them not to be surprised. Such comfort with angels made Kyrael's job much easier.

Greyson frowned. "I don't have a break for a while. Do you have a business card? I can contact you later."

"No need."

Kyrael offered a hand for shaking, and Greyson took it. The moment their hands touched, the two vanished from the pub and reappeared in Seattle. Kyrael selected the waterfront, and they landed on an empty pier. Greyson let out a scream and staggered away from Kyrael. He trembled and gasped like Kyrael were a gull who dropped a fish on the boards of the pier.

"Fuck me, what the bloody hell happened?"

Kyrael cocked his head at Greyson's reaction. Where was his excitement? Kyrael's chest pulled so tight it made him shift. "We have someone to meet with here in Seattle."

"*Seattle?*" Greyson shrieked.

"Why should that surprise you?" Impatience itched his wings, begging him to take Greyson straight to Adriel, then head to Gabriel. If he were working his old job, he'd already be finished. He wasn't Heaven's fastest messenger for nothing. "You saw one of my kind when you were small. So by my very nature, this shouldn't be shocking."

"Your kind?"

Kyrael flicked his wings in a noticeable manner. "Angels. Is that not obvious?"

Greyson sank to sit on the planks of wood. He tucked his head between his knees, drawing deep yet unsteady breaths. "This isn't real," he murmured. "Work and school. I should see the counselor. Stress. Pills."

Kyrael knelt beside him. "I don't understand. Why do you deny what's right in front of you?"

Greyson turned a derisive glare on Kyrael. "Don't be daft. The person in front of me is a strange bloke with crazy copper hair and violet contacts spouting the impossible. Besides, aren't angels supposed to have wings?" The anger on his face faltered. "Wait. How did you know about my guardian angel?"

Kyrael tilted his head in thought. "Well, he wasn't *your* guardian. You happened to witness him working when you were a babe. But that's how I found you. The angel in charge of the European guardians marked your name." He held out a hand to shake. "Let's try this again. I'm Kyrael, messenger angel. Pleased to meet you."

Greyson scanned his surroundings, silent and stiff. "This can't be real. But I'm sitting in the middle of a different city in my work uniform."

"I wonder why you don't see my wings. The guardian angel you saw had wings, right?"

Greyson's head jerked up. "Seriously? I was a toddler. It's not like I remember the incident, let alone the specifics. I have an impression of a glowing individual. That's it. No details. But that being made me feel good, unlike all the scary things I see. I assumed it was an angel."

"Scary things?"

Greyson frowned. "Spirits, haunts, demons."

Kyrael ruffled his feathers. "I guess it makes sense if you see the good, you can see the bad, too."

****

Nervous tension pulled all of Flick's muscles tight.

She stood across the hall from the open door to her English Lit class. Wade sat in his usual spot, chin resting in his hand, skimming notes.

"Go sit next to him," Adriel urged her while giving her a little push in the back.

"I wish you'd do this." She turned a pleading gaze on him.

"What meaning would it have if you weren't a party to the actions?"

"Huh?"

"If I do the asking and I do it with my personality, will you be sure he likes you or my version of you? This needs to be all Felicity."

"Then how are you planning to help?" She scooched backward, but Adriel pushed her forward again.

"I'll smooth the way and give you support. You stopped in traffic to scold me. I think you have plenty of nerve to talk to an older boy. Now hurry up and do this, or I'm going to feel guilty when you host me tonight. I want to uphold my half of the bargain." Adriel kept a hand in the center of her back, pushing her toward the empty seat next to Wade.

When she reached the desk, Wade glanced up at her and smiled. "Hi."

She froze.

Adriel whispered in her ear, "This is where you say hi back."

"Hi." Her voice came out a tiny thread.

Wade turned back to his notes after a moment of her continued silence.

"You're terrible at this," Adriel commented. "Why?"

She sat in a huff, pulling out her notebook. With her

pen, she wrote, *I tried to warn you.*

She handed him the pen, and he took it. She pointed to the paper. Having him talk about Wade out loud would be too embarrassing, even if no one could hear.

Adriel shrugged and put the pen to her paper. *What are you so worried about?*

*Rejection.*

*And he's so ideal you can't stomach even the possibility of rejection?* He shot her an incredulous glance. *Last I checked, there are over four billion males on the planet. Let's say a quarter of those are in your age range, and half of those are in a relationship, while a quarter of the remaining males harbor sexual tastes that don't include you, which leaves over a quarter of a billion young men to choose from.*

She rolled her eyes. *Yeah. Spread out across the whole planet. It's not like I can take my pick.*

*With my help, you could. We could teleport anywhere worldwide. So ask this guy, and if he's foolish enough to say no, I'll help you find someone better.*

*Foolish enough?*

He smiled. *I've seen a lot of humanity's worth. You're a good person. Whoever you choose will be a lucky individual. But please make sure they are also worthy of you.*

*What about him?* She made a tiny gesture in Wade's direction.

He shrugged. *I don't know him well enough to answer. All I can tell you is he's not currently slated to go to Hell.*

Flick snorted, choked, then coughed over Adriel's revelation. Wade turned to her, concern on his face.

"Are you all right?"

Flick wiped her watering eyes. "Yeah. Sorry."

Under the desk, Adriel nudged her with his foot. Around them, the rest of the class filtered in, but the professor had yet to arrive, and somehow, all the other students flowed past them, finding seats elsewhere in the classroom.

"Ask," Adriel hissed.

"Umm… Doyawanna, you know… " she mumbled.

"Was that even a human language?" Adriel grumbled. "I can only hold the gap around you for so long."

"Sorry. I didn't catch that," Wade said, a grin on his face.

Flick's stomach turned somersaults. Wade was so much cuter up close.

"You're Felicity, right?"

"Mmm." She nodded and blushed. "I… Uh… Do you wanna go to my Homecoming with me?" The moment the words came out, more followed, impossible to stop. "I know this might sound stupid since you've already graduated. And we've barely talked. Hell, I don't even know if you've got a girlfriend. If you've got a girlfriend, I'm sorry. I'm not trying to step on anyone's toes. It's just I don't have anyone at my other school to go with, or even someone I like. But you…" A squeaky giggle followed this.

Wade blinked at her for a moment before chuckling. "That was one hell of a ramble for a simple question. I graduated last spring, so I guess, yeah."

Flick's brain felt like mush. "What? Huh. Oh wait, for real?"

"Sure. A dance could be fun."

When had the python started squeezing her chest?

"Yes. Perfect. Good. Then yeah."

He reached over, putting one hand on top of hers. "Maybe you'd like to go out sometime before then? You know, get the jitters out of your system so you can relax and enjoy your dance."

"Ah, ha ha. Yeah. Good idea."

His eyes twinkled. "Tonight? I've got work the next four nights."

"I-I"—she glanced back at Adriel—"can't. I've got something I've got to take care of tonight. Um, this weekend?"

"I have Saturday free. What would you like to do?"

Something crinkled under her hand. Lifting her fingers revealed two concert tickets. She glanced back at Adriel, who nodded to her. Sliding them toward Wade, she asked, "Do you like the Pink Hedgehogs?"

"Yeah. I heard them over the summer at the concert in the park series. They rock."

"Tickets." She pushed them toward him. "I mean, I've got them. The tickets, not the band."

Wade chuckled. "That's good. I'd have questions if you had them tied up in your basement or something."

A weird fuzzy feeling brushed across Flick's skin, and a second later, the professor burst into the room, looking disheveled.

"I'm so sorry, class. It was the weirdest thing. After four years of teaching here, I got lost for the first time." She shook her head. "Let's get started since we're almost ten minutes into class."

Flick heard little of the day's lecture. She kept sliding sideways glances at Wade. On her other side, Adriel crossed his arms on the desk and tucked his chin in the divot. He never closed his eyes but never moved either, at least not until the class ended.

After exchanging cell numbers with Wade, Flick headed for her car, the end of this class setting her free for the remainder of her Monday afternoon. With the excitement of a first date buzzing through her, maintaining her composure while walking down the hall took work. But Wade paced behind her, so she didn't want to do anything to make herself appear stupid. This included talking to Adriel, who stayed at her left shoulder.

Rather than indulging her pre-date stomach butterflies, she took time to process Adriel in detail, like how tall he stood. She wasn't a short woman, standing five-eight, but her nose only reached Adriel's sternum.

He also had the smoothest walk she'd ever seen. Ghosts floated around, and monsters slunk, both very fluid in their motions. But Adriel's movements were lithe and graceful and full of confidence, the way a cheetah or a panther moved. Adriel hadn't told her why an angel would need a vacation from his job. Would he explain why an angel needed predatory grace? Every time she relaxed around him, he found a new way to make her nervous.

After they'd climbed into her car and shut the doors, Adriel started laughing, a deep chuckle first, which built into rolling mirth. He leaned against the dash of her car, gasping.

"What is so funny?" she asked, lost.

"My interactions with humans have never covered anything like what I've witnessed today. The school is fascinating. And you went from a spunky young woman to a girl with the conversational acuity of a goldfish simply because of the presence of a crush." He wiped his eyes. "I have no words."

She scowled at the traffic in front of her. "I don't know why you'd find my struggles so amusing. What? Don't angels ever have to date?"

"No. God hand-makes all angels on an as-needed basis."

"Are there female angels?"

"The Powers are all female." He shuddered. "Do not mess with them. They comprise Heaven's army, and they're terrifying in their own right."

"Huh. That's not what I would have expected. Men make up most of the armies here."

"That's because human men have failed to utilize the feminine fervor. Whether humanity ever realizes female potential is neither here nor there to me. I'm not an angel of judgment, at least not on such accounts. But in Heaven, you *do not* piss the women off."

He sat back, rubbing at his ribs. "But that's not your original question. Angels don't need dating, marriage, or sex because we're not in charge of making the next generation of angels. But we feel a whole spectrum of love, and we cherish those bonds."

"Weird."

"So was what you displayed."

"Thanks, by the way." Flick switched back to the subject of Wade. "I got some strange feelings before the professor arrived. I assume that was you doing your thing. You said you'd clear the path and came through. If the professor had arrived on time, I never would have gotten my question out. And thanks for the concert tickets. Do I owe you for those?"

"Don't worry about it. By letting me participate in your life today, you've given me experiences I would never have gotten and will probably never get the chance to do again. That's a huge gift to an immortal."

The car jerked under Flick's foot slip. "Seriously? You're immortal?"

"Mostly."

She frowned and accelerated back to the proper speed. "How can you be mostly immortal? Isn't that like being mostly dead?"

"Both are possible, but not in the absolute terms prevalent in this plane of existence. For example, when we exterminate the remalas, the laws of physics don't disappear. No one but God can remove energy from existence. Angels can, however, move, alter, or reassign the energy. In the case of the remalas, their energy is sent through a parallel dimension, which acts like a filter. When the energy returns to this plane, it is neutral, ready to be used by some force of nature. The round trip eliminates the original entity."

He crossed his arms. "Death for an immortal is a little more complicated, but in rough terms, it means getting deconstructed and too intermingled with other energy sources to be re-sorted."

"How would that even happen?"

"Not a discussion for tonight. Let's just say deconstruction is not a pleasant fate, and it occurs in horrific circumstances, all of which make everything you've ever seen lurking look like visions of Heaven."

"Understood. Don't pry into deconstructing angels."

"Do you believe I'm an angel, then?"

Flick gripped the steering wheel. "I believe you're benevolent. I believe you call yourself an angel, whatever entity classification that represents. Do I believe you're a robe-wearing, halo-toting, harp-playing angel? Not so much."

"Common misconceptions," Adriel muttered. "Except the robe thing. Those are still popular in Heaven. The breeze from underneath—"

"And we're done." Flick interrupted while pulling into the parking garage. Her muscles tightened, and she clenched the steering wheel. "Do we have to wait until after dark to do your experiment?" Letting Adriel take her to seek out those wicked things hadn't seemed so scary during the morning hours. But in the dim light of the parking garage, all the tiny hairs on her arms stood up in protest.

"No. We can go now if you don't mind entering their dark, daytime hiding spots. They're a lot closer at night."

"Letting you in will be like earlier, right? I'll be able to see everything?"

"You'll have complete autonomy of your body unless you wish otherwise."

Flick gripped her backpack. "I'll put my stuff in the trunk. Let's get this over with."

She dropped her bag in the trunk and turned to Adriel, waiting.

"Your hand." He held his up like he had at school.

She reached for him with more confidence than last time. Beneath her palm, his skin stretched smooth, flawless, and a little too warm to be a normal person's. They touched hands for a mere moment before he vaporized, and her skin absorbed him like smoke being sucked out of a vent. On her inside, a warmth spread, coating her innards.

A flaw in this plan drew up fresh nerves. He'd never told her where to seek out remalas. Did he want her to wander the city? Should she let him take over her movements and take her there himself?

*"Felicity?"*

"Holy crap," she gasped.

Adriel's voice spoke from within her head. *"Crap isn't holy. But it's not cursed either, so—"*

"I can hear you inside my head. It's freaky."

*"It's convenient. There aren't any angels in Heaven who've ever gone for a ride in a human before, so we're in uncharted waters."*

"Are there angels elsewhere who have? Ridden in a human?"

*"Yes. I mentioned previously they're fallen for crimes against humanity, meaning they're in Hell. That's why your permission is vital. Now, I'd like you to exit the parking garage and head north. We passed an alley that had prime hiding spots. We'll try there first."*

Since she'd stayed sitting on a bench during their last hosting, Flick expected moving around to feel weird. But nothing odd happened aside from the warmth coating her insides.

"What's it like in there?" she asked, hoping to dispel her nerves. Those went up a notch the moment she left the garage for the street.

*"A bit claustrophobic. I'm all constricted, and I can't see the appeal. But sometimes, the ends justify the means. If angels can take out more remalas by cooperating with a host, then a little discomfort is worth it. This is the alley."*

Flick dried her hands on her pants while still out in the long shadows of evening. Gray engulfed the alley, and for the first time, she couldn't soothe herself by hurrying past without looking.

*"I'm here with you. You'll be safe."* Adriel's words

helped—a little.

Forcing one foot in front of the next, she took the alley. By halfway in, she knew nothing lurked here. By the time she reached the far side, her eyes and throat burned. Giving up and going home to cry off her fears sounded perfect. But for whatever reason, she persisted.

*"Head farther north."*

She followed Adriel's instructions for several blocks, but it wasn't until they reached an overpass, the site of a cleaned and removed transient camp, that she felt the familiar sensation of evil watching. Her body froze.

"I can feel something in the shadows of the pillar to the right," Flick murmured. "Are we good now?"

*"Closer,"* Adriel urged. *"I need to see how close I can get."*

With leaden feet, Flick pushed herself toward the bridge support. Tendrils of a smoky substance drifted from the shadows. The evil aura they'd found was more potent than the sort of creatures who peeked at her from drainpipes.

Something out of sight gurgled and slid across the gravel. Flick whimpered and bit her lip.

*"Closer."* Adriel's demand came across like an order.

Though every impulse told her to run away, Flick took another step closer. Then, a second.

With a wet squelch, the creature slipped from the shadows. The thing shaped like a frog but the size of a bulldog with shaggy hair like a yak, locked its gaze on her. A grin spread across its face, flashing a mouthful of jagged teeth. Its froggy tongue smacked along them.

In the space of a single blink, the creature lunged for

her, its mouth gaping. Before she could run, Adriel burst from her body. In one swift, fluid movement, vapors around him took the shape of a scythe, and he swung it straight through the center of the creature. The frog screamed and ruptured like an overripe watermelon, exploding.

Flick flinched, expecting the pieces to spatter everything, including her, but they vanished into thin air. She squatted, clutching her knees and gasping. Adriel shook his hand, and the scythe disappeared. Crossing the space between them, he crouched in front of her.

"Are you okay?"

"What the hell was all that?" Her voice trembled over every word.

He pulled her to her feet and into his arms. The warmth of his proximity returned. She might not buy his claim to be an angel, but he was the antithesis of the creatures, and that made her feel safe. As a result, all the tension holding her body loosened, turning her joints to jelly.

"The experiment was a clear success. That was a mid-grade remala. Had I approached on my own, it would have fled, but you saw the result."

"What I saw was horrible." The tears started with a single one, then several, then a flood.

Adriel cradled her against his chest. "Shh. You're safe with me. I would never let them harm you."

"Can they?"

"Remalas feed off negative energy, so the more you output, the more delicious you are. If they consume enough to disrupt your molecular structure, they'll kill you. But as I said, you're safe with me."

Chapter 4

Greyson stared at the last sparkles of light glinting off the ocean. He'd taken a couple of hours to process, sitting on a bench overlooking the water and ignoring the self-proclaimed angel beside him.

No logical explanation of how he could have gotten to Seattle presented itself. But the surrounding city couldn't be anywhere else. Enough time had passed in this location to be sure he wasn't dreaming. The supernatural had imposed itself on Greyson for as long as he could remember, but it had never impacted his life in such an overt fashion.

"Are you ready to meet up with Adriel?"

Greyson frowned. Kyrael asked him this every twenty minutes to the minute for the entire time they'd been here. The two had several discussions about who this Adriel was and what Kyrael needed from him. If Kyrael told the truth, Greyson wasn't in any hurry to meet this other angel. But he didn't have the energy to weave away from Kyrael's persuasive attempts yet again.

"Fine. Let's go," Greyson conceded with a sigh.

Kyrael leaped to his feet in one motion like a jack-in-the-box popping up. Whatever sort of being he was, he had way too much energy. Greyson barely reached his feet when Kyrael grabbed him, and the waterfront disappeared.

They reappeared under a creepy, shadow-filled overpass. Not far from them, two figures stood, intertwined, a young woman and a man with metallic hair like Kyrael's.

"Ugh. You've got to be shitting me," Greyson groaned. "You're snogging an angel of death?"

The woman's head popped off the angel's chest, and she cast a horrified gape at the angel in question. Dropping him like a hot pan, she backed away, terror on her face. The angel, however, rounded on Greyson, looking livid.

Greyson's legs locked, refusing to move him away. Adriel drew up latent fear, not for being some muscular menace but rather despite his lithe build. Two minutes ago, he would never have imagined a death angel had such a mild appearance—but with the primal energy rolling off him...

"You and your big mouth may have ruined something vital," the angel snapped.

"Peace, Adriel." Kyrael stepped between them.

Adriel blinked a couple times, then relaxed to a state of cool composure. "What can I do for you, messenger?"

"I won't be a messenger for long," Kyrael trilled. "I'm running a few errands for Gabriel, then I'm getting reassigned."

"Fantastic," Adriel cut him off before he could get rambling. "But why does that bring you here?"

Kyrael's expression flickered. "Well, Gabriel wanted to know why you made contact after being seen. You could have walked away. But by the looks of things..." His gaze flipped between Adriel and the young woman. "I've been delivering bad news for a decade. I don't want to have to tell Gabriel you've fallen."

Adriel gave a little growl in Kyrael's direction. "I'm not seducing humans. We just completed an experiment. The whole experience left her distraught."

Kyrael frowned. "What sort of experiment?"

"She gave her permission and hosted me so we could track down a remala."

Kyrael took a quick suck of air between his teeth. "Why?"

"To get close enough to kill it."

"Can she see them?"

"Yes." Adriel turned his piercing gaze on Greyson. "I take it you found another like Felicity?"

"Indeed. His name is Greyson. Gabriel asked me to find out if there were more like her. After I made contact, I wasn't sure what to do with him, so I brought him along."

"I guess your timing is fortuitous after all. You may go back and tell Gabriel angels can work with humans like them. If we have willing hosts, the exterminators can get close enough to ambush remalas, making some headway on the backlog."

Kyrael shuddered. "I'm not sure telling him that will go much better than if you got frisky with a human."

"Don't use human slang on me," Adriel snapped. "Especially not that sort. I'll stay with these two while you report to Gabriel. Ask him what he wants me to do with them. Until then, I guess we'll go back to Felicity's apartment."

Kyrael nodded, then shot straight into the sky in a streak of light. Ignoring Greyson, Adriel approached Felicity as one would inch toward an injured animal.

"You don't need to be afraid of me," Adriel soothed. "I promised to keep you safe. That hasn't changed."

She took backward steps to match his forward progression. "Is it t-true you're an angel of death?"

"I'm sorry I didn't tell you sooner. I didn't want to scare you."

"Then the scythe, with the remala…"

"That's one of my tools. I can cause death to anything, but that's why I get vacations. Killing is hard, even on a death angel. So every couple millennia, I get a century or two off to recover." He held out his hands in a placating gesture. "I don't trail death around like slug slime. You've touched me and come out unscathed."

He took a step closer, but this time, she held her ground. "Please, Felicity. Flick. May I call you that, like the rest of your friends?"

She shrugged.

"Flick. Trust me. You are safe with me." His next step caught her in a hug again. "Thank you. Everything is done. I've turned the information over to the proper channels. And you never have to host again. As I suggested before, if you let me spend some time with you, those creatures won't come around, and you'll get a break from seeing the unwanted specters."

She backed up, nodding. "I'll think about it. In the meantime, what are we going to do with him?" She pointed in Greyson's direction.

Greyson folded his arms and scowled at the two of them. "*You* don't need to do anything with me. *He* can take me back home, assuming he's got the same capabilities as Kyrael. Then I'm returning to real life and pretending none of this ever happened."

Adriel had the decency to look contrite. "I'd like to honor your wishes, but until I get word back from Gabriel, you need to stay with us." He rubbed the back of his head. "Let's go back to your house, Flick. You can tell your parents he needs a place to stay until the exterminators do some work. That's enough of the truth."

"But I don't know him. What if he's a deviant?"

Greyson snorted. "I could say the same of you. I don't know you. What if you want to hurt me while I'm sleeping? You're chummy with a death angel, after all."

Adriel cast glares between Greyson and Felicity. "We're not throwing out accusations. This is an aberrant situation, and I've already gone far enough without Gabriel's authorization. I understand this is uncomfortable for you both, but please be patient. Kyrael could be back before nightfall."

"That fast?" Felicity asked. "Who is Gabriel?"

Adriel arched an eyebrow. "The angel Gabriel? The one who visited Mary in the Bible?"

Both Greyson and Felicity said, "Ah."

"I can see questions on your faces, and now isn't the time. Suffice it to say Gabriel is a big deal, even in Heaven. He asked for information on you, meaning it's best to wait for his instructions."

Greyson shrugged. "I guess waiting a few hours is fine. I've already lost most of the night's sleep. What does the rest of it matter?"

"You have an accent, and you lost the whole night. Where exactly are you from?" Felicity asked, her forehead scrunching.

"London," he tossed out, still focused on Adriel.

"Kyrael brought you all the way from London?" she yelped.

"Yes. And it was bloody annoying." He pointed a finger in Adriel's direction. "If Kyrael lost me my job because I disappeared, you guys get to fix it for me."

Adriel inclined his head. "I'll see your livelihood isn't affected. You'll have to excuse Kyrael. He's simply a messenger, so his trips to Earth are brief and limited. I doubt he understood the impact of his actions on your life. I may work with human souls, but I live here most of the time. I observe and learn."

Greyson followed the other two through the Seattle streets. Daylight had dimmed to twilight, and darkness spread under and around the city. They'd reached the time of day when things crawled out to watch Greyson. He braced for the appearance of anything from the minorly disturbing to the downright gruesome. But tonight, nothing lurked in the shadows, and no feelings of unease prickled his skin. Since Kyrael ran off with him, this was the best part of Greyson's day.

The fourth floor of a building on the edge of downtown held Felicity's flat. The building wasn't super swank, but it was nice and in a prime location. Her parents must draw in a comfortable income.

He used the elevator ride to get a few details about her, trying to put himself more at ease. "How old are you?" he asked.

"Eighteen. Why?"

"How do you propose knowing a twenty-year-old man well enough your parents will let him stay over?"

Her expression pulled tight with thought. "Are you closer to nineteen or twenty-one?"

"I had my twentieth birthday three weeks ago."

"I take classes at the community college. You could be in one of those. You're two years older than me, so you and I could end up in the same classes, right?"

Greyson nodded. "Which class? You heard Kyrael

say my name is Greyson, right? Why am I not staying with other friends or roommates?"

"What's with all the questions?" she threw back.

The elevator doors slid open, and Greyson stepped out. "You need the answers in your head already if the lies are going to look believable when you tell your parents."

"Smart." She grinned.

"Not really." He stuffed his hands in his pockets. "I spent too much time lying to my parents. I regret that now."

"Oh." She took a key out of her pocket and paused. "Dang it. I forgot my backpack in the trunk."

Adriel vanished and reappeared with a floral-printed backpack in his hands a moment later. "Here you go."

"Thanks." She unlocked the door and called, "Mom," on her way inside.

"In the kitchen," a woman called back. "Dinner's almost ready. Set the table, please."

"Come on." She gestured for Greyson to follow her.

Felicity led the way to the door of a small kitchen area. Inside, a woman with gray-streaked brown hair strained pasta in the sink. When she turned, Greyson saw what Felicity would look like in thirty years. The girl was a carbon copy of her mother.

The woman's gaze flipped from Felicity to Greyson and back, her eyes widening a bit. "You didn't tell me you were bringing anyone for dinner."

"Sorry, Mom. This is Greyson. He's in my English Lit class at the college. Um, I was wondering... Could he stay with us for a bit? I guess he can't go home. Exterminators."

Her mom frowned. "I suppose. We don't have much

extra space, though."

"Sorry for the inconvenience," Greyson said, emphasizing his accent. "I recently transferred to the community college here. I don't have many friends in the area yet. Felicity was kind enough to offer."

The woman's expression lightened. "Oh. Where are you from?"

"I'm from London. My trip was rather spontaneous, and I'm short on everything from clothing to cash." Not to mention my passport, he tacked on in his head. If the angels didn't come through, he was good and stuck. "The offer of a place to stay is generous." Hopefully the smile he pasted on didn't look too forced.

Felicity's mother rummaged through the refrigerator. "Well, you're welcome to stay for now. At least, as long as you don't mind the couch." She pulled out a bag of salad greens and a bottle of vinaigrette. "I'm Linda. My husband, Mark, will be home any minute now."

"Since I've got nothing else to offer, can I help?" Greyson asked.

The entire situation made him uncomfortable. He didn't want to be a charity case. He didn't even want to be here. These people were friendly, which made reciprocating necessary when he'd rather punch something. But it wasn't Felicity's fault he'd spoken to the angel in the pub. Her mother wasn't to blame. Lashing out at either of them wouldn't accomplish anything aside from making him look like an arse.

Linda smiled at him. "Not necessary." She handed Felicity a stack of plates. "Why don't you show Greyson to his seat at the table, then come back and get the silverware?"

The table stood in an open front room on the other side of the wall from the kitchen. "You can sit here." Felicity pulled out a chair and set a plate on the table.

Greyson nodded and sat while she set the rest of the plates out. "I'm sorry if I caused any trouble," he said.

She grimaced. "I understand getting swept up in their agenda. Don't worry about it. I just hope they get you home all right." She gave Adriel a pointed glare when she said this. The angel rested on the couch, where he could view the table.

"Do they even eat?" Greyson whispered, nodding his head in Adriel's direction.

"He didn't eat at lunch today. So I don't know."

"Flick," her mother called.

Felicity hurried off. Something in the kitchen clinked, and Greyson overheard Linda's irritated voice in the ensuing silence.

"You put me in an awkward position, Flick. How well do you even know this boy?"

Greyson flinched. Where was an angel to whisk him off to the other side of the planet when he needed it?

"I haven't known him long, but he needs a hand," Felicity answered. "I thought you and Dad were always on me about helping people."

"Not in our living room, overnight. What if he's dishonest?"

Greyson jerked to his feet and crossed the living room to Adriel. "Get me out of here. *Now*."

"I already told you why I can't."

Greyson rubbed between his eyes. A throb warned of an impending headache. "You're stationed in Seattle. Take me to wherever you're staying."

"I can't do that, either."

"Why the hell not?" Greyson snarled.

"Because." Adriel folded in on himself, shrinking and condensing into an orb of light the size of a tennis ball that hovered like a free-floating lightbulb. "This is how I sleep," the lightbulb said. "I don't need accommodations suitable for you." The ball unfolded until Adriel sat on the couch again. "I'm sorry we're inconveniencing you. Try to cope as best you can until Kyrael returns with Gabriel's instructions."

"Dinner's ready," Linda said, carrying a bowl of salad to the table.

Felicity followed her with a bowl of spaghetti. She cast one glance in Greyson's direction, then ducked her head and returned to the kitchen. After what he'd overheard, Linda's smile and gesture toward the table appeared forced. He wanted to tell her to piss off, but then he would be rude, too. A tiny, rational part of him understood Linda's hesitations. But she suspected the worst without knowing him, leaving the rest of him cross.

He hadn't imagined the night could get ghastlier, but it did. Mark came home right after they sat down, and he carried even more skepticism than Linda, wearing his distrust on his face. Greyson took long, steadying breaths, reminding himself if he had a daughter who brought home an unknown, older bloke and asked if he could stay, he would also be suspicious of the guy's motivations. If they could tell her parents the truth, all those suspicions could be set aside or at least redirected at the angels.

**\*\*\*\***

Flick waited until her parents were asleep before sneaking out of her room and into the living room. As suspected, Greyson sat up, staring out the windows at the city lights. She padded across the room and sat beside the couch on the floor.

"It's too bad Gabriel hasn't sent word back yet," she said.

Greyson grunted.

"I'm sorry my mom and dad were acting weird. But at least they let you stay."

Greyson grunted again.

"Is there anything I can do to make you more comfortable?" She paused, but his expression stayed tense.

"I want an outlet for my frustration. Maybe it sounds stupid to a girl, but I just want to hit something."

"I can arrange that," Adriel said, unfolding from the ball of light hidden in the folds of the curtains to dampen the glow. He pointed outside. "Would you like me to take you on a remala hunt? Not only will you get to destroy something, but you'll be doing the world a favor. You'll be able to see firsthand why I want to open connections between people like you and the exterminators."

"Why the hell not? I can't sleep."

"I guess I'll come too, then," Flick said, standing up. "You'll need a way back into the building."

"I can get him in and out," Adriel offered.

"If you don't mind," Flick countered, "I'd kind of like to watch and see if the whole thing is as scary as I thought."

Adriel squeezed her arm. "Come if you'd like." He turned to Greyson and explained how hosting an angel worked.

Greyson wrinkled his nose and stared at Flick. "You *let* him possess you?"

"It's not so bad, and it's not like a horror movie or anything." She scratched her head. "Though, coming to the defense of hosting another entity is not something I ever expected to do."

Greyson shrugged his shoulders. "All right, death angel. You can come in."

Adriel held his hand out, palm open. "Place your hand against mine. Once I'm inside, you are in command. All I'll do is ride along unless you offer me control. Even then, I'll only be able to operate the specific functions you've relinquished."

"So if I give you permission, you can take a shite with my body and nothing else?"

Adriel grimaced. "I'd pass on the offer, but conceivably. I don't have to do what you offer, you know."

Greyson reached out and placed his palm against Adriel's. Watching Adriel get absorbed into his body was fascinating. It gave Flick an unexpected thrill.

"Do you feel warm inside?" she asked.

"Like I gulped down hot tea too fast." Greyson stood. "Should we go? It's after eleven, and you have school tomorrow, right?"

"Yeah. Speaking of which, what will you do while I'm at school?" She grabbed her jacket off the hook inside the door and offered her dad's to Greyson.

"If all goes well, I'll be back in London."

Flick eased the apartment door shut. Sneaking out with the untrusted guy wouldn't go over well with her parents. By the time they'd reached the streets, her nerves hummed again.

"Adriel wants us to head west this time," Greyson informed her.

Flick should have taken the lead, being in her home city and all, but she hid behind Greyson, repeatedly bumping into him. Despite knowing Adriel was along for the ride, it didn't ease her fears of seeking out something as horrible as what she'd seen earlier.

"Are you sure you wouldn't rather stay at your flat?" Greyson asked the next time she stepped on his heels.

She shivered and knocked into him again. "No. I don't want to be afraid forever. Even though seeing the remalas up close is terrible, I want to see them destroyed. I need to know they aren't free to wander around with no check."

Greyson offered Flick his hand. "You can hold onto me if it helps."

She hesitated until a scratching noise from the sewer grate sent her past his hand to wrap her arms around his chest. Greyson put his arm across her shoulder.

"Adriel says not to worry so much. The noise under the grate was likely a rat."

She wrinkled her nose. "I don't know that I feel much better knowing there are rats large enough to make those sorts of noises lurking below us."

Greyson rubbed her arm and chuckled. "Then I suggest you skip the London underground tour should you ever end up there."

They chatted for three more blocks before an overwhelming stench of decay hit her nose. Flick gagged, and Greyson let go of her to cover his mouth and nose.

"Look down," Greyson hissed.

Barely visible in the streetlights stretched the slender threads of a webbed trap. A single spindly leg, like that of a spider but three feet long, reached out of the space between two buildings. They'd walked straight into a remala's alert system.

When the searching leg didn't find anything, more unfurled from the gap. Once five legs had ahold of the edge of the building, they hoisted the owner out of the space. But what followed wasn't the fat body of a spider. Instead, a long snake-like body slithered out, wet and slimy like a slug, slurping against the brick façade. Those sinister legs lined the entire length—a length that continued to grow five, six, seven feet, piling up on itself. Eight glittering black eyes focused on Flick and Greyson.

Flick ordered herself to move, but her feet couldn't. The creature's webbing held her fast.

Fangs popped from the mouth of the remala, and a chittering filled the street, bouncing off the surrounding buildings. It rubbed its legs together, excited about its prey.

Flick lost all feeling in her legs. As if terror had sliced her brain from her body, every muscle refused to respond to the urge to flee. Rooted to the spot, Flick prayed Adriel would go to work.

"Fine," Greyson blurted out of nowhere. "Try whatever you want as long as you kill it."

Greyson's hand glowed, and the tendrils which formed a scythe appeared in his hand. With a hiss, the creature reared back, and Greyson rushed in, sliding beneath the belly. In a blinding streak, the remala twisted, protecting its abdomen with countless legs.

Greyson pushed up on one foot, one hand on the sidewalk for balance, his opposite foot connecting with the side of the creature's head and three of its eyes. The hit made its legs flex away from the body. With an improbable twist, Greyson brought the scythe down the length of the creature's gut, opening a gap that spewed black goo for a second before the whole thing burst and disappeared.

Greyson gasped, and Adriel separated from him. "Well?" he asked Greyson.

Greyson turned toward Adriel, his eyes wide. "That was intense. I was scared half out of my wits. Then you took over and I felt like an action hero…like having an out-of-body experience or waking dream. We *killed* that thing. I can't feel any of the evil aura anymore." He faced Flick. "You were upset when you went hunting with Adriel. Was it as bad this time?"

Flick gripped the front of her jacket. "This creature was worse. But you're right. It was like watching something on TV. You were kinda kick-ass."

He blushed and tucked his hands in his pockets. "Well, it was all Adriel."

"No. You were brave," she countered. "You let him use your body against that creature."

A weak chuckle escaped him. "I was petrified. If Adriel hadn't moved my body, I'd have sat there while it wrapped me up for supper."

"We *were* pretty stuck," Flick agreed. "I couldn't move, either."

Adriel stepped in beside them. "Now that I know we can function as a pair, it opens up a whole new level for partnerships." He gave Greyson an intense stare. "Since you understand better, I'm hoping Gabriel permits exterminators to partner with people like you and create a hunting unit. If you liked the rush, you could be included." He held up a finger. "Assuming Gabriel deems this okay."

"Adriel?" Flick nibbled her lip. They'd started back toward her apartment, but her mind hadn't calmed at all.

"Yes?"

"If I let you control me, could I squash remalas like Greyson did?"

He cocked his head and stared. "It would work the same. But I thought the whole ordeal disturbed you."

"It does. Though, now that I've seen two destroyed, there's something cathartic about it. I think I'd like the chance to kill one, like killing fear, you know?"

"That might be therapeutic," Adriel agreed. "But not tonight. Tonight, you need to sleep. Greyson, if Kyrael hasn't returned in time for Flick to go to school, I'll take responsibility for entertaining you tomorrow."

"Thanks," Greyson said, "for the offer and for letting me blow off steam tonight."

Adriel nodded. "My goal was never to inconvenience those like you but to offer a mutually beneficial partnership. I'm glad you feel like participating is an option now. I understand today was hard on you."

"It was, still is. But for the first time, I feel like Kyrael running off with me might not have been all bad."

Chapter 5

The next morning, Flick wished she could take Adriel's scythe to her alarm clock. The hour felt utterly ungodly. She grabbed her clothes and headed for the shower. The grating whir of her father grinding coffee reached her in the hall. Poor Greyson wouldn't get to sleep in. Not that extra sleep mattered. Her parents had to expect him out when she left for school. Then again, was he even still at the house? Or had Kyrael taken him back to London? Would he be hunting the same creatures there with a strange exterminator angel?

The bathroom door pulled against her hand, and Flick found her nose in a whole lot of skin belonging to Greyson's chest. Heat fanned across her cheeks, and she jumped back.

"Oh. Uh. Good morning. Or maybe not so good since you still can't go home."

"I hope you don't mind that I borrowed your shampoo and stuff." He took a sniff at his shoulder. "I guess there are worse things to smell like than little girls."

She stuck her tongue out. "How's that for 'little' girl? I'm not sure what you're making fun of. It's not like I've got bubble gum scented stuff."

"It reminds me a lot of the stuff my ex-girlfriend used." He sniffed again. "It smells better on me."

Flick squeezed the folded towel in her arms. "I

didn't even think about that. Do you have a girlfriend or family who are wondering where you're at?"

"Nope. My parents live in Suffolk, so they won't notice if I'm not home. And no girlfriend. She liberated me not long ago."

"Me, too. We broke up at the start of summer."

"Huh. Well, good riddance, I say."

"Truth." She edged her way inside the bathroom. "If you're still here tonight, you can stay again. Have Adriel bring you to the community college campus. He went to class with me yesterday, so he knows when my class finishes and where to find me. It's kinda fun having someone my age in the house. I don't have any siblings, so…"

Greyson gave her a half-smile. "For the record, I think you're a kind person. None of my anger yesterday was directed at you. Though it sucks to even think about it, I'll crash here again if I'm still in Seattle tonight. I live by myself in London. The company is nice."

When she came out of the bathroom, washed and dressed, Greyson and Adriel were gone. The depth of her disappointment surprised Flick. But it wasn't until she stepped outside that the value of Adriel's presence crashed down on her.

Flick stood at the bus stop, fretting. No amount of mental scolding dispelled the tremors nor kept her from focusing on well-lit spaces. But that's because no amount of self-soothing got rid of the images in her head—the hairy frog or spider slug. Every whisper in the dark sent her cringing. Without an angel, she was nothing but food for these things.

Now that the window to the other side was open, was she doomed to spend the rest of her life with her stomach in knots, paranoid? What about Adriel's promise to stay with her?

No. That was selfish. Greyson didn't even have a home here, and he wasn't whining about his situation. In fact, Flick didn't know anyone else as persevering or brave as Greyson. Yet she was panicking over seeing things she'd seen daily until now? How disappointing. If Adriel left to take care of Greyson for the day, Flick should, no, *would* wait until they came to meet her after classes.

She fought with herself all the way to the school, trading the warm, illuminated interior of the bus for the dark and chilly early morning outside. As usual, her friends lingered, waiting to walk the last couple blocks with her. But even Jake and Marisol's enthusiastic greeting didn't push back apprehension, which now clung to her skin like cobwebs.

Marisol linked arms with her and pulled her close, peering at her face. "You look like hell. Is everything all right?"

"I didn't sleep well last night," Flick said, admitting what she could.

"You look stressed on top of tired," Jake observed.

Marisol gave her arm a shake. "Well? Tell me what happened yesterday."

Flick grasped the one thing she could tell her friends, which was significant enough to distract them. "I asked that guy, Wade, to Homecoming. He said yes."

The following shake Marisol gave made Flick take a sidestep. "The college guy?" she yelped. "Seriously?"

"He said it was no big deal since he graduated this spring."

Marisol hooked her arm around Flick's shoulder,

giving her a rough squeeze, her gaze gleaming with pride. "My Flick is all grown up and falling for older guys."

Flick pried her friend off. "I haven't fallen for anyone yet. He's just nice and good-looking. We've got a date on Saturday. Ask me after if he's more than eye candy."

"You two are both set. I guess I should get my butt in gear and find a date," Marisol said.

"You could always dance with us," Flick offered.

They were approaching the school, and an eerie feeling permeated the grounds. Since meeting Adriel she was getting a feel for the subtle differences in how otherworldly beings felt. This aura was more sinister than the small remalas which observed her but less evil than the spider-legged thing they'd fought last night.

Part of her wanted to ask Adriel what the differences meant. Another part of her fought the idea of knowing any more. What she knew already swamped her mind, threatening to overwhelm her. Like right now. She had to force her focus back on her conversation.

"As a fifth wheel?" Marisol was saying. "Whether it's at a dance or as that monstrosity my grandparents drag around behind their truck, a fifth wheel is lame. But a third couple, that's acceptable. Know anyone else from your college classes who might want to come back and relive high school for a night?"

Greyson popped into her mind. He was single, and at twenty, he was two years older than Marisol. That was a respectable age difference. And he had such a delicious accent. But he wouldn't be here in two weeks. Then again, maybe Adriel would fetch him from London for a visit.

"Well?" Marisol asked. "Was your big pause a good thing?"

Jake snickered. "The pause was her trying to let you down easy. College guys don't want sassy little girls like you," he teased. "We did suggest a middle schooler the other day."

Marisol made a face at him in answer.

They entered the bright corridors of the school, and a weight slipped off Flick's shoulders. She smiled at Marisol. "I can think of a guy. But I don't know if it would work."

Marisol bounced on the balls of her feet. "So? Tell me about him anyway."

"He's tallish, like six feet, and he's got dark brown hair that's kinda longish in front. And he's from London, so—"

Marisol groaned and shuddered. "A guy with an accent? I'm sold. Ask and see if he's interested. I'll pay for the whole night and pick him up in a limo, whatever it takes, as long as he spends the night talking so I can hear the accent."

"Good God, you're shameless," Jake quipped. "You sound ready to bear his children over word pronunciation. Man, why can't I have an accent? I wouldn't be stuck at third base." Mischief sparkled through his grin, and he waggled his brows. "Then again, I'm taking Kristin to the dance."

"Ugg." Marisol shoved him away. "Getting with her is like getting cheese in a can."

"Huh?" Jake scratched his head.

"In a world of gourmet options, you choose the easiest, grossest, fakest version."

His eyebrows soared. "You're comparing girls to

cheese?"

"Why not?" Marisol pressed her lips together in exaggerated thought. "That would make Ellen Haas something stinky, like Limburger."

Flick snickered.

"What would you call me?" Marisol asked through her own giggles.

"Swiss cheese." Flick decided. "You've got a bit of bite, but everyone loves you anyway. And your brain is full of holes."

Marisol rolled her eyes. "Then you're a Muenster."

"Naw. I'm Gouda."

"And we're done with the cheese puns." Jake rubbed his face with both hands. "It's too early to be that lame. But I don't care what you two think of Kristin. My night promises to be fun."

"Because you might get laid?" Marisol threw the question at him. "I hope you like something about her besides the fact she's free with herself."

"You know, if I acted like her, no one would think twice," Jake scolded. "Why can't she do as she likes?"

"She can," Flick countered. "So can you or anyone else. I question her motives because I don't trust she acts the way she does in a healthy way, mentally or physically. If she's not sexually liberated for a healthy reason, then you sleeping with her is adding to the problem."

"Like you're an expert," Jake grumped. "You didn't even sleep with Liam. What would you know?"

"I know it's a good thing I didn't. Liam's selfish, end of story. Every time we hung out, it was another opportunity for him to brag up anything in his life. I can't imagine what his behavior would translate into in bed.

All for him, and he'd brag about it after. The whole time, he'd never even realize to brag about one's prowess in bed, one needs to shake the foundations of their partner's world."

Jake blinked. "That's one hell of a lecture from a virgin."

Flick blushed. "Well, I did spend one sleepless night contemplating having sex with Liam. I made sure to do it when he wasn't around so I'd know my head made my decision and not my body. And all I could imagine was him getting his and leaving me out. Then, him telling his friends he was God's gift to the bedroom."

Marisol snorted. "I could so see Liam doing that. But I don't think unearned bragging about man-skills is a flaw restricted to Liam."

The three of them hiked up the stairs toward their classes. Halfway up, Flick walked straight into a chest, wobbled, and tipped backward. Kyrael caught her and pulled her back to her feet.

"Come with—"

Flick twisted out of the angel's grasp before he could run off with her.

Jake reached to steady her. "You almost fell."

She waved his helping hand away. "I'm good. Just klutzy from lack of sleep. Hey, you two head to class. I'm going to splash some cold water on my face in the ladies' room."

"If you're sure," Jake said.

"I'm sure. Marisol, if I see the guy, I'll ask, okay?"

"Thanks."

Flick turned and headed back down the stairs toward the closest ladies' room. Sure enough, Kyrael followed her, protesting.

"I need to take you to meet the others. There's big news."

She rounded on him and hissed, "Not here."

He remained silent, following her down the stairs and into the same corridor where she'd met Adriel. Two angels in two days. They were doing a good job keeping her on her toes. Above them, the warning bell rang.

"Hurry up," she ordered the angel. "I'm going to be late for class."

"Whatever you think you need to accomplish here can't be as important as what Gabriel wants," Kyrael pressed her. "We need to go *see* the others."

"You are like the chihuahua of angels. You're so twitchy." She scowled at the angel. "Adriel made it sound like being involved with you was a matter of personal choice."

The angel fidgeted, his copper hair vibrating in time to his squirms. "You do have the choice. But the news is *huge*. Explosive even for Heaven. Do you want to pass up such an opportunity?"

"Do Adriel and Greyson already know?"

Kyrael nodded, trading his antsy fidgeting for a solid, professional stance. "I went straight to Adriel, then came to see you. I am a messenger angel, after all. Delivering news is what I do."

"Are you always so annoying about it?"

"I'm Heaven's fastest." The statement carried no pride, just conviction. Then, a shamed look crossed Kyrael's face, and he stared at the floor. "I don't think I'm bad at it."

He looked so pitiful. Flick reached out and put her hand on his shoulder. "Why don't you tell me the news here, and we'll decide how to proceed from there. But you need to stop running off with people. You can't pull us from our everyday lives at random. You're creating situations we can't explain and can't fix. But excusing ourselves like this is fine, so relax and be patient with us."

Kyrael gave a put-out sigh. "Such a method is slow by Heaven's standards, but if that's what it takes. Gabriel is intrigued by what you guys did with the hosting and extermination of the remala. He's given permission to form an experimental squad of co-hosts. We shouldn't go around getting humans involved until we know your effectiveness against the remalas. So for now, it will be the four of us."

He returned to his antsy state, the speed of his words increasing. "Adriel's duties as a death angel translate into extermination, but I get to learn now. I'm so thrilled I can't even explain the feeling."

"I couldn't tell," Flick muttered.

"That's why we need to meet with the others. We have to decide on partners and begin hunting. If we take down the ripe remalas who are ready to contract with demons, then Gabriel might expand the program." Kyrael shivered with excitement. "Heaven hasn't restructured in ages, *literal* ages. This is huge." His gesture with the last word caused Flick to step back.

Flick reached around his arms and grabbed his shoulders to hold him still. "Okay. But this level of over-excitement isn't going to work, not for daily living or hunting remalas. And neither Greyson nor I can drop our regular lives and hunt nonstop. We have to eat and sleep. To do that, we need a job and money. To get those, we need to finish school. The hunting can happen in between."

He put his hands over the top of hers on his shoulders. "Adriel is already working on getting Greyson settled in Seattle. I'm sure he'd get you whatever you needed, too. See, so we *can* go meet up with them."

"Kyrael." She set a hard stare on the angel. "I'm going to lay something out for you right now. I can't work with you. If you're the other angel involved, then you'll have to work with Greyson or count me out."

Kyrael wilted. "But I took Greyson from London yesterday. He's still a bit upset." He drooped even farther. "I'm going to get sent back to being a messenger. No way will Gabriel overlook a failure of this magnitude."

Flick pressed a single finger to his chest. "Then, I'll make you a one-time offer. Follow me through my day without interrupting. Watch and learn—"

"But I already know the whole internet," he interrupted.

"And yet can't apply what you learned there to functioning in my reality," she scolded. "Watch what it's like to live as a human so you can match the flow. If you can adapt to a level where you're comfortable to work with, maybe one of us will reconsider."

\*\*\*\*

Kyrael's stomach churned with his unhappiness. A human had scolded him. Worse, there was a slim chance he deserved it. But to be told neither of the two humans who could see him would work with him cut deep.

His natural enthusiasm tripped him up with the other messenger angels. Now he was faltering in this new endeavor. Why had God given him this personality if it would leave him ostracized?

Disheartened, he followed Felicity from class to class, watching as she requested. The whole ordeal was tedious in the extreme. How could humans stand crawling when they ought to run? And why was the information being presented in such minuscule portions? While he understood humans couldn't touch a computer and absorb all the knowledge all at once, they had to be capable of going faster than this.

Felicity left the school after the third period, pausing at her house to grab a sandwich and get her car. True to his promise not to interrupt, Kyrael had said nothing to her all morning. When he joined her in the front seat, she sighed.

"I didn't mean you had to be mute. I wanted you to stop jumping all over like an excited puppy."

"You don't seem to believe I can maintain proper boundaries. So I chose to be—"

"Sulky?" She turned onto the street, leaving the parking garage. "I didn't think angels pouted."

"Distant, rather than risk angering you."

She glanced sideways at him. "I'm not angry, though Greyson might be. But the few times we've met, you're indelicate. The whole meeting angels thing and all that's followed is enough for me to handle. My gut said you were going to make it worse. Not through malice but through carelessness and lack of understanding. You can follow that, right?"

He nodded, staring out the window. This human girl's insightfulness unsettled him. She had a knack for cutting through and hitting him.

"Kyrael, you're a messenger, right?"

"That's correct."

She nibbled her lip. "Can you fight the remalas? I

mean, Adriel is fluid in his movements. It's unreal, and he took Greyson's body through fighting moves last night."

"I'm not the same. However, Adriel can teach me. I'm an angel, so learning the material won't take long. But no one is willing to work with me as of now. Training me seems pointless."

"Urg." She squeezed the steering wheel. "Stop sounding so pitiful. One of us will work with you. Just be calmer about everything, okay? How many people have you seen running about their day in a manic fashion?"

"None."

"Is frantic hurrying commonplace for Heaven? Because I haven't seen Adriel act so rushed."

"No."

She cast a smile in his direction. "Then what you need is an outlet. Maybe that's why you're being put on this project."

"Hmm. Interesting perspective."

She pulled into the community college's parking lot, and the two climbed out of the car. He hurried around to her side of the vehicle. The afternoon had grown dark with clouds, and the wind tugged at their jackets.

"What are the rules for me following you here?" he asked, falling into step beside her.

"Adriel and I used my notebook paper to write back and forth," she murmured. Her gaze flicked up to passing people. She must not want to be seen talking to herself. "We can do the same if you want to ask questions and stuff. I told Adriel and Greyson to meet me here after class, so I assume we'll see them before long. Then we can plan how to go hunting."

"Gabriel gave Adriel command of the unit."

She nodded and opened the door to a classroom. A pink blush spread across her cheeks when a young man smiled and waved. Before Kyrael's eyes, Felicity transformed from a confident young woman to a turtle, drawing within herself, shyness permeating her features.

Kyrael glanced between them several times, studying the interaction. He hadn't seen one like this yet. The young man shifted his books and gestured for Felicity to sit. Felicity took off her backpack and used it like a shield, clutching it to her chest. Yet, despite her hesitations, she took the offered seat.

Kyrael grabbed a spare chair and pulled it to the two-person desk they were using, settling himself at the end.

The young man frowned at Felicity. "Are we still on for this weekend?"

Shock flitted across Felicity's face. "Yeah. Why? Did something come up?"

"Well, you've shown up to class the last two days with two different guys in tow. They aren't even in this class and—"

Kyrael had stopped listening. He sprang from his chair and hurried out the door. He didn't want to make a scene in case Gabriel said no. If all he'd done was rush out of class, the encounter could still be explained away. Felicity was right. If he slowed down and thought things through, the fallout promised to be less messy.

This time, he wouldn't bother with the escalator of light. Concentrating on Gabriel's garden, Kyrael teleported himself there. The effort left him breathless but was worth it because Gabriel sat working in the shade of a tree.

"Back so soon?" Gabriel asked without looking up.

"I was accompanying the young lady through her day, and another young man saw me in one of her school classes."

"And?" Gabriel pressed.

"I was wondering if we should offer him the opportunity to be involved with the experimental team."

"Why would you think we should include him?"

Kyrael fidgeted, then stopped himself. Felicity had warned him to calm down. Taking a deep breath, he held himself steady. "He and the girl are friends. If she's going to be working with us, and he can see us, then keeping him out of the secret would be much harder than asking if he'd like in."

After a few moments, Gabriel peered up from his work. The smile he gave Kyrael set the angel squirming with its kindness. "I'm glad to see you maturing into this job. It's reasonable to assume the young man will find out. It's better to get him involved now to form a more cohesive unit. Assuming this new young man wishes to be a part of the hunters."

Kyrael dropped to his knees and bowed his head to the floor. "Thank you, Gabriel. Which angel should I contact about working with this new individual?"

"Do you have any recommendations?"

Now Kyrael was glad he'd knelt because a Seraph asking his opinion on something so monumental would have knocked him to his knees. "Niciel." Kyrael peeked up at the seraph to see his reaction.

Gabriel nodded. "He's suitable. Please contact him and let him know I'm pulling him from extermination in Italy and reassigning him to the host team."

The seraph had already returned his focus to his

work. Kyrael stood and centered on Niciel. Teleporting oneself to far-flung locations like Earth drained an individual, and very few messengers had the stamina for repeat trips. But Kyrael would put his talents to work for Gabriel. Once he'd sensed the other angel's presence, he teleported himself to Niciel's side.

Niciel jumped, smacking his head on the underside of a half-collapsed column. "Cheese and crackers, Kyrael. Don't barge in when I'm focused on hunting."

"My apologies. I have a message from Gabriel."

Niciel frowned, crouched, then swung a blade beneath a pile of fallen stones. He stood, shaking his hand to dispel the misty weapon. "There. Now we can talk. I'm impressed. Most of the time, you're all over me with your news."

"I've been told it's disruptive."

"By every angel you delivered messages to for how many centuries?" Niciel shook his head. "I'm sorry. I don't mean to offend. You are the fastest messenger, and I can't fault your speed."

"Thank you. Now, hear me out since time is short." He explained the job Gabriel had given them and how they needed to get back before Felicity's class ended.

Niciel snapped his gaping mouth shut. "That's a whole lot of change in procedure for Heaven."

"Can you process at the college?" Kyrael pressed.

"Sure."

Kyrael took a pinch of Niciel's shirt to guide him, and they both disappeared, reappearing in the hall outside her class. "We'll wait here for them."

Niciel stared at Kyrael. "Who are you, and where's the impatient Kyrael?"

"Self-reflecting on personal behaviors," Kyrael

answered, forcing himself to focus on the classroom door.

Chapter 6

Wade frowned at Flick, and her stomach sank. His was not a look of good news. "Are we still on for this weekend?"

Shock jolted through Flick. "Yeah. Why? Did something come up?" Was she being dumped before they even went out? His tone was downright chilly.

"Well, you've shown up to class the last two days with two different guys in tow. They aren't even in the class, and I wondered where we stand." He sighed. "Wait. That came out sounding way more jerkish than I meant. We haven't been out yet, and if you're dating multiple guys, that's your choice. But be fair and let me know. I don't want to go into our date with the wrong expectations. That's all."

Flick's face went numb. "Multiple guys?" she gasped out. "Um—"

The teacher walked in, and Wade shrugged, turning away from her. No. This was going all wrong. She caught at his sleeve and leaned to whisper.

"I'm not dating anyone. Extra boyfriends is so…brazen, uh, no. I'm mean, not something I have the confidence to do."

Speaking of confidence, hers was draining fast now that she could smell his shampoo. Liam had smelled like guy's body spray, but Wade smelled like an adult. Her cheeks warmed under a blush.

He turned, and they were nose to nose. Flick's blush deepened, and she jerked back away from him. How could he think she'd date other guys when he set her heart tap dancing on the back of her ribs?

Wait.

Her face numbed again. The professor had started talking, but the words bounced off Flick's brain. Without her focus on being dumped, the meaning of Wade's statement sank in.

She grabbed his arm. "*You saw them?*" she blurted.

The professor quieted, and the whole class stared. A new blush—one of deep embarrassment—settled, not just on her face but on her entire head.

"I'm so sorry," she murmured.

While the class went back to normal, she pulled out her spiral notebook and found a fresh page. Writing her question also gave her innards a chance to calm down after making a spectacle of herself.

*I need to know what the two men you saw looked like*, she wrote.

*We have class.* Wade chuckled while writing. *Maybe you should focus after grabbing the professor's attention.*

Flick shook her head and pointed to her request.

With a shrug, Wade wrote, *Both guys had their hair dyed with some metallic spray. And the first guy wore colored contacts in teal. Today the guy had violet contacts. Aren't you a little young to hang out with guys old enough to go clubbing?*

Flick's stomach bottomed out. Kyrael had hurried off, so she couldn't ask what she was supposed to do with this information. After twirling her pen a bit, she tried another angle.

*This might sound random, and don't laugh, but do you see spooky things?*

Wade read the question, his entire body going rigid. He sat in a frozen state for several minutes, staring straight ahead. Though, he didn't take any notes on the lecture.

After a pause, he wrote, *What do you mean by spooky things?*

*Like ghosts, or worse.* Flick didn't need him to answer. She could already tell by his expression—he saw terrifying things, too.

*Can we not talk about this now?* Wade shuddered and focused back on the lecture.

Flick let it go. The middle of class wasn't the best time to delve into such topics. Imagine how he'd react when she introduced those "clubbing" guys as members of the not-so-human society. She couldn't blame him for missing their absence from the land of the living. She'd missed it with Adriel at first, too. In so many ways, Adriel and Kyrael looked human. It wasn't until she'd tried interacting with them on a more interpersonal level that the differences became apparent.

The one conclusion she reached while keeping half her mind on her class, telling him about Adriel and Kyrael, wasn't her decision. *But*, she would try and find a way to bring him along when she met Greyson and Adriel after class. If Adriel wanted to drop the bomb of not being human and their capability of killing shades on Wade, he could do the honors.

She doodled wing shapes in the margins of her notes. While she accepted Kyrael and Adriel were not human, she still couldn't swallow the notion of them being actual angels. For one thing, she'd never seen so much as a feather clinging to them. Though, she'd seen and read enough fantasy material to know appearances weren't everything when it came to the otherworldly. Still, shouldn't an angel be a little more regal than the overexcitable Kyrael? Or a little less... Well, Adriel had a certain *je ne se quoi* that didn't quite mesh with being angelic.

When the professor dismissed class, Wade grabbed his stuff in a hurry and stood to go, but Flick caught his arm. "I see them, too."

He turned his face away, pulling his arm free at the same time. He headed out the far door, opposite the one Kyrael had exited through.

"You don't have to say anything," Flick said, following on his heels. "I saw it on your face when you read the question. For years I haven't talked in-depth with anyone about what I see." She ducked the door of the classroom on its swing shut. "The few times I had mentioned them when I was younger earned me a reputation as the kid obsessed with the occult. But I have a new acquaintance who sees the same things, and I can't tell you what a relief it is."

Wade spun, glaring. "What relief?" he snapped. "Now we can all shrink from the shadows together?"

Flick gaped, stammering over her response. "No. I meant that I don't question my sanity."

"How did you even know to ask me?" Wade had taken off down a side hall of the building, not waiting for Flick.

"A hunch," she hedged around the truth. "But here's the crazy thing. I'm meeting the guy who also sees them, right now, outside the building. Please come with me. You can tell us a little about what you see, and we can share how we're coping."

Wade jammed his hands in his pockets. "I'm coping well enough. I don't need to sit around telling ghost stories to make myself feel better."

Flick snorted, then caught herself when Wade shot her a sideways glare. "I'm not laughing at you, just at the idea you're coping well. Bringing this up has made you moody in a way I've never seen before."

He stopped at the inside edge of the exterior doors. Outside the glass, Adriel and Greyson stood in the shade of a tree, talking. They waited farther away than if Flick and Wade had gone through the main hall, but not too far for Flick to see Greyson was relaxed in Adriel's company. What a huge change.

"What would you know about my moods?" Wade accused. "We've talked like twice."

Flick twisted the straps on her backpack around her fingers. "I may have spent a little too much time watching you." A blush warmed her cheeks, and she gazed down. "Crushing on you. I understand it's not as if I know the real you. But I've never seen you this agitated. People who are coping don't flip moods like this." She glanced at her purple fingertip and untwisted the strap. "I know you have no reason to trust me or believe me or whatever. But I admitted what I see to you, so doesn't that earn me a few minutes of tolerance on your part? Please come meet my friends."

"Friends?" Wade's eyebrows lifted near his hairline. "Now there's more than one?" He frowned. "Are we talking about those clubbing guys?"

"Not just them, but they'll be there. Please?" She gave him her best puppy eyes and hoped she looked cute enough and his attraction was strong enough to override his objections.

Wade grimaced. "God. Cute girls get whatever they want. Fine. I'll meet your friends. Then I don't want to talk about this stuff ever again. I spend enough time looking over my shoulder without rehashing it in the daylight hours."

"If that's still what you want after meeting them, then you have my word." Flick pushed open the door and stepped outside.

****

Greyson and Adriel's conversation had waned to a comfortable silence. That morning, he might have been in a hurry for Felicity to come out of her class so he could move on, but after spending the day with Adriel, everything had changed. Except for one brief encounter earlier in the day, Kyrael, the agitating angel, hadn't been around. This left him and Adriel free to explore the city and discuss the full implications of Kyrael's news from Gabriel.

At first, he'd balked at the idea of becoming part of a ghost-hunting team with a pair of so-called angels and a high school senior. It sounded like the plot of a cheap teen-network drama. But arguing got much harder when Adriel made good on his promise to settle Greyson in Seattle.

Adriel's promise unfolded in a series of short disappearances by the angel. Each time he returned with some mind-bending piece of a stable life. First, he'd shown up with all of Greyson's documents: his passport and such. Then he'd brought back a green card with all the appropriate seals and verification. When he returned with a key and a copy of a lease, Greyson protested.

The key was to a flat in Felicity's complex—on the

same floor even. He couldn't afford the rent of such a nice place, even if he could have returned to his job at the pub. But in Seattle, he didn't have a paycheck. Adriel assured him Heaven would provide a salary for being a guinea pig in this trial. Living expenses were what they'd been talking about while waiting in the shade for Felicity's class to end.

Felicity lingered inside a door to an adjacent wing of the college rather than the one Adriel had indicated she'd come out. She appeared to be having a disagreement with a young man. If she looked distressed at any point, he'd interrupt. If the two of them were going to be partners, he might as well start having her back.

Without taking his eyes off the pair, he asked Adriel. "It's cool Heaven's going to cover my rent and pay me a salary for living expenses. But where does the money come from?"

"Uh, haven't you ever been to church? Congregants tithe. Their money belongs to the church to do God's work. This is God's work, directly ordered."

"Churches like the Vatican?"

"Among others. We have the Grigori in key positions in churches around the globe. They're well-suited to seeing God's will carried out in the physical world. They'll direct the funds to wherever I request. In this case, the money will go into your bank account."

"Grigori?"

"Another classification of angels specialized for work on Earth."

"Specialized? When you say it that way, it makes me think of E Squadron."

Adriel cocked his head.

"Special forces? Secret government ops?"

"Ah." Adriel smiled and shook his head. "I could tell you, but then I'd have to kill you."

"Did you just make a joke?" Greyson rolled his eyes. "Not funny coming from a death angel."

"I watch human movies, you know. And no, not *that* sort of specialized. The Grigori are on Earth long-term to monitor and advise. By specialized, I mean they've been altered to live amongst humans and serve effectively."

Greyson crossed his arms. "I'm still not buying the whole angels and God thing."

"I know." Adriel sighed. "Out of curiosity, why are you agreeing to my proposals if you don't believe we're good?"

Greyson shifted his weight from foot to foot. "Several reasons. First, I don't think you're bad. I just don't think you're divine. The money might even be coming from the church. Historically, religion and the occult are pretty interconnected. I'm sure plenty of otherworldly beings have links to one religion or another. As for skimming money off the church, people donated on the idea it would be used to do good works. If we banish these negative beings, then they're getting their money's worth, right?"

"I believe they'd be satisfied, yes."

A blush crept across Greyson's face, and he turned, studying the leaves above them. "The last reason is rather selfish. I liked taking the creature out. I've never gotten such a rush, and it's not something I could do on my own. To get paid to eliminate more and to stop flinching when I go past the shadows, I'd be crazy not to agree."

"Greyson."

He spun to face Felicity, and his torso stiffened.

Why in God's name had she dragged over the bloke she'd been talking with? How was he supposed to tell her about getting a flat on her floor now? They'd have to establish some system of keeping the rest of their lives out of otherworldly business.

"Wade, this is Greyson," Felicity introduced. "He arrived from London a couple days ago. And this is Adriel."

Both Greyson and Adriel froze. Greyson's shock was mirrored on Adriel's face. She wouldn't bother introducing Adriel unless this guy could see other entities, too. But he wasn't acting skittish. She must not have told her friend Adriel wasn't human. Either that or he had an envious comfort with angels.

Wade shrugged. His expression said he didn't want to be there.

"Greyson is the friend who can see the same things we can," Felicity explained to Wade. She turned a loaded look on Adriel before settling her attention on Greyson. "I thought if Wade knew others were suffering from seeing what we see, it might make him feel better. Maybe we can help him the way we've been helped." She murmured the last sentence, every word begging Adriel's permission to tell Wade more.

Conflicting feelings rolled through Greyson's stomach. On the one hand, he didn't want this poor guy to keep struggling with the same fears he'd just dispelled in himself. The relief was overwhelming—so much so he was now letting a strange entity pay him to live and hunt halfway around the world from his home. On the other hand, Adriel and Kyrael didn't split between the three of them for hunting. If this guy joined, someone would get left at home each time without an angel to keep the negative beings at bay.

One other feeling twinged in the middle of the mix. He enjoyed his conversations with Felicity, and he didn't know another human in Seattle or Washington State, for that matter. If she had a hunting partner she was already friends with… Loneliness panged in his chest. He'd assumed hunting would be between the two of them, and her attention would be his anchor to creating a social life in Seattle. Now he was going to end up a third wheel.

Before Adriel had time to delve into anything, the main doors burst open, and Kyrael rushed out, followed by another man Greyson assumed had to be another angel. The man following Kyrael had metallic gold hair and lime-green eyes. He had a very European look about him, wearing slacks, a t-shirt, and a dress vest.

Kyrael rushed straight into the middle of the three, his expression a bit manic. Greyson braced himself for the onslaught of Kyrael's next round of news, but the angel took one look at Felicity and pulled up. After several moments of silence, he spoke.

"I'm glad we caught you. Felicity, you didn't exit through the same door we used to enter your class."

"Sorry," she murmured.

"Niciel?" Adriel asked, cutting across Felicity, confused. "What are you doing here?"

Kyrael tucked both his hands behind his back. Then he rocked to the balls of his feet and back before speaking again. "When Wade saw me in class, I got permission to add a third. Niciel will join the team if everyone agrees."

Kyrael's efforts to hold back were apparent to Greyson. The angel squirmed, trying to keep control. Adriel nodded, his gaze flicking from person to person.

He also shifted positions several times, but his movements were more contemplative.

"Uh? Felicity, I'm gonna go," Wade said.

Adriel let him walk several yards away before vanishing and reappearing in front of him. Wade let out a shriek and staggered backward. He whirled around, glaring at Felicity.

"You could have warned me they weren't…that they're," he hurried back to the group and dropped his voice to an angry whisper, "not human."

Adriel reappeared right at Wade's shoulder this time. "Would you have believed her?" he challenged the young man.

Wade startled, jumping away, then scowled. "Maybe. What the hell are you?"

"Nothing from Hell, I assure you," Adriel said at the same time Kyrael burst out, "Angels." Kyrael bit his lip at a swift glare from Adriel and fell silent.

Wade broke out laughing. "I'm out." He turned and walked off again.

"They kill the creatures and get rid of them," Felicity called after him.

Wade paused in his tracks.

"Nothing has come near me since they've been around," she continued. "We can help them get rid of the nasty ones faster. If you're interested."

He turned back. "I'm listening."

Adriel put a hand on Felicity's shoulder. "Talking doesn't prove much, like Flick telling you we weren't human wouldn't have meant much without a little demonstration. Your name is Wade, right?"

Wade nodded.

"Do you have obligations this evening?" Adriel

asked him.

"I guess not, once I get off work. Why?"

"We'll take you on a hunt. You can see for yourself what getting rid of the negative entities involves. If you're interested in the process, we can talk further." He turned to Felicity. "Greyson didn't get a chance to deliver his big news." The angel stared at Greyson, waiting for him to tell her the details.

"Right. Since I agreed to stay and be part of this little experiment, Adriel set me up. He got my passport, a green card, and a flat near yours. He's even paying me a salary for the hunting."

"Sweet." Felicity's eyes shone. "Am I getting paid, too?"

"A college fund," Adriel answered.

Felicity drooped.

Adriel chuckled. "You'll get some pocket money, as well." He rubbed his hands together. "Right. We need to assign partners so we can begin training with one another."

"I call Adriel," both Greyson and Felicity shouted at the same time.

The others all stared at Adriel, who wore a bashful expression. "Given my normal job, I don't get much love. You guys are embarrassing me."

"What job?" Wade asked.

"I'll have Niciel partner with Wade for tonight," Adriel continued, ignoring him. "They'll stay together if Wade agrees to be a part of our efforts." He turned toward Felicity, his expression going soft. "Flick, what have you done to Kyrael?"

"Nothing." She looked confused. "I guess I did order him to calm down, or I said I'd quit. Is that what you mean?"

Adriel put his hands on her shoulders and stared her in the face. Greyson shuddered. The girl had serious pluck to stare at a death angel. She faced a reaper, even if he was on vacation, and he wasn't sure he could do the same despite liking Adriel better than Kyrael.

"Kyrael's reputation for excitability has preceded him for a very long time," Adriel said. "He's been the brunt of teasing and mild manipulation for it. Despite that, he's always rushed headlong into every encounter, never calculating the impact of his actions…until you."

"Me?" she squeaked.

"Somehow, your energy wavelength compliments his."

She looked lost.

"In other words," Adriel explained, "you can help him calm down when the rest of Heaven failed him. I know we met one another first, and you're more comfortable with our familiarity, but I'd like to see you work with Kyrael. He's been struggling to find his place. I have a feeling a partnership between you two could help him reach his potential."

She blushed scarlet. "Okay—"

Kyrael rushed her, stopping short when she held out a hand palm flat to stop him, then pointed. "No."

His head drooped. "I'll be calm. You won't quit even though you have to work with me?"

"Not as long as you control yourself."

"Shall we go see Greyson's new apartment?" Adriel suggested.

"Sure," Felicity agreed.

"What about me?" Wade asked.

Adriel turned, raising an eyebrow. "I thought you

had work. We can meet you tonight for the hunt."

"If you want me to be in on your project, whatever it is, shouldn't I see all of it? If you're paying, missing work isn't a big deal. I'll call in sick."

Adriel cocked his head. "If that's what you want. Flick, can you give Wade your address? We can meet at the entrance to the building." He wrinkled his nose. "Niciel, can you ride with Flick, Greyson, and Kyrael? I'll go with Wade in case he has any questions."

Greyson caught a flash of triumph crossing Adriel's face. He'd been manipulating Wade all along—he was far more comfortable among humans than he let on.

Greyson followed Felicity back to her car, walking next to the new angel. "I didn't quite catch your name."

The angel startled and bumped into Greyson's shoulder. "Niciel." He pronounced it Nih-seal. "Apologies. I've never spoken to a human before. Or touched one." He poked Greyson's arm.

Greyson ignored this. The fascination would pass faster if he allowed it to play out. "Do all angels have peculiar names?" he asked.

Niciel glanced sideways at him. "Humans have the odd names."

"I guess it's a cultural thing," Greyson mused. "What sort of angel are you?"

Niciel hesitated.

"It's okay. Adriel's a death angel. How much worse can it get?"

"I'm an exterminator. They get rid—"

"Of all the remalas," Felicity finished for him. "Adriel told us about you. At least he told us a little."

"Convenient."

Felicity pulled out her keys and pressed the fob,

unlocking the doors of her little silver sedan. "Angels in the back. Sorry, I don't trust you not to touch things or distract me while I'm driving."

Kyrael scrambled in due to his excitement, though he did manage not to run his mouth. A sharp intake of breath from Niciel gave away the calmer angel's excitement.

"Haven't either of you ridden in a car?" Greyson asked while buckling in.

"No," the angels answered in unison.

The ride back to her flat didn't pass fast enough for Greyson. Adriel had given him the key to his new flat, and while Greyson knew the building was very nice, he hadn't been inside his new place yet. Adriel promised he'd have everything he needed for a comfortable life. What that looked like in physical terms, he didn't dare speculate, which reminded him. If he was going to pick up here in the States where he left off in London, he ought to see about transferring schools. He'd ask Adriel after they'd toured his flat.

While Felicity parked, Greyson made a mental note to ask if a vehicle could be included in his adjustment package. Adriel could teleport him around, but that would get awkward when he made regular friends or started dating. Besides, the Vatican had an awful lot of money. What was a little economy car to them?

They waited by the front doors for several minutes for the other two to arrive. Kyrael and Niciel poked around in both the foot and car traffic. Their antics forced Greyson to keep up a conversation with Felicity so they wouldn't keep laughing at things other people couldn't see. The Seattle streets had their fair share of nutters, so maybe Felicity and he wouldn't draw attention. Still, he didn't want to look unhinged.

"They have to find parking on the street and walk back here," Felicity soothed when Greyson strained to look up and down the street for the hundredth time.

He put his right hand in his pocket. "I assumed as much. So…are you happy your boyfriend can join our team?"

She blushed and let out a random giggle. "He's not my boyfriend."

"Yet," Greyson tacked on.

She rubbed her cheeks. "Is it that obvious?"

"I've seen billboard advertising more subtle." He chuckled. "Well, maybe you two can make a connection while beating remalas into another dimension."

Felicity glowered. "I guess getting older doesn't help guys get more romantic. How would you turn a hunt into anything like a date? After kicking gross remala butt, are we supposed to go play video games? Eat nacho cheese chips and wipe our hands on our pants? Or find a sports game so we can yell at the tv?"

Greyson burst out laughing. "Where do I find a girl that cool? But as an older male, I'll warn you right now, if a bloke uses a bunch of romantic notions all on his own, you haven't found the perfect man. You've found someone randy, and each move he's used is a plea to get in your pants."

Her face took on an expression of mocking seriousness. "Let me get this straight. If a guy is a jerk to women, he's an asshole?"

"Yes."

"And if a guy is being super nice to a girl, he's an asshole?"

"A wolf in sheep's clothing. Yes."

She frowned. "Is there such a thing as a nice guy? As far as being a woman is concerned."

Greyson grinned. "You're looking at him."

Her laugh hit the glass walls of the building and bounced back at them.

"What's so funny?" Adriel asked, leading Wade around a corner.

Felicity snorted while trying to control her laughter. "Greyson was explaining the male MO to me."

Wade gave him a quizzical look. "Why do I get the feeling her hysterical laughter means the explanation wasn't in our favor?"

Greyson shrugged. "She's a high schooler hanging around two college guys. I just laid the facts bare."

Felicity stuck her tongue out at Greyson. "I'm eighteen, and you're twenty. And, Wade, have you turned nineteen yet?"

He shook his head. "I'm still eighteen until February."

"We're all close to the same age. But if there's a dirty old man here, it would be you."

Greyson raised his hands in surrender. "Guilty as charged, on occasion. But I didn't pick my partners in this little venture. Remember, a few days ago, I lived in London, unaware of this or you. Don't make me sound like I've been scoping out unsuspecting schoolgirls."

"And according to Greyson's definition, you'd just be dirty," Felicity whipped out at Wade. Her eyes widened and she turned plum red from her scalp to her neck. Spinning around, she busied herself, punching in the access code.

"I plead the fifth," Wade muttered.

Greyson pulled the lease papers Adriel had given

him out of his pocket and unfolded them. "I'm on the fourth floor," he informed Felicity, who waited to push the button for the elevator.

"Same as me," she chirped, avoiding Wade's gaze. "We're neighbors. How lucky is that?"

"I don't think luck had anything to do with it," Greyson said. The elevator doors slid shut, and they started their way up. "This was all Adriel's doing."

"Wait, wait," Wade said. "You're going to take an apartment from some random non-human guy?"

"I know it's hard to comprehend," Greyson admitted. "I waffled, questioning my sanity. But after tonight, I think you'll get a better idea why I might consider."

The doors slid open, and Greyson held up the paper. "Unit 404."

Adriel snickered, and Greyson turned a sharp look on him. "You're not screwing with me, are you? Like 404 doesn't exist, or it's the utility closet?"

Adriel looked aghast and pushed everyone out of the elevator so the doors could close. "No. I wouldn't dream of teasing you. The number is a joke, though."

"Because it's the unit right next to mine?" Felicity asked.

Adriel rubbed his face. "No. But the proximity was handy. In some cultures, four is a taboo number because of its close relation to death. The joke was for me. Your unit has the most fours of any in the building. *I* rented it for *my* hunter..." He fell silent, waiting for them to join him in the joke.

"Must be angel humor," Greyson said, rolling his eyes. "Now I get to live in the flat most representative of death. Dandy."

"Do you want me to switch you to another unit?" Adriel asked.

Greyson opened his door, the word yes resting on his tongue. But it never made its way past his lips. The flat was huge, with large windows looking out over the city. Between the buildings, he had a peekaboo view of the Space Needle. The nicest furnishings he'd ever been able to call his own graced the rooms, all modern and black leather.

"I can stay here," he choked out.

"Sweet place," Wade whistled from behind him.

"Oh. The floor plan is the same as my place," Felicity said. She put her hands on his shoulders and peeked over at the apartment. "Your furniture is better...*real* modern. Mom likes mid-century modern, but it just looks old to me. Mind if I poke around?"

"Not at all."

She slid past him, and he caught a whiff of her—tea tree and mint—fresh.

"You've even got a second bedroom," Felicity called from the far side of the apartment. "Planning on taking a roommate?"

"Will I need to in order to make the rent on a place this size?" he asked Adriel.

Adriel shook his head. "Not in the way you're thinking. But whatever angels are working on this project will stay here, as well. While we don't need a bed, we require space and other furnishings. This place is big enough to accommodate us all."

"Do you not sleep?" Wade asked, shivering.

"They sleep curled up as a floating ball of light," Felicity explained.

"Creepy," Wade said.

"Not to me." She started poking around the kitchen. "Did you know you're stocked in here, Greyson? Anyway, when they float like lights, they're the best bug lights ever. They keep away everything scary. It's awesome. I've never slept as well as when they're here. The angels are the exact opposite of creepy."

"Then you two believe they're angels?" Wade asked.

Greyson and Felicity exchanged a look. "Not in the way you're implying," he answered for them both. "Angels from God seems a bit far-fetched. But we're both sure they're good. And they're bloody effective at getting rid of the negative entities."

Wade shook his head and leaned against the wall. "This is nuts. Bonkers. I've broken down beyond repair."

Greyson rolled his eyes and waved Felicity into the living area. "Let him finish his meltdown in peace."

Chapter 7

Adriel spent the afternoon watching the three humans watch each other. Greyson and Flick chatted on the couch. While Flick had Greyson's full attention, she kept casting worried glances in Wade's direction.

Wade sat in a chair at the dining table. After calling in sick to work, he'd laid his face on the glass and stared at the other two. The young man's expression stayed distant and closed. But both the others had reacted with similar dispassion. Seeing the creatures that plagued them dispelled seemed to be the one concrete thing to change their minds.

Which reminded him. "What's the worst thing each of you has seen?"

None of the humans looked pleased, but Flick spoke first. "I was eight, and my nanny was walking me home from a playdate at Marisol's house well after dark. While we were waiting at a crosswalk, a delivery truck drove by. Sitting on the top, as big as the cargo portion, sat a remala that looked like a giant snail, except the body coming out of the shell wasn't covered in slime but human hands. These were moving the thing toward the cab of the truck. The shell had a pattern on it, like ribcage bones. I never saw the face, and the truck turned the corner just before we crossed the street.

"I don't know if it was going too fast or if the weight of the remala caused it to almost tip. My nanny hurried me across to the other side, muttering about drunk drivers. The truck must have crashed right after we crossed because my nanny grabbed me and ran up the street, telling me not to look back. I heard squealing tires, crunching metal, and shattering glass. The next morning, the street was still closed. People around the apartment complex said the man had died a messy death."

Niciel hissed. "The remala shredded his energy to get at the good stuff."

"Agreed," Adriel added.

Greyson tucked his hands under his rear, sitting on them. "I was twelve. The kids at school thought because I claimed I saw ghosts, that meant I'd like to be dared to go into a graveyard." He made a scolding click with his tongue. "That's the last time anyone ever took advantage of my ego. Like a bloody fool, I said yes. All I had to do was tag the tree in the center. But when I got there, the whole tree uprooted itself and chased me around the place, cutting me off from the gates. I ended up scrambling up some ivy and over the brick wall. The ivy covered a whole row of iron spikes. I still have scars on the backs of my thighs."

"Good thing you didn't get caught, or we might have met under different circumstances," Adriel commented.

"Hmm," Niciel added, "both haven't encountered anything above mid-grade remalas. Though, if the second pulled up a tree to chase a victim, it was getting close to ripe."

"Makes sense to me," Kyrael joined in. "After all, wouldn't there be a plethora of negative energy to feed on in a graveyard?"

"Only during funerals," Niciel countered. "Since regular human visitation isn't as common as, say, people walking over a city sewer, there's less concentration of negative energy but more regularity for feeding remalas outside a cemetery. We tend to find the ripe remalas in places with a steady flow of misery."

"Hospitals?" Flick guessed.

"Yes." The angel nodded. "Office buildings, subways."

"School?" Wade joked with a laugh.

"Schools are a perfect breeding ground," Niciel imparted. "What with anxiety over tests, friends, dating, and a dozen other things, schools provide a feast for remalas." He shook his head. "Teens, in particular, need to relax. They off-gas negative energy faster than a dairy farm sends out stench."

Wade wrinkled his nose. "Are you seriously an angel?"

"I spend my time killing what people build up. I wouldn't be very good at my job unless I understood where and why people radiate negative energy. I spend a good deal of time here on Earth. You pick up the nuances."

Niciel glanced out the picture windows. "We have an hour or so until twilight. Do you want to wait or hunt the long shadows now?"

"Wait," Adriel decided. "Let's let the big boys get hungry, then look for prey."

"Can these children handle it?" Niciel asked. "We've connected with humans who still have one foot in the cradle."

"I resent that," Greyson objected.

"I'm legally an adult," Flick protested.

"I don't even live with my parents," Wade complained. "Besides, I only agreed to watch."

"If you say so," Niciel responded, though he didn't indicate to whom he spoke.

"Flick is timid, but her heart is strong," Adriel said. "She'll be a fine hunter. Greyson gets a thrill out of helping conquer his fears. He'll also do well. I can't vouch for Wade. I met the boy on one other occasion, though I wasn't aware he could see me at the time. He's an unknown."

He spent the next few minutes explaining to Wade how the hosting worked so the hunting angels could go undetected. This was one of the last hurdles to gaining a third team member. They needed to see if Wade could handle hosting another being and if he could stomach chasing the things he feared.

"You never told me the worst thing you saw," Adriel urged him.

Wade flinched and looked away. "I don't want to talk about it."

"The more we know about your experiences, the better we can work with you."

Wade turned a glare on the angel. "I was six, and there weren't just monsters in my closet. My grandmother haunted me every night for a month after she died. Each night, she came into my room, passed through my door, and came back a little later. She grew more horrifying on every return trip through my room: flayed open wounds, extra random body parts, protruding bones, and gross things buzzed and crawled on her. My parents took me to a grief counselor, but I needed an exorcist."

"You needed an exterminator," Kyrael said, glaring in Niciel's direction.

"Anyway, after about a month, she stopped

appearing. No idea why. It should have been a relief, but it took years of hiding under the covers at every scratch coming from near my closet before I started sleeping through the night again. Not that the harm she did could be fixed by sleeping better. I don't like to think about her or anything else I see, but the damage is still there, deep down. I don't sleep soundly…ever."

"I remember your grandmother," Niciel murmured. "The whole department heard. It took too long for the local exterminator to corner the woman and destroy her energy imprint. She had such a bent to complete something on Earth she fused with any source of power, collecting remalas until she contracted with a demon to complete her task."

"What did my grandma…what?" Wade burst out, sitting upright for the first time since he'd lain on the table.

Niciel shook his head. "Her goals concerned the living. I can't tell you."

Wade stood up so fast the chair flew back, and he slammed his hands down on the glass, shaking it. "I deserve to know, damn it. I hate my grandmother now. She terrorized me. I need to know if she haunted me on purpose. If I ever said a prayer to that absentee calling himself God, I'd pray she's in Hell watching the same things I saw every night."

Niciel's expression softened. "I'm sorry. I never realized some could see the remalas and be affected by them." He crossed the room and put a hand on Wade's shoulder. "If I tell you what she sought, do I have your word, you will focus on hunting remalas and taking your anger out on generalized evil plaguing Earth?"

"Sure, sure."

"You will not seek retribution?"

"Fine. Whatever."

Niciel held out his hand.

"What?" Wade snapped.

"We're sealing this with angelic power. If you break your vow and seek what you've sworn not to seek, your joints will freeze, and you will experience pain unlike anything you've ever known. Only I will have the authority to release you."

"God. Drama much?" He held out his hand.

Niciel took the offered hand. On the backs of their joined hands, flowing symbols written in the angelic tongue drifted in a pulsing circle. Adriel flinched. If Niciel felt the need to go this far, whatever he had to tell the boy must be unpleasant. He had a feeling Wade had traded one form of closure for another open wound.

Niciel sighed, and his shoulders drooped. "I doubt your grandmother meant to terrorize you. She didn't pass of natural causes. We believe she was hunting for her killer."

"But she went down the hall to my parent's room—" Wade gagged. "Oh God. *No*." He turned for the door, went rigid, and dropped to the floor like a log—choked screams issuing from between his clenched teeth. Tears leaked down his cheeks.

Niciel crouched beside him. "I'm sorry. I agreed because you seem like the sort of man who wouldn't have stopped until you found answers. Try to find peace knowing your grandmother's soul was released from her torment when we exterminated the remalas fusing with her." He lay a gentle hand on Wade's head. "Heaven will settle the wrongs done to her in due time. Don't will your grandmother to Hell anymore. That spot is reserved for the one who deserves it."

"You've suffered enough." The angel snapped his fingers, and Wade's body sagged to the floor. Now, proper sobs tore from him. Niciel took the corner of his shirt and wiped the tears off Wade's face. "I meant to save you years of panicked searching only to find this same pain. Now you can heal and live the life your grandmother would have wanted for you."

"Am I following this right?" Flick whispered in Adriel's ear. "Did Niciel imply one of Wade's parents killed his grandmother?"

Adriel nodded. "Best to wait for further discussion until Wade deems the time right."

****

Kyrael tagged along after Felicity while she gathered her things. She paused to put a hand on top of Wade's, patting once before leaving to check in with her parents. Kyrael followed her next door and waited while she greeted her parents with long hugs.

"I take it your friend was able to go back to his apartment?" her mother asked.

Felicity paused for a moment. "Greyson's apartment had some trouble with the health department, so they canceled his lease. He got lucky and ran into someone on his way out this morning who fixed him up with a place in our building. Next door, of all things."

Her mother cocked her head. "Really?"

"Right place, right time," her dad said. "I hope he bought a lottery ticket."

"I'm not sure if he can." Felicity carried three glasses and a carafe of water to the table. "He's just got a green card, after all."

"How was school today?" he asked, setting plates

and silverware out.

"Fine." Felicity took a seat at the table. "The semester is heating up. I have a feeling I'll be crazy busy."

"Well, it is your senior year, honey." Her mom set a dish of salad on the table.

Her dad added garlic toast and sat. "Don't forget you need balance. If your grades are in hand, remember to take time to spend with your friends. You only get one senior year."

"You'd better only have one senior year," her mom teased, setting a lasagna on the table, then taking a seat.

Felicity grinned and held her plate out for a slice. "I'll graduate on time. No worries. But speaking of staying social, I got a date for Homecoming next week."

"Anyone we know?" her mother asked, adding salad to her plate.

"No. He's in my English Lit class."

"At the college?" her father asked, concern in his voice.

"Yeah, but he just graduated this spring, so don't get all parental. His name's Wade."

"Seriously?" Kyrael yelped. He'd been poking around the living room, looking at family portraits and souvenirs. "When did that happen?"

Felicity blushed and answered in vague terms. Kyrael had to give her credit for her delivery. Her parents would assume the conversation was meant for them, yet she could still answer him.

"I asked him a day or two ago. The week has been so crazy I've lost all track of time. But we're supposed to go out on Saturday to break the ice."

"I think the ice is broken," Kyrael quipped. "A

whole lake's worth."

"Where will you be going?" her father asked.

"I'm not sure. When I saw Wade today, he'd gotten some bad news about his family. We'll see what happens."

Kyrael spent the rest of their meal lounging on the couch. Life as a messenger kept him pretty busy, so he knew to appreciate these down moments. Once Wade had his feet back under him, training would begin, then hunting in earnest. Gabriel might authorize additional teams if they made a significant dent in the quantity of ripe and mid-grade remalas or maybe send their team around the globe to hot spots. Humans liked traveling, right?

"I don't have any homework tonight," Felicity informed her parents. The three were clearing away dinner. "May I go next door and see how Greyson is settling in?"

Her father glanced at the clock. "Okay. But be home by ten. It's a school night."

"Thanks, Dad." She rinsed her plate and headed for the door.

Kyrael slipped after her, unnoticed by either parent. "You guys are a nice close family."

Felicity closed her front door behind them before speaking. "My parents work a lot, but otherwise, yeah. I'm lucky."

"You and Wade will have children?"

Felicity paused with her hand raised to knock on Greyson's door. "Seriously, Kyrael? We haven't even been out on a first date. I thought you'd read the internet. You should know people don't get together like that."

"According to many sites, it only takes once."

Her hand went from ready to knock to smearing down her face. "While you're correct, biologically speaking, a first date doesn't mean we'll do what it takes for children to happen. Even a first month of dates doesn't mean we'll sleep together. Kyrael, dating is definitely a watch-and-learn thing for you. Or ask Adriel or Niciel. They seem to know human behavior well enough."

Kyrael fidgeted. "Well, they do their work on Earth. I work out of Heaven, so I don't linger where I can people-watch."

She patted his arm. "Don't worry. I'm not mad or anything. But sex is an awkward topic like ninety-nine percent of the time. If you're unsure if a moment is the one percent where it's okay to bring it up, check with someone discretely until you get a feel for how humans handle the topic."

"But Greyson joked about men's desires with you earlier."

"There's the subtlety you don't get. He was both generalizing and making jokes about no one in particular. You implied Wade and I would be procreating, and soon. That's just *no*. Especially when we haven't even been on a date. Oh, and it's pretty much never okay to discuss anyone's parents regarding this topic, so never go there."

"Noted."

Felicity knocked on Greyson's door, and he answered. "Oh good, you're back." He stepped into the hall and pulled the door most of the way shut, lowering his voice. "Your boyfriend is pretty messed up, though that's understandable. After the third time Niciel promised him the murderer is indeed going to Hell, he finally agreed to hunt remalas, no observation necessary. I think he just wants to kill something."

"Maybe hunting will be therapeutic for him. It certainly did wonders for you."

Greyson grinned. "We're splitting up tonight. Niciel is taking Wade out for a hunting free-for-all. You and I are hosting so Adriel can start training Kyrael. We're going after some local small-fry."

Kyrael drooped. "I want to be a useful hunter."

Felicity poked his arm. "You'll be fine. Adriel doesn't seem like the type who'd let you stay if you couldn't learn. So learn, then we can start beating back the big remalas."

He gave a sharp nod, heartened. "You're right. We can do this. *I* can do this." He held out his palm. "Can I go inside you?"

Felicity flinched, and Greyson snickered.

"What?" Kyrael asked.

"It sounds dirty when you use those words," Greyson pointed out.

Kyrael's mouth dropped open. "But, I don't...angels don't... How did you come to that conclusion?"

"Your wording. Remember, you look like any other bloke," Greyson said. "Human males only go inside a girl when they're, well, there's no hosting. You get what I mean, right?"

Kyrael gave a swift nod. "Watch for vernacular overlap."

"Exactly." Felicity paused, a horrified look spreading across her face. "I never even thought of that. Even if we call it hosting, I let Adriel inside my body. Do I still count as a virgin? If I let Kyrael inside, does that make me slutty?"

Greyson knocked his head against the doorframe. "Since we're the first to host angels willingly, I don't think there's solid precedent for what you're asking. But my gut says you're safe. They're going in through your palm and hanging out... Well, it felt like someone wrapped a heating pad around the inside of my torso. That's not the locale in question, so yeah. You should be fine."

She heaved a sigh of relief and pressed her palm to Kyrael's. "Come on then."

Kyrael let himself relax and shift, absorbing into her skin. This was his first time in a host. He spread along the underside of her skin throughout her body until he felt like a mirror image reflected inward.

"*Felicity?*" he called. Would she hear him? Would he hear her?

"Right here, Kyrael. Adriel said you'd be able to talk to my mind."

Seeing through her point of view, their gaze turned to Greyson. "Are you already hosting?" she asked.

Greyson nodded, then opened the door and called inside. "We're heading out. Are you taking Wade back to his house when you're done?"

Niciel answered. "I think he'd do better with another person around."

"I have a roommate," Wade protested.

"A human who understands what happened to you," Niciel countered. "Can he stay here tonight?" he asked Greyson.

"Fine by me." Greyson patted his pocket, and keys jingled. "I've got the keys, but I'm sure we'll be back before you. Hope the hunting helps." He shut the door and turned to Felicity, smiling. "Adriel wants to go back to the overpass from the last time. He figures in the power vacuum left by the remala you defeated, others might have moved in. And there's plenty of room to maneuver and fewer people to stare."

Not having any control over his movements or the flow of conversation annoyed Kyrael. Then again, Felicity had told him to watch and listen. Trapped and seeing the world through the windows of her eyes, he was forced to do just that.

Several things impacted his thoughts. His ability to flit from plane to plane or place to place usually left him frustrated with the plodding pace on Earth. Now that he was stuck in a human body with heart rate and movement sensations flooding him, he finally understood why people moved so slowly. This was the constraint of their biology.

Slowing down this much also allowed him to take in other details. For example, the nervous trip of Felicity's heart each time she passed a shadowy recess, though she didn't stop her conversation or break her stride. Had she been living with this low-grade fear her whole life? No wonder she and the other two were so willing to work toward a solution, or more specifically, keen to keep an angel around. With angels present, nothing would creep from the shadows.

Also, Kyrael observed the easy flow of conversation between Greyson and Felicity. If humans and angels were the same, he'd say they were fast becoming friends. All these pieces put together left a fresh seed of determination in Kyrael's stomach—a desire to excel at the task Heaven had placed on him. In one evening, he'd seen the emotional aftermath of living with seeing remalas. Now he could feel the biological response in a simple walk down the street. Kyrael wanted to gift Felicity a life free of fear. She deserved to be lighthearted with her friends for real.

They came over a rise, and ahead of them loomed the overpass where Kyrael had first met Felicity. Her stomach tightened, squeezing him, and her palms broke out in a sweat. Her breathing quickened, and her muscles tensed.

"*Relax,*" he soothed, breaking the silence he'd held since they'd left the apartment. "*Adriel and I won't let anything happen to you.*"

"I know. But can you feel the remala while you're inside? Something moved in up under the shadows. Either the remala is big, or there's a whole lot of them. The malice is rolling out from under the overpass in waves."

Kyrael shook his head no, remembered she couldn't see, and switched to a verbal answer. "*No. Your body works like a shield in both directions. If it can hide me from the remalas, it can hide the remalas from me. Speaking of which, remind me to have Adriel teach me how to track them while I'm being hosted.*"

Felicity's next breath came out with a funny squeak and a shudder.

"Adriel wants to know if you're sure you're up for hunting," Greyson asked for the angel inside him. "No one is demanding this of you."

Felicity nodded. "I can be nervous and still want to hunt. Adriel, I know you'll protect us. You did last time. It's just…I wish I could see you, or feel you, or get a hug or something."

Greyson shifted his weight from one foot to the

other, then opened his arms. "I'll hug you for him. I mean, if you're that scared, I'd hug you anyway. I don't let girls freak out on their own. But you don't know me very well, so—"

Felicity wrapped her arms around his chest and squeezed hard enough to cut him off. She trembled against his body. Tears stung at her eyes, and inside, Kyrael startled, once again moved. He could feel physiological responses but not the emotions behind them. She'd been holding herself back.

Greyson hugged her in return, patting. "I'm with Adriel. Are you sure this is what you want?"

"Yes." She drew back from Greyson, blinking to clear her eyes. "What's the plan?"

"Adriel says if the remala is large, you and Kyrael stand back. Kyrael's supposed to watch and be ready to act the next time."

"Can an angel learn that way?" she mused.

"*Yes*," Kyrael answered. "*Showing us a skill once is enough.*"

"Lucky bastards," Felicity muttered.

"What?" Greyson asked.

She made a face. "Kyrael says angels can see a skill once then do it. I wanna learn like that."

"No kidding. Oh, Adriel says if there's a small remala, he and I will demonstrate for Kyrael, then we'll find more for him to practice on. Ready?"

"*You can do this*," Kyrael encouraged.

Felicity nodded, and the two stepped toward the overpass. Evening blanketed the city in blue light punctuated by the harsh orange glow of streetlights. But under the overpass, no streetlight infiltrated the thick gloom.

An unaccustomed anxiousness permeated Kyrael. He wasn't used to going into a situation like this blind. Since he was a messenger, he'd never needed to go into a fight at all. But he wouldn't be blind to danger should it exist like when he was inside Felicity.

The two humans crossed into the darkness of the overhead-cement like ringing a dinner bell. None of the remalas were large, but dozens of them surged from crevices, scuttling, creeping, oozing, and scurrying toward Greyson and Felicity.

Felicity stared at them, her heartbeat racing and sweat beading out all over.

"*Watch Greyson*," Kyrael barked. "*I can't see.*"

She turned her head in time for Kyrael to watch in astonishment. Greyson materialized a smoking scythe, cutting through the closest remala. His slice took out four of them, then a kick, in which Adriel had concentrated angelic energy, exploded a fifth.

The remalas turned to the easier target, rushing Felicity. The mob flashed toward them in a blur of fangs, slime, crawling legs, and too many eyes.

"Kyrael, help," she screamed, "however you need to!"

Adriel had taken control of Greyson's body. Using that as a benchmark, and with her permission given, Kyrael forced his will over her nervous system. Once in control, he ordered angelic energy to create a weapon he could handle. As the remalas contacted her, electric crackles covered Felicity's body, resulting in an explosion of negative energy as a sticky shower that disappeared the instant it touched material from the Earthly plane.

He flexed her hand, concentrating those electric

sparks, then tossed them at several retreating remalas. With a sickening hiss like water over hot coals, the remalas exploded. The rest had fled, at least out of his visual range.

Stars burst in Kyrael's consciousness. Every joint in his body quivered like jelly. His hold on Felicity snapped, and he fell from her body to the pavement in front of her.

"Oh heavens," he gasped, not even bothering to get up. "Why do I feel mushy?"

Adriel crouched next to him, his head between his knees, breathing hard. "Some side-effect of controlling a host." He groaned and pushed himself to stand up. "Last time, it went away in a couple of minutes. But to get so close to a den, the side-effect is worth it."

"A den?" Greyson asked.

"Yes. Those were all very low-level remalas. There's safety in numbers until they've eaten enough negative energy to protect themselves." Adriel closed his eyes. "I don't sense any additional remalas nearby."

Felicity bent, offering Kyrael her hand. "Need help up?"

He took her hand and let her help hoist him to his feet. The jelly feeling had faded into a prickly sensation. "Thank you. I'm sorry I let you get so scared. I've never been in a host before, let alone controlled anyone. It took a second to figure out the right way."

She nodded, her lower lip trembling. "You kept me safe, as promised."

Two tears accompanied the tremble, and a surge of remorse and protectiveness moved Kyrael to her side. He scooped her up and hugged her with one arm while drying her tears with the other hand.

"You're my partner, and I let you get so scared you're crying. I promise to do better next time. I may not have been blessed with the best self-control in Heaven, but I swear I'll make you proud to be my hunting partner."

She pressed her face to his shoulder, sniffling, but she nodded. He let her cry, not like he had a plan for distracting her. What did one do with a human in this state?

After a few minutes, she rubbed her cheeks dry on his shirt, then lifted her face. Felicity's eyes widened, and her mouth dropped open. She scrambled backward, away from Kyrael so fast she ran into Greyson, who caught her and held her up.

"What?" he asked, looking alarmed.

"Holy fuck!" she screeched. "He's got wings." Her head whipped around in Adriel's direction, and she squirmed in Greyson's grip. "Him, too."

She shut her eyes and drew several deep breaths, which shuddered on their way out. "It's true," she whispered. "Angels. Like the real deal, angels."

Greyson squinted and frowned. "I still don't see wings."

Adriel's gaze flipped between Felicity and Kyrael. "I don't know what to tell you other than they seem to have a special connection. It's why I paired them together in the first place. Somehow, their connection made a believer out of her."

Felicity pushed away from Greyson and inched toward Kyrael, stretching her hand out. "Your wings are stunning. I-I don't have words. Can I touch them?"

"Of course. You've hosted me. It seems fair. Touch whatever you like."

Greyson snorted on laughter, and Kyrael eyed him. "Did I make another misstep?"

"Ambiguous wording," Greyson said, laughing.

Adriel palmed his face. "I had to sit through this already, and once was enough. Kyrael, we need to talk. But for now, we should get Flick to bed. She has school in the morning."

Chapter 8

Friday morning, Flick woke for school, excitement buzzing in her stomach. Today they had an assembly before school to announce the Homecoming royalty, so her classes were all ten minutes shorter. After lunch, she'd have English Lit at the college.

Wade skipped class yesterday. According to Adriel, he was still healing. She hadn't seen Wade since they'd left the apartment after his disastrous revelation. So she hadn't had a chance to ask if they still had a date tomorrow.

Flick and Greyson hadn't gone hunting since the last time because Wade spent so much time hunting the local area was getting thin in remalas. Between their hunting and Kyrael accompanying her everywhere except the shower, she hadn't seen a single remala, leaving her floating like a balloon.

She grabbed the English muffin Kyrael had set out for her in the kitchen. Her parents were already gone for work, not that they would have seen him anyway. Taking a bite, she grabbed her bag.

"Let's go a few minutes early. I want to ask Adriel a question on our way out."

"I'm ready when you are." He flexed his wings and settled them on his back, then slipped past her into the hall.

Flick braced to get hit with feathers, but Kyrael

117

didn't touch her. His wings still startled her on occasion. Getting used to them had taken a bit since the white-feathered appendages took up a good deal of visual space behind him. Like the rest of him, Kyrael's wings slid around objects in the Earthly plane unless an effort was made to connect with them like she had when she'd first touched them.

No substance in nature compared to the indescribable softness of Kyrael's feathers. Flick would encase herself in those feathers and live in there if it were an option. Her fingers itched to touch Kyrael's wings every time she saw him. Somehow, she managed to hold herself back.

Marisol and Jake met her at the bus stop. Marisol scanned her head to toe. "Are you taking some new supplements? In the last couple of days, you've looked rested, and relaxed, and calm. I need me some of that."

"I'm not taking supplements, but things have taken a turn for the better."

"So true." Jake jumped at her, grabbing her hand. "Kristin and I are going out tomorrow. Maybe I don't have to wait for Homecoming if you know what I mean."

Marisol rolled her eyes. "We know what you mean. You haven't talked about anything else in forever. I'm considering setting up a pool with all your friends so we can hire you a hooker and get you laid just to shut you up." She turned to Flick. "Don't you have a date tomorrow, too?"

"Maybe. I haven't been able to get ahold of Wade to set it up. How about you? Any luck finding a date?"

She frowned. "You said you would ask the other guy you knew."

"Oh. Right. I'll see him later today. I'll remember to

ask this time."

"I'm calling you to make sure you do." They turned up the path leading to the gym. "Otherwise, I'm going to get stuck taking some wallflower who didn't have the guts to ask anyone else."

"Mmm." Flick nodded. "Like the self-proclaimed 'God-daddy' Bruno."

Jake busted out laughing. "I'd love to see you dancing with *Dog*-daddy. I think his nose would fit right in your cleavage."

"Is he short, or is our Marisol just super tall?"

Marisol scowled at Flick. "They didn't call me Tall Marisol until eighth grade for no reason. *And* he is super short."

"That's what makes you two such a beautiful combination," Jake said. "Juxtaposition in motion."

Marisol stopped dead in her tracks, throwing her arm out across Flick's chest to stop her, too. "Call the Vatican. We've seen the first sign of the apocalypse. Jake used juxtaposition correctly."

"That's not a sign of the end times," Kyrael said.

Flick snorted with laughter, and both her friends stared. "Jake is notorious with big words, but I don't think his malapropism counts as cataclysmic."

"Huh?" Jake scratched his head.

"There's the proof." Marisol poked his arm. She opened the door to the gym and waited for the others to go in. "Who do you think will end up Homecoming queen?"

"Duh." Jake rolled his eyes. "Lena Agassi. She's like sniffing permanent markers, so bad for your brain yet so hard to resist."

Flick choked on a laugh. "There's more competition

for the guys. Will the king hail from the football team? That is, Scott Flint. Or will he be the soccer darling Teo Reyes?"

"All balls and no brains," Marisol grumbled.

"But they have pretty faces. Who said good looks only work for girls?" Flick took a seat as high on the bleachers as she could get. Her friends sat close on either side of her, other students crowding the rest of the row.

"Just because people don't bump me doesn't mean I can pull extra seating space out of nowhere," Kyrael whispered in Flick's ear. "Can I hitch a ride until there's more space?"

Flick nodded and held out her hand beside her hip and out of notice. Kyrael touched it, absorbing into her body. The warmth of hosting an angel filled her chest, then her limbs. She'd have to invite him in more often on cold days this winter.

The principal started the assembly with the usual plea to be quiet, then some random announcements. Flick settled in to watch the last spectacle of popularity bias during her public school career. If nothing else, she'd have the stories for later in life.

Sure enough, Miss Permanent-Marker won the crown for Homecoming queen. Homecoming royalty won based on student votes and were approved by the staff. The female students would have been split on who should win, but not the guys. All of Lena's qualifications were on her body.

The Homecoming king was a little more surprising. AJ Tran won. Then again, he made smart look easy, and from the few times Flick had classes with him, he seemed authentic and kind. Good for him.

Within a minute of the two taking their places at the

front of the assembly, an overwhelming wave of malice rolled through the gym. Flick gagged, and Marisol glanced over.

"I know, Lena, right?"

"Lena," Flick huffed.

"*Your heart rate is through the roof,*" Kyrael commented from inside her mind. "*Is it a remala?*"

Flick nodded.

"*I'd guess it's hiding below the seating, feeding on sore feelings,*" Kyrael said. "*Do you want to go exterminate it? Or do you want me to exit your body and scare it off?*"

"I need fresh air," Flick informed Marisol. "I'll be back in a minute." She worked her way to the side of the bleachers to come down less noticed. On her way, she murmured, "Can we kill it without causing a scene?"

In her head, Kyrael chuckled. "*That's my hunter. I think I can keep others from noticing.*"

Flick nodded and ducked behind the bleachers. She could almost smell the remala. A putrid aura clung to the air, making it heavy like humidity. Her breakfast threatened to come up again.

"I've never sensed anything this strong."

"*Even if the remala is ripe, don't worry. I've gone out the last few nights with Adriel, training. There will be no hesitation on my part today, and I'm sure I can destroy it.*"

Flick threaded through the steel supports under the bleachers. The closer she got to the center, the sicker her stomach got. A constant taste of vomit coated inside her cheeks, pulling the moisture out of her mouth.

The staff had switched to another activity for the assembly, dimming the main lights and making the darkness under the bleachers even deeper. Shafts of weak light pierced the gloom but didn't do much to illuminate her surroundings. Several yards in front of her, a figure leaned against the wall, but the silhouette was human.

Running across a person wasn't what surprised Flick. Students sometimes snuck behind the bleachers to do things the staff wouldn't let them do if they were in the open. This man standing alone surprised her. Based on what she sensed, the place ought to be crawling with remalas or hosting a big one.

While she could still sense the foul aura, she couldn't see a source. No slinking, nasty creature lurked in the shadows, nor could she zero in on the center. Still, the negative energy ricocheted off the undersides of seats and walls in a frenzy, drawing in energy from all sides like a vacuum.

The young man pushed off the wall and wove his way in her direction. An occasional shaft of light crossed his face, and Flick tried to place him. He was too old to be a student, but not all that old, almost the way she'd thought of Adriel when she'd first seen him in the school. However, this man didn't give off an angelic aura. He didn't give off an aura at all.

Flick shuddered. She'd gotten far too paranoid if she was looking for reasons people might not be human.

The young man stopped a few feet away from her. "What brings you down here?"

"Same to you," she retorted. Something about his demeanor drew out a scowl and a mood to match.

He chuckled. "Mr. Ostanes. Freshman History teacher. New this year. I got monitoring duty."

Sheepishness washed over Flick. "Sorry. I got up to

use the restroom and smelled something nasty down here. I thought I'd make sure no one was pulling a prank or something for Homecoming." She tossed out the first lie to pop into her mind.

"A nasty smell?" Mr. Ostanes raised an eyebrow. "Should I be offended?"

She blushed. "You don't smell it?" How could he? He was just a teacher.

"I smell the usual sweaty feet from bleachers, and while it's not pleasant, I wouldn't say it's remarkable." He took a step closer, scrutinizing her. "Students aren't allowed under the bleachers. Shouldn't you be heading back?"

She fell back a step. "Yeah."

He took another step closer. "I'll be seeing you around."

Flick faltered another step farther away before turning and hurrying back to the edge of the bleachers. "What the hell?" she muttered.

"*No sign of the remala?*" Kyrael asked.

"No. But don't come out yet. The evil energy was almost a physical force like being rolled under a wave on the beach. That didn't come from nowhere. I just didn't see the remala." She nibbled her lip. "There's no way it sensed you, right?"

"*It's possible. Using a host to hunt is all speculation. There's no precedent and no data. This is why we're doing a single team, to see if there are holes in our theory.*"

"Well," Flick said, "if the remala comes back, we'll be ready. Stay inside until after lunch, just in case."

"*Will do.*"

"There you are, Flick." The assembly had let out,

and Marisol worked her way through exiting students toward Flick's spot at the corner of the bleachers. "Did you get sick?"

"No. Almost, though."

Jake followed Marisol. "That's good. I'd hate to see you miss your date 'cause you had your head in the toilet."

"Thanks for the loving support." Flick took her backpack from Jake.

"I do what I can." He peered at her face. "You don't look so well. Maybe you should go to the office."

"Maybe I will." Two things about going to the office appealed to Flick. First, she could walk through the school and ensure the remala wasn't skulking about. Second, she didn't think she could focus on first period. Her head and gut both churned, not in the vomitous way they had under the bleachers, but something about the missing remala nagged her.

"I'll walk you," Jake volunteered. "My class is in that direction anyway."

"See you at lunch?" Marisol asked her.

"Unless something unpleasant happens, I'll be there." Flick turned for the office.

Jake fell into step beside her. "Is everything all right, Flick?"

"For the most part."

He caught her arm, pulling her to a stop. "Knock it off. Marisol is letting you off easy, but we've both noticed how different you've been for like a week now. Is everything okay at home?"

Flick opened her mouth to lie, then stopped. Jake deserved better. Besides, if he and Marisol noticed her shift in behavior, then they'd catch a lie.

"Want to skip out on a bit of first period to help a sick friend?"

He grinned. "Sure."

They entered one of the unisex bathrooms together, and Flick locked the door to the private space.

Jake settled in, leaning against the wall. "Well, this must be good."

"We've known each other for how long?"

"How many years has it been since pre-k?" He ticked off fingers, keeping count. "Thirteen years."

"Right, and how long have I seen things that freak me out?"

He nodded. "I thought this might be the case."

Flick crossed her arms. "Look, I know you've never believed me—"

"Hold up. I never said I didn't believe you. I just said I was skeptical of anything I couldn't see for myself. Whatever you see scares the hell out of you, and I've never thought you were crazy or playing at seeing them. Whatever they are, they're very real to you. Don't think I discount your experiences."

Flick's eyes watered. "Why didn't you ever explain it like that before?"

"Because you stopped telling Marisol and me about seeing things in the seventh grade. Even though we knew you still did, do." He rubbed his hair. "I even think I know why. Our class watched a spooky movie as a treat for Halloween, and afterward, Henry Ferris said anyone who believed in ghosts and crap was a loser and a freak."

"I don't care what Henry thinks." Flick tightened her crossed arms.

"Not now. Maybe not even then. But lots of people did care. Middle schoolers are dumb. If Henry thought believers were stupid, other people would, too, in order to suck up. I think you knew that well enough. Because after Halloween, you never mentioned your specters again."

"Yeah, well…"

Jake left the wall and hugged Flick, crossed arms and all. "We both figured you needed some space, and you would tell us anything important. Is this important?"

Flick nodded, her chin knocking into his shoulder. "I, uh…wow, this is weird to say out loud. I still see everything all the time. But not for the last week."

"What changed?" Jake went back to his spot on the wall.

"I found something that keeps them away from me."

"That's good, right?"

Flick shrugged. "It's got ups and downs. I've also gained a lot of understanding about what I see. It turns out they can cause harm to people. And the ones I see are the baby version. They get a lot worse."

Jake frowned. "Where are you picking up the information? Is it a reliable source, or some random crap a wacko posted on the net?"

"I'd guess it's pretty much the highest authority." She rubbed her face. "Jake, you and Marisol have been patient beyond normal friends. You are the best sort, and I'm so lucky to have you. But I need to keep testing your patience. I'm not ready to tell you the details. Hell, I don't know if I'll ever be. But please hang in there with me. I'm trying to fight these things head-on, so maybe I can relax and enjoy life a little for a change. I mean, like being relaxed enough to fully enjoy, not like my life has been miserable or anything—"

Jake put his finger on her lips. "You're babbling.

And as long as you swear you're okay, Marisol and I will hold our peace. But no matter what, we have your back. You don't have to be alone and afraid."

Flick reached over and squeezed Jake's hand. "I'm not. Thanks."

"So do you want to tell me the truth about what happened in the gym? Or is that part of the secret?"

"Are you sure you want to know?"

Jake sighed. "Let me guess. The students and staff weren't alone in the gym?"

"Nope. I couldn't find the cause, but the air got nasty. Bad enough that I was telling the truth about almost puking."

"Why would you even go looking for it?" His voice cracked on incredulity. When Flick didn't respond, he shook his head. "Fine. Tell me when you're ready. Anything else I should know?"

"Like?" Flick asked.

"Like you're actually a superhero sent to purge the world of evil spirits? After dark, you're out hunting the things that bump in the night?" He chuckled. "Ooo. Maybe you're secretly training as a medium. You're tired of seeing them slink around without knowing what they want, so you're planning to séance them all and speak to the dead." He smacked the palm of his hand to his forehead. "Oh. It's so obvious. This is one of those twist movie endings. You've been a ghost this whole time, and I'm the one seeing and talking to the dead."

Flick rolled her eyes. "Right. You've been watching too much tv."

Someone knocked on the door, and Flick pulled it open to find herself face to face with Mr. Ostanes.

"We meet again," he chuckled. "Scoping out under

the bleachers and now locked in the unisex bathroom with a young man?" He put his hands on his hips. "Please don't make me have this phone call with your parents."

Flick scowled at having to deal with him again. "Jake came to make sure I was all right. After the smell in the gym, I got sick. He can take me to the office."

Jake's eyebrows soared over wide eyes. She never let sass into her tone when talking to teachers. But Mr. Ostanes' easy, teasing, young-person manner rubbed her fur the wrong way. Jake could just get over his surprise.

Mr. Ostanes pulled a slip of paper out of his pocket. "Nope. The young man can go back to class. Here's your pass." Mr. Ostanes took a careful look, head to toe, at Jake, then Flick. "I guess you're not hiding anything. Run along. I'll take Miss…"

"Felicity."

"I'll take Miss Felicity to the nurse's office."

Jake shrugged. "I'll see you at lunch. Feel better, Flick."

"Flick?" Mr. Ostanes pointed her toward the office, blocking the way Jake had gone with his body.

"A nickname my friends call me." She turned on her heel and marched straight for the office.

"You've got a lot of spunk for someone who was sick mere minutes ago," Ostanes observed.

"You've got a lot of free time for someone who's supposed to be teaching."

"Ouch. She's feisty." He pointed her into the office. "Put your energy into feeling better rather than snapping at teachers." He gave her a mocking salute and sauntered off.

"*The line between child and adult blurs here,*" Kyrael said.

"That's because I'm almost done with school, and so are my friends. He's pretty young. If he just graduated from college, Ostanes would have been in my grade like five years ago, give or take a year."

"*Ah.*"

Flick lay down in the nurse's office and pulled out her books. She might as well keep up on homework while she got her head and gut under control. Searching the halls for the remalas fell through the cracks.

Chapter 9

Greyson sat on the floor, leaning against his couch. In front of him, all across the coffee table lay notes he'd been taking. Every paper dealt with the remalas. Adriel had assumed the role of teacher. This allowed the two of them to compile a wealth of information the angels took for granted.

The two had drawn up papers on size, attributes, power, and preferences for feeding and hiding. The picture was much broader than Greyson had first grasped and far more complicated. Remalas weren't strictly creatures born of negative energy who ran around sucking up more until they got super powerful.

He'd considered them a bit like a virus, a biological entity without a brain. But it turned out the more power they got, the more like real animals they became. They went from existing off pure instinct and the drive to feed to a thing with a goal—gain enough power for a demon to contract with you.

Once the contract was formed, a remala functioned as a host, much like he, Felicity, and Wade did for the angels. Since demons couldn't leave Hell to raise hell on Earth, they would transfer a bit of their consciousness to the remala and, from there, use the host to complete whatever work on Earth they had, none of it good.

Greyson stretched his legs out long, pushing paper away as he did. "Okay. Tell me some of the more notable catastrophes caused by possessed remalas."

Adriel turned from where he'd been staring out the window at the city. "The stock market crash in 1929, the burning of Rome, the black plague."

"Wait. Isn't the plague bacteria carried by rats?"

Adriel's stare went hard. "A bacteria whose genetic path was altered by a possessed remala to carry out the gruesome wishes of Hell. Why do you think it cropped up out of nowhere, killing hundreds of millions over repeated infections? Yersinia Pestis existed in rodent populations before the plague went viral to borrow the expression. A demon turned it into a weapon of mass destruction. Via a remala, of course." Adriel frowned. "We also suspect there was a remala involved in the atrocities of World War Two."

"Why aren't angels hunting the possessed remalas, then?"

"Two reasons. First, we hunt the ripe remalas, hoping none get strong enough to appeal to Hell in the first place. Second, once possessed, the remalas become arduous to track. It's difficult to catch them until after they've started wreaking havoc. Letting things get bad so we can hunt isn't our thing, so we're back to picking off the ripening remalas before Hell finds them."

"And that's where we come in as hosts." Greyson pulled his knees up, wrapping his arms around them. "If partnering with willing humans works, you might be able to avoid any remalas ripening to the point they get possessed."

"Right."

A shudder shook Greyson. "The mid-grade remalas are so horrible. What does a ripe remala or a possessed one look like? Would I seize up at the sight?"

Adriel knelt in front of Greyson. "The closer they get to being ripe, the more humanoid their features get." He frowned. "Remember Wade's description of his grandmother's ghost? That was a different type of possession. But you get the idea of looks based on what he said. In their case, his grandmother wasn't the remala. A human soul can't be one. But she fused with remalas to gain the same power remalas are after."

"Then she could have started the next plague?" Greyson asked.

"No." Adriel shook his head. "Hell and its denizens can manipulate humans, but not the same way they can inhabit a ripe remala. They would have been limited to the scope of her last wish, the one which trapped her on Earth. Since she sought retribution of a violent nature, Hell employed her, but it's not the same."

"That's a bit of a relief." He tipped his head back until it rested on the seat of the couch. "So to summarize, if we see something that looks like a rotting human, we've found one of the bad boys, so kill on sight."

"Right—"

Whatever he was going to say next got cut off by a knock on the door. Greyson stood and crossed the flat to open it, confused. Felicity and Wade ought to be in class, and he didn't know anyone else in Seattle. Wade breezed in the moment he opened the door.

"I left some stuff here the other night."

Greyson trailed after Wade. "Aren't you supposed to be in class with Felicity?"

"She's a big girl. She'll be fine."

"My concern was aimed at you. Adriel said you're hunting so much you don't sleep, and now you're dropping your other activities?"

"I've got a job. What do I need college for?" Wade rummaged through a drawer in the guest room.

"No one told me we'd be abandoning our lives in favor of hunting. Felicity is still attending school. If you quit everything, how are you going to keep friends? Start a family? Even if you don't want a regular job, don't you want hobbies?"

"None of that stuff matters in the grand scheme of things." He slammed the drawer shut. "Have you seen my driver's license?"

"No. And how can you say it doesn't matter? Adriel started this project to improve our quality of life, not turn us into mindless hunting machines." Greyson stepped in the doorway, blocking Wade's way out. "What you're doing isn't good for your mental health. You're going to hurt yourself."

Wade's jerk toward Greyson stopped just shy of aggressive. "What the fuck would you know? I'd moved on, pushed aside all the crap from my past. Then you guys waltz in and not only dredge it all up but drop a nuclear bomb on me. One of my parents is a murderer, for God's sake, and I can't do a fucking thing about it. Now get the hell out of my way and let me cope the best way I can."

Adriel peeked over Greyson's shoulder. "I thought this might be happening, so I did some research. Exterminators like Niciel aren't adept at human emotion. Being a death angel, I see a bit more, and I figured you might need help."

"How can you help?" Wade snarled. "Even killing the murderer won't untangle the mess I'm in."

"No. But when Niciel forbade you from going after the living, he left the details vague. I'm sure he wanted to keep you from obsessing over trying to find a loophole. But after looking into the incident, I think there was a bit more he could have shared, information which might give you some marginal peace of mind."

"And you waited this long to tell me?" Wade shouted.

Adriel put protective hands on Greyson's shoulders since Greyson stood between the two. "I didn't intend to wait. You haven't responded to anyone trying to reach you, and you disappeared from your usual routine. Don't blame me if your desire to vanish worked too well. Now, can we have a civil conversation?"

Wade's eyes still burned with fury, but he backed down. Adriel shifted Greyson from the center of the doorway and took his spot, keeping Wade inside the guest room.

"That's better," Adriel soothed. "Your grandmother was indeed looking for her killer in your parents' bedroom, but she kept returning because she never found the culprit." Wade opened his mouth, but Adriel held up a hand for silence. "Your parents aren't innocent of everything, but they didn't murder anyone. You were too young to put the other pieces together, but do you remember the frequent business trips your father made?"

"Yes, but—"

"Your mother was having an affair when he was out."

Understanding dawned on Wade's face. "Mr. Zeller, her co-worker. She was sleeping with him?"

"Serially. And your grandmother caught them in bed together. Being your father's mother, she threatened to tell her son. Harold Zeller is not a good man. He orchestrated her demise to keep her quiet so he and your mother could continue their affair. After your grandmother's death, your mother suspected Harold and grew afraid of him, cutting ties."

"And we moved to Oregon from New Jersey. That must be why. Mom said it was for her job, but…"

Adriel's face was full of sympathy. "I understand these facts don't absolve your mother or unsnarl the situation. But if you're outraged, I believe you deserve to direct the anger in the appropriate direction. Your grandmother never got her revenge because your mother had already stopped seeing Harold. He was never in the room with her daughter-in-law as she'd hoped to find. But as Niciel pointed out, retribution wasn't your grandmother's to dish out. Heaven will handle Harold."

Wade sobbed. "I thought…"

"I know," Adriel soothed.

Wade's whole body shuddered under his emotions. "Niciel and I were planning a hunting road trip. We were going to go indefinitely, but I don't think I want to leave forever anymore. But I'm not ready to join the team yet."

"Go for as long as you need to heal, then come back to us," Adriel said. "We'll welcome you home whenever that happens."

"Really? None of you care?" His question was directed at Greyson.

"Why would we care?"

"Because I haven't been pleasant about any of this."

Greyson managed a grim smile. "None of this is pleasant to start with. We've seen evil as it grows into servants of Hell. Your story is more personal and gruesome, so it's natural your feelings will be rawer. I think Felicity and I can handle that truth. She's been trying to get ahold of you, you know. Can you text her or something before you leave?"

Wade grimaced. "She asked me to go to her Homecoming dance, and I can't. I'm not ready. But I can't handle letting her down on top of everything else, either. Can you pass along my apologies?"

"I guess."

"She'll understand it's not personal, right?" Wade asked.

"It isn't?" Greyson clarified. "I'm not pacifying her with lies. If you resent her because she introduced you to the angels and opened this can of worms, then she deserves to know."

"I feel a little bit that way, or at least I did until the stuff Adriel told me. For the first time, I feel like I might be able to heal. If I work things out, she'll have been the one to facilitate it. For now, give her my apologies for the inconvenience. I'll sort out how I feel about her role in all this with everything else. There are always other dances if I ever feel ready."

"Fair enough," Greyson agreed. "I hope you find the healing you need. We'll see you when you get back, right?"

"Probably, no, definitely. If I decide I can't be part of the team, I'll at least come back and say goodbye."

"Here's a license." Adriel handed him the plastic card.

"You had it?"

"I made you a new one the same way I made the papers for this apartment. Call it a goodbye present."

Wade nodded.

"Where's Niciel?" Greyson asked.

"Waiting in the car. I should go." He exited the bedroom and crossed the flat to the door, pausing with his hand on the knob. Turning, he said, "Thanks for the rest of the truth, Adriel." Then he left.

Greyson heaved a sigh. "Was that good or bad? I can't tell."

"Good, I think." Adriel returned to the living room, and Greyson followed. "Did you want to keep working?"

"I think my brain is spent at the moment. I'm going to lay down and rest if you don't mind."

Adriel shrugged. "Do what you like. You'll need it. With Wade and Niciel leaving town, their relentless hunting will stop, and it won't take long for remalas to move back into the area. We'll need to hunt in a few days."

Greyson stretched out on his leather sofa, enjoying the scrunch of the material under his shoulders. He closed his eyes and relaxed, pushing aside all thoughts of remalas and hunting. He'd picked up meditation early in secondary school to drive away the memories of the things he saw. Pulling this skill for the first time in a while, he focused on his breathing, letting his mind fill with his favorite shade of green.

He wasn't sure when he passed from meditating to napping, but the knock on his door woke him from sleep. Stretching, then standing, Greyson left his imprint on the sofa. Had he been asleep long enough for Felicity to come home, do homework, and pay a visit? Or had Wade forgotten something else?

The peephole warped Felicity's face, making her look a bit like a goldfish. Greyson opened the door and prepped himself to dump her on Wade's behalf. At least she wasn't one of those super-sensitive girls.

"Hi," he said, opening the door. "Come on in."

Felicity had been home because she didn't have her

school stuff. She peeked behind him at the living room floor, carpeted with his papers. "Were you attacked by a ream of printer paper?"

He shut the door behind her and went back to the sofa. "Adriel has been giving me detailed information on remalas, and I've been taking notes for us all since I don't start back into college in person until winter quarter."

"On paper?"

He rubbed a hand across his hair, eyeing the mess. "It seemed natural. But now I feel like one of those detectives in the movies. I just need red yarn, and I can start tacking these all to the wall."

"I don't think the remalas count as a crime family. They are their own brand of nasty." She sat on the other end of the sofa. "You start school in the winter? Then Adriel helped you get transferred?"

"I'm losing a bunch of credits because they don't transfer well from England to America, but for our purposes, it's convenient enough. The easiest place to make them up is your community college. Then I'll shift to the University of Washington or whatever university you choose since we'll need to stay close to hunt together."

"When you said taking notes for us all, does that mean Wade, too? Have you talked to him? He wasn't in class today."

"That's because he stopped by during your class time." Greyson then explained what had happened with Wade. "Anyway, he asked me to give you his apologies. He won't be going to Homecoming with you. He said maybe another dance later in the year if he feels up to it."

Felicity wilted, sliding down his leather cushions.

"Dumped before we even went out. Is that a world record?"

"It wasn't like he dumped you for being you. This was all him," Greyson pointed out.

"But Homecoming is a week away. Marisol was complaining about how all the decent guys will be taken." She pushed herself up and gazed at Greyson. "Which reminds me, I promised I'd ask if you'd be willing to go with her."

"Me?" Greyson jerked back in surprise. "Is that even legal?"

"You're twenty. I looked into it. School rules allow exceptions for eighteen-year-old students to bring a date up to two years older if they ask permission from the staff first. You'd get a pass along with your ticket. The rule allows students who started dating before one graduated to continue attending events together. But we can use the rule, too, right?"

"But I don't even know your friend."

Greyson's mind swam. Part of him acknowledged this might be an opportunity to meet other people in Seattle. On the other hand, did he want to befriend a bunch of high schoolers? He'd be starting college after the new year, and he could make friends there.

Dating one of his teammate's friends could get awkward. Then again, these were Felicity's friends. He was going to meet them at some point because of how much time he and Felicity would be spending together. But she'd leave for school in a few months, so how long could the weirdness last?

He was closing in on a year without a girlfriend. Getting a little… No. For God's sake, what was he thinking? This was a schoolgirl he was considering. *But she's only two years younger,* a little voice pointed out. *Even her school will make an exception for you to date her. And she's eighteen. She can make her own choices as an adult—*

"Greyson?" Felicity cut off his thoughts. "Did I offend you?"

"No. No. Just weighing it all out." He leaned back against the sofa. "Is this Marisol eighteen?"

"Since the end of August."

"Is she pretty?"

Felicity scowled. "Why should looks matter? Shallow much?"

"I'm human, not shallow. Even I'd have a hard time faking my way through a date with an unfortunate-looking person."

Felicity's scowl deepened. "Beauty is subjective."

"But ugliness is pretty universal. If she's not ugly, at least I can work with that." He tapped his fingertips on his thigh. "How about this? Is she at least as pretty as you?"

"How would I know how pretty I am?" Felicity said, exasperated. "I can't compare myself to others."

Greyson laughed. "All girls compare themselves. Take a crack at it."

"Fine. She's not ugly at all. I wish my nose were as straight as hers. Her eyes crinkle up when she laughs, but it matches her dimples and makes her look all adorable. She's tall, but so are you, so height wouldn't matter. And, um, she's got dark wavy hair and dark brown eyes. She can be a bit blunt, like when she said she'd date you for your British accent."

This made Greyson laugh even harder. "She sounds interesting. But why don't the two of you go as friends?

You're both without dates now. I'd feel bad leaving you home to take out your friend."

"*No*," Felicity whined. "It's our senior year. It's supposed to be great. Going with your friend because you both can't get dates isn't memorable in the right way. Going with your girlfriends is what desperate freshmen are supposed to be doing." She crawled toward him. "I have an idea. Why don't the three of us go out tomorrow? You can meet Marisol, and she can help me think up ideas of who else to ask."

"I think you should ask your friend, Jake," Kyrael said, crossing the living room to sit on a dining room chair.

"You said you were staying at my place. And butt out." Felicity made a face at him.

"Your parents were… Wait, I saw a delightful descriptor for it on the internet. Afternoon delight."

Felicity clapped her hands over her ears and shrieked. "You did *not* just tell me that. Adriel, fix him. These moments are getting worse."

"You wanted a reason I didn't stay at your place," Kyrael protested. "Did you want me to lie?"

"In this case, *yes*." This time, her whine was real. "Now I can never go home or even look at my parents again."

Kyrael huffed. "Anyway, this Jake is already accepting of you and your ability to see extra stuff."

"We've been friends since preschool. It's like suggesting I date my brother."

"I'm just saying, from a comfort standpoint, he's convenient. He's aware and accepting of your contact with the otherworldly. Your involvement in the otherworld might scare some suitors off."

She turned her scowl on the angel. "Since when did you become an expert at human compatibility? First, you asked if Wade and I… You know what, never mind. You don't get it." She turned back to Greyson. "Don't listen to him. Jake isn't an option. Not only do we know each other too well, but he's already got a date. So would you go out with Marisol and me tomorrow?"

"I guess. But please don't promise her anything. I can make up my own mind on this, okay?"

"Understood." She whipped her phone out of her pocket and started typing texts. A minute later, she smiled at Greyson. "There. We're all set to walk around Seattle Center with you tomorrow. We'll show you a bit of the city."

Greyson gave her a half-hearted nod. Something about his decision gnawed at his stomach, though he couldn't pinpoint a specific reason. It was probably Marisol's age. He'd never intended to date someone still in high school. Right. That was the issue.

****

Flick fussed with her hair. She was supposed to pick up Greyson right now so they could meet Marisol, but selecting her outfit had taken so long she was running late. Kyrael sighed and tapped her head. Her frizzies disappeared, and her hair glossed on its own.

"That is a handy trick. Why didn't you use it sooner? I could cut off like twenty minutes in the morning."

"I'm not here to be your stylist. But you're going to be late. I read girls spend a good deal of time prepping for dates, but this isn't for you, so what's the worry?"

Flick blushed. "I'd feel weird going out with Greyson and Marisol if they were both dressed up and I looked like a slob."

"Can we go, then?" Kyrael pointed at her door.

Flick grabbed her purse and dropped the strap across her body. "Yeah." She took a jacket and an umbrella from the hall closet. Drizzle soaked the city. Of course, they'd planned an outdoor date today.

Crossing the hall, she took a few steps and knocked on Greyson's door. When he opened it, Flick nipped her lip to keep back her initial impression. He'd dressed up in a casual, sexy way that seemed so natural to European guys. Marisol was so freakin' lucky. Now, she needed another Euro-hotty to drop into her life in time for the dance.

"You look nice today, Felicity," Greyson said, grabbing his jacket and umbrella.

"Thanks. You, too."

"Adriel left for the day." Greyson turned to Kyrael. "Are you good keeping the creepy things away while we go out?"

Kyrael nodded. "Just don't split up unless you don't care what you see because I'm sticking with Felicity."

Flick reached out, grabbing both their hands. "You guys can call me Flick if you want. I think we're plenty close." Holding both their hands made Flick pause. "Kyrael, why are you so much warmer than humans?"

"Energy output. Like touching a lightbulb."

"Ah." Flick let go, and both her hands went cold.

Disappointment tickled Flick's stomach for the first time. She was setting Marisol up on a date. If things went well, she'd be the third wheel. Images of Marisol and Greyson holding hands, laughing, and snuggling raced through her mind, and loneliness settled in behind it. She'd gotten used to being Greyson's sole friend. The idea of sharing his time disappointed her, a feeling exacerbated by guilt. She shouldn't want him to stay alone. He deserved friends and a life. At least if he were dating Marisol, Flick could be included in all parts of his life.

She led the way to the bus stop. Fifteen minutes later, they got off at Seattle Center. Flick and Greyson popped open their umbrellas, even though the floaty drizzle drifted in from the sides as well as coming down from the top. The tree they were supposed to meet by was empty. They'd arrived before Marisol.

"Things got crazy with Wade yesterday," Greyson said, huddling under both the tree and his umbrella. "I never did ask how school went. You prattled for a long time about the Homecoming assembly. Was it as predictable as you thought?"

"As far as the Homecoming royalty goes, yes." She paused, frowning. "I forgot to tell you and Adriel about the weird thing that happened, though. I hosted Kyrael for the assembly so he wouldn't have to avoid people while sitting. After his presence disappeared, the gym filled with a massive, menacing aura. The energy got so thick I almost puked. I went looking for the source and couldn't find anything."

"Nothing?"

"No. And there was even bait. The staff posted a teacher under the bleachers to ensure no one escaped down there to screw around. But even with all the negative energy getting sucked under the bleachers, no remalas were stalking him.

"He sent me back to my seat, but I think he was a bit suspicious. Now he really has the wrong idea about me because Jake and I stopped to talk in one of the private unisex bathrooms after the assembly, and the teacher caught us. Jake has been worried about me. I guess I haven't been acting like myself since I met Adriel."

"Understandable. Though, so is the teacher's misunderstanding if he caught you locked in the lavatory with a boy. I'd wonder."

"This is the same undatable Jake I mentioned before. Nothing happened, nor would it. Anyway. This teacher bugs me. He's too young and tries to act all cool and casual. It's annoying. I'd wanted to check the school for the remalas, but he escorted me to the nurse's office, and I didn't get the chance. So Monday I will have to host Kyrael again and see if we can remove the remala before it feeds on a whole school's worth of negative energy. Or worse, before it attacks a student."

"Want me to come?" Greyson offered.

"Under what premise? But I guess if I haven't caught it by the Homecoming dance, we could step out for a minute and hunt."

"Flick!" Marisol yelled her name and waved from down the block.

"That's my friend, Marisol." Though, Greyson didn't need the explanation.

Approval was evident in his eyes, which, for some reason, annoyed Flick. She could always hope the two didn't get along, but then how would they hunt at the dance if he didn't go with Marisol? And she ought to work on this selfish streak.

Marisol joined them, tipping her umbrella so it didn't knock theirs, then stuck out her free hand in Greyson's direction. "Marisol. And you must be Greyson."

"A pleasure." Greyson shook her hand.

Marisol shot Flick a delighted grin the moment his

accent was unmistakable.

"What should we do?" Flick asked the two of them. "Everything I thought we could see is outdoors, and the damp is starting to soak into my clothes."

"We could take the monorail to Westlake Center, then take the train to the International District. The monorail would give Greyson a good view of the city. Then we could find lunch in the International District. All the best Chinese restaurants are down there."

"And we'd stay drier," Flick agreed. "Okay. Wait. Greyson, do you like Chinese food?"

"Yes. And I'm great with being indoors instead of out in the rain."

"Maybe we can get pastries at Pike's Place after," Marisol suggested. "A hot double dark chocolate brownie a la mode."

Flick's stomach growled. "Okay. Enough talk about food. Let's make it happen."

They worked their way across the Center toward the Space Needle and the monorail station. True to her fears, Flick found herself walking behind Marisol and Greyson while they chatted. Kyrael walked beside her.

"You look sad," the angel observed.

Flick dropped back far enough to whisper to Kyrael without calling Marisol's attention. If her friend asked her about the distance, she could always fib and say it was so Marisol and Greyson could have privacy.

"I want them to get to know each other, but I also didn't want to be left out," she murmured.

He took her hand and squeezed. "You're not alone, though."

"I know. But you're not the same as a date." She squeezed back, whispering her responses so Marisol wouldn't ask questions she didn't want to answer. Not that she needed to worry. Marisol was engrossed in plying Greyson with questions designed to make him speak, then drooling over his accent.

"I'm not the same." He smiled. "You wouldn't want a date with me anyway. Imagine the awkwardness of dinner out, talking to yourself."

"And a plate for no one," she added in a whisper, giggling.

"Did you say something?" Marisol asked, glancing back.

Flick shook her head. "Just musing some things over. Add talking to myself to my list of quirks."

"I ran out of room on the page," Marisol teased. "But don't let us ignore you." She waved Flick closer to her and Greyson.

"I'll let you pester him a bit longer, then join you two," she said. Flick waited until Marisol's attention was caught again, then dropped even farther back. "Kyrael, I've never asked, what do you eat? I've been assuming you leave and get something specific to *angels*."

"We generate our own energy in a similar way to a star."

"You're a walking nuclear reactor?" she yelped without thinking.

Marisol stopped and turned around, which might have been a good thing judging by the aghast look on Greyson's face. "Seriously, Flick, what are you going on about?" She put a hand on Greyson's arm and said, "Give us a sec."

Marisol closed the distance between her and Flick and leaned by Flick's ear. "Jake said you wouldn't talk to him but were having some of your old *troubles*," she whispered. "Are you all right?" She glanced around. "Are we all right here? Is there anything I can do? Woman to woman? Because if you need me today…"

Flick swallowed hard, trying not to shrink back from Kyrael. "N-no, I'm good. I swear. Go on your date." She flinched, and Kyrael sighed.

"I'm not harmful to you. I thought we had already established that. You won't get any radiation from me."

Flick huffed a deep breath, shoulders unknotting, then tensed and jumped when her phone beeped the arrival of a text. Marisol's phone rang at the same time, saving Flick from further questions.

Flick glanced at Jake's text but looked up when Marisol said, "Jake?" Marisol made a face. "You got it backward. Flick is free, and you're interrupting my date." She scowled at the phone. "No, I'm not out with *Dog*-daddy."

Greyson raised an eyebrow, and Flick rolled her eyes. "Don't ask."

Marisol thrust her phone in Flick's direction. "Jake wants to talk to you. He needs a free friend." She pointed a finger at Flick. "This doesn't mean I'm done with you."

"What's up, Jake?" Flick asked, ignoring Marisol and her can of worms.

His sigh made the phone crackle. "My date went to hell. I don't want to be alone."

"Where are you?"

"Almost to Marisol's. I thought she'd be home."

"You're close enough to my place. Why don't you head there instead? I'll meet you."

"Are your parents home? I don't want adult intrusion."

Flick gripped Marisol's phone. "Jake, you're

worrying me. What went so wrong you don't want any parents around?"

"Not over the phone."

Greyson held his keys under her nose. "You can use my place."

"Right." Flick took the keys. "Jake, my neighbor said we can use his place. He's a student. In fact, he's Marisol's date. There won't be anyone at his apartment. Will you meet me?"

"Yeah."

"Do you want Marisol to come?"

Marisol nodded her willingness and gave Flick a thumbs up.

"No. She can finish her date. No offense to Marisol, but I'm glad you're the one free. Talking might be easier without her abrasive analysis. I'm gonna go. See you at your place."

"Wait. I'm in Seattle Center right now. You've got to give me about twenty minutes to get back. Don't leave thinking I stood you up."

"'Kay." He hung up.

She handed the phone back to Marisol. "I wonder what went wrong? Wasn't his big day with Kristin supposed to be today?"

"Does he want me there?" Marisol took her phone and tucked it in her pocket.

"He said to finish your date." She pocketed Greyson's key. "Thanks for letting us use your place. If I'm not there when you get back, I'll be at my house."

"Okay."

They both glanced at Kyrael.

"I'll be fine since I'm just going back to the apartment." She made it look like she was speaking to

Greyson but gave Kyrael a slight wave in Greyson's direction.

He nodded. "Adriel ought to be home soon, so if you're sure, I'll make sure they get an undisturbed date."

"I'm sure," she muttered.

"Huh?" Marisol asked.

'I'm sure," she said louder. "I was thinking about bus routes. You guys have fun. I'm worried, so I'm going to get back."

Chapter 10

Jake waited at the door to Flick's building when she arrived. He looked all sorts of miserable. She put her arm around his shoulders and led him inside the building.

He stayed silent to Greyson's door, speaking when she pulled out Greyson's key. "This guy knows you well enough to give you his key?"

"It's complicated, but we trust one another, so yeah."

"How does a college student afford an apartment in this building?"

"Rich relatives?" She opened the door and let him in.

"Are you over here often?" Jake's gaze ran all around the main living space. The more of the space he took in, the farther his eyes widened, and his lips parted.

But what a question to ask. Her answers would give him the wrong idea. That seemed to be an ongoing theme.

"Jake, you're avoiding the elephant in the room," she scolded. "What was this morning's disaster?"

Jake crossed and sat on the sofa, slumping down into a ball of misery. "Kristin happened."

Flick took the seat beside him. "I thought she was your golden ticket, your guaranteed home run."

He opened his mouth but didn't utter a sound.

Flick squeezed his hand. "What happened?"

"I got used and abused."

Flick started to laugh, then caught herself. Jake didn't have a single trace of a joke on his face. Instead, she reached over and pulled him to lean on her.

"I'm sorry. You can tell me the details if you want. Regardless, I've got you."

"Don't tell Marisol. Please?"

"I won't if you're sure that's what you want."

He shrugged. "I went to see Marisol because I didn't want to be alone. But you're different. I don't know. You seem to soften the negative somehow. Marisol sharpens edges to a weapons-grade razor."

"What did Kristin do to you?" Flick grumbled.

"She kicked my manhood in the teeth."

Flick gasped, and Jake rushed an explanation.

"No, not a physical hit to my goods. I mean she emulated me."

"W-what?" Flick stammered. Her brain fished for the word he was trying to use.

"I know, right? The day started awesome. When I went to pick her up, she invited me in, saying her parents were gone. My moment had arrived. She took me back to her room. Then we kissed. I got her top off—"

"Those weren't the details I was asking for."

"Anyway, she insisted I go down on her before we did anything else. If I got her off, she'd do the same. So I obliged. Then she has me strip. I'm super excited. But she takes one look and bursts out laughing."

He turned his face, stuffing his nose into Flick's shoulder. "She ordered me to put my clothes back on. Said I don't measure up. When I suggested a hand job as a trade for what I'd already done, she literally fell to her bed laughing." His whole body shuddered. "Said she had to have enough to put her hand around for that to work."

He groaned. "I couldn't go home. Mom would know something was wrong, like I can tell her. Not to mention, I'd rather be buried alive before telling my guy friends about this. So I had to find you or Marisol."

"Oh. She *emasculated* you."

He nodded, a dozen shades of miserable.

"Jake." Flick's heart broke a little. "Kristin's a bitch. Don't listen to her."

"She's slept with like half the school. Yet, I'm not good enough."

Flick scooted so she could wrap her arms around him. "And the half of the school she's slept with, I wouldn't touch with a ten-foot pole. She wouldn't know quality if it slapped her in the face."

"When it comes to personality," he complained. "She does know size. She's seen more dicks than a men's locker room. And mine's not..."

Flick patted his back. "Skill at any physical activity is partly about the equipment. The rest is practice and talent. You could give a pro football player crappy high school supplies, and he'd still be awesome. But you can't give a high school player pro football supplies and expect him to play like a champion."

"That's a crappy analogy, but I see what you're getting at." He drooped against her. "How am I supposed to get skills when I can't get a girl into bed?"

"I don't have the answer." She rested her cheek on his hair. "Practice on a mirror?"

Jake gave a grudging laugh. "That's for kissing. The other isn't a pretty visual."

He let go of Flick and went to the kitchen. "Does this Greyson guy have any alcohol? That'll make me feel better."

"Drinking isn't a productive solution. Besides, Greyson's only twenty—"

"Found it." Jake pulled a fifth of vodka out of a cupboard. He clinked around until he located glasses, then opened the fridge and pulled out orange juice. "Screwdriver?"

"Who are you?" Flick asked, wandering into the kitchen after him.

He poured a little vodka into the glass, tipped it into his mouth, then swished. He swallowed, then did this twice more without the swishing. "There. Sterile enough for surgery. All traces of Kristin gone."

Flick wrinkled her nose. "Nasty."

He closed the three steps between them. "Are you sure about that? Don't knock it 'til you've tried it."

"I meant the Kristin part. But the other part, too." He stood so close she could smell the vodka on his breath. "Anything sexual is gross if you think about the rituals and the parts used and—."

"You said the same thing about kissing right before the first time we kissed," he pointed out, shifting so he rested all his weight on one leg. "We were nine, and you didn't understand then either. Told me putting a mouth on a mouth was icky. I believe you've since changed your mind. I think you'd change your mind about the rest, too."

"Probably. But I can't take your word for it for two reasons," she teased. "First, you haven't even done the deed, let alone play with variety. So what would you know? Second, you chose Kristin. Eew."

Jake's lids lowered. "She wasn't my first choice."

In one swift movement, his lips connected with hers.

The kiss at nine years old had been under the mistletoe to see what the fuss was about. It had been a dry little peck of lips on lips. No big deal. And while it proved kisses weren't so icky, it destroyed the magic movies attributed to mistletoe. After all, they had sparkles and cheering and magic. She got Jake.

This kiss, however... She'd been kissed before by several different guys. If skill mattered in such endeavors, then Jake was a contender. In her shock, she let the kiss continue long enough to register his kiss was light and full, forming to her lips. She fell back until the counter stopped her.

"Well, this was not the pairing I would have placed bets on."

Flick jerked away from Jake, smacking his chin with her head. "*Adriel*," she squeaked, a wild blush flaming across her entire face. "You're back."

"Is someone there?" Jake asked, holding his chin, eyes watering.

"Uh, well." Flick searched the room for anywhere not embarrassing to look.

"Don't mind me," Adriel said, heading for the bedroom. "I'll watch tv and let you two do whatever."

"We're not... That was just..." Flick's protests fell dead around her feet.

Adriel shrugged. "No judgments. I'm not that sort of angel. Besides, you have free will." He glanced inside the bedroom and came back out. "What happened to Greyson?"

She glanced at Jake, who stared hard at the spot she spoke to. Whatever. He knew she saw other beings. Why not converse and let him wrap his mind around everything?

"Greyson and Marisol are out on a date," she answered Adriel. "Kyrael is with them. But Jake had a bit of an incident. I told him we could talk about it at my place, but he didn't want parental distractions."

"I can see why he wouldn't," Adriel observed.

Flick's face burned red with irritation and a blush intermixed. "Greyson offered us his place," she continued, ignoring his comment. "They'll be back after lunch and dessert."

Jake interrupted, tapping Flick's shoulder. "Who? What?"

She rubbed her face. "One of the details I didn't want to get into yesterday. This is Adriel. He's an angel. I mentioned him to you once before. Remember I told you I almost hit some dimwit playing in the street? Adriel's the dimwit. But he's not really since cars can't hit him. I just didn't realize when I went out of my way to avoid him."

"Angels?" Jake choked on the word.

Adriel appeared beside Jake and blew on his neck. Jake shivered and swiped at the spot. "What the?"

"Adriel blew on your neck."

This time, Adriel plucked a feather from his wing and ran it across Jake's neck. Jake's whole body shuddered, and he stumbled back into the kitchen counter. His wide eyes searched the general area where Adriel stood but never focused on anyone.

"The fuck," he breathed. "It's true. Everything you've ever said is true."

"I thought you said you believed me?" Hurt laced Flick's tone.

"I did. I mean, I believed you thought you saw things. But I didn't apply them as real to the rest of the world, you know? *Angels*?" His voice cracked.

"Yeah. Greyson can see them, too. We're helping them with a project."

Using the counter to keep himself upright, Jake worked his way out of the kitchen toward the sofa. When he got there, he collapsed to the leather seats and draped an arm across his eyes.

"Jake?"

"I need a few minutes."

"He still can't see you, right?" she asked Adriel.

"Most people can't. Niciel, Kyrael, and I discussed this, and we're unsure what the catalyst is for being able to see the otherworldly."

"This guy can have a conversation?" Jake looked out from under his arm at Flick.

"Yeah. He was saying he doesn't know why Greyson and I see the things we do."

Jake nodded without moving his arm. "Is he your expert on the nasty things you see?"

"Yes."

"Are you ready to share the details with me?"

"Maybe. I'm closer. But Adriel made me wonder. Jake, did you set today up to be alone with me?"

He jerked upright, glaring. "How would I have put that together? I thought you were out on a date."

"Right." She crossed the room and sat beside him on the sofa. "Then what happened in the kitchen?"

"I've been waiting for an opportunity and the guts to do something, anything, so you'd know you're the one I want to be with." His gaze held sincerity.

"When did your feelings for me change?" she murmured.

"They haven't. In kindergarten, I told Ms. Kelley I

was going to marry my best friend, Flick. The problem was Flick never showed she would return my feelings, so I kept them to myself. If I took advantage of anything today, it was the chance to kiss you. I might never have gotten another shot."

"But I don't feel the same." Flick squirmed back away from him.

"But now you know it's an option," Jake pointed out. He sat up and ran a hand through his hair. "You and I have always had truth between us. So here's the truth. Kristin did everything, just as I told you. But it didn't crush my spirit. I played the hurt up a bit because you were pampering me. Being used sucked, don't get me wrong. I didn't want to go home. I thought Marisol would let me raid her parent's liquor cabinet, and we could abuse Kristin together. Then you were available, and the chance to indulge myself in your care was too strong to resist." He tucked his head down. "Are you mad at me?"

"I'm speechless but not angry so much as shocked. Being together with you would mean a huge and permanent shift in our relationship. I've never considered you an option, so I'll need time."

"But you're not opposed?"

"I don't know, Jake."

Someone knocked on the door, and Adriel left to answer it, swinging it open seemingly on its own.

Jake cocked his head. "The angel answers the door?"

"He lives here, so yeah. Well, if it's Wade or me. Or, in this case, Greyson."

"Wade?"

"He was the guy I was going to go to Homecoming

with. He sees the angels and creepy things, too. He's away, taking some time to adjust to everything. We might be the only three on Earth who can see the otherworldly. Oh, and there are three angels with us. Adriel is here. Kyrael is with Greyson, and Niciel went with Wade."

Greyson breezed into the living room. "You two can keep your friend Marisol. She's not for me, thank you."

Flick blinked in confusion. "What went wrong?"

"It would be quicker to tell what went right. The best explanation is we are incompatible. Think fire and ice, if the ice were something off-putting like frozen clam chowder."

Jake burst out laughing. "Marisol is an acquired taste. She's blunt, bossy, and hella loyal." He held out his hand. "I'm Jake."

"The distraught friend? You seem to be doing well."

"Flick is an excellent nurse for the heart." He chuckled. "I had a run-in this morning with a bitch who thought taking shots at my manhood was acceptable. I needed to vent without my guy friends giving me crap about it. It pays to have a couple of girlfriends for such moments. They're the perfect amount of sympathetic, you know?"

Greyson pulled a dining room chair over and sat. "I know what you mean."

"So what's it like living with an angel for a roommate?"

Greyson half-toppled from his chair in surprise. "You can see them?"

Jake shook his head. "Flick and I have been in school together since pre-school. I know all about what she sees. Then today, she's having a conversation with thin air, then the air starts tickling my neck. Creepy as hell, I tell you. But Flick says it's angels, and you can see them, too."

Greyson took a second, getting his bearings, then nodded. "Yeah. One of the angels transplanted me here about a week ago without notice and without asking. Now I live in the States, partnered with an angel, on a team with Flick to hunt those creepy things."

Flick shot Greyson a dirty look, but not in time to shut him up. Jake's mad scramble off the sofa knocked her to the floor.

"Shit, is he serious?"

Flick got up, rubbing her butt. "He's telling the truth."

"So I was kinda right yesterday about being the superhero? You're fighting evil with angels?" He drew up. "Are you safe? If you're in any danger at all, I don't think it's a good idea."

"There's only a little danger," Flick soothed. "Kyrael does all the fighting for me."

"How does that work?" Jake asked.

"I, uh"—Flick blushed, hot—"kinda host him inside my body. He can emerge and face the thing head-on or move me to do it."

Jake's hands shifted to his temples, rubbing in circles. "Tell me I didn't hear you right. You, who ghosts and shit have plagued for your entire life, are letting a self-proclaimed angel possess you? And *control* you?"

"It sounds bad when you say it that way."

"It sounds bad no matter how you say it, Flick." He turned to Greyson. "Don't tell me you're dumb enough to let a strange entity take over your body."

Greyson pressed his lips together. "Flick's right. It

sounds bad, the way you put it. But the reality is bloody awesome. Adriel is my partner, and he's a death angel. He just whips out this scythe and cuts the creatures down. I'm like Flick. I've seen crappy stuff all my life. Having the upper hand for a change is liberating. I'll put up with sharing my body for that."

Jake walked over to Flick and took her hands in his. "I've always worried about you, but this, Flick, this pushes the limit."

"The limit of what?" She didn't like the sound of his statement. "You're not going to be my friend anymore? You're not going to care enough to worry anymore? Write me off?"

"No." He leaned toward her, eyes pleading. "I'm going to have to take some kind of action. Call a priest or a medium or something. This can't go on. You're scaring me, and this latest decision says your judgment might be questionable."

"Are you saying you think I'm *crazy*?" Everything from her neck to her toes tightened, trembling under the pressure. She and Jake had their disagreements, but he'd never questioned her sanity before. Talk about crossing lines.

Kyrael nudged her arm. "Get me paper and a pen, like we used in class."

"Greyson," Flick couldn't keep the edge from her voice, "I need paper."

He grabbed some of the stack he'd used earlier to take notes, along with the pen, and handed them to Flick. She took the materials and slapped them down on the counter, then grabbed Jake around the waist, hauling him in front of the writing supplies.

Kyrael had the pen in hand and wrote, *Greetings,*

*Jake. I'm Flick's angelic partner, Kyrael.*

"Oh! That's how you spell it," Flick said, reading over Jake's shoulder.

Jake had gone rigid, his eyes bulging. "The fuck…" he whispered.

Kyrael kept writing. *If it helps, I* am *an angel. Flick is safe with me, so you don't need to worry about her safety or who is inhabiting her body. She's got the final say in anything we do together, and expelling me takes a single thought.*

Jake's gaze flipped up to Greyson, then to Flick, with only his eyeballs moving.

"Adriel," Flick called. "Do you want to say anything to Jake?"

The angels switched out, and Adriel took over writing. The first thing Flick noticed was how different their handwriting was. The distinction would be hard for Jake to explain away.

*This is Adriel, death angel by trade. Flick is precious to this team and me. We don't let team members get hurt. Know I'm watching you, young man.*

"What's he talking about?" Greyson asked.

"Maybe later," Flick said. One uncomfortable topic at a time. "Adriel, play nice."

Tremors shook Jake, knocking him into Flick, who stood at his back.

Adriel rolled his eyes. *If you worry about Flick's safety, let her know if you see anything unusual happen at your school. She sensed a great deal of negative energy at your school yesterday and found no being to attribute it to.*

"Is he being serious?" Jake asked, squinting at the paper. "I can't see any of this crap. What am I going to notice?"

*Damage to people or the building. Unexplained air movement like when I blew on you. Hot spots. Though, those would be a bad sign. The more harmless a being, the colder they run.*

Jake gripped his head with both hands and huffed. "I can't believe I believe this." He started muttering rapid words meant for no one in particular. "But I can't deny what I felt, and the writing appearing is almost indispensable."

"Indisputable," Flick tossed in, earning her a glare.

"There's no way someone could preprogram something when they have no idea what I'm going to say. The responses are so specific. Then two different kinds of handwriting. And...tell me something only I would know," he blurted.

Adriel huffed. "He doesn't want me to do this. I deal exclusively with the dead, you know."

"Adriel warns you he deals with the dead, and you might not want to know," Flick repeated so Jake could hear.

He tapped the paper. "I want to see this Adriel write something no one but me could know. Now I'm feeling better about my doubts. I don't know anyone dead, so how could he answer? Ha!"

Adriel gripped the pen for a moment before scratching out, *I don't like being challenged. I'll be back in a few minutes.*

The angel disappeared.

Chapter 11

Greyson watched this exchange with a sense of detached reality. He wished he'd had anyone who believed him the way this guy believed in Flick. On the other hand, Jake could disrupt the flow he and Flick established.

Jake crossed his arms, pouting. "Did the angel leave? Where did he go?"

*Heaven,* Kyrael wrote. *You've got serious guts provoking a death angel. Even the other angels don't mess with them.*

"This is the second time you've said something of the sort," Greyson remarked. "Why?"

Kyrael spoke and wrote to include everyone. *"For a human, a death angel is the one who calls their soul from their body. There's no medicine to help you recover from a reaping. From there, they send the souls Heaven or Hell-bound. The souls going to Heaven are available for conversation if an angel chooses.*

"I assumed as much. I can see why a human should be afraid of a death angel, but why are the other angels skittish around them?" Greyson asked.

Kyrael shuddered. *Death angels are notorious for their short tempers due to the nature of what they do. As a result, they're the one classification of angels who get regular vacations. For the most part, angels and joy go hand in hand. But death angels drag sorrow around with them. Even if it's human sorrow, it still takes a toll.*

"Adriel mentioned being in Seattle on vacation," Flick said.

*If the death angels get cranky, they can rain down all sorts of unpleasantness. One of my fellow messengers had to deliver bad news to a death angel once. He came back with all the feathers singed off his wings. Took him eleven months to grow them all back.*

*The rest are all one-off stories, but they include things like an angel who was rendered as mute as the dead for suggesting a death angel was too uptight. The death angel left him speechless for days after returning to Earth. The mute angel was too scared to track him down and ask that he lift the curse.*

Greyson took the pen from Kyrael. "We get the idea."

"They can't be too wicked with their retaliation against perceived slights. They're angels, after all," Kyrael added.

"I don't know," Greyson said. "I've seen Adriel materialize and swing his scythe."

"He'd get cast into Hell if he took his scythe to another angel with the intent to kill and no permission from Heaven," Kyrael said. "Heaven has some very absolute laws on conduct."

"Angelic ten commandments?" Greyson asked.

Kyrael laughed. "Something like that."

Jake had been watching the visible half of the exchange. "Really convincing."

"Your doubts are getting annoying," Greyson said, eyes narrowing. "I thought you believed Flick."

"But angels? Seriously?"

"Don't be too hard on the boy, Greyson. You still

have doubts," Kyrael pointed out. "You can't see my wings."

Greyson turned his head away. Watching Flick find her faith when he still couldn't see irked him. But it drove home what he'd been told as a child. God was a personal thing. You could follow others who believed without questioning, but the truth was in your own heart, not theirs. And his truth still waffled. The weirdest and most frustrating part was once Flick had seen their wings, he wanted to, too. But for all his efforts, he saw nothing, and he couldn't for the life of himself figure out what he was missing.

Adriel reappeared and snatched the pen off the counter.

"He's back and ready to write," Flick informed Jake.

The group crowded around the paper, curious to see what Adriel had found to convince Jake. *Your grandfather passed when you were five. Your parents had an open casket service for him. When they sent you to pay your respects, you stuck your finger up the nose of your grandfather's corpse. He said he's never laughed so hard at a funeral. He's waiting to give you a hard time about it.*

Jake stared open-mouthed at the paper. "How…" His voice trailed off.

"Seriously, Jake?" Flick shot him an exasperated look.

"I was five, and his nostril was huge!" Jake trembled. "After, I thought I was going to go to Hell for the longest time, so I never told anyone what I did."

Shaking, he crossed the room and dropped to lie on the sofa. "Holy crap. There's an angel in the room. Like a real angel who went to Heaven and got my dead grandpa to dish up dirt on me." The blood drained from his face, leaving him ghostly pale. "A death angel."

*Reassigned. And I thought of one other thing you can do for Flick. Help shield her so she can converse with Kyrael at school.* Adriel let the paper flutter down on Jake's head.

He looked at it, then nodded.

Flick's phone beeped a text. She tapped a text back, then looked at Greyson. "Marisol wants an update on everything. Can I call her from your room?"

"Whatever."

She took the phone and hurried off. Lucky for her. The next moment, Jake rushed from the sofa, puking all over himself and the kitchen floor. Greyson grimaced at the mess.

"What the hell?"

"Sorry," Jake panted. "I guess all this affected me deeper than I thought." He made it to the sink for his next heave.

"I'll clean up the kitchen for you," Adriel offered. "Can you loan the boy fresh clothes?"

"Fine, fine." He turned and headed for his bedroom. Adriel had somehow transported all his clothing from England, so he had plenty to choose from, and Jake was a little smaller than him, so it ought to fit.

Greyson paused at the door to his room. Through the crack, he could see Flick lying on her stomach on the bed, kicking her feet up behind her. Her back was to him, and her phone lay propped up on the pillow, Marisol visible on a video call.

He paused, unwilling to let Marisol see him. His feelings about their date were one-sided, and her next comment confirmed his fear.

"I'd so give him a bunch of babies if they all came with his adorable accent and tight ass."

"Why would you want to look at your kids' asses?" Flick teased.

"Well, I'd want them to be sexy in their own time, of course."

"You're so weird."

Marisol laughed. "You're the one who sees ghosts. You calling anyone weird is like a turtle making fun of a snail for his shell."

"You come up with some strange analogies." When Flick spoke next, hesitation slowed her words. "So…what are you going to do about homecoming?"

Marisol disappeared from the screen and returned a second later with her face buried in a pillow. "Do? I'm going with Greyson. He didn't say we were yet, but I'm positive he's about to ask."

"Based on?" Flick prodded.

"He rode the bus and got off at my stop to see me home, then waited for me to open my door and go inside. You don't do that for someone you don't want to spend more time with."

Greyson gritted his teeth. He'd been making sure she got in safely, nothing more. Marisol and Flick were young ladies living in a big city. Who knew what weirdos lurked looking for a lone girl like them?

"Maybe he was just being nice," Flick hedged.

"Girl, you're hopeless with boys, which is why you don't notice anything. I'm telling you, Greyson might be all British aloof, but he wants me."

Greyson palmed his face. She'd twisted everything he'd said.

"Speaking of boys, what was the whole deal with

Jake?" Marisol asked.

Flick growled. "Kristin used him for oral, then told him he was too small to get anything in return and sent him packing."

Marisol frowned and made a show of snapping her fingers. "The term I'm looking for, would it be Bitch-slut, or Slut-bitch?"

Greyson cringed. There was her mouth again. How abrasive.

"I don't know what name suits her best, Marisol. But I think he was more angry at being used than hurt about the insults." Flick's voice had gone very tight. "Things with him just got weirder from there."

"Like what? Dish, girl."

"I'll tell you soon. I need to sort through some stuff to find the right words before speaking them."

"You and your secrets, Flick. You've got a stockpile of skeletons. Someday, that closet's going to burst open on you."

Flick sighed. "I need to go. Jake and I are still over at Greyson's."

"Okay. But tell Mr. Reserved Brit to get his ass in gear and commit in time for me to find a killer dress."

"I'll pass your message along." She hung up.

Greyson pushed the door open, leaning on the frame. "You didn't show me the skeleton closet the last time I was over."

Flick stared at him, mortified. "You were listening?"

"I came in at the very end of the conversation, which confirmed what I feared. I was too gentle with her while trying not to hurt her feelings, and she misinterpreted." He took a seat on the edge of the bed near Flick. "You didn't want to tell Marisol that Jake likes you?"

She startled. "How can you tell?"

"Adoration practically shines out his arse. Something happened today with him, didn't it?"

Flick sat up and scooted closer, sitting hip to hip with Greyson. "He told me he liked me," she confessed. "I didn't know he wanted more until today." She trailed off, her tone indicating much unsaid, and her body drooped.

"I take it you don't reciprocate?"

She shrugged. "We have this huge history. I don't remember a time when Jake wasn't my friend. He's been planning this future with me, and I…" She stopped, falling silent.

"What do *you* imagine your future looking like?" Greyson asked.

"I have no idea. Everything has changed."

"Okay, before the angels and stuff."

Flick tucked her hands under her legs, brushing his in the process. When she stopped, her pinky rested against his. Greyson registered this, which set his stomach buzzing.

"Before the angels," Flick said, "I was planning on attending the University of Washington so I could be close to family and friends. I wanted to get a degree in environmental architecture. I thought I could squeeze in a husband and maybe a kid later."

"In your imaginings, was Jake ever the husband?"

She shook her head. "Jake and Marisol are in my vision, but it's as guests in my fabulous backyard. They bring their families, and we all celebrate the Fourth of July."

"Does he ever make your heart beat faster or your stomach flutter?"

She blushed and turned her head away. "No. Not like with Wade. Why are you asking so many questions?"

"I figured you could use a little help sorting your feelings. Ever since I got back tonight, you've been tighter than a stretched rubber band. It's how I deduced something happened with Jake." He took a deep breath. "I think you owe Jake the truth, and soon, like I should have been firmer with Marisol. Now I'm going to hurt her worse because I wasn't clear to start."

The door swung open, and Adriel shot Greyson an exasperated look. "I had to clean Jake's clothes myself. Did you forget what you came in for?"

"As a matter of fact, I did. Sorry."

"Well, he finished vomiting all over himself and passed out. No matter how much he'd convinced himself he believed Flick, his faith only went so far. Reality overwhelmed him. I put him in the guest room and texted his parents, saying he was staying the night with friends."

"Sorry for all the trouble, Adriel," Flick apologized. "Would it have been better if I hadn't told him?"

"I'm not asking you to lie to your friends. He was going to question you. It was inevitable. I expect Marisol will do the same."

"Do I need to brace for telling my parents, too? They're going to be a hard sell."

"We'll worry about that when and if sharing with them becomes necessary. But I texted your parents, too, and told them you were staying at Greyson's to watch a movie. Kyrael and I would like you to host us and go to your school. I'm curious if the remala is active on the weekend. After dark is the perfect time to investigate."

"What if Jake wakes up while we're gone?" Flick asked.

"I'll be sure he sleeps."

Flick's stomach growled. "Greyson might have gone out for lunch. But I haven't eaten. Can we eat before we go?"

Adriel nodded. "I'll order something for you. Are you hungry, Greyson?"

"Get me a little something. Lunch wasn't enjoyable because I wanted to get out of there."

When Adriel had gone, Greyson lay back on his bed and sighed. "Hunting is fun, but kicking back and enjoying life while Wade cleared the area was more fun."

Flick joined him, turning her head to focus on him. "It's just hard to find the motivation to walk out the door and search for trouble. But at the school, when I could sense the remala, I didn't hesitate to go looking. Besides, I'm not having any fun today. Can I confess something?"

"Sure."

"I'm glad you didn't get along with Marisol. I felt all horrible and selfish when you met up with her and started talking. I've gotten used to being your only friend, and I didn't want to share. I think it's because no matter how much my other friends say they understand, they'll never get me, like Jake. Look what trying did to him. But you…"

She grabbed his hand and squeezed. "I know you can't go through life belonging to me. That's not healthy for either of us. When you start college, you'll meet more people, and I'll try to be happy for you. But for the time being, can I be selfish?"

Greyson returned the squeeze. "I'm all yours for the time being. If we're confessing, I kept quiet, too. I should have been more direct before and suggested I take you to the dance. I don't mind going, but with you, not because I want to go to a high school dance with just anyone. You adopted me as a friend from the moment Kyrael brought us together. I'll return the favor of being there for you."

"I'd like to go with you, but…" She wilted, her head resting against his shoulder. "What about Marisol and Jake?"

"Marisol will have to accept she made up my feelings for me. I'll tell her in no uncertain terms I'm not interested. From there, what she feels is her own problem." Greyson paused. "Jake is a little trickier. As I said, you need to tell him how you feel sooner rather than later. I hope he's a big enough man to accept you taking a friend to a dance."

The moment the words left his lips, Greyson knew he'd be all right if Flick took him to the dance as more than a friend. His hand itched to take hers. If he angled his head, they'd be close enough to kiss. He closed his eyes on his impulses and tried to sigh them out.

Jake had already dumped enough on her tonight. There would be a better moment to suggest switching the direction of their relationship. Besides, such a shift would have to be weighed out. If anything went wrong, working as a team might get tricky. Then again, Wade was out hunting on his own. If things went pear-shaped between them, they could always part ways.

Flick may have had a point about regular friends understanding their circumstances. In which case, Flick might be the one girl who could ever really connect with him. And what if they did get on together? They couldn't hunt forever. The angels weren't going to be hiding in an eighty-year-old while they shuffled around looking for remalas. So once they got too old to be effective hunters, who would they have then? With Flick, he could have a partner in so many senses of the word.

Carrying that further, if the job of hunting fostered such a unique connection between them, how would regular spouses react? He had an advantage as a man. He could hunt until he got too old, then still take a younger wife and father a family. But would Flick have to choose between hunting and family? Would the choice play out the same for her if she was with him?

He squeezed his eyes tighter shut and groaned. Regular relationships carried enough weight. Trying to balance dating and hunting promised to be twice as bad.

"What's wrong?" Flick asked.

"Just trying to sort through the reality of being a hunter. Some new things occurred to me."

"Anything I should know about?"

He shook his head. "Nothing you need to worry about. Don't take on my anxieties. I'm sure you've got enough of your own."

She was eighteen. She had plenty of time to worry about a family later. Besides, the angels seemed keen to make sure their participation was voluntary. Either of them could bow out if life turned away from this path.

The doorbell rang.

"That's our food," Flick said, hurrying off the bed. "I'm starving."

Greyson's stomach growled, but he would have been happy to stay on the bed with her for much longer.

\*\*\*\*

Flick sat on the bus, her knee bouncing out her nerves. The closer they got to her school, the more her stomach churned. She prayed they wouldn't find anything once they arrived. But despite her hopes, memories of the oppressive miasma at the assembly crept in around the edges.

Greyson reached over, putting a hand on her knee. "Adriel and Kyrael are with us. This will be fine, like all the other times."

"You didn't feel the aura the day of the assembly. I've never felt so much malice concentrated in a single place."

"And you didn't see anything either. Maybe with the student body together, and now that you're more in tune with these things, you're just seeing the buffet drawing in the remalas. The angels have said places like schools are a remala feast."

Her knee quieted under the weight of Greyson's hand. Having him there was reassuring. And, of course, he was right. No matter what they encountered, the angels would drive it off.

The bus pulled to a stop, and the doors swung open. Flick stood, exiting, Greyson right behind her. A flitting desire to hold his hand tickled her brain, but she shook it away. She wasn't a baby who needed to clutch an adult's hand. She was an angel's partner and a hunter. If she couldn't walk to the school of her own volition, what right did she have to continue down this path?

Jutting her chin forward, she marched in the direction of her school. The walk encompassed the same two blocks she walked each morning with Marisol and Jake, but tonight, the sidewalk seemed to stretch for miles into engulfing darkness.

A block from the school, Greyson frowned. "Do you smell that? It smells like something dead."

"Just a little whiff." Rocks settled in Flick's

stomach. "It's the same as what I smelled during the assembly."

Moving forward now proved much more difficult, and her feet dragged. The start of the next block marked the outer edge of the playing field for her school. The moment they crossed the street, a wall of negative energy engulfed them, so thick it almost felt viscous like glue.

Greyson put his hands over his mouth and gagged. "Oh God," he choked out.

"Is it the same as before?" Kyrael asked inside her head.

"Worse." She clutched the fence and fought her stomach.

Greyson sagged beside her, gasping for breath. "Are there usually lights on at this time on a Saturday night?"

She glanced up at the school. Several windows glowed. "Staff or janitors, maybe. I don't hang out at school at this time." She tightened her grip on the post. "Do you think any staff is safe?"

"Adriel figures they are. Since the effect is so profound, he wants to come out and feel what we're feeling."

"But won't his presence send the remala running?" Flick asked.

"He doesn't care. He says this might be more than a one-night job."

Tears stung Flick's eyes. "I don't want to keep facing this. I'd rather just get rid of whatever is causing this pollution. I feel like I'm surrounded by evil gelatin."

"I didn't realize that was a flavor here in the States. Weird." Greyson grinned. "Look, I don't want to submerge myself in this filth ever again, either. But I don't need to see the thing to know this isn't some ordinary remala. We've seen up through mid-grade beasties, and they're bad enough. We should know what we're up against before we go rushing after whatever this is."

"Okay." Flick meant her words for both Greyson and the angels.

Half a second later, both angels stepped from their bodies to stand on the sidewalk beside them. Like a sea anemone retreating within itself, tendrils of the miasma pulled back, reeling into their source.

The air around Flick lightened, and she drew a clear breath of wholesome air.

This lifted an invisible weight on her body. Her stomach settled, and she switched to leaning on the fence, her muscles having gone rather gelatinous—at least until she saw Adriel's face. If his smile could manifest light, this expression brought out lightning.

"This is not a remala."

"What?" Both Flick and Greyson yelped together.

He shook his head. "This is going to be at least a three-part mission. I need to call Niciel and Wade back. I'm not an exterminator, and we need one to identify this entity."

Flick held her phone out to Adriel. "I have Wade's number. I had it for…" She blushed, not wanting to recap getting dumped.

Adriel took it and dialed Wade, putting the call on speaker.

"Felicity?" Wade sounded groggy and confused. "'Sup?"

"Is Niciel available?" Adriel asked.

"Adriel?" The grogginess was dropping away, but the confusion lingered in his voice. "He was sleeping, too. We're on the East Coast. It's the middle of the night. He can hear you. I put you on speaker."

"Niciel, we need you and Wade back in Seattle. Flick encountered what she thought was a remala at her school, but on her first inspection couldn't find the source of the negative energy. The four of us returned to investigate, and Niciel, it wasn't a remala. It wasn't anything I've ever encountered. The miasma was thick enough to feel semi-solid and so vile, I can't describe it. I need someone who's been in the field with these entities to identify what's lurking here."

"You came out of your host to feel the aura?" Niciel clarified.

"Yes."

"Hmm," he grunted. "Then I need a week. Don't reveal yourself anywhere near the school in case that's its lair. We don't want whatever this is to run off on us. A week ought to be sufficient to get it to let its guard down. Then I'll need to feel the aura for myself. From there, we'll make a plan, okay?"

"A week from now is the Homecoming dance," Flick said. "If my school is its lair, is it safe for all the students and staff to be there after dark?"

Silence for a moment, then Niciel said, "Checking its type after the dance will be better."

"Won't any negative emotions feed the thing?" Greyson asked.

"Assuming it's a remala."

"What else could it be?" Flick asked, not really wanting the answer.

"The miasma disappeared when the angels came out?" Niciel asked.

"Yeah," Flick confirmed. "It kinda curled back like

tentacles."

"It could be several things, none of them good. It might be a familiar. Those are entities akin to demons who do a demon's bidding. They don't pack as much power as an actual demon, but they have physical bodies and can exist outside Hell, and so cause more trouble. Those are rare, though. Only a couple have turned up during my hundreds of years as an exterminator.

"It might be a hive of remalas. On occasion, they collaborate. Our worst-case scenario is a contracted remala. I've been on two teams dealing with those. It's not pretty. So let's hope you found something less sinister."

"You're not convincing me it's safe," Flick said.

"It's not," Niciel answered. "No matter what you found, it's a whole lot of trouble. But here's the tricky part. If you found a contracted remala or a familiar, they're intelligent enough not to get caught with their pants down. One sign of interference from Heaven, and they'll pack their bags and skip town."

"I didn't already ruin our chances to catch it, did I?" Adriel asked.

"Probably not. Angels have business on Earth all the time. Don't hang around the school or show up again unless it's dire."

Adriel waved the group to cross the street and start walking away. "Can Flick still attend?" he asked. "We've promised not to put them in harm's way."

"She might be in danger if she was suspected of being in league with angels. She's not immortal and could be used as leverage in a tight spot. But that's pessimistic thinking on my part because people who can see us aren't supposed to exist, so why would another entity suspect?"

"Unless her being able to see remalas is obvious even to an observer," Kyrael pointed out. "I don't like the idea of sending her to school."

They passed the bus stop, but Adriel kept them walking.

"She needs to keep living as if she's noticed nothing," Niciel ordered. "If she acts strange and the entity already suspected she could see, it might be enough to tip it off. Finding a familiar or contracted remala again could take years and lead to disaster. *Don't lose track of this thing.*" He grunted. "Don't poke me, Wade. Flick will be safe as long as either Adriel or Kyrael stays hidden inside her. They can reveal themselves and scare it off if her life ends up in the balance."

"Oh," Niciel added. "Don't under any circumstances engage this entity. If it's a hive, you'll need me and a few more exterminators to route them all. If it's a contracted remala…"

He stopped speaking.

"That bad?" Greyson murmured.

"If it's a contracted remala," Niciel finished, "we'll have to involve the Powers. The two times I was party to a contracted remala's extermination, it took the angelic army's intervention. And a familiar is even worse. Good luck, and see you in a week." The phone call ended.

Chapter 12

"An entire army?" Flick whispered.

Adriel shook his head. "No. The entire army isn't sent out for something like a single remala, even if it is contracted with a demon. A unit of Powers would suffice."

Adriel turned, fanning his wings to help him balance while walking backward. "I should go do some research in Heaven. Flick, is there any way you can stay with Greyson until school on Monday? I'm sure I can be back by then."

"I doubt it. My parents aren't going to agree to me staying two nights with an older guy when my house is right next door."

Greyson put a hand on her shoulder. "If Adriel needs to go back to Heaven, we'll figure something out. I can stay alone for a couple of nights if worst comes to worst. Kyrael will be next door."

Adriel folded his wings and stopped walking. "I'll go as fast as I can. With two angels in and out of your apartment building, I'm sure everything has given your place a wide berth." He moved in and hugged Flick. "Be brave."

She tucked her arms around his ribs and under his wings, letting the feathers caress her hands. "I will."

Adriel let her go and clapped Greyson on the shoulder. "You, too. Be brave. I'll be back soon." The next moment, he'd vanished.

Kyrael glanced around at the street. "I should go back inside, Flick. We don't know where the thing has gone, and I don't want to be the reason we can't catch it later."

"But I can't feel the aura at all," Flick protested. She felt better with the angel where she could see him. "Doesn't that mean the creature is long gone?"

"Not necessarily. A hive would scatter, but a contracted remala or a familiar would be able to suppress their energy."

"To the point we can't even feel it?" Greyson asked. "And angels can't do the same? How does it work when they have powers above yours?"

"Not above." Kyrael held his hand toward Flick. "Their power is a sidestep. Nature is full of measures and countermeasures predators and prey take with one another. Abilities are never the same, just balanced. Angels are capable of much that no one in Hell can match. Hence, the evil entities' ability to employ stealth to avoid being overpowered."

Flick touched his palm and absorbed the angel.

"I guess his explanation makes sense," Greyson said. He shivered, his whole body shaking. "I feel cold and alone with no angel holding the darkness at bay."

Flick reached over and took his hand. "Do you mind? I wanted the connection earlier but felt like a baby asking you to hold my hand to make me feel safe."

He wrapped his fingers around her hand and squeezed. "Thanks. It makes me feel better, too."

"The next bus stop for my route is up about two and a half blocks. I guess we can use the walk to figure out how to angel share for the night."

"Adriel told your parents you were staying at my place to watch a movie. I'll text them and explain you and Jake both fell asleep, so everyone decided to stay the night. They don't have to know the other party in 'everyone' is an angel. Besides, what better chaperone than an angel if they're worried about your honor?"

"*I don't care what humans do with other humans,*" Kyrael said inside her mind. "*I'd only intervene if someone were going to hurt you.*"

"Intervene like how?" Flick asked.

"Huh?" Greyson stared, waiting for her to supply the other half of the conversation.

"He said he wouldn't intervene to *save my honor*, as you put it. He'd only keep me from getting hurt."

"That's vague given the number of ways one person can hurt another," Greyson said. "But on some level, it's good to know having angels riding along in our lives won't interfere with how we want to date. I'm not interested in adopting celibacy because Adriel and Kyrael are around."

"Then you're not a…I mean, you're experienced?"

"You sound surprised."

Flick blushed. "I never thought about you that way. I mean, as someone who dated and more." Her blush deepened over her inadequate description.

Greyson drew his head back. "I'm mildly offended. To never be thought of that way makes it sound like I'm lacking any appeal."

Flick rubbed at the blush on her cheek with her free hand. "No. I meant—"

He laughed and swung their joined hands. "I'm teasing you. I get the general idea."

"Oh. Then, can you convince my parents not to

come barging over and collect me?"

"They wouldn't trust you? You're eighteen."

She shot him a sideways glance. "No. They trust me. They don't trust *you*, or any other guy for that matter."

"But shouldn't your activities be your choice?"

They reached the bus stop and paused under the streetlight. Constant illumination felt good.

"For the most part, they don't interfere," Flick explained. "But imagine you had a daughter. Now imagine some guy doing to her what you've done to past girlfriends. In the bedroom, I mean. Not that you've done anything wrong."

Greyson made a face. "I'd want to pound the guy." He chuckled. "Point made. I'll try my best to sound harmless when I petition your parents."

Flick pulled out her phone and checked the bus schedule—they had about five minutes. The two stood waiting, her hand warm in his. Between Greyson's touch and the circle of light surrounding her, the tension gripping Flick released. She sighed, leaning against his shoulder, exhaustion pulling at her.

"Are you still good?" he asked.

Flick yawned so wide her eyes watered. "I think telling my parents I fell asleep at your place won't be too far from the truth. I could almost curl up here and nap."

"You *must* be knackered," Greyson huffed. "I can't forget we're mere blocks from where we encountered something so evil even angels are cautious. A something which is unaccounted for at the moment."

The bus pulled up, and Greyson nudged her to climb aboard. They sat together, and Flick let herself lean on him, tucking her head to his shoulder. He smelled like his apartment—laundry detergent and the essential oils

Adriel used in place of air fresheners.

Greyson wrapped his arm around her and pulled her against him. "I'll wake you when we get to the stop."

"I feel weak," she mumbled around a yawn. "It's barely after midnight, and I'm making you hold me up."

"Not to worry. I'm a night owl, and I've been used as worse than a pillow."

Greyson kept a steadying arm around her all the way back to his flat, where Kyrael let himself out of her body and got the doors for them. Inside, Greyson laid her on his bed and pulled off her shoes.

"You can have my bed. I'll take the sofa. I refuse to share with your puking friend in the guest room."

She slid her phone in his direction. "Text Mom, not Dad," she murmured.

The bed creaked, and the soft beeps of his texting punctuated the otherwise silent room. Darkness slipped over Flick, and she let herself sink in.

Illuminated in the blackness, Jake waited. He sat up on the sofa in Greyson's living room. "I can't deal with all your craziness anymore, Flick."

Marisol joined him, perched on the edge of the sofa. "How could you drag Jake into your mess?" she accused. "You're a horrible friend."

"And a heartbreaking tease," Jake added to the accusation. "You kissed me. You led me on and made me think we might have a chance together. Then you pull the rug out from underneath me, crushing my dreams."

"You're the one who kissed me," she protested.

"And you said you'd think about being with me. Then you spend the night in the room of a guy you've known for less than two weeks? You're worse than Kristin."

Something scratched in the shadows, and Flick bit her knuckles. "You're upset and calling them to us, Jake. Please calm down. You're still my best guy friend."

"If you love me, if you want to keep me safe, then make me happy. Date me. Marry me."

Slime oozed down the walls of Greyson's apartment, and from within the drywall came the skittering of remalas feeding on Jake's distress and Marisol's indignation.

"See what you've done to him," she scolded. "When Kristin hurt him, we all knew she had the potential to be a bitch. But you, you're worse. You've broken a friend. There's a special circle in Hell for women like you. I bet it's infested with all the creeping things you've ever seen."

Out of nowhere, Mr. Ostanes appeared. "You've not only broken a boy, you little deviant," he reprimanded. "You've been sneaking around where you shouldn't be, keeping secrets and lying to everyone: friends, parents, teachers. I know you lied to me."

The finish on the drywall crumbled and gave, opening a wide hole the size of a coffee table at the seam with the ceiling. Remalas, like blood-sucking bugs, tumbled out, raining down inside Greyson's immaculate living room. It was the hive. The hive had been in the living room all along, waiting for Flick to reveal her horrible side.

The wave of insects rolled across the floor, undulating and swelling. Flick tried to run, but her feet were glued together. She shuddered and fell. The mob of remalas engulfed her, and only a sadistic laughing permeated the crawling darkness.

Flick woke screaming, covered in sweat. The door

to Greyson's room burst open, and Kyrael and Greyson rushed in.

"What happened?" Kyrael asked in alarm.

Flick clutched at her chest, panting. "Nightmare."

Then the tears flowed, streaming down her cheeks. She gasped for air, and the sweat on her body turned icy.

Greyson sat on one side of her and Kyrael on the other. "Want to tell me about it?" Kyrael asked. "Sometimes dreams are the subconscious trying to tell you something. I could help you sort it out."

"It was a pretty cut-and-dry nightmare." She rubbed at the tears, but they didn't stop. "Jake accused me of being a tease, then breaking his heart. Marisol said I'd ruined him. Mr. Ostanes pointed out all my rule-breaking and lying. Then, feeding off everyone's negative energy, the hive of remalas erupted from the living room walls and swallowed me alive."

Kyrael smoothed his hand across her head. "Sounds like raw fear. I've never tried sleeping in the human fashion, but if you want, I'll let you curl up with me here. I know you want to snuggle my wings," he tempted.

Despite being a little embarrassed at having her desire caught, Flick nodded. Kyrael lay out on his stomach and lifted the wing toward the inside of the bed. Flick crawled over and tucked herself in beside him. Like snuggling in a chick, Kyrael folded his wing over her and pulled her against him.

Greyson stood, and Kyrael pointed across Flick to the far side of the bed. "You can join us. I don't want you to have any nightmares either."

"I don't know." Hesitancy laced Greyson's voice. "It seems…"

A moment later, the mattress jiggle told Flick he'd

given in. She didn't blame him. If it weren't for the angel wing over top of her, she doubted she'd go back to sleep. And Greyson must have similar images in his head.

"Seriously, Flick?" Jake's voice cracked between the words.

Flick's eyes opened, her body protesting the lack of sleep. Kyrael's wing blocked her view, so she wiggled up enough to peek out. "Shh..." she admonished in a whisper.

Jake stood beside the bed, glaring down. Oh, right. This would look compromising. All Jake could see was her, still in yesterday's clothes, in bed with Greyson. She went to sit up, but Kyrael's wing pinned her down. She struggled to get the appendage off her, but between the feathers and structure, it weighed way more than she would have thought.

She shoved against him. "Kyrael. Let me up."

"You can stop whispering," Greyson grumbled into his pillow. "I'm up."

"Yeah. But Kyrael isn't, and he's super heavy. I don't understand how someone who can slip through crowds like a leaf on a river current can have a wing weighing as much as a great dane."

Greyson shrugged and shifted, then yelped and scrambled off the bed like a doused cat. "What the bloody fuck?"

Kyrael sat, stretched his wings, then tucked them against his back. "I guess you can see them?"

Greyson pointed a trembling finger at Kyrael. "I suspected, but they're huge, and feathered, and..." He garbled off before falling silent.

Kyrael smiled at Greyson. "You've let belief into your heart, but I hope your desperation over last night didn't push you to that point. I'd rather have you fall into faith with a happy heart."

Shivers shook Greyson's body, and he wrapped his arms around himself. "I guess I believed Adriel went to the real Heaven to try and help. Or maybe having you sleep with us gave me so much comfort..." He shook his head. "Give me a minute to process."

"You know what, no." Jake jammed his hands in his pockets and turned. "Just, no. I'm not doing this. I don't see Flick in bed with a strange guy, pinned by a disembodied voice-on-paper that the strange guy suddenly believes has wings."

Flick hurried around Kyrael and grabbed Jake's shirt before he left the room. "Jake. Stop, please. I know yesterday was overwhelming for you, but I need you." She bit her tongue, realizing how he might misinterpret those words despite their truth. But she also didn't want him to make up anything untrue and leave with his feelings bent out of shape before they could even talk. "We went on a hunt last night. It was alarming, and I was having nightmares. Kyrael stayed to keep away those thoughts."

Jake didn't say anything or turn around, but he stopped trying to leave.

"I know how you must be feeling," she sympathized. "But Greyson is just a friend. He sees what I see and knows the fear I feel. That's why he was here with Kyrael and me. He started in the living room, but neither Kyrael nor I wanted to leave him alone to face his fears. There's nothing else."

She glanced over at Kyrael and Greyson. "Can you guys give us a few minutes alone? Please?"

Kyrael nodded and left the room.

Greyson went to the closet and pulled out fresh clothes before also heading for the door. His whole body sagged.

"Greyson?" Flick called after him. "Did you have bad dreams, too?"

"Something like that," he mumbled, leaving.

Flick shook her head. She'd figure him out later—one emotional man at a time. Pulling the side of Jake's shirt, she led him over to the bed and sat on the edge. When Jake didn't sit, she patted beside her.

"Jake, don't be a pouty baby. Sit down so we can talk like grown-ups."

He still didn't speak, but he sat.

"You believe me now, don't you, all of it? Even though you say you don't want to."

He shot the bed a frightened look. "Either you're one hell of an actor, or something invisible was pinning you to the bed. And the writing last night." He shivered. "I meant it. I can't handle this."

She took his hand. "Jake, I don't think we should date each other."

"What?" he yelped, and a pathetic look took over his face. He gripped her hand in return. "Why not?"

"First, because I don't feel that way about you."

"But the kissing yesterday, you liked it."

She met his gaze. "Jake, you're good at kissing. Kristin missed out. But your skill doesn't change that I didn't feel a romantic draw during or after." She played with his fingers. "You are one of my best friends, and I see you in my life forever, but not as my husband. I can picture barbeques, vacations, and game nights, but you're always there visiting my family and me with your wife and kids."

He caught and stilled her fingers. "Maybe you've never thought about it because you've never considered me a possibility. If you gave us as a couple some thought for real, you could change your mind."

"I don't think I will."

He sagged. "It's Greyson, isn't it?"

"It's not. I had a crush on the other hunter, Wade. But he dumped me. You know all this, so stop creating crap to make yourself miserable."

Jake stared at the spot where Greyson had slept. "But last night—"

Flick clapped a hand over Jake's mouth. "Stop right there. I've never lied to you, Jake. I told you the absolute truth. Greyson gets as scared as I do. You don't see these things, so you don't know."

She let go of his hands and tucked hers between her knees. "And that's another reason I don't think being with you is a good idea. I can see all of the otherworldly stuff disturbs you. But it's not going to stop, and it's not going to go away. Being with me will torture you."

"So you'll what? Pick one of the two hunters? Or will you be living as a warrior nun?" Bitterness laced his tone. "At least I know your truth, even if I struggle."

Flick blinked at a sudden burning in her eyes. "What I see and what I do is going to make life more complicated, but I don't think those are my only two options. I could meet a guy and keep this away from him. If it got serious, I could walk away and choose him instead. He'd never have to struggle with this part of me."

Jake scoffed. "That's freaking brilliant, Flick. Meet a guy and build a relationship based on half of yourself. Lies of that magnetism will hold up long-term for sure.

191

What will you do when you're married with kids and trying to pretend you can't see the things slinking toward the nursery? You're talking about building a house of cards."

"Lies of that magnitude?" She'd meant to correct his misstep, but while the words were on the way out, their truth and weight hit home. During her talk with Greyson, walking away from Jake had sounded so easy. But if Jake was right, maybe she should try to love him back. It would be weird for her and difficult for him. But it might be better than being alone.

"Urg." She flopped back to lie on the bed. "I'm *so* confused."

Jake settled in beside her, propping himself on one elbow. With his free hand, he smoothed her hair back from her face. "Flick, I love you. I don't want to add to your trouble. I want to walk through it *with* you. All of this spiritual stuff," he waved his hand around at nothing, "will be hard to get used to. I'm not promising to jump on board and be happy about it. But I promise not to run away and to do my best to understand what you're dealing with." He leaned close, his breath warm on her lips and nose. "You're worth whatever I have to do."

Trepidation slammed Flick's heart against her ribs. She slid past him and over the edge of the bed to the floor.

"Jake, I can't. You made a good point, and if my feelings for you ever change in your favor, you'll be the first to know. But I don't want to get involved because of desperation, or panic, or fear of the unknown. You deserve better. For now, I need you as my friend, so give me space and don't ruin things. Okay?"

Jake sat and sighed. "Okay."

She pulled her knees up and tucked her face into them. "Don't sound so sad. Please. I can't bear the thought of hurting you. But I also can't be with you just to make you happy. That'll blow up in our faces." She chanced a peek at him. "Look, I have an idea to get us headed back in the right direction. You, Marisol, and I are all single, and Greyson is alone in a new country. He has zero interest in Marisol and zero interest in me. But all four of us want to have fun. I think we should all go to Homecoming together. You can go with Marisol, so you don't get your hopes up. I know the heart can be stupid about misreading things. But a night out doing normal, fun activities would be good for all of us."

Jake shrugged and stood. "If that's what you want."

His tone drew out a scowl. "What I wanted was to go with Wade. I wanted you to get with Kristin. I wanted Marisol to have a date. No one is getting what they want. I just thought we could take all the lemons and make lemonade, you know?"

He paused at the door and looked over his shoulder, his whole body sagging. "You're right. We should try to make the best of things. If Marisol agrees to the whole four pathetic losers on a pity date thing, I'll go with her. I'm going to go home now and try to put the pieces back together. See you at school tomorrow."

"Wait, Jake." Flick hurried to her feet. "Be careful at school. There's still something there. Follow Adriel's advice if anything gets weird."

He shot her an inscrutable look. "Unlike you, I can choose to walk away and never see any of this again."

The moment he left, she slumped back to the floor, tears streaking her cheeks to drip from her chin. A few minutes later, Greyson appeared in the doorway.

"Your friend went home." He rubbed a hand on his face. "Want me to listen?"

Flick nodded, and Greyson sat beside her.

"Telling Jake I'm not interested in dating sounded way easier when you suggested it last night."

"Because you are interested?"

Flick shook her head. "Because I hurt him even though I do care."

"You guys have a lengthy history together. As long as you don't cross your signals with him, he'll get over it."

"I already crossed the signals. I let him kiss me last night. I mean, the kiss was a shock, but I didn't stop him, at least not until Adriel caught us."

"Ah." Greyson stared straight ahead of them.

"He wasn't pushy about it. I'm not even sure why I didn't run away sooner. And even though we weren't kissing for long, I'm sure it was long enough to make everything more complicated. Then, this morning, he said some things about living with what I see and the possibility of a normal life. But with him…"

"He swayed you." Greyson didn't even ask it as a question. "How manipulative."

"Maybe. But, regardless, he got me thinking. Even if we walk away from hunting to try to live a normal life, it will never be normal. Something will always lurk in the shadows, and we'll see it. We can't leave our family out of our other world because pretending those things aren't there will be nothing but lies. And if we tried to include them, how many people would believe us?"

She sighed. "If those thoughts are true, then I have three choices if I ever want to date long-term. Wade dumped me, and I wouldn't dream of putting those sorts of expectations on you, which leaves Jake. Maybe I *should* date him."

Greyson stiffened. "If you're right, then you're the lucky one. If you can force yourself to love Jake, then Wade and I had better learn to love each other."

Flick's hand shot to her mouth. "Oh, I'm so sorry. I didn't even think about that. There's always Marisol. I know you don't like her, but she likes you—"

"Flick, I'm not asking you to set me up. I just wanted to point out Jake left you with a bleak scenario. Don't let his pessimism talk you into something you don't want. Right now, he's desperate not to lose his chance. Make sure you don't lose your choice in the process."

She nodded. "Then you're not worried about finding someone?"

Greyson shrugged. "The dating scene is stressful enough without adding in the rest of what we live, so I'll worry about the whole remalas factor after I meet someone I get along with. You have Marisol and Jake, who believe in you. But they can't be the only two understanding people on the planet. Somewhere, someone will desire you as a partner *and* understand your situation. Don't panic because Jake is. I'm not."

Flick nodded. "I'm glad all I said was I'd let him know if my feelings changed. You've made me feel much less desperate." She blushed. "He tried to kiss me again, but I didn't let him. Oh, and I suggested he take Marisol to the dance while you take me, and we can all go as friends. He agreed but sulked. Are you still willing?"

"For you? Sure. But only if you're positive that won't hurt Marisol and Jake."

"I'm not stupid enough to vouch for other people's feelings. But if they agree, then I'll trust them."

Chapter 13

The silence of the archives surrounded Adriel like a cocoon. White marble columns supported the upper floors, and between them were nestled countless shelves of records on every conceivable event in the cosmos. Here, one could find the precise chemical combination and reaction to create a new star. Or maybe the history of a civilization in the third quadrant of the Centaurus A galaxy.

But he was looking through more relevant records, at least as far as his experiment was concerned. Adriel moved the book he'd been reading to the top of the stack on his left. Off the pile on his right, he took another and opened it.

"Adriel the Executioner," a hard feminine voice drawled. "Aren't you scheduled to be on vacation? And I thought people who read were supposed to be intelligent types. Yet, here you are, working toward getting cranky instead of recharging. Smart."

Adriel grimaced at the all-too-familiar voice. "And I thought Powers were supposed to be the combative type. Yet, here you are spreading joy and love in your wake, as always, Serai."

Serai snatched the book from him and scanned the first page. "Why are you researching contracted remala?" Her gaze snapped up, fierce. "Did you see something while on Earth?"

He stood far enough to reach and take the book back. "Nothing in particular."

"If you suspect the whereabouts of a contracted remala, you're obligated to tell Gabriel so a unit like mine can be deployed."

"What I'm working on carries no such obligations."

"You're a death angel," she hissed. "This is not your duty. We already have one rampant messenger angel flitting between assigned duties. It's unnatural. Don't add chaos to Heaven." She crossed her arms and glared. "But you might be better in tune if you were vacationing like you were supposed to."

Like lightning, she flipped one stack of books, spine up. Before he could cover the titles, she'd skimmed enough to scowl. "I'm reporting this to Gabriel and assembling my unit."

Adriel stood, slapping his hand over the spines of the books. "Report me, and we'll find out who's crankier, a death angel whose vacation got cut short, or a Power, who's always bad-tempered." His eyes flashed, provoked. "At least human women have an excuse. But you don't menstruate, so why the permanent PMS?"

Her arm twitched, and Adriel responded. His energy flowed, solidifying in a scythe, which he arched around, stopping it just short of her throat. The tip of her sword snagged his shirt right at the ribs, a little to the left of center.

"Tsk, tsk, children." Gabriel gave his fingers a flick, and both weapons disappeared. "Being the most mercurial angel in Heaven isn't a competition." He strode across the floor of the archives, trailing glory behind him like a monarch's robes. When he reached the table, he paused, scanning the titles of Adriel's stacks.

"It appears our project is yielding interesting results."

Adriel bowed his head in respect. "Perhaps. Identifying what we've found is going slowly as we're being cautious not to send anything fleeing."

"Niciel couldn't identify it?" Gabriel asked.

"Niciel's partner had an emotional crisis. They are on a road trip while Wade copes. I've contacted Niciel and explained. He advised waiting a week before revealing another angelic presence, hoping the arrivals would appear to be random duties."

Gabriel rubbed at his chin.

"Wait!" Serai protested, stomping her foot, then bowing in apology. "What business does a death angel have with an exterminator? I wasn't made aware of any project that might require my unit, and it sounds like this may. Exterminators and Powers have jurisdiction over such things."

"Little sister, are you so bloodthirsty? Isn't it better if the Powers see no action?" Gabriel's soft scold hit Adriel, too. Amazing how the seraph's words could draw up contrition, regardless. Gabriel went back to thinking. After a minute, he spoke. "How is the rapport with your partner developing?" he asked Adriel.

"Well. As I would have expected."

Gabriel nodded. "And Kyrael? How is his training coming along?"

"He's hardly the same angel."

"Kyrael's involved?" Serai snapped. "Gabriel, how can you sanction this unnatural experimentation in switching jobs? Send him back to being a messenger. Heaven doesn't make mistakes. He was assigned there for a reason."

Gabriel cut a stern look in her direction, and she

stepped back, swallowing hard. "Angels grow, sometimes in unexpected ways," he admonished. "Flexibility is a desirable trait in a commander. You've been alive long enough to realize nothing in this universe always behaves the same. He's evolving, not toppling the natural order, and if I, a seraph, am monitoring his progress, then you can rest assured he's headed in a proper direction."

She dropped to one knee. "Apologies, gracious one."

"Kyrael's progress?" Gabriel asked Adriel again.

"Since beginning work with Felicity, he's calmed to what I would call a normal level. His drive to protect her might lead me to believe he ought to be a guardian, but he's adapting to killing remalas like a natural. He's even manifested a weapon I've not seen before."

"Oh?" Gabriel arched a curious eyebrow.

Adriel snickered. "I'd describe the pair like a divine electric eel. He's using sparks of angelic energy."

"Interesting."

Gabriel turned to Serai, tucking his hands behind his back. She was on her feet again but wouldn't look at him. Her downturned face carried rabid curiosity, and a moment of gloating triumph zipped through Adriel's chest. One didn't have the Powers jealous of them very often. Especially not Serai.

To Adriel's shock, Gabriel filled Serai in on their experiment with the three humans. He'd thought they were keeping it quiet until they were sure the experiment provided results. Serai was known for speaking her mind. Secrets and bluntness made bad bedfellows, at least with a woman like her.

"Serai," Gabriel said. "You are not to take your unit

in until Niciel and Adriel give the word. The whole point of this experiment is to see how close to these types of entities having a human partner can get us." His tone left no question that disobedience would be punished.

"But," she protested, "a delayed response could be catastrophic."

"And a response by a unit of Powers will also have significant consequences. Either way, this is going to be an impactful incident. Let's see what we can learn from our new unit this time." He untucked his hands and pointed first to Adriel and then to Serai. "Can the two of you set aside whatever is ruffling feathers between you?"

They looked opposite directions. "Fine," they answered in unison.

"Good." A smile rippled through Gabriel's voice. "Serai, I have two tasks for you. First, I'd like you to ready your unit discreetly. Tell them there are warning signs on Earth but no actionable intel. You will be ready. Adriel, hers is the unit you will call if Niciel deems backup necessary."

"Yes, exalted one," Adriel said through clenched teeth.

"Serai, your second task is to train Kyrael for a real battle."

Her mouth dropped open. "But—"

"Enough." Gabriel's voice rolled with thunderous authority.

She dropped to both knees, and even Adriel found himself in a low bow.

"He has my blessing on his journey to discover himself. You have my order to train him. Is there any issue?"

She shook her head.

"Keep me posted, little siblings."

Gabriel's turn to leave washed the archives with glory in motion. The wave of power ruffled Adriel's feathers and tugged at his hair. Maybe he'd been wrong. If there were angels you didn't want to anger, the seraphim fit the bill.

Serai stood, whipping a braid of iron-black hair over her shoulder. "Have you done enough research? Will you be returning now?"

He went back to his chair and took a seat. "I have a few more hours until I promised to be back."

She leaned forward, putting her hand over the books. "Which do you think will be more useful, researching something you still won't be able to identify without Niciel's help or sending Kyrael up for training?"

Adriel sighed and rubbed his face. "I'll return and send Kyrael your way." He stood and glared at Serai. "Kyrael has become my friend. Bully him, and you mess with me."

She huffed. "As if that's a deterrent. But even I wouldn't tangle with Gabriel. No matter what I think, I'll keep my mouth shut around Kyrael."

"Angels see so few true first-time events. I look forward to being witness to one," Adriel snarked.

He vanished from his seat before they ended up pulling weapons on one another again. Angelic weapons were lethal to nearly every form of life in the universe except other angels. To actually kill another angel with an angelic weapon, one had to focus energy and release a safety on the weapon. This manifested in an automatic request to the seraphim. If they denied it, the weapon would only be a nuisance. But even without a deadly edge, both their weapons could make the other's life miserable for a while.

**\*\*\*\***

Adriel appeared in Greyson's living room, and Flick jumped off the sofa. "Thank goodness you're back. My parents insist I come home, and we couldn't think of an excuse for me to stay over again on a school night."

Adriel flinched. "Then you're not going to like my news." He shot Kyrael an apologetic look. "Especially not you. Gabriel commanded you back to Heaven. You're doing battle training with Serai."

Kyrael groaned. "What did I do to warrant punishment?"

"He ordered her to play nice."

Kyrael slumped in the chair he occupied. "You might as well order a snapping turtle to be a lap dog."

This drew a chuckle from Adriel.

"Who is Serai?" Flick asked.

"The most ferocious Power in Heaven," Kyrael answered. "She's got a bent for battle, a fuse so short you can't even see it, and a tongue sharper than a knife. And I have to train with her," he wailed.

"Don't start," Adriel snapped. "I vouched for how much you've matured while working with Flick. If you disgrace me or this project—" He stopped and changed tactics. "Flick is trying so hard to face these things bravely. Would you belittle her efforts in the eyes of Heaven?"

Kyrael paled and shook his head. "Never."

"Then train with Serai, and if she gives you shit, electrocute her." A wicked grin spread across Adriel's face. "I pulled my scythe on her in the archives, but it wouldn't have done much. She's prepared to block weapons attacks. I doubt she's seen anything like your sparks."

"You pulled a weapon on one of the Powers?" Kyrael gasped.

"That attitude is going to allow her to walk all over you."

"You're not cursed?" Kyrael poked all around Adriel's body.

Adriel swatted him away. "Knock it off and get going. You might still be back in time to go to school with Flick. Don't make me leave Greyson alone for the day."

Kyrael nodded and disappeared.

"Sorry, Greyson," Adriel apologized. "With the nest at the school, it would be you who went without an angel for the day."

"No. I'd want you to go with her. Whatever hangs out there is nasty. I'll be fine in the flat."

"Now, what do we do for the night?" Flick asked.

Adriel considered this a moment. "For now, I'm going to stay in Greyson's house. You've got family to socialize with, and he's otherwise alone. But I'll sleep along that wall." He pointed to the one separating the two apartments. "Greyson, if you sleep in the living room and Flick gets as close to that wall as possible, I should be able to keep things away from you both."

"I think the laundry closet is right there, but I'll see what I can do. I'm going to go. You'll be there if Kyrael isn't back in time for school, right?"

Adriel put a gentle hand on her head. "Of course."

"Do you want to hang out here after school tomorrow?" Greyson asked. "We could do homework together. I still have to complete my courses online for the term."

"Sure."

Flick left Greyson's and took the few steps down the hall toward her place. When she walked in, her mom smiled. Both her parents were in the kitchen dressed for going out.

"We haven't seen you all day," her mom said. "And you missed a call from Jennie and Fred. We're meeting them for dinner. There might still be time for them to drag Paisley along if you want to come."

Flick smothered a laugh. "If Paisley and I want to hang out, it won't be at dinner with our parents. But you guys go and have a good time."

Her mom pointed to the fridge. "We had pasta for lunch, and there are leftovers. You can reheat those, okay?"

For a moment, Flick considered returning to Greyson's and eating there, but her mother must have caught the look.

She shook her head. "You've been out all weekend at Greyson's, and I'd like to see you spend some time away. I understand your friends were there yesterday and overnight, but give the poor man some space. He might not want to host the high school hang-out."

Her dad made a funny noise in his throat.

Her mom put a hand on his arm. "She and Marisol are eighteen, and Greyson is only a little older. Don't get all bent out of shape. He's not a deviant. But he is living in the adult world, where you're not." She'd turned her attention back to Flick. "So make sure you're leaving him the space to live an adult life, okay?"

"And make sure there's a chaperone," her dad added.

"*Dad*," she groaned. "We're not like that."

Her mom patted her dad's arm and picked her purse up off the counter. "Just let Greyson breathe and stay here tonight, okay?"

"Okay."

Her parents left, and deep loneliness blanketed her for the first time since the angels had come into her life. She didn't like the sensation. But what would take her mind off unpleasant things, both those lurking in corners and her shredded romantic life? Escapism. She gathered the necessary ingredients: a bar of her mother's expensive chocolate from the stash under the kitchen towels, a mug of chai tea, and a book she'd taken from the free book exchange locker at school. It was the sort of romance one didn't admit to their friends they read.

She took these to the bathroom and turned the hot water on, adding enough bubble bath to send fluffy white mounds all over the tub. Since the apartment was empty, she walked to the laundry closet to take her clothes off. If her sense of direction wasn't skewed, Greyson's living room was right on the other side of the wall. His formal dining room also sat along there. Her parents used the spare room along that wall for an office, each keeping a desk in the space along with a few random pieces of workout equipment her mother never used since she had a gym membership through her work.

If Flick shoved aside the elliptical, she might have enough room to sleep on the floor. Now, all she had to do was think of an excuse to sleep on the office floor that wouldn't lead her parents to schedule a session with a counselor.

After dropping her clothes in the color-coded bins in the closet, she returned and turned the water off. The bathroom had several candles in it. And though they weren't necessarily set there for bath time, they might work well. Flick lit those and left them where they would illuminate her book, then flipped off the overhead light—ambiance set.

She climbed in and let the bubbles engulf her. Snapping off a piece of chocolate to suck on, she opened her book and sought to lose herself in another world. And boy, was getting lost easy. The book opened, and in a few pages, the protagonist and her love interest were involved in a scene that added steam to the mirror.

Flick set the book on the floor, shut her eyes, and put herself in the protagonist's stilettos. She let her imagination carry her through to the inevitable end of the scene. All the heat in the tub left her breathless, so she stretched out, pressing her foot against the chilly porcelain at the opposite end. A push of her toes thrust her torso out of the water into the cool air of the room. Her foot settled to the bottom, the drain holes forming to the skin on her heel.

She drew a few deep breaths and steadied her heart. This book might turn out to be awesome.

Bubbles drifted up out of the drain holes, popping at the surface. A grotesque stench filled the room from each ruptured sphere, like the inside of a rancid trash can.

Shit.

Flick tried to get her feet under her and rush from the tub, but something caught her left ankle and held it under the water against the drain.

Flick whimpered and jerked her leg, but it didn't budge. Whatever held her was twisting itself around her leg. Now her knee wouldn't bend.

Another bubble popped, and a voice drifted into the bathroom. "Smells pure." The words hissed.

Flick got her other foot under her, clutching at the side of the tub. "Adriel," she yelled. "Help!"

Like a squeezing tentacle, the force wrapped itself up her thigh. A serpentine shape lined with tiny hooks like rose thorns peeked through the bubbles. These barbs cut into her skin. Little wisps of blood tainted the bathwater and turned the bubbles red.

Flick took the deepest breath she could and screamed. If only she had some power of her own. She'd kill the thing, no hesitation. But without an angel, she was helpless.

"So delicious," the voice hissed again.

Flick tried tugging herself away again, but the effort left her arms shaking. She'd have to use her brain. Light. Grabbing a shampoo bottle, she chucked it at the light switch. Nothing. She grabbed the conditioner and tossed it. The bottle hit the button, and the light blinked on. The tentacle recoiled. Flick scrambled from the tub and snatched her towel, knocking the candles into the red-tinged water.

She got three steps outside the door when the lights in her apartment flickered and went out. "If the angels like you, you must taste extra good." Now, several voices hissed the threats.

Flick bolted for the front door, slipping and sliding across the laminate floors on the water she dripped. Each stumble ratcheted up her heartrate by providing an extra second for something to catch her. The shadows reached around her, trying to block the way out. Flick screamed again. Someone hear, please.

Her foot skidded across a puddle and slid out from under her, taking her down. She crashed on the kitchen tiles, bruising several places.

"Flick!" Greyson yelled, bursting through the door, scythe in hand.

He moved like an action hero or a martial arts star, wheeling the weapon through the air and slicing the tendrils, reaching for her. Each one touched by the scythe exploded and vanished. After three, the lights flickered back on, and Adriel erupted from Greyson's body. He streaked toward the bathroom without even touching the floor, still armed, wearing death on his face.

Greyson hurried over to Flick. "Oh God. Are you all right?" His jaw tightened. "So much blood."

Flick looked down, bewildered. The puddle she'd slipped in was all blood. "Is that mine?" Her brain felt detached. "I'm cold."

"You're going into shock," Greyson said. He pulled out his phone. "You need an ambulance. You've lost too much blood."

Adriel returned, taking the phone from his hand. "Human doctors can't heal these."

A flash of light went out from his body, and a second later, a female angel stood in the kitchen beside him.

"Serai," Adriel snapped. "Remalas inflicted the wounds. You heal these, right?"

"I can, but—"

Adriel let out a vicious snarl. "This girl is part of the program. Heal her."

Serai shot him an evil glare but knelt beside Flick. The angel touched her leg, and warmth spread across her whole body, followed by searing pain. Flick thrashed, screams tearing the back of her throat.

"Hold her still," Serai barked. "The purification is painful."

Greyson gripped her shoulders, and Adriel pinned

both her legs. Still, Flick squirmed as far as she could. From the dozens upon dozens of slashes, fire cut through her flesh and into her bones. Her cries turned to gasps, and she struggled to stay conscious.

Despite her efforts, blackness encroached on Flick's vision, and the room grew very far away. Unconsciousness smothered her, and she let it have her.

## Chapter 14

"Flick?" Greyson touched her cheek. "Flick, can you hear me?"

"Yeah," she murmured. Her lips were hot and threatening to crack.

"*Thank God.*" He pulled her up from where she lay on the couch and hugged her, tucking his chin over her shoulder. "I thought I'd lost you."

"I'm fine," she soothed, then stopped. "Am I?"

He put an icy hand on her forehead. "You still have a fever," he said. "But your wounds are healed."

"Flick, I—" Adriel's voice broke, and he dropped to both knees beside the couch, pressing his head to the floor in abject apology. "I broke my promise and let you get hurt. I'm so sorry. Please forgive me."

"An angel asking a human for forgiveness?" Serai taunted. "This takes irony to a whole new plane."

Adriel turned his face, scowling. "Make yourself useful for a change and report this to Gabriel, then bring Kyrael back. They each need an angel with them at all times."

"Before you go." Flick struggled to sit up because Greyson wouldn't let go of her. "The thing that attacked me spoke."

"It what?" both angels gasped, focusing their attention on her.

"It said I smelled pure and delicious, and anyone the

angels favored must taste extra good." She frowned. "I don't understand why it attacked. I thought they liked negative energy, and I was super relaxed and happy in…the…bath…"

Flick looked down at herself, and heat crawled up her neck to set her cheeks blazing. Someone had dressed her in loose-fitting pajamas. This meant not only had everyone seen her stark naked, but someone had rifled through her drawers, then clothed her.

"How did I get dressed?" she whispered—as if that made the bad news less embarrassing.

"Greyson kept your towel over you, and I dressed you when Serai finished the healing," Adriel explained. "You have many scabs on your leg. I would recommend loose clothing for a while."

"Everyone saw me," Flick wailed.

"Everyone was scared shitless for you," Greyson countered.

"I wasn't," Serai replied. "This is why you panicky males aren't enlisted in Heaven's standing army."

Greyson frowned. "Men seem to handle blood well enough here on Earth. But it's different when someone you care about is bleeding."

"Until that someone gets a period or has a kid," Flick muttered. "Men are big babies. We'd go extinct if reproduction were up to you."

"See," Serai trilled. "God does know what he's doing. Now, if humans could stop screwing the divine plan up."

Greyson rolled his eyes. "If it's such a divine plan, how are humans capable of screwing it up? Doesn't sound like a very good plan to me."

Serai hissed. "Sacrilegious fool. It's called a plan

because it was a blueprint or guide. But humans have free will, and that means plans can go awry. Imagine creation like a puzzle. With their free will, humans took the box, shook it up, and threw the pieces all over the floor. We, in Heaven, try our best to put the pieces back together, but sometimes, they get lost under the sofa or bent out of shape. And the picture will never be the same. It's all messed up, and there are holes."

"Enough, Serai," Adriel ordered. "Arguing the ins and outs of the universal order with humans is against the rules." He stooped and took Flick's hand. "I'd like to leave and go report this and get Kyrael. Prodding Serai into action will take longer than the task itself. Can I leave you in her care? She's a Power, and very little on Earth would dare mess with her." He made a face. "In Heaven either, for that matter."

Flick glanced at the austere Serai. "Hurry back. She's a bit...rough."

Adriel smoothed a hand across her head. "I promise."

He vanished, and Serai scoffed. "How far the mighty Adriel the Executioner has fallen."

"Executioner?" The trepidation in Greyson's voice mirrored Flick's unspoken tremor.

"Oh, ho, ho," she crowed. "He didn't tell you?"

"We know he's a death angel," Flick said, protectiveness for Adriel cropping up.

Delight rippled across the angel's face, and Serai perched on the edge of the dining table. "Adriel isn't your average death angel. He's not escorting little old ladies across the divide. Adriel is a specialized death angel. He's called the Executioner because he's the one who handles mass casualty events."

"How do you mean?" Greyson asked.

"I mean, if there's a shooting event, or war, or genocide, that's all Adriel's work. He handles natural disasters, plagues, and mass extinction, too."

Greyson and Flick exchanged a look, then Greyson shrugged. "Are you trying to make us dislike him? Because it's not working."

She tipped her nose up and crossed her arms. "Not at all. I'm trying to help you see who you're dealing with and what you've done to him. The death angels are from the choir of Virtues."

"And that's supposed to mean what?" Flick asked.

"The universe has a hierarchy, child. God, angels, *then* sentient beings such as humans. And within the angelic hierarchy, Virtues are halfway to the top."

"And you're a Power, correct?" Greyson asked.

"Yes."

"And those are above or below Virtues?"

She shot him a condescending look. "We're partnered beside each other and under the Dominations. Virtues control all aspects of nature, including death. Powers beat back evil in all its forms." She scowled. "This is why I disapprove of Kyrael. He was assigned to the archangels when he was formed. He's a messenger, period. Trying to change his destiny is—"

"Gabriel's choice, not yours," Adriel replied, cutting her off.

"How long were you listening in?" Serai snapped, swiveling to glare at him.

"Long enough." Adriel nudged her aside and pulled a rather awed-looking Kyrael inside the main room from the kitchen.

He took one look at Flick and rushed her, plucking

her off Greyson's lap and wrapping her in a hug that included his wings. Flick nestled her chin on his shoulder, letting the feathers caress her face.

"Flick, I'm sorry. I feel horrible."

"Why?" she whispered. "This wasn't your fault."

"But I left you." He shook his head enough she had to dodge. "Never again."

Serai hmphed. "It's catching. I'm going back to Heaven."

Adriel made a face. "As much as I'd prefer to see you leave, you still need to train Kyrael. Set up a barrier in the living room. Do the training here instead."

The front door opened, and Flick's mother let out a scream. "Flick," she shrieked. "Where are you?"

"In the living room?" Flick glanced at Greyson in confusion.

Her mother rushed into the room, grabbing Flick and scanning her head to toe. "What happened?" she fussed. "Are you hurt?"

"W-why?" Flick stammered, still trying to keep up.

"There's a pool of blood in the kitchen. What happened?"

"Tell her the truth," Adriel advised. "She knows you see these things, correct?"

Flick nodded.

"Nothing good comes from lies," he reassured. "If we need you to get them out of the building for any reason, they might as well be prepared."

Flick's mom was looking more worried with each passing minute of silence.

Greyson broke the silence. "You know she sees spirits, right?"

Her mom frowned. "Not that again."

"I see them, too," he rushed. "She was attacked while you were gone. I heard her screaming and came to help, but she'd already made it to the kitchen. I guess they attacked in the tub. Flick, you should show your mom your leg."

Her dad hurried from the kitchen, his gaze on the floor. No doubt she'd left a trail of blood from the bathroom. While he investigated, Flick pulled the loose leg of her pajama pants up. Her mother gasped at the twisting spirals of scabbed-over slits. For a second, her gaze slid sideways to Greyson, accusing.

"Don't even think it, Mom. Greyson saved my life. I could have bled out if he hadn't heard me and gotten to me."

Her mom ran her hands across the scabs. "They look like a sea creature or something made them. What makes perfectly spaced cuts in a spiral like this?"

"They're evil beings called remalas, Mom." A shudder shook Flick's body. "It came out of the drain and tried to—" She frowned and looked at Adriel. "What were they trying to do to me? I thought they wanted negative energy."

"You're tainted with angelic power," Serai answered. "If angels were passive and laid out like a plated dinner, the remalas would consume us for the divine power."

"Honey? Who are you talking to?" her mom asked.

"Shh. It's just the angels." She rubbed her temple. "You're telling me we've been tainted with angelic power, and now we're twice as delicious?"

"More like delicious to the tenth power," Serai answered. "Hosting angels the way you have has never been done before, so there's no precedent for what it's doing to your mortal bodies." She shrugged. "Hazard of the job."

"Unacceptable," Adriel hissed through clenched teeth. "I kill enough humans in the course of their own evil. I'm not throwing the good ones in the line of fire."

Serai hopped from her perch on the table and squared off against Adriel. "You're too involved with these mammals. So what if they're good? They do their part, then end up in Heaven. It's not like there aren't plenty more where they came from. Three hundred and eighty-five thousand humans were born today alone."

"But we've only found three who can do what they can." Adriel's tone carried a soft warning. "They are irreplaceable."

"Do they know you're just protecting a tool?"

Adriel clenched his fist, and his scythe appeared. "I'm going to teach you a lesson in compassion, you frigid hag."

Serai snarled back, raising her sword.

"This whole notion is ridiculous," Flick's mother snapped. "I want to know the truth." She stood and took a few steps forward at the same time the two angels swung.

Flick screamed and threw herself at her mother, knocking her out of the way. The furniture on either side of the room exploded with the force of the blows.

Flick scrambled to her feet, red rage blurring her vision. Limping to Serai, she caught the neckline of the angel's shirt. Then she stalked, as best she could, over to Adriel and grabbed his shirt in the other hand, glaring between the two.

"*Look what you've done to my house*," she yelled. "Adriel, that's a reaping tool. Don't fucking use it near my parents. And you," she rounded on Serai, "I was told female angels were cranky, but you are a complete bitch. You could have killed my mother. This is an unacceptable way to treat your hosts and their houses. What would Gabriel say about this behavior? Huh?"

Both angels stared at her, open-mouthed and silent.

"That's what I thought." She glared at her mother. "I understand you can't see it, but you walked into the middle of an argument between angels and nearly got hit with a death angel's scythe. I'm pretty sure that's instant death." She trembled, adrenaline and anger still driving her.

"But—"

"No, Mom," Flick snapped. "I don't have time for going around about personal realities. If you get in the way, this is real, even for you." She let go of Adriel and yanked her pant leg up again. "Just because you can't see something doesn't mean it's not there, and you can't get hurt. The results are plenty visible."

"What do you have to say about all this, young man?" Flick's dad asked Greyson from the entrance to the hallway. His expression flickered between angry and shellshocked.

"Everything Flick said is true. The angels pay my bills, otherwise I'd never afford the flat next door. They teleported me here from London not too long ago. All because I can see them. She and I are two of the only three they've ever found like us."

He glanced over at the rather sheepish-looking Adriel. "The one Flick held in her left hand was Adriel. He's the death angel. He's a head taller than me, with metallic silver hair and teal eyes. He's living with me next door."

He jerked a thumb over his shoulder. "Behind me is Kyrael. He's got metallic copper hair and violet eyes. He lives here with you guys, but he was in Heaven on an errand tonight—lousy timing.

"The one Flick is still holding onto is Serai. She's a warrior angel and evidently wears her combative edge all the time. She's got a long iron-black braid and vivid green eyes. She picked the fight with Adriel." He stared at Flick's mom. "And yes, they came close to hitting you with their weapons."

He shot the two angels dirty looks. "What the hell kind of bad blood is between you that you'd use divine weapons in the house?"

Adriel's contrition disappeared, and a sour look crossed his face. "She fancies herself my rival. She leads the Powers. I lead the Virtues. Or rather, based on raw ability, we're the best in our choirs, so even though Heaven appoints the leader, our advice is the rule."

Greyson huffed. "If this is how quick you are to destroy crap, I can see why neither of you has been appointed to lead your choir." He heaved a heavy sigh. "I know Kyrael has training, but Serai, I think you'd better go back to Heaven until tomorrow and cool off."

"I'm not taking orders from a human."

Greyson strode across the room and got in her face. "Try me. You have all the tenderness of a scorpion, and so help me, I'll find a way to get a message to Gabriel about how you're acting, even if I have to wander the streets looking for an angel who's free to run the errand."

"Hmph. I'm not hanging around disrespectful mammals any longer." Serai vanished.

"Adriel," Greyson continued all business. "I think you and I had better go home. Kyrael, can you clean up all the blood and repair the damage to their flat? And will you be all right looking after Flick for the night? Can those wounds get infected or contaminated or anything?"

Kyrael shook his head. "Serai may be condescending and cold, but she's good at her job. Her healing will be deep, pure, and flawless. Even earthly bacteria shouldn't be able to get in."

"Perfect. Mr. and Mrs. Landon." He ducked his head in their direction, then left.

Flick's eyes stung, and she blinked back tears. What she wouldn't have done to have him stay.

Kyrael snapped his fingers, and all the blood trailing through the house disappeared. Everything that had exploded when the angels exchanged blows righted itself. Her mom and dad gasped, and her mother wobbled, grasping the counter for stability.

"I'm exhausted, and I almost died of blood loss tonight," Flick said. "I'm going to bed. Oh, and in case you're still suspicious, Adriel let Greyson into the apartment when they heard the attack." She turned to Kyrael. "Can I sleep under your wing again tonight?"

His expression went indulgent. "Of course."

"Mom, Dad, good night." She limped across the living room, away from her still silently shocked parents, and shut herself in her bedroom.

\*\*\*\*

"Flick has nerves of steel," Adriel said for the hundredth time. "Imagine butting in between Serai and me. No one in Heaven would dare, except a seraph like Gabriel."

Greyson tried to sigh out his irritation. "Why did you let Serai get to you?"

Adriel ran a hand through his hair. "I cut my

vacation five hundred years short, so I didn't clear away all the negative emotions I built up from being forced to cull so many people. Serai gets under my skin even when my mood is level. If our current endeavor involved killing humans, Gabriel would have put anyone but me on it, even if I did make first contact. But killing negative energy beings is somewhat cathartic. It's not the same as the forgetful bliss an angel's vacation stores within them, but it's not the same old job."

"I don't like Serai," Greyson said. "Not even a little, which is a bit surprising. She has to be the most beautiful creature I've ever seen."

"She is that," Adriel agreed.

"And she ruins it in a single expression."

"Also, true."

"Wait, if you can admit she's sexy…I thought you said angels don't have sex."

"I said she was beautiful. That's not the same thing. I'd liken her beauty to watching lava flow. It's mesmerizing, hypnotic, dangerous, and attractive."

"I can see that."

"As for angels having sex, no, not as humans do. As I said, God creates new angels as needed. Also, we're not biological beings like any life on this planet, so even if we did do our own replicating, it wouldn't be a biological process like conception and birth."

Greyson took off his soiled clothes and tossed them outside the door to his laundry closet. He thought about a shower, then changed his mind. Adriel was with him, but after seeing Flick, the tub came off dodgy.

On the upside, this conversation was a good distraction. "I remember you said you didn't eat because you manufacture your own energy, like the sun. If you tried to reproduce, would you create a black hole or something?"

Adriel laughed. "No. I've never asked, but I doubt we're even capable of reproduction. Whether we tried to split the core of our being or procreate with our genetic material, I'm sure it would be a spectacular failure. What interesting questions you humans think up."

"Eating, sleeping, reproduction. Those are fundamental processes for humans. It would be an easy way to relate. I guess that's what drives the curiosity." Greyson stopped talking to brush his teeth. When he left the bathroom, Adriel's ball of light floated in the corner.

"Um, I don't suppose you'd be willing to hover over the other side of the bed for the night, would you?"

Adriel drifted to the side opposite Greyson and hovered. Greyson climbed in, and fatigue drew his eyelids down before he even registered his head hitting the pillow.

"Greyson?" Flick called from somewhere outside Greyson's sleep.

"Greyson?" This time, the caller was Kyrael.

Greyson took a foot to the rear, which shoved him out of bed and to the floor. He landed with a thud and a groan.

"Get up, human." Serai's voice hit his brain like a cheese grater.

"What?" he griped, keeping his face pressed to the floor. Was it too late to fake falling back to sleep?

"The little girl is here. You two are switching partners for the day." Serai grabbed the back of his t-shirt and jerked him to his feet like he weighed no more than a pillow.

"Why does that warrant abusing me?" he grumped.

"You were disrespectful to me yesterday."

He turned and glared. "As if nearly killing Flick's mother and destroying their house was respectful?"

"I'm sorry, Greyson," Adriel apologized. "I'll take Serai out to the living room, and we'll work out the plan for training Kyrael today. I'm sure Serai came to collect him."

Greyson might have continued venting a growing sour feeling at the angels, but Flick poked her head in the bedroom door at that moment. She blushed and pulled back until just her eyes were showing.

Adriel put a hand on Serai's back and shoved her out of the room. Flick, however, stayed in hiding.

"Is something wrong?" Greyson asked, flopping back into his bed. He'd been through an utterly unpleasant wake-up.

"I, uh."

"Aren't you going to be late for school?"

"I'm going to skip today, at least the high school portion, to give my leg another day to heal. Kyrael made a doctor's note for me. Then I hoped maybe you could give me a ride to my college classes later. You know, my leg and all."

Greyson closed his eyes, trying to find a more relaxed place to start his day. "You can come in, you know. I don't bite."

"Yeah, but..." She spoke the following words so softly he couldn't hear.

He cracked his eyes open. Flick had turned an admirable shade of magenta. "Sorry. I missed that."

"You saw me naked," she whispered, her mouth half obstructed by the doorframe.

"Oh. Is that why you're acting all shy? Don't worry

about it. I was rather distracted by all the blood and the avenging angels."

When she stayed hidden by the door, he sighed and got out of bed. Crossing the room, he grabbed her and hauled her inside, swinging the door shut. He didn't stop until they reached the bed, and he pushed her to sit. Thankfully, she acquiesced because he didn't want to be too rough and hurt her leg.

"Now. Let's talk about this like adults, okay?"

Flick nodded, her eyes wide and full of unshed tears.

Greyson's heart swelled with concern. "What is it?"

"A bunch of stuff. You did so much for me last night, and I'm so embarrassed. Not only did you see me naked, and you're the only guy who ever has, by the way, but you were forced to take care of me like a baby. I'm sure my blood ruined your clothes. My parents nearly accused you of being the problem. But most of all, I never even said thank you."

She glanced up at him, and a tear slipped down her cheek. "Thank you for rescuing me, Greyson."

"The angels did most of the work."

"Don't sell yourself short. You helped. I was in an awful state, and you could have walked away from all the carnage and let them handle it. But you stayed with me. Then you even set my parents straight so they wouldn't doubt me."

He reached for her, hesitating a moment before lifting her chin so they could see eye to eye. "Of course, I'm going to help you. You are my friend. No, more than my friend. You are a partner and the only person in the world who can understand this half of me. After being alone with my demons for twenty years, to have you understand what I go through means more to me than if you could recite all my favorite things."

She nodded against his hand, her eyes still wet.

"When I saw you in all the blood yesterday." He blinked back burning in his own eyes. "I've never been so scared for anyone. Flick, I…"

He inched the distance between the two of them closed. Stopping just shy of her lips, he hesitated. His breath caught in his throat and came out rougher than usual. He hadn't expressed his feelings yet, but she wasn't backing away. Her breath whispered across his mouth, warm, inviting. Greyson's heart thundered, urging him to cross the last inch and seal the kiss.

The bedroom door creaked on its way open, and Greyson dropped his hands, jolting back away from Flick. Adriel walked in, took one look at the two of them, and turned around.

"What do you need, Adriel?" Greyson asked, his voice catching. He cleared his throat. "Flick, I just wanted to tell you how happy I am that you're all right."

Flick nodded with wide eyes and stood, tripping on the loose covers. She blushed and straightened up, pulling her ankle from a corner of the sheets. "Right. Okay. What's the, uh, plan for today?"

Adriel turned back around, looking sheepish. "There wasn't one. I'm sorry if I interrupted."

"It was, um, n-no problem," Flick stammered. "We were, ah, just clearing the air. From last night. You know?" She made a show of stretching. "You know, if Greyson is okay with giving me a ride to school, I can go for second and third period. If Serai is training Kyrael, they can wait 'til after I'm at school and Greyson gets back here, right?"

A wild giggle escaped her. "I'd have Adriel drive

me, so Greyson didn't have to, but he can't for obvious reasons. Though, watching people stare at a supposedly driverless car on its way through the city would be funny."

Greyson couldn't help laughing. "That would be bloody hysterical." He shot Flick a tender look. "But I have to agree with the angels on this one. You should rest today. There's no shame in giving yourself a bit to heal."

Adriel nodded. "I have an idea." He flicked a couple of fingers at the bed, and a stack of books and papers appeared. "Why don't the two of you complete your homework for the day this morning? I've imported the assignments from all of your teachers. Once you're finished, if Flick feels up to afternoon class, we can discuss it. Otherwise, you should be much better tomorrow. On that note, the other two will train in the living room under a barrier. You won't be able to see them, but they'll hear you if you speak their names."

"You sound like you're leaving." Worry tinged Flick's voice.

"I am, but not for the full day. I ought to be back after lunchtime. I'm going to ask if there's anything more we can do for your leg."

"Ask who?" Curiosity prickled at Greyson. The angels kept leaving on errands, and he wanted to see where they went.

"I want to ask Raphael. He's the angel of healing. If there's more than what Serai did, he'd know." He crossed the room and hugged Flick. "Two angels will be in the apartment with you. We won't leave you alone again. I'm so sorry your trust in me is shaken. I'll do my best to rebuild it." He kissed her forehead. "Peace."

He shot skyward in a beam of blinding light.

Greyson made a mental note to ask one of the angels what the deal was with their travel methods. Sometimes they went in a beam of light, and sometimes they vanished without a trace. Flick limped around to the far side of the bed and climbed on, wincing when she moved her left leg. Pulling over assignment sheets, she started reading.

Awkward silence pounded in Greyson's ears. The perfect moment had died with his hands on her chin and his lips close enough to feel the heat of hers. Now she'd retreated, and he hadn't spoken his feelings. He wanted to take his textbook and smack his forehead with it. Instead, he opened the book and let his mind wander to what could have happened if Adriel hadn't opened the door.

Chapter 15

Sweat trickled down the side of Kyrael's face, but he didn't dare wipe it away. He heaved deep breaths, trying to steady his body. A gash on his side dripped blood to the floor, and none of the knuckles on either hand had any skin left. At the other side of the barrier, Serai crossed her arms, expression unimpressed.

"Please tell me you're ready," she snapped.

"Almost." His lungs burned in protest of wasting air on speaking.

"It took you three hours to master a sword." She hissed across a scolding click of her tongue. "That's got to be a new record. I don't think any of the Powers has ever taken longer than an hour and a half."

He glared and gasped out, "I'm not a Power. I'm an archangel, and I'm doing my best until Gabriel officially promotes me. I learned, didn't I?"

She sniffed. "If it takes you three hours to master hand fighting, then another three to develop your sparking power, we'll be training into a *second day*."

She yelled the last two words at the same time she threw her next attack. Her fist came straight for his right ear. Kyrael swiveled back and downward out of the way. He brought a foot toward the rear of her legs, but she jumped, avoiding the kick.

Serai landed like a cat and swung around, the heel of her open palm connecting with the bridge of his nose.

Kyrael ignored the crunch of his nose breaking and brought his fist up into her sternum, using her proximity to finally land a blow.

She stepped back, a wicked grin spreading. "Better."

Without warning, she came at him again. He blocked her blow with his forearm, caught her arm with the crook of his elbow, and swung her across himself, hoping to take her to the floor. She twisted out of his grip, coming up from underneath, elbow aimed for his gut. He dropped down, opting for the ground and throwing his hip into the back of her knee to take her with him.

Her knees landed beside his ribs, with her hands on his torso, one on the gash. Kyrael cried out even though he knew it would entice her to go harder against him. Sure enough, she flipped to her feet like a cat, bringing her foot down where his head had been a second before.

"Land one hit on my head, and we'll move on," she taunted. "How many hours will that take?"

Kyrael grunted when her fist connected with his spine.

"Or maybe I should get the little human girl of yours in here with me. The women of Heaven dominate the army. Maybe she could do better. You could host her, and she could move your pathetic body for you."

Kyrael gritted his teeth together. Serai wouldn't drag Flick into training like this. Would she?

He had a fraction of a second to react to the kick aimed at his gash. He dropped, grabbing Serai's leg on the way down, then yanked with all his strength. The move took them both to the floor. But he landed on top, knocking the air out of her. Before she recovered, he slammed his raw knuckles into her jaw.

"There," he panted. "Leave the humans alone."

She laughed and shoved him off. "Well, at least now I know what motivates you. Are you sure you don't want to be a guardian angel?"

He curled around his injured side. "And move down from archangel? Not a chance."

"Ambitious. I guess I can respect that. Though I still hold being the best in your choir ought to be enough satisfaction."

"Then why do you compete against Adriel?" He focused healing power on the gash.

She stood and, with a snap of her fingers, had herself clean and unruffled. She turned her back on Kyrael. "He's blocking my light."

Kyrael sat and started repairing his knuckles. "What the heck is that supposed to mean? You're a Power, the only female angels in existence. And you're their brightest star. How could he block your light?"

She glared at him like he was stupid. "People know his work, even if they don't know his name, the way people know Gabriel, Michael, Raphael, and a dozen others. But I'm the pinnacle of the angelic army. I've led the charge against dozens of contracted remalas. Who knows my work? Who speaks my name or discusses my deeds?"

Kyrael stared at her, aghast. "But you're not supposed to want glory for yourself. That's a fallen angel's sin."

She huffed. "I don't want it for myself...precisely. But when great deeds are whispered in God's ear, will he even remember me? Have I made him happy at all?"

Understanding dawned on Kyrael, insight inspired by time spent on Earth. "You want love."

She scowled. "Don't make me sound like some

desperate human woman. I simply don't want to be overlooked."

"And you think Adriel is blocking the view."

She snapped her fingers, and the barrier disappeared. "We're done for today."

Without another word, Serai vanished.

Kyrael tucked this away to ponder later. Whether she yearned for recognition, acknowledgment, praise, or love, Serai was missing something. Perhaps he wasn't the only one who had needs outside his station. One thing he'd learned on Earth was humans were both flexible and full of holes. They twisted and wormed their way through life, adapting themselves to fill those missing pieces. What if angels had missing pieces, too, and all they had to do was flex a little to fill them?

****

Flick sat alone and deep in thought on the bed in Greyson's room. Kyrael had been half beaten to a pulp by Serai. And she'd vanished without a word to anyone else in the house. Greyson was tucking the ball of light, which comprised a sleeping Kyrael, into the folds of the curtain so he wouldn't drift around the living room—poor angel.

But Flick wouldn't let his suffering go to waste. If he was willing to go through such pain so they could function as a team, and so he could protect her, then she'd rise, too. She wouldn't let the remalas' attack make her retreat. Kyrael deserved a partner with the same strength he put out. So, like him, she'd pick herself up and move forward. The next time they needed to hunt, she'd be at his side—sort of, since he'd be inside.

At two in the afternoon, Adriel still hadn't returned. From time to time, worry over having a single exhausted angel to guard them bothered her, but trying to make good on her promise to herself to persevere, she let something else dominate her thoughts.

Had Greyson almost kissed her?

Heat crept across Flick's cheeks at the mere thought. Her heart had flustered her over Wade. And her head agreed Jake had positive benefits even if her heart wasn't on board. But what about Greyson? He cared for her, and he made her feel safer. They were fast becoming very close friends. But more?

She flopped down, burying her face in his pillow. It smelled like him, and her stomach squirmed.

"Flick?" Greyson called. "Are you awake?"

She lifted her head from the pillow. "Yeah. Just thinking about things."

"You're not dwelling on the negative, are you?"

She shook her head.

He glanced back at the door to the living room. "Kyrael's asleep and recuperating. I have to wonder if Serai enjoyed beating on him a little too much. But regardless. Adriel isn't back yet, so would you like to watch a movie?"

"Sure."

"Here or in the living room?" he asked.

"Um. Let's not wake Kyrael. We can watch it here." She grabbed the spare pillows and propped them against the headboard.

Inside her head, a giant question mark floated. What the hell was she doing suggesting they sit on the bed to watch a movie? What if Greyson tried to kiss her again? More heat crawled across her cheeks. What if he tried more?

She jolted when he crossed the room, coming close

enough to her so their shoulders bumped. He grabbed the remote and turned the tv on, pulling up the streaming service menu.

"What should we watch?" he asked.

"Comedy," she answered. "I need to laugh."

"Rom-com? Something raunchy?" He paused, waiting for her to answer.

"Nothing with violence. I've had more than enough."

"Okay, action comedies out. Let's go with this." He selected a movie about a girl who took a job as a bodyguard under the pretense of being a boy. They didn't even have to play the film for Flick to know the protagonist would fall for her employer—very *Twelfth Night*.

Greyson helped her settle on the bed so her leg was comfortable. But before he could join her, the door opened, and Adriel walked in. He glanced at the television and the two of them.

"I'm glad you talked Flick into taking it easy." He tossed something to Greyson. "That's cream Raphael made especially for Flick. It needs to reach every single hole, so why don't you help her get the back of her leg where she can't see?" He stared straight at Greyson. "A little gift to make up for my timing today."

"What does he mean?" Flick asked, looking up at Greyson.

He stood statue-still, holding a small jar in his hand. All the while, his face turned deeper and deeper red.

"Is something wrong?" she asked. "I can put it on if you don't want to."

He shook his head. "Why don't you lie down on your stomach and, uh," his blush intensified, "Remove at least the one pantleg."

"Oh right." She blushed, too. That's what he'd been embarrassed about.

A moment of hesitation held her. She didn't want to embarrass him further nor embarrass herself either. This morning had been awkward after last night's naked rescue incident. But if she didn't get her leg healed, how would she keep up with Kyrael? He hadn't let all the wounds Serai gave him hold him back.

Gritting her teeth against both embarrassment and pain, Flick tried to wiggle her bad leg out of her pants. It didn't take long to give up on the idea of removing a single leg. The raw burning alone made pulling the fabric off in such a way impossible.

"It's going to have to be my whole pants," she muttered, unable to look at Greyson. "Will it bother you? 'Cause I can do this."

"I won't be bothered." Greyson's ears glowed crimson when she peeked up to see why his voice sounded funny. She was troubling him, but he was determined to help. How poised. Now she had two people she had to live up to.

Keeping her gaze on the covers, she slipped her pants off and lay flat on her stomach. The mattress moved under Greyson's weight. The heat on her blush ramped up, and her heart threatened to beat a hole in her ribs. Why was she this embarrassed?

"I'll, uh, start at your ankle. If that's okay."

"Uh-huh."

Flick closed her eyes and waited for his touch. The scabs all burned where the fabric of her pants rubbed her, so having him touch them all to rub in cream didn't sound pleasant. But she'd hang in there, just like everyone else.

The scrape of metal on glass of the lid opening preceded a wonderful aroma. She could smell everything she loved about lazy summer days: warm air, trees, flowers, grass, the pool, sunblock, barbeques, campfires, and so much more. How could the scent of a summer afternoon come from a jar?

Greyson's first touch made her jerk, but she firmed up her body so he could work. After an initial sting, the cream brought relief. Not a lessening of pain but a deep relaxation as if she could feel her damaged cells releasing their anguish. Flick's body threatened to melt into the mattress, loosened by all-encompassing tranquility. This was better than sleep, or meditation, or yoga. Through her closed eyes, Flick could practically see her body's energy aligning with the universe's energy.

The spiral of cool healing followed Greyson's hands as they smoothed cream along the line of wounds. When his hands reached the back of her thigh, she jolted again. A whole new awareness permeated her mind and body, driving out the tranquility and replacing it with electric bees. His hands were so close to *things*.

His palms were soft and warm, smoothing the spiral of cuts toward her inner thigh. Greyson's head touched her back between her shoulder blades, and the exhale of his deep breaths washed warm across the back of her neck.

*Oh God in heaven.* Her stomach burned, and Flick squeezed her eyes shut. *Kiss me.* The plea ran through her brain. *Brush your lips against me so I know for sure that's what you want.* If she thought this hard enough, would he hear? She didn't dare move because if she was wrong, she might never get the guts to look him in the eye again.

If she'd read into this morning incorrectly and he wanted nothing more than their friendship, she'd feel like a total idiot. And she knew plenty of people who got signals wrong, including herself. Hadn't she missed Jake's massive crush on her? What if she was doing the opposite this time? The idea Greyson didn't want her stung. Dear Lord. When had she developed a crush this big? It had snuck up on her out of nowhere.

His whole chest lay along her back, and his smoothing hand traced from the back to the front of her thigh. When his fingers went between her and the mattress, she gave up her hesitation. If his fingers pulled, she'd go with, rolling to face him.

Pounding on the front door.

Greyson's nose crushed into the back of her neck, and he went limp. "You've got to be fucking kidding me," he muttered. "I'm almost five thousand miles from home, know at best a handful of people, and still can't get a moment."

He pushed away from her. "You'd better get dressed. We don't want to give anyone the wrong idea."

"Shut the door so I can put cream on the front." She hadn't missed the disappointment in his eyes, had she?

"Flick!" Marisol's voice screamed through the front door, loud enough to hear. "Are you here?"

"Crap. Never mind the cream." She whimpered the whole while she dragged her pants on. The back of her leg felt perfect, but the front was as raw as ever.

Greyson had already left for the front door. By the time she'd reached the bedroom door, both Marisol and Jake rushed into the house, straight for her. They tackled her, hugging wildly. Someone's knee hit her leg, and she cried out, dropping to the floor.

"What?" Marisol asked in a panic.

Flick whimpered and pulled her pant leg up. Marisol's hand flew to cover her mouth while Jake groaned and reached for Flick's leg, his face contorted.

"How?" he murmured.

"One of those things I see attacked me in the bathtub last night. I'm okay, though."

Jake turned an evil glare on Greyson. "How did this happen with everything?"

He crossed his arms and gazed back. "Her parents were out to dinner, and she was home *alone*." He emphasized the word so he didn't have to have the whole "angels" discussion with Marisol there. "But don't let her fool you. She stayed here with me today because she nearly bled out. I don't know what would have happened if she hadn't made it to the kitchen, where I could hear her screaming. Stupid expensive soundproofing."

Marisol jutted her chin forward, eyes flashing. "I'm glad."

Everyone gasped.

"No. I'm not glad you're hurt, but I kinda am." Her eyes filled with tears, and her chin trembled.

Flick cast a glance between her friends and the clock. "Wait. There's no way you should be here this early. Did you skip to see where I was?" No, that was stupid. They'd text if they were worried. "What happened?" Her lips had gone numb.

Marisol burst into tears. Jake pulled her into a hug, soothing their friend, but he shocked Flick when tears started dripping down his face, too.

"There was… Something happened today at school,

Flick." Jake's voice trembled. "Someone brought a gun to school and—" He choked off with a sob.

"We had to see you with our own eyes," Marisol bawled. "We had to be sure you were still alive. So many…"

"Damnation," Adriel swore.

Jake jerked up, staring hard at the spot where Adriel stood.

"What?" Flick asked either of them.

"I swear I saw. Or heard." He shook his head.

"If I were active," Adriel said, "an incident like a school shooting would be my job. And no one thought to alert me, though I'm in the same city?" He paced the living room. "This can't be a coincidence. We find a hive or worse at your school just in time for a shooting? This is a disaster. All that fear and pain will cause whatever's living there to swell with fresh energy."

Jake tapped Flick's shoulder. "I saw something, didn't I?"

"Adriel," she murmured. "Neither of you were hurt? Were you, you know, close?"

Jake shook his head. "I was in the gym on the opposite side of campus."

"I saw some blood." Marisol shuddered.

"This happened during second period," Jake explained. "By the time the police caught the shooter and the lockdown ended, this was the soonest we could get here. We knew you weren't on the bus but didn't know if you'd come late." Jake hugged her again, burying his nose in her hair. "I was so worried."

"I wonder why my parents didn't call?" Realization jolted through Flick, and she lurched to her feet, hampered by pain and her tangle of friends. "My parents!" she shrieked. "I didn't plan on staying here all day. My phone and pack are at my place. They've got to be panicked."

When Adriel dropped her phone into her hands, Jake's jaw tightened, and Marisol gasped. But Flick ignored them and dialed her mom. She picked up immediately.

"Flick?" The noise of people, sirens, radios, and activity drowned out her mother's voice.

"I'm here, Mom. I'm at home and safe."

"Thank the Lord." Her mother burst into tears. "When you didn't answer, and we couldn't find you, we thought you were... Twice in two days, Flick. I ca-can't." Her mother dissolved into unintelligible sobbing.

"Where's Dad?" Flick asked.

"I'm at the school. We were waiting for police to identify... If you were one of them..." She broke down again.

"Mom," Flick snapped. "Where's Dad?"

"If he's not at home, he'll be there in a sec, baby."

Adriel grabbed her, and Greyson's apartment vanished. They reappeared in her living room just as the front door burst open, and her father came running in, yelling her name.

"Here, Dad."

He rushed her, scooping her off her feet into an uncomfortable hug. His whole body trembled, and he kept murmuring, "Thank God," over and over.

She patted his back. "Dad, this hurts."

"Are you injured?" he asked in alarm.

"No. I mean, I'm still cut up from last night." She hung her head. "I should have called you. I wasn't even at school today."

"Y-you weren't? Why?"

"I thought I'd tell you when you got home. My leg was too bad. I couldn't hobble to the bus stop, and driving was out of the question. So I stayed next door to let Greyson and the angels take care of me." He looked ready to lecture, so she pulled up her pant leg again. "Look. See on the front how they're still raw?"

She turned so he could see the back of her leg. "But Adriel visited the angel of healing today and brought me a cream to fix them. I only got it half rubbed on when Marisol and Jake showed up. They're still at Greyson's. But Mom said you were on your way here, and I didn't want to miss you. I left my phone here. I'm so, *so* sorry."

He gripped her shoulder a little too tightly. "I'm so relieved to find you unhurt. I should be furious about the rest, but if you'd gone to school today, we might not be having this conversation." He crouched, looking at her lower leg. "This is all real, isn't it?"

"Why would you say you believed me if you didn't?"

He turned a sad gaze up on her. "We always had faith in you. But the things we couldn't see, well, there's a big difference between faith and proof. Your mother and I both believed that you believed what you saw was real. Am I making sense?"

"Yeah."

He stood and hugged her again.

"Dad, can I bring everyone over here?"

"Of course. But make sure—"

The front door opened. "Flick, we're coming in," Jake called. He entered the living room, followed by Marisol, Kyrael, and Adriel. "Greyson said everyone here knows, and we just finished telling Marisol. So it's okay for me to let you know that Greyson and Serai, the psycho angel, went to get as close to the school as possible."

"I thought we had to wait a week?" Flick asked Adriel.

"Things surrounding your school are out of hand. I never thought I'd live to see this day, but I agree with Serai. We need to identify whatever's inhabiting your school and deal with it."

"There's really something lurking at our school?" Marisol asked, shrinking in on herself.

"Yeah, and it's going to feed off this chaos like nobody's business," Flick informed her.

"What are the angels going to do about it?" Marisol whispered.

Flick caught Kyrael's eye. "We're going to help the angels get close enough to send whatever it is to Hell."

He returned a gleaming grin, his eyes narrowed and excited. "I'm so glad you're on board."

Adriel patted her shoulder. "From the moment you stopped traffic to scold me, I knew you had a steel spine. But don't go getting all bloodthirsty on us. We have to proceed methodically so it doesn't run first."

"What do you mean you're helping?" her father snapped. "We don't want you becoming a casualty."

She turned to her father, willing him to understand. "I'm already a casualty, Dad. I have been since birth. True, I didn't die in the tub yesterday or at school today. But what kind of life do you think I'd have even if I turned my back and closed my eyes? The creatures still find me. However, if I help Kyrael and Adriel, I have a chance to do something besides be a victim until the day I die."

He looked like he wanted to argue, so she took her father's hands in hers. "Dad, you're always on me to bring good into the world. Imagine the impact this would have. Maybe no one will see the work I help with, but they'll feel it. Peace and safety will reside in the shadows instead of unease."

He cocked his head, gazing at her. "You amaze me." After a pause, he asked, "The angels pay for Greyson's apartment? For real?"

"Yeah. Why?"

"If this job you're helping with interferes with school or work, they'll see you're taken care of?"

Flick smiled. "Adriel promises."

Her father smoothed a loving hand across her cheek. "Imagine my daughter saving the world, for real."

She blushed. "Not saving it, but making it better."

Flick's father, Marisol, and Jake all jumped and yelped when Serai appeared in the living room, dropping Greyson in a heap on the floor. Ignoring all the humans, she spoke to Adriel.

"We have a huge problem. A contracted remala inhabits her school. But that's not the worst of it. The smell Flick has been reporting. It's because the remala is contracted by the King of Rot, Astaroth." She paced around the living room. "I fled the instant I touched the miasma. We can't afford to lose such a potent entity. But we also need to figure out what the remala's goal is. Astaroth will have something in the works, and it won't be pretty. Last time, it was the mutation allowing the black plague to jump from rats to humans. I don't need to tell you how that turned out."

Adriel looked sick. "I worked the plague. I know the toll very well."

Flick staggered over to the couch and sank onto a cushion. All the bravado and conviction she'd felt moments before leached out of her. How was she going to stand in the face of a creature contracted to the demon responsible for the plague?

"What's wrong, Flick?" Jake asked.

She glanced at Greyson, who sat in a listless ball on the floor. Through numb lips, she summarized. "The being in our school works for the demon who caused the black death, the King of Rot."

"What's he doing in a school?" Jake shrieked.

"The school is nothing but a feeding ground," Flick relayed for Serai. "The being is likely manipulating something else in the area, but the goal would be mass casualties, destruction, or both. What in our area would be capable of mass destruction?" Flick asked everyone.

"Taking out the shipping ports could cripple commerce not just on the west coast but worldwide," her father suggested. He fumbled with the wall, steadying himself on it. "There are also major military bases nearby, and just across the ocean are China and Russia. It would be easy to start a world war by launching weapons from here."

He took several deep breaths. "You said he's the king of rot? What if, instead of real viruses, he worked with computer viruses? Major software players have headquarters here. He could do something to electronics that use their operating systems. Or there's airplane manufacturing. We already know what a disaster airplanes can be in the hands of evil. Messing with any of those could bring the world to its knees."

Flick took several swallows as bile backed up in her throat. "Serai said thank you. She left to take those ideas back to Heaven and begin assembling the necessary units of the angelic army."

Someone knocked on the door, and Flick went to open it, dazed. It took her a moment to register Wade and Niciel standing in the hall. Shaking her head to clear it, she waved them in.

"You're back early." Her tone was dead.

"Serai ordered us back," Niciel said. "I take it the news isn't good."

Flick shut the door and led them into the living room. "For those of you who haven't met, this is Wade. He's the third and only other person like Greyson and me that Heaven is aware of. And because you can't see him, Niciel came back with him." She sighed. "Adriel, my brain feels like oatmeal. Can you tell them what Serai reported?"

She sat on the sofa while Adriel dropped the bad news on the last two. Somewhere in the middle of his doomsday talk, her mother came home, and a fresh round of being hugged by parental pythons began.

Chapter 16

Adriel perched on the sofa, which still sat against the living room wall out of the way of training. After school had been canceled for the next day, Flick's parents agreed to let everyone stay the night. Marisol and Jake's parents grudgingly agreed. They were worried about their kids but willing to do whatever they needed to help them cope.

He gazed over the group. Five sleeping bags were lined up in the living room, and the five young people had stayed awake whispering amongst themselves until quite late. Jake and Marisol were safer, having been made aware of the angels and the true nature of events around them. Now, it would be easy for Flick to warn them away from anywhere or anyone of suspicion.

Flick, Wade, and Greyson were another matter. If the angels were altering their energy makeup by using them as hosts, then the risk increased every time they paired up in that manner, which got Adriel thinking. Since they'd been found, no one had asked why they existed in the first place.

What gave Flick, Greyson, and Wade the ability to see all these things? If angels knew the cause, could they reverse it so they didn't have to see? And even if Heaven could blind the humans to evil, what would that gain them? They'd still know and worry. In which case, if angels found the cause, could they catch others and blind them to the otherworldly when they were small enough to go on and live a normal life?

Concentrating, Adriel made three glass vials and used his power to pull blood from each of the three humans. Gabriel was now referring to them as witnesses. He would have someone in Heaven test the witnesses' blood and compare it to typical human blood. Hopefully, some simple explanation existed, and these three would be the only ones trapped in the world of the remalas.

He sent out a pulse of energy, a call, a request for a messenger. When this experiment began, Gabriel instructed as few angels as possible should be aware of the experimental unit, so Adriel had been doing all the communication himself. But now that Serai was mobilizing angelic warriors, the whole thing would soon burst wide open. So what was one more messenger?

Abrasael appeared before him and bowed.

"Shh," Adriel warned, pointing to the sleeping youths. "Three of them can hear us."

"Seriously?" Abrasael yelped, pressed his fingers to his lips, then whispered, "Sorry. What can I do for you?"

Adriel held the vials toward Abrasael. "Take these to Raziel for me. It's blood from the three humans who can see and talk to angels. I want to know what makes them different from other humans." He gazed past the messenger. "I want to see if we can do anything to keep others from suffering the way they have at the hands of negative beings."

Abrasael gaped.

"What?" Adriel snapped. "This needs to be completed in a hurry. If Raziel doubts this, have him check with Gabriel. My name and the fact it involves these humans will be enough to get an immediate audience."

Abrasael shook his head. "I understand. It's just you look…tender. The mighty Adriel the Executioner is in love with some humans?"

Adriel flicked his wings and shot forward, grasping the messenger by the throat. "I want this clear to all you petty angels. These children are under my protection. You mess with them, and you mess with me." He let go and stepped back, leveling an icy glare on Abrasael. "I also know the messengers have given Kyrael decades of harassment. He's working for me at the moment. My protection extends to him, as well."

Abrasael bowed low. "Understood."

"Tsk," Adriel clicked his disappointment with his tongue. "Kyrael would have already delivered."

Abrasael glared in Adriel's direction and disappeared. Adriel let him go. With eons of time on angels' hands, his and Serai's combative relationship wasn't the only tense one in the heavens. For whatever reason, messengers seemed to like being petty. But none of them would dare to mess with the Executioner. And by proxy, his companions wouldn't be harassed either. At least as long as his threat seemed real.

He crossed to stand over the sleeping humans. On second thought, his threat was accurate. If anyone equal or below him messed with these children, they'd face his displeasure. If anyone set above him tried, he'd advocate in their favor until ordered to stand down. Now that he thought about it, Abrasael had been right about one thing. He, Heaven's Mass Executioner, had fallen in love with a couple of humans.

Stooping, he smoothed a hand across Flick's cheek, then moved to do the same on Greyson. These children were precious. He'd drawn them into a dangerous world, and he'd see they made it out the other side. He would ensure their final date with a death angel came at the end of a long and satisfying life. Well, gaining satisfaction was up to them, but he'd see they got the chance, like giving the healing cream to Greyson this afternoon. Adriel glanced between Greyson and Flick. Had his gift worked out for them? The two had many solid points of connection. They ought to do well together should they choose one another. He'd just set the scene.

Adriel started rearranging his energy to fold into his regenerative ball of light when Serai reappeared in the living room. He rolled his eyes and grabbed her arm, hauling her from the front room. She had all the subtle quietness of a garbage disposal full of rocks. Whatever she needed, she was sure to wake the humans while making her request.

Once inside Flick's room, Adriel shut the door. "Now what?"

"I wanted to give you a rundown on procedure. You and your little team will be vital in tracking down the contracted remala. For once, we have the opportunity to stop the creature before the demon's plans come to fruition."

Adriel felt like making a face at her, human-style, and yelling, "Duh." But he refrained in favor of more pointed barbs. "Congratulations, you've finally realized the potential Gabriel and I saw at the beginning. But don't worry, it only took you," he crossed his arms and raised one pondering finger to his chin, "several days? I think that might be a record for tardiness."

Her glare twisted. "*What?*"

He matched her sourness. "I heard about the crap

you gave Kyrael. I don't appreciate having members of my team bullied in my absence. As you just proved, you are not so insightful as to be ahead of anyone on this project. So I would appreciate a little more cooperation going forward, or you and I will tangle for real." His eyes narrowed. "And I'll be sure to give you your spanking where the rest of the Powers can see."

She stepped so close her nose nearly touched his, her eyes alight with challenge. "Try me."

He tipped his face away from her and swiveled out of her space. "I'm tired of asinine messengers tonight. Tell me what you came to say, or go back to Heaven."

\*\*\*\*

"I'm bringing a full unit back to the apartment in three days," Serai explained to everyone gathered in Greyson's living room.

Flick's friends had gone home, but they would be back later in the day. Greyson shuddered. He didn't know how many powers made up a unit, but if they were all as rough as Serai, one was more than enough. Besides, the substantial two-bedroom place seemed small, with everyone using his flat.

"Won't that be too much power concentrated too close to the school?" Kyrael asked.

"Keep listening, little pigeon. I was about to say they would disperse across the city and gather information to be studied for anomalies. In addition to the suggestions of Felicity's father, we'll be investigating the University of Washington's medical research facilities, the train lines, the geological systems monitoring local volcanos, and the nuclear power plant near Hanford. We realize this is far from Seattle, but anything which has the capability of mass destruction is a site of interest."

She crossed her arms and leaned against the wall to continue lecturing. "My unit will pull all records, paper and computerized, and bring the information to Heaven for faster sorting. Once anomalies have been found and tracked, that information will be brought here along with the entire unit, at which point we will construct the plan for actual containment and disposal of the creature." She glared a challenge at Adriel. "My team has the expertise in this matter. Do be a good boy and listen to those with more experience."

"And what will my team be doing?" Adriel gritted out.

"While my team figures out the creature's larger goal, your team will identify the contracted remala and, if possible, get it to talk."

Greyson burst out laughing. "You want us to meet with the mastermind and get him monologuing? What do you think this is, a cheap superhero movie?"

"Besides, what does a contracted remala even look like?" Flick asked. "I've had weird feelings at the school all year, but I've never seen anything out of the ordinary, let alone more horrifying than the mid-grade remalas we've exterminated so far."

"That's because once contracted, the remala can take on whatever form best suits its goal," Serai said.

"Like a shapeshifter?" Wade asked. "Will it be changing on us mid-search?"

Serai contemplated, then her wings sagged. "I don't know. We've never gotten to a contracted remala before it put its plans in motion. In the case of the plague, the remala took the form of the initial infected rat, harboring and spreading the fleas. In other cases, the remala has looked human to blend in and cause damage directly amongst the population. The one thing I can say for sure is you're looking for a sentient living creature hiding at the school."

"And how are Greyson and I supposed to stake out the school anyway?" Wade asked.

"The same way I created all of Greyson's necessary documents," Adriel chimed in, "I've altered the appropriate records so the two of you will pose as high school seniors. Cousins, so your familiarity will be explained."

"How will their looks be explained?" Flick muttered. "There's no way Greyson still looks like a high schooler."

"I resent that," Wade protested.

"Sorry." Flick shrugged. "You're still eighteen. It makes a difference, biologically speaking. Your diploma is a piece of paper that has nothing to do with your looks."

"Can Jake and Marisol manage a secret like this?" Greyson asked.

Adriel sighed. "I hope so. I'm counting on them wanting to be helpful. A task might keep them from trying anything stupid."

"Will the school even open tomorrow?" Flick asked.

"Yes." Adriel and Serai exchanged a glance before Adriel explained. "Serai went to the school last night and finished the police investigation, the cleaning, the necessary paperwork, and such. Then she modified notices from the district saying it was necessary to open the school as soon as possible to allow students access to friends and counselors for their mental health."

"Ah. And the remala won't notice?" Greyson clarified.

"We can't be sure," Adriel hedged. "If it were so easy to predict a contracted remala's actions, we wouldn't have so much trouble eliminating them. I'm hoping it will be greedy enough not to question why the feast is returning so soon."

Serai pushed away from the wall. "I've got business elsewhere. See you in three days." She vanished, leaving Greyson, Wade, and Flick with their angels.

"Well." Wade stretched, then leaned back on his hands where he sat on the floor. "Tomorrow is accounted for, but what do we do to kill time today? I'm used to continuous hunting now, so this whole sneaking around thing is weird."

"Have you been back to your place yet?" Greyson asked. "I'd bet your food is growing biology experiments in your refrigerator."

"Naw, my roommate would have eaten everything long before then." He stared at the ceiling. "But I should go back and let him know I'm alive. I burned off a lot of bad feelings while I was out with Niciel. I think I can face living as normal a life as possible around hunting. Thanks for taking me back, no questions asked."

"Will you be coming back to school at the college?" Flick asked.

He nodded, his gaze still on the ceiling. "Niciel and I talked a lot about my future. Living the whole college experience and getting a chance to finish growing up will be important for healing. I can hunt on the side. You guys do." He huffed a laugh. "I went nonstop, but you two found a contracted remala."

Greyson reached over and patted Wade's shoulder. "We told you we were here for you. I'm glad to hear you're healing."

"I think I might ask Adriel if he can get me a place in this building, too. It would be nice to be close to you guys, convenient for hunts, too. But no offense, Greyson. I'm not interested in rooming with you."

"Who asked you to stay, anyway?" Greyson asked in mock indignation.

His stomach unclenched. He would never have said no to letting Wade live with him, but he hadn't had a chance to solidify anything with Flick yet. The last thing Greyson wanted was for her to remember her crush on Wade before Greyson had her heart.

"Greyson, could you give Felicity and me a minute before I leave?"

"Sure." Greyson stood and went to the bedroom, closing the door most of the way. He wanted to turn on the tv, but his feet wouldn't move. Listening in was rude, but if he did, he'd know what Wade had to say to her and where that left him.

"I wanted to apologize once again," Wade said. "Even though you didn't complain, I'm sure you were disappointed, especially since I left in such a rush. I didn't do anything right that night."

"It's fine. I understood. Or, I mean, I understood you needed the time. Not so much the circumstances. I wouldn't presume to—"

She kept prattling like a nervous little girl, and Greyson's heart constricted. She never acted flustered around him. What if she didn't like him the way he wanted her?

"Felicity," Wade cut into her babble. "I'm still not ready to go out with anyone. I'm not done fixing myself. I've started down that road, but I still have a long way to go."

"It's okay," Flick muttered. "My road has gotten pretty bumpy. I'm honestly not sure what I want right now. So don't stress on my account."

"Good. Not that things are unsettled, but you're not sad or anything. I don't want to make you unhappy." Wade's jeans rustled. "I'm leaving, Greyson," he called loud enough to reach the bedroom.

Greyson took a few extra moments coming out of the bedroom. He didn't want them to know he was at the door already. Wade stood at the flat's entrance with Niciel behind him.

"Before you go, ju-just be careful," Greyson muttered. "The last time I sent a teammate home for the night, she got attacked."

Wade smiled. "Thanks for worrying about me, but Niciel's not going anywhere. And if for some reason he needs to, I'll come over here first." He paused with his hand on the knob. "I'll have Niciel teleport me over in time to go to school tomorrow morning. Flick, I'll leave it to you to fill me in on your school."

He left, and Greyson kind of missed him. But only a little because when he turned around, Flick sat on the couch gazing at him. Adriel and Kyrael were nowhere to be seen. They must have gone to the guest room.

She waved him over to sit beside her. "Wade was right. What do we do with today?"

Swift and dirty thoughts of how to kill time hit Greyson's brain, but he shook those away. "We can't go too far from the flat. Adriel and Kyrael won't want to be stuck in our bodies all day. And we told your friends we'd be here when they came back this afternoon." He fidgeted on the sofa cushion. "We never did watch a romantic comedy. Are you up for a movie?"

"I am, but…" She hesitated, and Greyson wilted a little. This didn't sound like an opportunity. "I feel guilty," she whispered.

"About what?" Greyson asked.

"Wanting to have fun when the rest of the school is traumatized." She turned to face him, her expression torn. "I wasn't there, and I don't think I feel the event the same way. Just like I know Marisol and Jake were horrified by the cuts on my leg, but they're never going to feel the way you or I did being involved in the attack, you know? And worse, *my* friends are safe and accounted for. No one has called to tell me I know any of the victims. So I'm sad thirteen students died, but…"

She leaned toward him. "I also have something that worries me about the shooting. The angels can take over our bodies and do as they like. They wait for permission, but what if the remala could do the same? It wouldn't wait for permission. What if the remala caused the incident in the first place? Is some poor kid from my school going to prison for something a remala did?"

Greyson took her hands in his, rubbing the backs with his thumbs. "First off, don't feel guilty for your feelings. That's a bad downward spiral. Everything you feel could change when you arrive tomorrow. But heartbroken or just a little sad, they're your feelings, no one else's, which makes them just right for you. As long as you acknowledge the way others feel with the same respect you give your emotions, you're doing fine."

He flipped her hands over and smoothed his thumbs across her palms. "Second, it might be possible for the remala to possess someone, but I think the angels would have warned us if they could. There are plenty of people who break for whatever reason. It sucks, but that's life.

Not everything bad results from some evil infestation."

He paused a moment while his words sank in. "I think it's the other way around. Adriel said negative human emotions create the remala in the first place. This means those evil things result from what we, as humans, do."

"I never thought of it like that. How did you get so smart?"

"Just born that way." He took one hand away from hers and used the remote to find the movie they were going to watch the other day.

She didn't pull her other hand away, and tiny sparks of pleasure zipped through Greyson's hand. But he'd sat in the center seat and had nowhere to lean. Keeping her hand in his, he shifted along the couch until he could lean back in the corner of the armrest. To his delight, Flick followed, though she stopped with her hip to his, sitting upright. Another gentle pull on her arm got her to lean against his chest.

Okay. These weren't the actions of a girl with zero interest. They were making progress. Squirming, he shuffled until their bodies aligned more naturally, and she was tucked in along his chest. Multiple internal organs got slithery and turned circles behind his ribcage until everything felt in knots.

It had been a while since Greyson had gotten so churned up over a girl. His last girlfriend had been one of convenience, with very little physical between them. She was saving herself, and he wasn't interested in making an effort to try to be that man. His interactions with the girl before had started hot and heavy, sleeping together on the second date. But he'd let something about seeing spirits slip, and she left the same night.

His last meaningful connection with a girl happened in his final year of secondary school when he'd convinced himself Whitley was his soulmate. He'd been in knots over her, then her devotee when she said yes to dating. They lost their virginity together. But on holiday with her parents, she met someone who made her heart beat faster than he did.

Now the heady feeling of being untethered around a girl had returned. And it was so much better than plain lust.

The movie started, but Greyson couldn't focus on it. What caught his attention was the shape of Flick's body against his, her silky hair on his cheek, and her hand still in his. Interspersed with those sensations were calculations. Which slight movements would bring her closer? Where could he place his face to invite a kiss?

He was an idiot because when he'd settled Flick on him, her head was too low, and his face could only reach her hair. So he rested his nose against her hair and drew in deep breaths. She smelled like mint shampoo.

The writhing in his stomach demanded an outlet. He ran his lips across her hair, and his eyes slid closed. He tightened his arms around her, pulling her close.

"Greyson?" she whispered, tipping her head.

It was all he needed. He ducked his head and pressed his lips to hers. Flick let out a little sigh that excited him to his core. He deepened the kiss, and she responded by twisting so she lay across his chest.

Everything outside the sphere of the couch disappeared.

Chapter 17

Kyrael peeked out of the guest room, but Adriel grabbed him and pulled him back in, clicking the door shut.

"I want to see," Kyrael protested. "I've never seen human courtship."

"You're being weird again," Adriel admonished. "Poor Greyson has been trying for a while to get a kiss. We're not going to be the interruption."

Kyrael peered at the door, wishing he could see through. "Do you think this means they'll marry? Reproduce?" He squirmed in delight. "Wouldn't it be wonderful to see a tiny blend of Flick and Greyson?"

Adriel lightly smacked the back of his head. "Stay out of their business. Flick may have helped you get control, but the twitchy old Kyrael still lurks in there."

Kyrael turned an exasperated look on Adriel. "Even you would melt for a baby belonging to those two, Mr. Death Angel."

"Without a doubt. But you've learned enough about humans to know one kiss on a couch doesn't mean they'll date and marry and have children."

Kyrael snickered. "I've also read enough to know one kiss on a couch can turn into more, and it only takes once to get a babe. You were providing them the opportunity to come together. Did you happen to provide your boy with a prophylactic?"

Adriel palmed his forehead. "No." He started for the door. "Do you think it would be necessary? Should I drop one out there? I can do it unnoticed."

Kyrael laughed. "You're worse than a parent. And you call me awkward. What will be, will be. We aren't meant to interfere, so don't fret. They're grown up enough to face their decisions."

Adriel made a face at Kyrael. "Stop sounding so wise. You're throwing me off. Kyrael isn't that mature."

Kyrael tipped his head, appraising Adriel. "You have a monster reputation in Heaven."

"So do you," Adriel quipped back.

"I just wondered if you worked friends in around your Adriel the Executioner wall? I may get picked on for my overexcited nature and out-of-proportion curiosity, but I've got several friends. I even spent time with Niciel. But I've never met anyone who says, 'I hung out with Adriel today, and we did *x*,' you know?"

Adriel scowled. "So? I'm exactly the angel I'm meant to be."

"But are you the angel you want to be?" Kyrael climbed up on the bed and sat cross-legged.

"What's that supposed to mean?"

"It means no one said angels have to be static beings. You are free to grow and change without losing Adriel the Executioner. I don't feel lost at all anymore. Personal change doesn't have to happen alone. You, Flick, Greyson, without you three, I would still be lost."

He held his hand up and let the air swirl above his palm, taking the form of a star-shaped board studded with dozens of amethyst and sapphire pieces. "So I'm asking you again. Do you have any friends? Because if you're willing to let me, I'd like to be the angel who goes back and says I hung out with Adriel, and we had a blast."

He set the gameboard on the bed and waited for Adriel to choose.

"No one wants to spend their free time with the Executioner."

"I do." Kyrael patted the bed. "I've met this so-called Executioner, and he's got some prickles, but he's a fiercely fair and loyal individual. His heart is guarded but soft inside the walls. It's said he has no patience, which can't be true because he helped one of the most overzealous and annoying angels in Heaven calm down and find his fit. If that isn't love and patience, I don't know what is." He pointed to the opposite side of the board.

Adriel hesitated a moment, his eyes meeting Kyrael's. The unspoken question of "Is this all right?" screamed itself at Kyrael. Kyrael gave him the most reassuring smile he could.

Adriel climbed up on the king-size bed and settled across from Kyrael. "Don't think I'll go easy on you because of all the flattery."

"I'd be insulted if you did." Kyrael pointed at the board. "I'll take amethyst, but you can go first."

The game ebbed and flowed as they worked pieces in four dimensions. The board actually warped in on itself, but that made the game more interesting. Adriel was one move away from cornering Kyrael when Abrasael appeared in the bedroom. He took in the two playing games and startled.

"Yes?" Adriel snapped.

"I have the results of the blood tests. Gabriel says the results change nothing about the experimental group."

"And those results are?" Adriel demanded. He leaned back on one arm, gesturing to hurry up with the other hand.

Abrasael dropped to his knees and bowed his head. Kyrael's stomach clenched. He could spot the posture of a messenger with bad news a mile away.

"The three are not meant to be among the living."

Kyrael kept his gaze on Adriel, and though the other angel didn't react much, his body stiffened—all the way down to the feathers on his wings. Not good. News like this could draw out the prickly side of the Executioner.

"Explain yourself." Adriel's order carried quiet menace.

Abrasael took a gasping breath. "At some point during the gestation, their fetuses should have perished. The medical science now, it keeps alive those meant to die."

Adriel leaped from the bed, scattering the game, and stood over the cowering angel. "There's a list of those meant to die. Are you suggesting the Virtues are incapable of reading a simple list? Or do you have the audacity to suggest the list we get is wrong? You know who makes the list, correct? You realize what implying it's wrong also implies?"

Abrasael whimpered. "Please. I'm just the messenger. Even Raziel can't understand how, for the entirety of human evolution, one set of rules can apply, then in the last century, half a century, those rules change. Individuals like those three humans are an abomination."

Kyrael scurried from the bed and placed his hand on Adriel's back between his wings. "Brother Abrasael doesn't live here and doesn't understand the swift adaptability of the humans. He can't wrap his mind around the speed these changes happen and how the old way can become irrelevant in a cosmic millisecond."

Under his hand, Adriel shook with barely suppressed fury. But Kyrael understood. Maybe even better than Adriel did since Adriel watched human growth and change firsthand while working on Earth. Kyrael had been working with the humans and Adriel for mere weeks. The changes in the humans, Adriel, and himself were mindboggling. Yet undeniable. But it was only through experiencing this he could comprehend it. Yes, he'd been changing before, but at a pace so slow it seemed tedious by comparison.

"Think, Adriel," Kyrael murmured. "Set aside Abrasael's discomfort with the circumstances and tell me what's left behind."

Adriel drew a shuddering breath and said nothing.

"Then I'll start," Kyrael said. "It means their mothers had troubled pregnancies. When faced with such difficulty, I imagine a human mother would be quite distraught."

"Which," Adriel drawled out, "would call to remalas." The tension around him shifted. "If those remalas got too greedy and fed off the mother—"

"The fetus could be contaminated," Kyrael finished.

"Yes. Thank you, Kyrael." Abrasael looked up with profound gratitude on his face, which startled Kyrael this time. Except for his friends, the messengers never looked at him that way. "Those humans are contaminated. In such a way, they have one foot on the other side."

Adriel rubbed his chin, nodding. "In the past, such babes would have perished either while still in the womb or shortly thereafter. Which explains why Heaven never had incidences of humans interacting with remalas and angels this way before."

"But it also means there might be others." Kyrael crouched beside Abrasael. "Be careful your expectations don't lead you to be unreasonable or judgmental. We're looking at a whole new type of individual. Heaven will have to adapt as humans have, or we will condemn an entire section of the population. These individuals have done nothing wrong. An unborn babe commits no sin to warrant being written off by the angels. The reverse. You should feel deeper compassion for these poor souls who have to cope with circumstances even Heaven isn't prepared to face."

Abrasael wrinkled his nose. "Are you seriously Kyrael?"

Kyrael smiled. "I'm just a better version of me. And it's all because I was willing to get swept along in this change." He winked at Abrasael and stood. "Adriel, there are a few deeper implications here."

Adriel scowled down at Abrasael. "Was there more to the message?"

Abrasael shook his head.

Adriel crouched and brought his face very close to Abrasael's. "Kyrael was too kind. Gabriel has given his approval to these humans, and an angel of any rank foolish enough to need more reason to accept them is worthy of punishment in my eyes. Go home and use your spare time to stop being a fool." He put a hand on Abrasael's head, and Abrasael cringed. "Since this news is sure to pass through Heaven like a wildfire, you make sure the angels know *I* will protect the human witnesses. And I won't be soft-spoken like Kyrael."

263

He removed his hand, and Abrasael vanished.

Kyrael sighed. "I guess you're a work in progress. Just like me." He shot Adriel a wide grin.

Adriel rubbed his face. "Please don't lump us together." He glanced over at the bed. "I'm sorry I ruined our game."

Kyrael clapped his hands together in excitement. "That's okay. I have another pastime for us. But it all depends on what's going on in the living room. I'm going to peek."

Adriel huffed. "What a blatantly weak excuse."

Kyrael chuckled and opened the bedroom door, peeking out. Despite Adriel's initial protest, he peered over Kyrael's shoulder. The television had returned to the streaming menu, and Kyrael couldn't see Flick or Greyson anywhere. Raw panic clogged his throat, and he hurried to the living room, stopping short at the edge of the sofa.

Greyson lay on the sofa, a peaceful expression on his sleeping face, his arms curled around Flick. She lay along his side with her head tucked on Greyson's shoulder. She, too, slept peacefully.

Kyrael took a blanket off the floor and spread it across their bodies. He paused to pull some of Flick's hair away from Greyson's nose, then bent and kissed Flick's forehead. Kyrael followed Adriel's wave back to the bedroom.

****

A weird sense of being awry nagged Flick. She'd never felt so nervous and so confident at the same time. She waited outside her building at the bus stop, Kyrael riding along inside her. Beside her, Greyson and Wade waited to make their debut as high school students.

Somehow, having those two at her side gave her courage.

She also had to work to shove back her draw to Greyson. She wanted to hold his hand, to kiss him, to ride the bus snuggled against him. But they'd talked about PDA last night. Wade would probably be okay with them together, but he had enough on his plate without adding anything. And Jake might be a bit of an issue. He was still hoping Flick would consider him. So they'd be discrete until she got a chance to explain things to the others.

Then there was the whole matter of everything she would face at school. Along with a being so evil it had direct ties to Hell, the place was likely swarming with remalas looking for a piece of the feast.

All of these bits gave Flick a sense of being outside her real life somehow. Today's situation wasn't normal, but she had no idea what real was anymore, nor how to get back to normal, even if she could identify it.

The bus pulled up, and Flick sat between Wade and Greyson. She kept her backpack on her lap and poked Greyson's leg in the cover it provided. A zip of heat rushed through her stomach when he slid his fingers between hers, holding her hand. She closed her eyes and tipped her head back, focusing on the delightful sensation of his skin on hers. The giddy feelings Greyson drew out shoved back all the negativity swirling around her.

"Still tired?" Wade asked her.

"Yeah," she murmured.

He cracked a huge yawn. "Me, too. I forgot how frickin' early high school started."

Flick stayed quiet, her innards going gushy. Greyson was running his fingers along hers, caressing. How distracting.

"I hope your friends can keep their mouths shut," Wade said, glancing out the window. "I haven't spent any time with them, and trusting them with something this big isn't coming easy."

"I'll vouch for them," Flick reassured him.

She worked to keep her voice and breathing steady. Greyson's fingers had moved from her hand to her leg beneath her pack. He massaged her thigh, and memories of her on the bed with him rubbing the healing cream into her leg flooded her mind. Never in a million years would she have pinned such a moment as romantic, but something about it had been so hot, and the heat lingered. She wanted to go back and see what would have happened if her friends hadn't come over and turned her already upside-down life on its head.

Flick fought a blush. She had a good idea of where it would have gone. On the sofa yesterday, Flick had let Greyson touch pretty much everything as long as his hands stayed outside her undergarments. She hadn't gone that far with any of her other boyfriends. Then again, she'd never felt so connected to any of them.

It wasn't simple attraction or desire between her and Greyson, though those were both present. Something much deeper tied them together and made being involved with him intoxicating. She'd told Jake she spent a whole night thinking about whether sleeping with Liam was the right idea, but she already knew what she'd do with Greyson. Now, it was a matter of waiting. There was no rush or need to force the "perfect" moment because, in her core, she knew whenever it happened, the moment would be perfect because it would be with Greyson.

Then again, this knowledge did nothing to calm her

heart when she was with Greyson, which made functioning difficult. On one side of her, Wade kept up a stream of small talk. On the other, Greyson did everything he could get away with unnoticed to distract her.

The bus stopped, and Flick rushed off, relieved in part and disappointed in another. She wouldn't see much of Greyson after classes started. Adriel had set the three of them as far apart on campus as possible so they could cover more ground in searching.

Wade gagged and rushed past her, vomiting in the bushes.

"Oi, are you okay?" Greyson called.

Wade held up his thumb despite heaving into the bush again. A moment later, he righted himself and wiped his mouth. "What the fuck? Has that stench and aura been around the whole time?"

Flick swallowed the sick feeling tickling her own throat. "Sort of. It's getting worse. But it's been around a while. How do you think I found this thing?"

Wade shuddered. "I have a much greater appreciation for what you two have been doing."

"Flick."

Jake and Marisol walked into the circle of light a streetlamp put out. Marisol waved, but Jake looked annoyed.

"What's got your panties in a twist?" Flick asked him.

"Is it you in your body, or am I talking to something else?" He crossed his arms. "The annuity is driving me nuts."

"Annuity?" Wade stared at Jake with unfettered confusion on his face.

"I think he meant ambiguity." Flick giggled. "Jake has the most epic malapropisms."

"Whatever," Jake snapped. "It's the same for all three of you. How the hell am I supposed to know who I'm dealing with?"

"Go ahead," Greyson muttered. The next time his body spoke, even his accent disappeared. "Jake, this is Adriel. It doesn't matter who is speaking. Both our consciousnesses are here and listening. And regardless of who is in control of our bodies, you need to be in control of yourself. You promised me you could handle acting as if you knew nothing about any of this. You said having Greyson and Wade join you at school as high schoolers wouldn't trip you up. And we've not even arrived, yet you're already struggling."

Marisol rolled her eyes. "If you can't tell the difference in speech patterns, you're an idiot." A shudder shook her body. "I-I don't want to go." She stared at the lights of the school in the distance. "The shooting ought to cover for all my feelings, and dealing with the memory of that would be bad enough. Now there's all this other piled on top."

Greyson snapped his fingers. "Thanks for reminding me. I thought you and Jake might need a little good news to shore you up. I checked on them, and I'm allowed to tell you that all thirteen young souls have been transitioned into the afterlife and are connecting with others there."

"Really?" Marisol's expression went desperate and hungry. She clutched at Greyson's shirt, and he stumbled back a step.

"Why would I lie to you?" Adriel asked with Greyson's delicious lips.

"To make me feel better, or to calm me down, or to, I don't know."

"Lying isn't in an angel's nature, though we are capable. But such a monumental deception would be cruel. I simply used my connections as a death angel to bring good news for once."

Marisol hugged Greyson, and a flash of jealousy surged through Flick. Sucking in a deep breath, she calmed herself. Marisol was hugging Adriel, not Greyson. And since Marisol wasn't the huggy type, she must feel immense relief.

"This is still way weirder than I thought it would be," Jake muttered.

"Are you capable of handling the acting?" Adriel demanded, somehow giving Greyson's voice the edge he carried when he entered death angel mode. "Or should I fix the school records allowing you to stay home for mental health reasons? Our task has serious worldwide implications. Humanity can't afford for you to waffle."

Jake clenched his fists and tipped his chin up. "I can do this."

"Good." Greyson let out a sigh. "I'm back as the speaker." His tone had shifted, and his accent returned.

Flick sucked in a deep breath. "Okay, then. Let's get this over with."

Despite her momentary conviction, it wavered with each step closer to the school building. Everything had changed. The doors had temporary metal detectors set up, and police pulled the students through one at a time. Students' faces were pale, pinched, and worried.

Usually, the halls were loud with boisterous conversation and joking. Today, everything was muted. An occasional titter of laughter promised resilience and hope. But the atmosphere was so heavy Flick was sure she'd have felt it even without her connection to the otherworldly.

"Felicity."

Flick turned when Mrs. Dennis called her name. Her second period teacher hurried over. She gripped Flick's upper arm and gave it a slight squeeze.

"Somehow, just confirming…" Her teacher's eyes glittered with suppressed emotion. "I didn't see you Monday, so…"

Flick stepped in and hugged her teacher. "Thanks for worrying about me. I'm glad you're okay, too."

Mrs. Dennis moved back, wiping her fingers across her eyes. "I'm sorry. I just—"

"It's okay," Flick reassured. "I don't mind. We're all trying our best."

"Yes. Exactly." She peered at Greyson and Wade. "I'm not familiar with these young men."

"This is Wade and Greyson. They're new. It's a crappy time to transfer in, I guess. I offered to show them around since I was home on Monday, and I'm a little less upset."

Mrs. Dennis rubbed Flick's head. "You're such a good girl." She shot the boys a sad look. "Don't judge our school by this one incident. It was a fun place to learn, and it will be again."

Greyson and Wade both looked at the floor, mumbling something, and Mrs. Dennis wandered off a little dazed still. Flick rubbed her face.

"This is so bad." She dropped her voice to a whisper. "Did you see those things that looked like spiders with fishtails clinging to her back? Screw Marisol and Jake's acting. I don't know if *I* can do this."

"Ah, Miss Felicity." Mr. Ostanes stepped up from behind, joining them. "Glad to see you thriving despite the circumstances."

Just as some of the students stood out thanks to their happy countenance, Mr. Ostanes seemed unruffled as well. His over-casualness still clung to him, though Flick was pleased to see none of the remalas did. If nothing else, those who were less affected would avoid the remalas, even if they didn't realize it.

"Good morning, Mr. Ostanes."

He drew a deep breath. "It is, isn't it? People are focused on the wrong thing. There's so much life in this place. Don't you think? Dwelling on the negative never leads to anything good. I, for one, encourage you, students, to count your blessings and focus on those. After all, life is a gift. It would be a shame to squander it." He shot her one last smile and walked off through the crowd of students.

"I think all the teachers are off the deep end today," Jake muttered.

"Not just the teachers," Flick said, turning to smile at the fourth person to touch her arm on their way past. This time, it was Heather from her first period class. "This is going to make searching out someone acting strange damn near impossible."

"Worse," Wade added, "since Greyson and I have no idea what anyone acted like before the shooting. And we don't know who's supposed to be here and who's not."

"Based on that, you and Greyson are the most likely suspects," Jake snarked.

Greyson rolled his eyes. "Grow up. If you can't help, at least don't get in the way."

"Jake," Flick interrupted. "Wade's first period class is right next to yours. Can you show him the way?"

"Right." Jake jerked his head in the direction they needed to go. "Come on."

"I'll show you your classroom, Greyson," Marisol offered, fluttering her eyes. Evidently, Greyson's message of disinterest was not received.

He shook his head. "You go ahead. I want to ask Flick a couple of questions."

She pouted, and Flick leaned over, whispering, "Guys don't like sulky girls."

Marisol pulled her posture and expression back to normal and flashed a grin at Greyson. "Maybe I'll see you at lunch, then."

He gave her a wave. The moment she was out of sight, he slipped his hand in Flick's. "Got a private spot?"

She nodded and led him to the unisex bathroom. They snuck inside and turned the lock. She internalized an eye roll at the thought of Mr. Ostanes catching her in here with a different guy.

"What did you want to ask m—"

Greyson grabbed her, pinning her against the wall and kissing her. Flick wrapped her arms around him, twining her fingers through his hair.

"That's not a question," she gasped between kisses.

"But it *is* important," he whispered, running his nose along hers. "I didn't see you alone at all this morning."

His lips stayed on hers even though he started to back up. When they couldn't get any farther apart, he broke the kiss. He tidied the hairs she'd mussed and sighed.

"I guess we should go."

She nodded. If she opened her mouth, she'd beg him to stay. If they stayed, she'd let him do things. And even though she didn't need to wait for a movie-perfect moment to have sex with Greyson, she wasn't losing her virginity in the bathroom at school.

"Yeah." She unlocked the bathroom door. "I'll see you at lunch. You can find your way, right?"

"Sure."

She left, and the lock clicked with Greyson still inside.

Chapter 18

Greyson leaned against the door to the bathroom, sucking in steadying breaths. Holding back was both delicious and difficult.

"*Is everything okay?*" Adriel asked. "*Your body seems to be under considerable strain.*"

Greyson clenched his teeth. "I want to... I need... Get the hell out of my body for like five minutes."

"*Oh. I won't watch, so you can use the facilities.*"

Greyson grabbed his cheeks in frustration. "It's not that. It's...urg. It's something I can't do with you here. Okay?"

"*Oh. Oh!*" Silence permeated his brain for a moment. "*You're going to be late for class.*"

Greyson turned on the water and splashed his face, then mopped the back of his neck. "All right. I'm going."

"*Greyson?*"

"Yes." He opened the door and exited into the thinning mass of students. Overhead, a warning bell rang.

"*Your feelings for Flick are genuine, right? Not just arousal?*"

"Nasty. Don't describe it like you're a professor. And yes. I think I'm in love with Flick."

"*How do you not know?*"

"It's complicated for humans, and stop making me talk to myself."

274

"*Please watch out for you both. I can't fix a broken heart.*"

"Maybe you should warn her to watch out for me. I'm sure of my feelings. But there are never any guarantees. Jake is still in love with her, and she knows it. And she still gets all flustered around Wade. If anyone is in a danger zone, it's me."

"*Noted. I'll be quiet for you now.*"

"You can talk. But don't make me respond until I can write it where you can peek."

He found his first class and settled in, trying to ignore the other students' stares. Flick had never struck him as young, being two years his junior. But sitting in the classroom, he felt ancient. Every face that turned his direction seemed to hold an unspoken accusation toward the old bloke trying to hide in their midst.

He pulled out a notebook, opened it, and wrote, *I feel sketchy as hell in here.*

"*Sorry,*" Adriel said. "*As soon as we pinpoint the contracted remala, Serai and her warriors will come crashing down on its head, and this will all be over.*"

*Until next time.*

"*It never ends. Such is the nature of creation. There's a balance of good and evil.*"

*I thought God was supposed to wipe all evil out.*

"*You don't want him to do that. Because of how the universe is balanced—*" He fell silent without finishing his statement, but Greyson could fill in the missing piece. The utter destruction of everything as they knew it.

"Hi," a girl beside him whispered. "You're new, right?"

He glanced at the teacher, who had opened the floor for people to share remembrances of those lost on

Monday. Some students were crying, others lay with their heads down, and a few had either given up or taken advantage and sat whispering.

If he was going to learn enough to find this remala, this girl was as good a place to start as any. "Yeah, I moved here from London," he answered.

Her gaze turned covetous. "R*ea*lly. That explains it. You look so mature, but it's because you're not one of the American dumbasses I'm stuck with. I guess they do breed them better in Europe."

Greyson paused. Did she just offer a compliment?

She grinned. "I'm Kristin, and you're hot."

"R*ea*lly?" He mimicked her fakey emphasis. "Kristin?" So this was the chick who sank her fangs into Jake. She wasn't pretty enough to play those sorts of games. She'd learn when she left high school. "You're pretty perky, all things considered."

"Bad things happen. I choose not to wallow. Besides, I didn't know any of the kids. There are fourteen hundred students at our school. Was your school at home this big?"

"No. Not even close." He had no idea Flick's school was this large. Their task suddenly felt much heavier. "Are you pretty popular? I'd like to hear about the school. I mean, the way it was. Things will go back to normal, right?"

"I assume so. And sure, what do you want to know? It'll be a nice change to talk about something normal. No one else wants to."

"Who are the smartest people in the senior class? I was always at the head of my class."

Her lips turned out in a thoughtful pout. "We don't have class ranking or anything. But I guess Tori Kenyon and Anthony Chung both have 4.0's. They've gotten straight A's since middle school. They'd faint if they saw a minus after one of those A's."

"Then what about the prettiest girls?"

"*Ask her about weird things*," Adriel demanded.

He gave his head an imperceptible shake.

Kristin tapped her chin to exaggerate her thinking. "You mean aside from me?" She giggled and reached to put a hand on his arm. "No one worth mentioning." She gave an exaggerated sigh. "I guess Brianna, Ferrah, and Jocelynn are pretty enough. But *I'm* special." She stuck her lower lip out. "They postponed the Homecoming dance. I'm going to be stuck at home on a Saturday night. If you don't have plans, maybe we could be stuck together." She laced the words with innuendo.

Greyson internalized a groan. How cheesy. Jake had questionable taste. Greyson would write him off as a total loss if it weren't for his attraction to Flick.

"A date's not going to happen," he said. "But I'm enjoying the gossip. Why don't you tell me who the weirdest people are? Start with staff."

"That would take longer than we have left in the period." She laughed at her attempt at a joke. "Staff, huh? Well. Mr. Vargas, the janitor, is so old we're pretty sure he's drinking the cleaning fluids to pickle his body and stay alive. Mrs. Langer has an unhealthy obsession with kittens. There are posters and figurines all over her classroom. And the new teacher, Mr. Ostanes, is some weirdo trying to be friends with all the students. They shouldn't hire anyone fresh out of college to teach high school. He thinks he's our age, and that makes him cool. Instead, it makes you wonder if he drives a van full of candy to school."

Greyson bit back a laugh. Imagine what she'd say about the college student posing as a senior.

"As for the students," she continued, "there are different classifications of weirdos. I'll give you the star in each category. You can figure out the rest from there. Tom Wallis is the leader of the park losers. They dress up and take their foam swords to the park to play pretend on the weekends. They're *never* getting laid."

Fresh excitement had entered her eyes. This girl got off on gossip. "Willow Stark is the leader of the new age crew. Don't touch their crystals. You might muddy the energy." She snickered at this. "But it's worth it if you want to see chicks who fancy themselves as practical witches try cursing you with herbs from their moms' gardens. Gretchen Walsh is the head of the next generation of crazy cat ladies. Henry Gershwin is a poster child for math geeks."

She licked her lips and kept going. "Oh, let's see…the crowning jewels. Garrot Morcos only emerges from his basement and video games to attend school. He's like a reverse vampire. He'll never even speak to a female besides his mom. Then there's Jake Polanski."

Greyson tensed at this. How had poor Jake gotten on her list?

"Jake thinks he's hot stuff because his two best friends are girls. He's always trying to use big words and screws up, making himself look twice as dumb as if he'd stuck to smaller words. He's also beyond desperate and the epitome of gullible." She put a hand on her chest. "I have a bit of a reputation. I'm sure you'll hear about it because I sleep with whoever *I* want on *my* terms. Guys have been getting their kicks off women, so welcome to equal opportunity. Jake fell all over himself to get with me. But in the end, he wasn't good enough."

She eyed him. "Good thing or I'd still be tangled up with that dork rather than free to be with you."

"And you think I'd trust you after you admitted to leading him on?"

"Yes, but you're not a loser with a crush on his best friend. See, Jake can't get with her. So he's desperate. He thought he'd use me, but I beat him to it. Since you're not playing stupid games with me, I won't play with you, either."

"Why can't he get with his best friend?" Greyson wasn't sure why he was asking. This could cross into dangerous territory full of hurtful details.

"Felicity Landon," Kristin said her name with a hiss. "I hate her."

"Really?" Greyson asked in surprise. "Why?"

"That stupid bitch is so full of herself. Ever since grade school, she's claimed to see ghosts to make herself seem special. Oh, everyone thought she was cool or spooky. Either way, they were fascinated by her and her blatant lies. I can't stand people who make shit up to get attention. I guess I can see why, though. She doesn't even count as cute, let alone pretty. Telling stories is the only way she can get anyone to look twice at her. If she knows what's good for her, she'll get a clue and take Jake before he loses interest. No other guy on the planet could swallow her bullshit and date her."

By this time, Greyson had shoved both hands under his butt to stop the shaking. This was the crap he'd taken the whole time he grew up. To hear it slung out at Flick made him mad enough to consider hitting a girl.

The teacher had given up trying to teach and had long since turned the class over to study time without trying to stop the blatant conversing. Kristin leaned her chin on one hand, elbow on the desk.

"So why is a date not going to happen? We seem to get along fine."

The bell rang, and Greyson stood, stuffing his notebook in his bag. Kristin stared, waiting.

"Because I happened to move into a flat next door to someone awesome. I'm kinda dating her."

Kristin trailed after him to the door. "Someone from our school? I can tell you if they're good enough or if you can do better. Well, of course, you can do better. *I'm* offering to date you."

Greyson had joined the stream of students and caught sight of Flick. A wicked tickle of vengeance sparked to life. He reached between people and grabbed Flick's wrist, pulling her over. With a glance behind him to be sure Kristin was still watching, he kissed her, taking an obvious lick at her lips as they broke apart.

"Are you acquainted with my neighbor?" he asked Kristin's back as she flounced off in a huff.

"What's gotten into you?" Flick asked him.

"Kristin was saying horrible things about you at the same time she was trying to get her hooks in me. It was an impulse to rub her nose in—"

"Greyson," Flick groaned. "How could you? The first place she's going to go if she wants to sharpen her claws is Jake. If she's miserable, he's easy to make miserable, too."

"Crap. I'm sorry. I wasn't thinking."

She waved him off to his next class. "I've got to find Jake and tell him about us before Kristin does. He'll be so hurt if the news comes from a source like her."

"Right. See you."

\*\*\*\*

Flick had to wave Jake out of his classroom. The whole way, his face carried hope, which made Flick feel worse. Thanks to all the chaos that day, no one stopped them. She took Jake back to the bathroom. Maybe she should call this place her office. She seemed to be having a lot of meetings here.

"Yes?" Jake asked, locking the door.

"I have something important I need to tell you, and it can't wait because mistakes were made, and, um, yeah."

His eyebrows knit together in the front. "Okay."

"Greyson and I are together," she blurted. Getting the words out had to be an all-or-nothing deal, and she couldn't afford to choke for his sake.

Everything about Jake withered before her eyes. "For real?"

She nodded.

"Why? When?"

"Yesterday. Do you need details on why? Because I don't want to hurt you."

"Sounds like you didn't need time to think, after all," he said, his voice heavy and bitter.

"And you pleaded with me rather than taking no for an answer. I don't think either of us handled your confession well." Her heart tightened. "I know it doesn't feel like it at the moment, but I care for you *so* much. I wanted you to hear my choice from me." She turned her head and stared at the floor. "Kristin was badmouthing me to Greyson, and he may have blabbed about the two of us to slap back at her. But she's petty enough to try hurting you with me."

"Then why haven't you said anything until it was

almost too late? Why wait for someone else to force the truth from you?"

"Don't be a brat, Jake. I'm not hiding things. Nothing happened between us until yesterday afternoon, okay? Last night was too busy when you were over, and when did I have time this morning? I would have liked a better place to talk this out than the bathroom. So in that respect, yes, Kristin forced my hand."

Jake slumped, leaning against the door. "I-I." A tear slipped down his cheek. "I feel like I'm losing you. More than just with Greyson. I can't be a part of your world anymore, and you're leaving me behind."

"Jake." Flick's heart cracked. "I'm sorry. I can't help any of it."

"You could have let me be your boyfriend. I'd have stayed at your back, even if I couldn't be at your side. Hell, I'd let an angel possess me if it meant I could stay with you."

Flick blinked back tears. "Don't say that, Jake. I don't want you by my side for this."

"I can tell. You'd rather trust a virtual stranger."

Her temple twitched. "I didn't mean I want to replace you," she snapped. "I don't want you or Marisol involved because I wouldn't wish what I see on anyone. Not even Kristin. It scares the hell out of me, and watching is worse than acting. But I don't want you at my side or my back. I want you safe. If I could go back, I never would have told you anything. And I mean way back, all the way to preschool. The remalas are that terrible."

"Whatever, Flick. I get it." He went to unlock the door.

She caught his arm. "I don't think you do."

The glare he gave her sent her tripping backward. He undid the lock.

"No matter how mad at me you are, don't let your guard down," she pleaded. "The remalas are preying on people who are upset. They're riding on people in the halls, and we can't even get rid of the small ones right now."

His cold expression broke her heart. "I told you before, I have the option of walking away from all of this. You've opened the door and pointed me out."

As if illustrating, he walked out of the bathroom without looking back.

Tears dripped down Flick's face.

"Trouble in paradise, Ms. Felicity?"

Flick wanted to dissolve into a puddle. Mr. Ostanes stood outside the door, arms crossed.

"You're supposed to be in class," he scolded, "and I find you closeted in here with the same boy? You really do like looking for trouble. You'd better break that habit before it bites you."

"Like last time," she muttered, "nothing was happening except a private conversation."

"Students can have private conversations on their own time. And don't get me started on your gross disrespect for the mood today. Your sordid little bathroom affairs, good or bad, can't wait while you at least pretend to have respect?"

She glowered up at him. "Things happen that we don't plan for. This was damage control, and it was important to me. Give me detention if you need to." Flick chewed the inside of her cheek. What had gotten into her? She was never so disrespectful to teachers. Ostanes brought out the worst in her.

"You're a bit feisty today. How about I grant your wish? You can spend your detention at lunch in my classroom with me. I have a little project you can work on to keep you out of trouble." He tucked his hands in his pockets and walked away, adding, "See you at lunch, or I'll turn this detention over to the principal. Calls will be made to parents, who I'm sure would like to know their daughter is skipping classes to lock herself away with boys."

Flick bared her teeth at his back. Everything about him pissed her off.

"*Flick?*" Kyrael asked. "*How are you doing? Having a close friend so mad at you can't be easy.*"

"I don't think I have a close friend anymore." She bit back a sob.

"*He's hurt. But if he's a good friend, he'll be back.*"

"How would you know? It's not the same for…your kind."

"*It isn't? Angels ebb and flow through friendships, albeit at a much slower pace. But I think my experience is applicable here. Look at everything your friendship has weathered to this point. He'll be back. Just make sure you don't close him off in the meantime.*"

"Thanks." She glanced down the hall. "I don't want to go to class. Wanna poke around?"

"*If you don't think it will get you in more trouble.*"

"I kinda don't care at the moment. We can't track this thing by its aura because it's damn near overwhelming. And with all the small remalas crawling around, I can't sort anything I feel. So how do we pin it down?"

"*That's the problem. We don't know because we've never done it before. Convenient for Serai to leave the most difficult task in the hands of amateurs. She'll come out looking the best at the end."*

Flick headed for the gym. Even if the bleachers were folded, she could still squeeze behind to find a space to think uninterrupted. The best part was she had to cross the whole campus to get there.

While she walked, Flick tried to focus on the swirling miasma engulfing the whole school. It still swirled too fast for her to pin anything down. Without students in the hall, she could see the small crawling things crowding the shadows. Compared to their bigger counterparts, they gave off more of a feeling of being spiders now, not pleasant, but not horrifying. However, the sheer quantity made Flick's skin crawl.

After several minutes of silence, Kyrael spoke inside her head again, *"I'm curious about something. These small remalas evolve into the larger ones, all the way to the contracted remala, but wouldn't it be reasonable to assume the small ones aren't unintelligent?"*

"I guess." Flick opened the doors to the gym.

*"Well, they must have some way to communicate. After seeing them all over the school like this, it's clear they're cooperating, or at least not stepping on one another's toes. Because small remalas can feed on one another to get larger."*

"Kyrael, make your point." She squeezed behind the bleachers, ignoring the things that looked like rotting crabs crawling up the wall at her back.

*"If we could find a way to monitor this communication, maybe they could lead us to the contracted remala."*

"Like police surveillance. That could work. But how

do we follow communication even your kind can't identify?" She didn't use the word angel in case anything might be listening. If small remalas could communicate, mentioning angels would be bad. And plenty of remalas were scuttling around under the bleachers to overhear.

"*That's where I was leading. My kind* can't." He sighed, and a ripple of warmth radiated through Flick's body. "*We got one other piece of important news, and Adriel hasn't yet shared it with you three.*"

Hurt panged Flick. "Why would Adriel keep something from us?"

"*Because it's a bit unpleasant. It's the reason the three of you can see the otherworldly. He didn't want you to be unhappy in any way. I'm sure he would have said, eventually. But it ties into my idea. Without modern medicine, you and the others would have died in the womb or shortly after.*"

"I know." Flick frowned. "Mom's always told me she had a rough pregnancy."

"*Not just a rough pregnancy, Flick. A mortally critical one. At some point, she must have despaired of you or her or both of you surviving. She had remalas feed on her while you were developing. Somehow, the energy from the remalas got tangled in the energy your new body was knitting together. Flick, you see them and us because you have traces of remala in your blood. It's left you straddling planes of existence.*"

"I-I what?" she gasped. Her whole body tingled, and the space around her head spun.

"*This is why Adriel didn't want to tell you. It's unpleasant. But you need to keep in mind this doesn't affect your soul or your afterlife.*"

"But." She glanced at a gecko covered in cactus

spines dripping something the color of dried blood and shivered. How could part of her be something so horrible?

"*Flick.*" Kyrael's voice was firm. "*This changes nothing. Heaven is not abandoning you because of it. On a physical level, you are the same as you were a moment ago and the same as you have always been. All that changed is your knowledge. Adriel and I sought this knowledge to help others like you. We had to know what caused your ability to track those like you, not for any other reason.*"

Hot tears filled her eyes, eyes that kept searching out the terrible things and imagining them as part of her.

"*I was wrong,*" Kyrael sighed, "*and I'm sorry. I shouldn't have told you. I meant to help find this remala and end the situation faster. You are the only individual I know who's ever heard the mid-to-low grade remalas talk. During your attack, remember? If there's something innate in their communication you happened to tap into that night, maybe you can use this deliberately, as well. But I should have come up with a different idea. I love you, Flick. Focus on that.*"

Flick shivered and wiped her eyes. "If I have kids, will I pass this mess on?"

"*We don't know. All we know is the three of you are the same, and we know the cause. We tested your blood in Heaven.*"

Her next breath was deep and fueled with a spark of determination. "So your idea is to see if I can connect with them? How?"

"*I don't know the method. It's just an idea. But you know animals have many communication methods humans can't use, right? For example, echolocation in bats and a shark's ability to sense the electrical fields of other living things. No one teaches them to use these senses to understand their world. It's possible if you find this part of you, some instinct could be unlocked. Who knows, maybe you've been using it all along, unaware of what you were doing?"*

"I think I would have noticed if I was communicating with evil spirits."

*"Unless you suppressed this early on. You were scared as a child. The human mind can protect itself by burying the unwanted."*

"Okay, let's pretend you're right. How do I even find this in myself? It's not like I can pay close attention and locate my spleen."

*"But it's not an organ,"* Kyrael countered. *"It's energy. How do you pinpoint a remala so you can avoid it?"*

"Wait, before I try this. You're inside me, and you destroy remalas. Am I in danger?"

He chuckled. *"How many times do I have to promise not to hurt you? Though, it's an understandable fear. But you already know the answer. I'm not remala poison. None of the angels are. The remalas flee because we're hunters. And since you're not a remala, I'm not going to hunt you. You're safe.*

"Right." Flick didn't acknowledge her lingering trepidation. "Here goes."

Chapter 19

Flick shut her eyes and tried to block out the miasma around her in favor of her own body. The first thing she found was her breathing, a little too fast and a bit too rough. Next, her heartbeat filled her senses. Each thud pushed her blood throughout her body—blood that carried traces of remala.

At this thought, her blood hummed with an energy she'd never noticed before, like being nervous, except she wasn't. Now that the energy had her attention, she could feel the slightest similarity to the force swirling around outside her. Next came the whispers. A rock settled in her gut. While she had no specific memory of the murmurs, she knew they were familiar and unwanted.

Flick wrapped her arms around herself and forced her head to allow the voices in. The noise grew and swirled. "Dark angel. Savior. Feast giver." The words beat down on her in a hushed cacophony, pushing in through the pores in her skin rather than her ears.

She gasped and resisted crying out. There were people at the other end of the gym in class. "I can hear it or feel it. The words are vibrations on my skin."

"*I know. I'm getting all the physical sensations your body is, remember? But my brain isn't wired to translate, so it sounds like crackling to me. Though, it makes sense for energy beings to communicate with energy waves. Interesting.*"

He continued to muse. "*Angels wouldn't be able to hear it because, outside a host, the remalas would flee or be destroyed. Inside your body, I was able to access your ears and now your skin, but I'm not privy to what your brain is doing, which is taking those signals and turning them into messages.*" He chuckled. "*It's a good thing I'm in here. I'm feeling rather squirmy and overexcited. In here, I can't bother anyone.*"

"You don't bother me," Flick said. "Not anymore. I even like the fidgety little kid side of you, in moderation. Now hush so I can eavesdrop."

The remalas continued to buzz about a savior, but none of them said who that was or where to find the savior. It was like listening to a parrot repeat its three favorite phrases.

The end bell rang, and Flick used the opportunity to leave the underside of the bleachers. She could walk around unnoticed for the next five minutes, then go to third period. Eavesdropping in the classroom would be as easy as anywhere else.

Halfway back to the main building, she bumped into Wade, who looked distressed. "What's up?" she asked.

He pulled her over to the wall behind a trash can. "It's so disturbing watching all these people getting preyed on and not being able to help. I'm struggling. Please tell me you found something so we can end this."

"Maybe." She glanced around. "But it's not something I can tell you here."

"Please," he begged. "I'm not accomplishing anything. I can't sit back and watch the carnage for three days until the cavalry arrives."

She clenched her teeth, knowing full well where this was taking her. Two minutes later, she shut the door to the bathroom. Hurrying, she told Wade about their tainted blood.

"I wondered if it might be something of the sort," he said.

"How?" she gasped.

"You don't watch enough science fiction." He grinned. "I take it you found a way to use this?"

She rushed the explanation of how, as well. There was no way she wanted to get caught in the bathroom with a guy twice in one day. Wade closed his eyes for a minute, then let out a whistle.

"Damn. You're right. I can hear them…in a manner of speaking." His eyes flew open, and he grabbed Flick, hugging her. "Thank you. Thank you. *Thank* you." He set her down and rubbed his head. "I was worried when I came back whether I'd be able to integrate into the team. You and Greyson get along so well. I felt like an outsider, like I'd missed my chance."

She drew a breath and let it slide out. "About that. Greyson and I are kinda involved. It's new and all. But if you're part of our team, you should know."

"Oh." He startled back a bit. "Well." He shook his head. "I'm glad. I didn't want you sitting around, hoping for something I might never be able to give you."

"But we're a team, not a couple. Or at least that's the way it should be. Don't let us make you feel like you're not needed because I can't tell you how many times I've wished you were back. Two of us are not enough. We *need* you. But a team also needs honesty, so I figured someone should say something, and since we have a private moment—"

"Felicity. You're babbling." Wade grinned.

"My close friends call me Flick, Teammate."

The warning bell rang. Wade unlocked the door and waited for her to exit into the scurry to reach class. He gave her a little salute.

"We'll compare notes at lunch."

Keeping an open channel to the traces of remala in her alleviated the stress the miasma pressed on her. She felt less suffocated. Unfortunately, the sensation was replaced with head-throbbing quantities of information, none of which seemed helpful. Over and over, the stupid things kept chanting about their feast giver. Knowing what feast the remalas were talking about sickened her, and knowing what feasts might be yet to come threatened to overwhelm her. She finally laid her head on her desk in her arms and tried to find a way to shut out the superfluous the way she could in a room crowded with humans.

When the bell rang at the end of third period, Flick left the classroom feeling ragged. However, she had learned to turn her remala sensing on and off. At the moment, she had it off to give herself a break from the nonstop adulation that led her nowhere.

Hopefully, she could control her temper while she did detention with Mr. Ostanes. He seemed to bring out the snippy side of her, and she didn't have the reserves of patience necessary for complete self-control.

Someone grabbed her arm from behind, and Flick tensed. "It's me," Jake whispered. His voice carried a strange edge.

Great. Just what she needed to deal with. Flick plastered a smile on and turned to face him. "Yes?"

"Mr. Ostanes told me you have detention with him now."

"Yeah. Getting caught with you in the bathroom a

second time didn't go over well."

"Tell me about it. The guy is relentless. I guess he has second period as a planning period. Anyway, he pulled me out of class to lecture me."

"Sorry about getting you in trouble."

Jake shook his head. "Listen a sec. He kept me for the rest of the period, and it wasn't for some impressive lecture. He spent it grilling me about you, and not in a 'what do you see in her' sort of way. It was more like, never get in a car with him." He gripped her arms. "Adriel said to tell you about anything weird. Well, that was weird."

"Ostanes asked you about things you can't see or religious stuff and me?"

Jake frowned, thinking. "Not so much. He did ask if you went to church. But even though it wasn't specific to the current, you know, situation, the conversation was bizarre. If nothing else, make sure you leave the classroom door open. Maybe he's nothing more than your run-of-the-mill pervert, but take precautions."

She patted his hands on her arms. "I'll be careful. Thanks for caring."

He let go of her and tipped his face away. "Of course I care."

She went for broke and gave him a firm but brief hug. "I care, too. Don't forget that part." She stuck her tongue out in disgust. "I guess it's time to go serve my sentence with Mr. Sketchy. Wade knows I've got detention, but will you do me a favor and make sure everyone else knows? I'll catch up with them at the bus stop afterward."

Jake nodded and left her to her detention.

The doorway to Mr. Ostanes' classroom looked like

it had been decorated for Halloween. Macabre creatures clung to the frame, milling about. They represented a mishmash of animal and human parts, studded with decay spots, mushrooms, maggots, and slime. The king of rot must be something to have drug these creatures out of hiding.

Flick walked under the grotesque arch without flinching because Mr. Ostanes watched her from his desk. Inside, his room seemed clear of the remalas, so the atmosphere provided a modicum of relief. He stood when she entered, and he grabbed a stack of papers and books off his desk.

"Ms. Felicity. I'm so glad you decided to follow the rules for a change. Take a seat." He pointed her to two desks he'd pushed together. She sat at one, and Mr. Ostanes sat across from her, setting his materials between them.

"You're going to help me sort these for my class's upcoming project. These are articles on various events in early American history. I'd like you to put them in chronological order, please. While you work on those, I'll flag other events in the books."

She took the stack of papers and read the first article's title. It was about the Salem witch trials. Flipping through the stack revealed they were all about the occult.

"What kind of project is this?" she asked.

"One I thought might tie into Halloween. Students get restless around holidays. This will give them a related outlet. We'll be discussing myth and folklore and how it's influenced the culture of Americans."

He stuck a sticky note to a page and pointed to her stack. "It's not getting any smaller." Flipping to another page, he said, "I find it all fascinating. Freshman history focuses on American history, but the story of Halloween doesn't stop there. Humans have been enthralled with what's beyond our existence for the duration of recorded history. Geographical location, culture, none of it seems to change the resulting legends much. Though, the same can be said for themes in storytelling. For example, humans overcoming nature or outwitting the trickster."

"Mmm." Flick shuffled a few papers. "Can I borrow sticky notes? If I post the event date at the top in bold, it'll be easier to sort."

"By all means." He pushed the stack of sticky notes toward her. "What do you think?"

"About?"

"Are these themes some intrinsic part of the human psyche, or are we passing on the same ideas over and over with each generation modifying the theme to fit their taste?"

"I don't know. I never thought about it."

He tagged another page. "Exactly. I want my students to expand their thinking, extrapolate, and not just be told how the world is. So we'll do it with a Halloween theme. They'll believe they're having fun, and I'll challenge their brains."

She wrote dates on several of the notes and stacked the papers in order. "Don't you think there are too many events here? It's a lot of material to cover."

"We'll be looking at each briefly. But you can't find a pattern until you have enough data to see the bigger picture. Do you see the bigger picture?"

She bit back a flash of irritation. Jake was right. Mr. Ostanes asked weird questions. "Concerning what?"

"Life. For example, is what you see all you get? Or

is there more to this world?"

Flick's skin prickled with heightened alertness. If he could see what was going on and suspected she could too, was he trying to connect with her? Or was this some sort of eccentricity? Or…could he be…

She glanced up at him. Mr. Ostanes studied a page in his book. Nothing about him looked weird or grotesque. He had skin with a light tan, dark brown hair, and a hint of afternoon stubble. He was completely ordinary.

"There might be more," Flick answered. "Isn't that what religions have been about since the beginning?"

"Are you religious?" His gaze snapped up to her.

"Not so much."

"Then do you believe in the existence of the sacred and the profane, at least?" He marked a page as if the question he asked had no meaning. And in any other situation, it might not have. But Flick couldn't let the coincidence go.

She poked at the traces of remala in her, allowing it to awaken. The energy gave a momentary low hum before crackling to life like high-voltage lines. Traces contained inside her body slammed against her skin, trying to get out and join with Ostanes.

The pull aimed his direction, but more so, her ties carried an absolute conviction Ostanes was the savior, and she'd beaten out the hordes in getting close to him. All she had to do was finish connecting, and she, too, could have a seat at the final feast. Or, if she pleased him and the demon he hosted, she might host one herself.

The knowledge of what she'd uncovered threatened to paralyze her, and she slammed the connection closed by ordering the energy to be dormant again. Sweat beaded out across her top lip, and she crossed her legs to keep from wetting herself.

She was alone in a room with a host and a demon.

"Felicity?" Mr. Ostanes eyed her.

She wanted to scream. How could something so average-looking be so evil? Forcing calm on herself, she gave him a bland smile. "Yes?"

"You spaced out on me there for a moment. Everything all right? I know the last few days have been traumatic, though you seem to be coping well enough. At least you don't seem consumed by the negative."

The urge to vomit tickled the back of her throat. "I was at home, sick, two days ago, so I'm not as bad off."

"Ah." He shuffled through to a new stack of papers.

Sitting still and answering his questions took a monumental effort. But Flick had already resolved to be a worthy partner for Kyrael. Somehow, she managed to slog through lunch to the warning bell.

"Leave the papers there," Mr. Ostanes instructed. "I'll tidy them up. You leave campus now, right?"

"For the community college." She tucked her hands in her pockets to stop them from trembling.

"Excellent." He'd pressed his fingers together, and a strange gleam entered his eyes.

Flick hurried from the classroom before he could do anything else weird or sinister. She waited until she was a whole hallway away from his classroom before speaking to Kyrael.

"Oh my God. That's him. That's the—"

"*I know,*" Kyrael answered. "*I felt your blood react, which was unsettling, to say the least.*"

"He knows," Flick murmured. "I don't know how much he knows, but he's obviously suspicious."

*"I think it's a safe assumption he knows you see things other humans don't. But I don't get the impression he knows you dally with angels. He didn't seem either on guard or defensive enough to know that part."*

Greyson and Wade waited for her at the bottom of the front steps. One look at her had Greyson uptight and stepping in her direction. She waved for him to stay silent.

"On the bus," she shushed them both.

\*\*\*\*

Greyson settled himself on one side of Flick while Wade took the seat on the other side of her. She leaned forward, bracing her elbows on her knees, head down, breaths shuddering. Neither he nor Wade said anything, but Wade had to be thinking the same thing he was. Flick had found the contracted remala.

She held her silence for one full stop before lifting her head. "Mr. Ostanes is the contracted remala."

"Are you sure?" Adriel asked with Greyson's lips. Greyson was getting used to sharing and the little nudges, which indicated the angel's desire to control some part of him.

"Did Wade tell you about using our blood to feel the conversation of the remalas while you were waiting for me?" she asked.

"In theory. I didn't get a chance to try it out."

"Well, I tapped into the remala connection while I was doing detention." She rubbed her face with both hands. "I could hear, or sense, or understand a pull to him. Intrinsically, I knew *he* was the savior they were all talking about. He'd done something so none of the remalas could get inside his classroom, but the energy in my blood was thrilled to have bypassed this. It wanted to join with him and get some of the glory. Or to get his attention and have him recommend me to the demons. I think the lower-grade remalas are smarter than Heaven has been giving them credit for, and I don't think it takes much energy to tap into their consciousness. It came way easier than I want to admit."

"Tapping in *was* easy," Wade agreed. "And they spent a lot of time whispering about the savior. Weird to think he's a teacher. What does that say about our education system? They're hiring servants of Hell to educate the next generation."

Greyson barked a laugh. "I think old people would say they've known that for a long time."

Wade snickered along with him.

"What do we do now?" Flick asked no one in particular, meaning her question was directed at the angels.

Adriel spoke through Greyson. "I need you three to stick together. Let's return to Greyson's apartment, and I'll contact Serai. Hopefully, her ladies are ready to go."

"I'm going to be a bit later," Wade explained to Greyson and Adriel. "Since I don't know how long this will take, I want to run back to my place and bring a few changes of clothes. Then we can all be headquartered at Greyson's, and I'll still have fresh boxers."

Greyson nodded. "Adriel says that's fine. Since Serai's unit hasn't done their investigation, he figures you'll have at least an hour or two before she starts throwing out orders for our team."

At the bus stop by their building, Greyson and Flick said goodbye to Wade, who took Niciel to a private spot so they could disappear for his house. Greyson reached for Flick's hand, slipping his fingers through hers. He contented himself with caressing her hand until the elevator doors shut. Then he kissed her, tripping them both into the handrail at the back.

Flick put her hands in his jeans pockets, pulling him as close as their clothing allowed. When his hips met hers, excitement pulsed through him, and Adriel toppled from his body, stumbling across the elevator. Kyrael appeared, scuttling back from them both.

Greyson swallowed his irritation at the interruption. It didn't matter much because the doors slid open, and the two angels fled to the fourth floor without waiting for the humans. Greyson kept Flick's hand, and she followed so close she threatened to trip him.

"What?" he snapped at the two staring angels. He pulled out his key and strode to his door, Flick following along.

"Remember, we, uh, we can feel all your body's physiological responses," Adriel said, staring at the ceiling. "You had a, um, swift and strong response. Could you please refrain? At least while we're sharing bodies?"

Flick's hands covered her mouth, her eyes wide. "That's right. You feel what I feel. So you could feel Greyson's, you know…"

Kyrael took the key from Greyson and unlocked the door. "I'll be watching television in the guest room. Human life just got way too real. But I sympathize with your friends and family a little better. There's a huge difference between knowing something and experiencing it for yourself." He hurried across the apartment and disappeared.

Adriel followed right behind him.

Greyson waited until the guestroom door shut and

sighed. "Well, that was embarrassing."

"Just a bit," Flick whispered, blushing.

Greyson tipped her face up with a finger under her chin. He gave her a soft, lingering kiss. "How long before your afternoon classes?"

"My professors emailed me. Thanks to the school shooting, I can take all the time I need out of class as long as I turn my assignments in online."

Greyson kissed her again, closing his eyes. "However shall we kill time?" He slid his hand across the skin of her waist beneath her shirt and above her pants. The mood the angels had killed came rushing back.

She sucked in a sharp breath and leaned toward him so they touched from the shoulders to the hips. With his fingertips, he traced the line of smooth skin that marked her spine. He paused when he reached her bra, then fumbled with the clasp. The next sweep of his fingers took them under the silky fabric and to the tip. She flinched when he tweaked, and he pulled back, but Flick leaned into his hand.

"Flick," he murmured between kisses. "If you need me to stop, tell me."

"Mmm," she mumbled.

She didn't stop him when he slid her shirt over her head, nor when he kissed down her collarbone and moved lower. She didn't say no when he took her breast in his mouth or when he slid his hand down the front of her jeans. He struggled to keep enough willpower to halt himself should she ask, the whole while praying she wouldn't.

He locked the front door between kisses and took her around her waist, guiding her to the bedroom. Too many people came and went at random for them to continue out in the open. Besides, this was her first time. He needed to take his time to be gentle with her body. She should enjoy herself. Assuming she let things go that far, he chastised himself. Though, holding onto the possibility of not having sex was getting difficult.

Flick was willing and trusting in the bedroom, letting him kiss and caress everywhere and tentatively returned the touches. Her innocent trust put an even deeper burden on him. If he hurt her, the angels wouldn't have to punish him. He'd be plenty disappointed in himself. Taking the lead meant not only did he have to get her to climax because she deserved that, but he had to care for both their health and futures.

So he dug deep for the willpower to spend a great deal of time on her. When she didn't bat an eye at him putting on a condom, he knew he had the green light. Now, to make sure she finished with him.

By the time he had her pleading for him to go all the way, he barely held himself together. His first movement inside caused her to cry out, and he pulled away. That wasn't pleasure in her tone.

"Are you good?" he panted.

Flick bit her lower lip and nodded. He'd needed the disruption anyway. It doused him in figurative cold water. When he moved into her again, he went slower. After one more sharp intake of breath, Flick relaxed, melting into their rhythm.

She gave a shuddering sigh, constricting every grip on his body. In response, he let go of everything he'd held back. After several moments of mutual release, he dropped to the bed beside her, kissing her face and neck.

"You're happy?" he murmured. "Satisfied?"

She drew three long breaths. With each, she ran her fingers across the muscles of his chest. "That was...*wow*." She gripped her forehead.

He grinned. "I'll take wow."

She grabbed the back of his neck, kissing him hard. "I think I get what all the fuss is about. I'm also glad you were my first. I don't think Liam would have been so"—she wrinkled her nose in thought—"attentive."

He traced all the bare curves of her body. "As long as you're happy, I'm happy." The flush of new romance clung to him, permeating the air between them until everything crackled. The once-upon-a-time when he'd convinced himself Whitley was "the one" paled compared to this. She'd been sparkling cider, and Flick was champagne.

Chapter 20

Adriel knocked on Greyson's door and entered without being invited, shutting the door behind him. "You might want to consider a top," he advised Flick. "Serai returned with Wade and Niciel. She has a request for you." He rubbed his face, fidgeting. "I want to say right now I disagree with her. And no matter how bossy she gets, you are free to refuse. It's not a request she can carry out without your help."

"What does she want?" Flick asked while snapping her bra back on. She had her back to him, her neck very red.

"She wants you to ask Jake to carry her into the school."

Greyson made a bit of a growl, and Flick spun, appalled.

"No." Flick yanked her shirt over her head and scrambled off the bed. "Absolutely not. Jake can't see what he's getting into. Greyson, Wade, and I are already vulnerable enough. I mean, I saw what came after me in the bathtub and still barely got away."

Adriel shrugged. "This is why I said the choice is yours. Tell Serai to stuff it. Maybe she'll listen to you. I tried and stopped arguing before I lost my temper inside Greyson's apartment."

"Thanks for that," Greyson muttered. He stood, retucking his shirt.

Flick marched out the bedroom door, and Adriel trailed after, trying to cram back a smirk. Serai might have met her match in Flick. The girl did need angelic assistance to take down remalas, but the guts to do the job were all her own. And she had a trump card Serai couldn't override. Free will. Actually, two trump cards because Serai couldn't interact with humans without the help of Flick, Greyson, or Wade. The stubborn and bossy Power would discover this relationship with the humans wasn't as one-sided as she thought.

"*You what?*" Flick shrieked.

Wade held up both hands in surrender. "Sorry. I didn't realize you'd have a problem with me using your phone."

"Use my phone all you want," she snarled. "But don't throw my friends into the middle of a battle when they're blind."

"Serai says he'll be fine," Wade soothed.

"Right. Serai has the compassion of a piranha. She's a calculating, battle-hardened angel, and she wants to use my friend as a *tool*." She spun around on Serai, furious. "Did you consider the fact that hosting angels has further altered us? The thing that attacked me was drawn to the residual power you leave behind. I saw it coming, but if you alter Jake, how's he supposed to cope when you leave? It's not all about this one moment. Think ahead a little."

Serai's expression turned cold and haughty. "I do think ahead, little human girl. I think ahead to the survival of your species, to the balance of positive and negative on the cosmic scale. Try considering the good of the many before nagging me."

The doorbell rang, and Flick tore across the house to

beat everyone else there. She blocked Jake from entering, shoving herself into him and out into the hall. Adriel glared all the others down and followed her, slipping through the crack of the closing door.

"Jake." Flick's voice broke. "Whatever Wade said to get you here, forget it and go home."

"He said you needed help, a volunteer to host one more angel." Jake's face was pale and clammy but resolved. "I want to do this. I told you I'd have your back in any way I could. I paid attention for the rest of the day. After the weird lecture by Mr. Ostanes, I got close when passing him in the hall to see if anything felt off."

He shuddered. "If Adriel hadn't written about warm spots, I might have assumed I passed him under one of the heat vents. I got a gust of scorching air on his way past. No vents. Then the message from Wade on your phone. Ostanes is the thing, isn't he?"

Flick nodded. "Jake, you need to understand. Something about hosting the angels makes us appealing to the remalas. It's what drew them to attack me in the tub. What if the same happens to you? You won't be able to see what's trying to consume you. Tell Serai no. You said you could walk away and be blind to all this. Do that. *Please*."

She was begging, tears in her eyes. Adriel placed a hand on her shoulder, and she turned her head, rubbing her cheek against his hand, a cheek damp with tears.

Jake reached for the spot, his hand stopping on top of Adriel's. Jake flexed his fingers. Though Jake couldn't see the angel, Adriel could see and feel Jake's fingers running the back of his hand.

"There's warmth on your shoulder. I can feel it even though I'm not touching you. It's different from the hotspot by Mr. Ostanes."

Flick's laugh quavered. "That's because you're playing handsies with Adriel."

"Oh." Jake jerked his hand back. "I thought maybe one of them was close since you rubbed your face on nothing."

"Adriel's trying to make me feel better. He agrees with me and thinks you're better off walking away."

Jake nodded, taking his time before speaking. "I think I'd like to ask Serai a few questions. I hear your concerns. Do you hear me when I say I want to help?"

"I guess," she whispered.

He patted the top of her head. "Don't worry so much about me. I'm not going to rush into danger, but you can't keep me in a padded bubble either." He sighed and tucked his hands in his pockets. "I was wrong, you know, about being able to walk away. Just because I can't see them doesn't mean I can unknow what I know. Trying to pretend set my skin crawling because my imagination ran away with me."

He gave a whole-body sigh that left him an inch shorter. "Asking Serai for more details is only half about having your back. I have it, but being involved with Serai would also benefit me. If I know this creature is gone, maybe I can relax and forget enough to enjoy the rest of the year. And when I say knowing the remala is gone, I mean like knowing the creatures and the angels are real. If I want to move on, I need to see the proof of this being over with my own eyes."

"I want to argue with your logic, but I can't," Flick conceded. "If you need to see whatever proof you can, then do what you have to do."

She opened the door to the apartment and waited for

Jake to go in before following. Adriel closed the door as the last one through. He, too, couldn't argue Jake's points. Though he had the nagging feeling if anything went wrong with Jake, he'd be the one left to fix things.

Flick had been spot-on about Serai seeing the humans as tools. But Flick hadn't carried Serai's thinking far enough. Greyson, Wade, and Flick were all tools, too. Serai didn't care about them as Kyrael, Niciel, and he did. While Jake didn't hold the same special place in Adriel's heart, he still wouldn't leave the boy to be preyed on by smaller remalas.

Flick gathered up the paper, a pen, Serai, and Jake. "There, ask your questions, Jake. Serai can write her answers for you to see."

Serai picked up the pen, a distinct look of irritation on her face. "Hurry up and ask, human."

"What do I have to do besides carry you around inside my body?" Jake asked.

Serai wrote, *I need to confirm this teacher is indeed the contracted remala. None of the other angels here has ever encountered one. I'll call in my unit once I'm sure we've got an exact location on the entity. All you and Felicity need is to use your rapport with this individual as a teacher to keep him in one place until my team arrives.*

"What happens if what Flick says is true and hosting you makes remalas want to eat me."

*I don't have a contingency plan for this scenario.*

"But you won't let things nibble on him for the rest of his life, right?" Flick demanded.

Serai wore a noncommittal look, but Jake couldn't see it.

Adriel snatched the pen and wrote, *If Serai doesn't*

*see you cared for, I will. (Adriel) But I'm not going to cast plans at random. I'd have to wait and see what effects there are, if any, and then deal with that reality. Just know you won't be abandoned.*

"Fair enough," Jake said. "So how does possession work? Will the cranky angel be running my mouth off at random people?"

Adriel laughed in Serai's direction before writing, *Serai will ride along like a virus.* He snickered. *Or a fungal spore. You won't notice her much at all. But unlike a virus, at no point will she be able to try taking over your body. You have to give permission for her to control any one part of you or all. However you want to divide it out.*

*Greyson once put it succinctly, saying that if he permitted me to defecate with his body, it would be the only function besides riding along I'd be able to perform. Though, I decline such an offer.*

"Huh." Jake huffed a laugh. "So...do angels crap?"

*No. We generate our own energy, like a star. It's a very efficient process with zero waste. You don't see star turds floating around space, do you?*

"I don't?" Jake asked. "I suppose if science knew what I know, questions might be asked and alternate possibilities considered. For example, is our solar system's asteroid belt the debris field for an unformed planet? Or is it actually the sun's litter box?"

Adriel, Kyrael, and Niciel burst out laughing.

Flick giggled and filled Jake in. "They must find the idea hilarious because all three angels are doubled over. Not Serai, so much."

Jake let out a wistful sigh. "I am kinda sad I don't get to see this part."

"Me, too," Flick agreed. "I like the angels."

"I hope you're not offended, Flick, but I'm going to let Serai ride with me."

Flick reached out and squeezed his arm. "I already knew. Hopefully, this all turns out okay."

**\*\*\*\***

Flick tossed and turned, unable to sleep. Her alarm clock blared 2:13 in blue numbers. For the past four hours, she'd tried every conceivable trick to empty her mind and sleep but hadn't succeeded. Tired of suffering alone, she got out of bed and rummaged in the folds of her curtains until she could cup her hands around the glowing ball of Kyrael.

Drawing this over to the bed, she lay back down, snuggling the ball under her chin. With soft whispers like fresh laundry in a warm breeze, he unfolded until it was her head tucked under his chin.

"You won't sleep with my light in your face," he whispered.

"I'm not sleeping anyway."

He wrapped his arms around her and cradled her against his chest. "Don't fret about tomorrow. Worrying won't solve anything. Focus on my promise to protect you."

She pressed her face to the base of his neck, trying to draw comfort into her core. "I know. But fear is stupid that way. It gets at you even when you're sure you're safe."

He kissed her forehead, and from the spot where his lips touched her skin, spread a deep heat like being wrapped in a soft blanket on a winter day. The sensation didn't stay confined to her skin but soaked into her, smoothing across her agitated heart, coating and comforting.

The next thing Flick registered was her alarm on her phone chiming. She stretched, feeling far more rested than her short night should have allowed for. Whatever Kyrael had done was nothing short of a blessing.

Her clothes lay across the back of her desk chair where she'd laid them last night. She'd slept through ten minutes of her alarm and used up all the extra time she'd left for herself. Flick hurried to dress and made for the kitchen. A steaming bowl of oatmeal topped with sliced figs and melting crumbles of brown sugar stood on the counter.

Kyrael must have done this since her parents would have left for work almost an hour ago. But she didn't see Kyrael anywhere, and she didn't feel him inside her. Trepidation set in. The last time she'd been alone in her apartment, the remala had attacked from the tub.

Something thumped, and the door to the spare bedroom opened. Kyrael walked out, looking nothing like the angel she knew. Instead of pants and a shirt in a very human fashion, he wore a kilted tunic with a breastplate of shining metal scales. He finished preening the feathers on his right wing, let it snap back into place, then looked up at Flick.

"What do you think? Do I look like a warrior angel?" He made a face and picked at the kilt. "Personally, I think it's a bit archaic."

Flick gaped, eyes wide. Each metal scale zipped with the electric power he used as a weapon. The only thing about him that looked safe was his friendly smile. Was she supposed to let him ride around in her, looking like a fresco of an avenging angel?

She trembled through her response. "Y-you

look…terrifying."

"Sorry about that. Serai said we need to be armed already. The milliseconds it takes to both exit your body and pull up weapons was too much of an advantage for a remala. By being armed already, we cut the lag time in half. You won't feel the difference carrying us." He pointed at her bowl. "I made you breakfast."

"Thank you," she murmured, sinking into her seat.

"Are you going to be all right?" he asked, glancing at the spoon she hadn't touched. "You need your strength, and we have to meet the others in ten minutes."

Tears stung Flick's eyes. "I'm so tired of reality shifting beneath my feet. Every time I feel like I know my world and I've adjusted, it changes."

"How do you mean?"

She waved a hand in Kyrael's direction. "Look at you. A couple of weeks ago, I had no idea angels were real. Then you were, but you were mostly carefree. Then you took on the remalas around me and became a source of peace. That turned into being friends. But now you look like a figure from a legend and all, I don't know, badass."

Her next breath caught, then hissed out in ragged whispers. "Do you realize we're going to be trying to kill the host of a demon today? A *demon*." She pointed at his armor. "I thought I understood. But seeing this, you, it's sinking in for real. That's what I meant about reality shifting. How could I not comprehend this yesterday?"

Kyrael caught her chin, tipping her face so she stared into his violet eyes. "Yes. This is deadly serious not just for us but for countless people on Earth. Remember, Heaven trusts you can do this. *I* believe in you. You might be scared by this transformation in me, but this is because of you and your strength."

"I didn't want you to be all…" her shoulders flopped through a shrug, "battle-ready."

He leaned closer so his breath brushed across her cheeks when he spoke. It drew up images of summer breezes. "When I first met you, I was lost, adrift in my reality. You took an angel who drove others away, calmed him down, and gave him purpose. The magnitude is still lost to you because I don't know how to show you the impact in a way you can grasp. But it's even more significant in the grand scheme than facing a mere demon."

Words escaped Flick. She was sinking into the purple of Kyrael's eyes. In their depths was so much he seemed to want her to understand, yet she simply couldn't comprehend it.

"And if you doubt your bravery," he continued, "remember you stepped into the middle of a fight between the two most feared angels in the lower six choirs. Serai still sets me trembling when she's irritated, and you grabbed her and scolded her. If you can shove Serai around, you can face a remala hosting a demon."

Flick trembled. "I want to believe you. I mean, I do. But trust doesn't stop my stomach from buzzing, my nerves from humming, and fears from gnawing at the back of my mind."

He tipped his face so their foreheads rested on one another. "How can the human mind cheat you so badly?" he lamented. "How is it not enough that an angel, no, all of Heaven, trusts you with this task?"

Flick burst into tears, and Kyrael jerked back.

"Now what?"

"I'm disappointing an angel," she sobbed. "I can

hear in your voice you're sad, and I'm the one doing it."

He gathered her in his arms and wrapped his wings around her. The brush of his glorious feathers across her face paused the tears. Shame wormed in. Some partner she was turning out to be. All the time she'd spent hardening her resolve to rise to his level was crumbling beneath her feet, and she had no idea how to get it back.

Kyrael glanced at the clock. "We've got four minutes until we need to leave. How do we find the brave Flick I'm so used to?" He snapped his fingers. "I have an idea." Grabbing her shoulder, he pulled her from the chair and guided her down the hall toward her bedroom.

What he had in mind, Flick couldn't guess. But she hoped it worked. They were down to the wire, and she was still failing him.

He stopped her in front of her full-length mirror and stood behind her, all glittering and hard. "On the internet, they say the clothes make the man, and so I would assume the woman. If your confidence is faltering inside, let's bolster it from the outside."

He tapped her shoulder, and her jeans and sweater disappeared, replaced with a tunic and armor that matched his. Flick gasped and staggered back, running into Kyrael and making their armor clink.

"This is what Serai is wearing."

Flick snapped her mouth shut and shook her head. "I can't wear this to school."

"I know. So let's try something more human."

He tapped her shoulder again. Her outfit morphed. Flick gawked at this transformation, perhaps even more astounded than with the angelic armor. She looked like a femme fatale. He'd put her in leggings with a black-on-black snake print. Her form-fitting black t-shirt had a metallic shimmer, and he'd topped it all off with a black leather moto jacket. She wiggled her toes inside pliable, black leather shoes that felt like wearing air.

"I look like a secret agent," she said with a giggle.

"And we've successfully redirected your attention." Kyrael nudged her along, transforming her bowl of oatmeal into a breakfast bar on their way past.

"I didn't know your powers worked like this," Flick said, taking a bite of her breakfast.

Kyrael locked the door to her apartment behind them. "How do you think I get dressed?"

The door to Greyson's apartment opened, and Wade stepped into the hall, followed by Greyson. Their angels must have already been riding along because Greyson locked the door.

Wade raised a hand in greeting, stopping halfway through, "Good mor—" His eyes went wide. "Holy Hell."

"What?" Greyson asked, turning around. He froze mid-spin.

Flick glanced over at Kyrael. "He said Serai wanted all the angels dressed this way to start. Didn't Niciel and Adriel wear their armor?"

Greyson's mouth moved without speaking.

"We saw the angels," Wade said. "But you look…" Air huffed from him.

Flick tilted her head, glancing at Greyson. He blushed and turned back toward the door, readjusting his jeans.

"It's stupid, isn't it?" Flick drooped. "Kyrael thought maybe—"

"She was having a crisis of confidence," Kyrael finished. "I thought if I gave Flick an outfit to match her intended mood, she might be more secure. But I could change the clothing if I failed to make her look strong."

"No need." Wade shook his head, then strode to the elevator, pushing the button. "Though, she's going to call attention at school."

"Do I look too goth with all the black?" Flick fretted, following him to the elevator.

"You look like a dirty fantasy," Wade muttered, turning away from her. "It's, uh, *hot*."

She laughed. "I'm not that type."

"Dressed up in those clothes, you are." Wade rubbed the back of his neck. "Fate sucks."

The elevator doors slid open, and he hurried inside. Flick went after him, and Greyson followed, sliding his jacket off and hanging it from his arms so it dangled down in front of his waist.

"Aren't you going to get cold?" Flick asked.

"Leave it," he ordered.

The elevator doors opened again, flooding the interior with outdoor light from the lobby windows—this illuminated Greyson's crimson face.

Wade huffed on his way past Greyson out of the elevator. "Lucky bastard."

"I'm so lost," Flick grumbled, following Greyson into the lobby.

Kyrael chuckled. "It's better that way." He held up his hand. "Ready?"

She drew a deep breath of warm air from the lobby laced with cold air from the outer door Wade had opened, then reached for Kyrael's hand, touching him so they could meld. True to his word, she couldn't feel anything different because he was armed, just the usual warmth spreading inside her ribs.

Flick sat between the two young men on the way to school. Everyone seemed to be staring. Then again, she accompanied two handsome guys. If she were a third party, she'd stare at them, too.

To her disappointment, Greyson refused to touch her, even drawing his hand away when she tried to take his. Maybe he didn't want to make Wade uncomfortable, but there were half a dozen reasons she'd like to hold his hand at the moment, which had nothing to do with anything romantic.

Instead, she turned to Wade. He always seemed ready to carry on a conversation, at least. "Did you sleep all right last night?"

"Good enough. You?"

"Kyrael did something to knock me out halfway through the night," she admitted. The bus was packed, and the subject matter toed the line.

"I had the same thing happen a couple of times when I left you guys. It's nice, but he said it's not something I should rely on."

"I suppose natural sleep is better. Where did you go while you were gone?"

"All over the place." Wade frowned. "Before you start getting curious, that was a deeply personal journey I'm not ready to share."

"But who would understand better than me? Or Greyson?"

"I've given Greyson enough," he mumbled. Louder, he said, "I know about the incident in the bathroom. Did you feel like discussing those details with me?"

Flick shook her head. "I don't even discuss that with Greyson, and he was there."

"Right. Some things are too personal, even for those

who know our truth. But I know where to find you if I ever change my mind. The same goes for you. You're always free to lean on me if you need to."

"Thanks, Wade."

"Hey, I mentioned this to Greyson already, but thanks for taking me back, no questions asked."

"There's only three of us. If we can't forgive and accept one another, we'd be in for a difficult and lonely life."

"Man, you're smart. Sometimes it's hard to remember you're a high schooler."

She made a face at him. "Big talk from someone just a few months older than me."

The bus pulled to a stop, and they stood to get off, Greyson tugging his jacket back on. Through the windows, Flick could see Jake standing in the circle of light cast by the streetlamp. His hands were in his pockets, and he shifted from foot to foot.

He'd spent the night at his place with Serai. But unlike Flick's night with Kyrael, there wasn't much Jake could do but converse with her on paper. So he couldn't have drawn much comfort from her presence. Then again, knowing she was lurking in the room would be like keeping a pet tiger—great, unless she turned on you, and God only knew what move would set her off.

The three from the bus joined Jake in the circle of light. His eyes widened as he looked Flick over from head to toe.

"Damn. Did you wake up this morning and decide to torture every male you encounter?"

"Torture?"

"You look so hot it's pretty much indecent. And it's hella distracting." He blushed and rubbed the back of his neck. "And since you're kinda involved, yeah, it's torture. Anyhoo," he sighed, glancing around, "hosting is the freakiest shit. I can hear Serai. Inside my head. It's like thoughts but in someone else's voice."

"We can all hear them when they're riding along," Flick explained.

"There've been a few times when I thought I heard or saw... But this is something else." Jake shivered. "And she's all hot in my chest, like drinking coffee too fast."

"Adriel says on occasion regular people catch glimpses of angels," Greyson said. "That's how you get the stories of people who thought they saw them. They did most of the time. Whatever you think you saw or heard was probably them."

"I'm glad he can hear her," Wade said. "Otherwise, communicating and coordinating with Serai would have been difficult."

"Serai says it's because she's now connected to my body. Fuck, wouldn't that be nice? Getting with an angel. Is she hot?"

Greyson scowled at him, then spoke in Adriel's accent-free voice. "Not advisable. The only angels who ever tried intimacy with humans are in Hell. As for her attractiveness, she's got the cold beauty of a black hole, and she's just as deadly."

Jake let out a gasp. "She said that's rich coming from the Executioner. What does she mean by Executioner?" The color drained from his face. "Holy fuck. You killed everyone during the bubonic plague? Pompeii? The Titanic?"

Adriel soured at the sight of the expression on Jake's face. "Serai, focus," he snapped. "You're not helping the boy through his job."

Jake backed away from Greyson. "Then it's true? Did you all know this?" He cast glances around the group.

"I didn't," Wade said. "But it doesn't matter. Niciel says Adriel's on vacation and off-duty when it comes to reaping human souls. He also says we need to get moving."

Jake nodded, stepping back toward the others. "Serai, too. She wants to confirm and get this creature destroyed first thing…before it has a chance to get suspicious and flee. Her unit is waiting around the city, ready as soon as we call. She wants me to remind you as soon as her team is called, you need to step back, or she can't guarantee the safety of the humans, I mean, of Flick, Wade, Greyson, and me. She's sure her team can take the creature down. You three angels just have to keep us four humans safe from any fallout."

Flick grabbed Jake and gave him a long hug. She moved to Wade next, hugging him, too. When she got to Greyson, she wrapped her arms around his neck and used the hug to pull him close enough to kiss.

"I'm glad I have you guys. Thanks for being awesome."

What followed was a silent walk toward the school. This time, when they crossed the road and stepped to the corner where the field started, the waves of negative energy sent Flick's body reeling. She gasped and clutched her head.

As if taking a cue from her reaction, a manicured hand reached from Jake's chest, then disappeared. Jake held up a hand, panting and massaging his ribs with the free hand.

"That might have been the most disturbing thing I've ever felt," he snapped, but clearly to himself. "At least warn me if you're going to be exiting and entering my body like a horror movie." He gave a put-out sigh. "Fine. But you can only use my mouth to speak."

"The aura is a contracted remala, no question," he said with Serai's speech pattern. "And one of the strongest I've encountered in a long time. Though, I think we can safely proceed with the plan. My unit ought to be enough to combat this evil. Felicity, you and Jake get the remala to a location where you can keep him until my unit arrives. Greyson and Wade, you two stay nearby in case Felicity and Jake need help."

"Let's do this," Adriel ordered through Greyson.

Chapter 21

Greyson fought back growing nausea. The miasma at Flick's school was thick and lumpy today, like bad gravy. It left a sour taste—the sort which precedes vomiting—in his mouth, puckering his cheeks.

He'd spent every moment from the time he left his flat until they'd crossed to the playfield fighting back dirty thoughts of Flick. The outfit Kyrael had dressed her in made her look like an action heroine or a spy. The looks of open desire on Jake's and even Wade's faces hadn't escaped his notice either. This had added a measure of pride to his thoughts. He'd been the one lucky enough to grab and hold her affection.

But once they'd crossed into the miasma, he couldn't distract himself anymore, not even with Flick and her naughty curves. Nervous sweat coated the palms of his hands, leading him to dodge Flick's attempts to hold his hand. If she'd been so scared, Kyrael had dressed her to kill, he didn't want her to feel his fear and make it her own.

Somehow, the distance to the school had doubled and yet wasn't anywhere near far enough. Long before he felt ready, they mounted the steps to the school. The walk had been silent, augmented by the fact that Flick had ordered Marisol to stay home for her safety. At least the girl had listened. The angels already seemed resigned to the possibility of collateral damage. Despite not getting along with Marisol, if she were hurt, Flick would be sad. Greyson would do almost anything to keep Flick from being upset.

Inside the door, Flick gripped Jake's wrist hard enough her knuckles turned white. "Let's head for his classroom."

Greyson grabbed Flick's shoulder and stopped her, kissing the top of her head. "Be careful."

She nodded and headed out for the creature's den.

"She'll be fine," Wade said, watching her go. His voice held zero conviction. "Just so you know, I'm waiting in the wings for you to screw up with her. She's special, and I won't let a second chance slide by."

Greyson crossed his arms over a jealous surge. "Why tell me?"

"Because I'm not trying to undermine you or sabotage you. She was forthright with me about the two of you getting together, so I'm returning the honesty. I'm not going to interfere or anything. I wasn't ready for a relationship before, and I'm still not. But that doesn't mean I can't see what I missed out on. Keep her happy, or I'll pick up the pieces, that's all."

"Hmph." Greyson bit back numerous sarcastic and rude comments.

He'd never had a declared rival for any of his girlfriends before, and he wasn't sure what to do. Wade would have to be watched now to ensure he didn't try subverting their relationship. Even a little harmless flirting could get out of hand. He knew from personal experience.

\*\*\*\*

Flick's heart thundered, filling Kyrael's senses. Through his connection to her body, he caught all the signs of her anxiety, like the sweat on her hands, her increased breathing rate, and the pressure she put on Jake's wrist.

"*Let go of your friend,*" Kyrael advised. "*You might be hurting him. You're squeezing a little too hard.*"

She dropped her hold on Jake, but none of the other symptoms abated. The school was still overrun with small remalas, feeding on the despair and heartbreak of the students and staff. The sight disgusted Kyrael, but like yesterday, he could do nothing. The only way to alleviate the problem was to destroy the contracted remala. Then they could purge the school. A purge would benefit everyone because with the hordes of small remalas gone, the energy surrounding those in the building would clear, and their paths to healing would open.

A macabre assortment of remalas still clung to the doorway around Ostanes' room. Flick wouldn't understand their presence, but Kyrael did. When he'd first seen them, he'd assumed they weren't entering because the teacher acted so happy compared to many of the humans in the building. The remalas were put off by the positive energy, which was their polar opposite and would neutralize them the way an acid neutralized a base.

Knowing Ostanes' true identity changed everything. Those remalas avoided getting too close to a true predator as reef fish shied away from passing sharks. Should they enter his haven, they would face his displeasure or, worse, become a snack.

Flick stuck her head inside the classroom. Ostanes sat at his desk, red pen held over papers. One deep breath, and she spoke, breaking his silence.

"Good morning, Mr. Ostanes."

He looked up from his paper and smiled. Kyrael shuddered. How had the remala perfected its disguise to such a degree? If it weren't for the contamination he put off, Kyrael would have no idea who or, rather, what Ostanes was. Also frightening was this creature's ability to suppress an aura of this magnitude. Adriel and Kyrael had both been in the building unhidden, and neither of them had sensed anything. Moreover, this entity was so sure of its power it hadn't been scared off by their presence.

"Good morning, Ms. Felicity." His eyes crinkled with some unspoken mirth. "Here to surrender for whatever detention you intend on earning today?" He glanced past her. "I see you brought your partner in crime."

Flick's breath caught, and she glanced back at Jake. "Jake and I aren't planning on causing trouble. He's my best friend and support." She waved Jake closer inside the room.

Kyrael's heart hammered in time with Flick's. Jake was on his phone, texting. He'd given the signal. In a few minutes, Heaven's warriors would swoop down and take out this monster.

Flick moved closer, pulling over a chair and setting it opposite the teacher's desk from Ostanes, then sat with a sigh. "I'm super confused, and I could use the advice of an adult. The counselors are extra busy right now, so can I ask you?"

Ostanes startled. "Uh, sure."

"Those times you caught Jake and me in the bathroom, he was helping me cope with things going on. But this time, my issue isn't something he can offer advice about."

"Ah." Mr. Ostanes twined his fingers together and rested his chin on them. "I can try."

"I feel conflicted about the shooting. Since I wasn't here and didn't know the victims, I'm not miserable like many students. Then I feel guilty for not feeling bad enough. Does that make sense?"

"Why don't we start the conversation by cutting the bullshit?" Waves of energy rolled off him, shimmering across every surface in the room.

"Wha-what?" Flick stammered.

Kyrael's heart sank. Without feeling those waves, he couldn't tell what the thing was up to, but it couldn't be good. Nor could his interest in Flick. This creature knew something about her.

His smile turned sinister. "I've been curious about you for several weeks now. Then, yesterday, I finally caught you in a lapse. Who is your master, and how is your suppression so flawless?"

"Excuse me?" Flick's confusion was evident.

Kyrael, on the other hand, had to suppress wild laughter so she could focus. How ridiculous. The creature thought she was like him. He must have felt her remala energy connect with his yesterday and misunderstood.

"Your master," he snapped. "You can drop your act. After interviewing the boy yesterday, I'm positive he's part of your ruse. I never imagined taking a human subordinate. How ballsy of you. Then again, perhaps your contract helps. I'll go first. I'm contracted with Astaroth. I'm aware he's not the most powerful master. So is your bravado due to a more powerful being backing you?"

"I don't have a—"

"*Don't stop talking,*" Kyrael ordered. "*Our backup isn't here yet. Keep the conversation going.*"

"—a reason to trust you with such details," Flick said, switching gears.

"I understand being a bit skittish. If you hadn't leaked the remala energy yesterday… well, I was getting concerned. I was sure you could see more than the other students here. And there have been angels about." He shook his head. "It makes far more sense knowing you're contracted. I'm relieved. I didn't want to leave. Astaroth's wishes are nearly complete."

"And those would be?" Flick brazened.

Ostanes shook his head. "I'm not sharing anything else if you're not opening up. I'm not even sure why your master would allow you anywhere near someone else's project anyway."

Kyrael glanced at the clock, worry settling into his stomach. Where was Serai's unit? They ought to have been here by now.

Behind them, Kyrael could hear Jake fidgeting. Unfortunately, this caught Ostanes' attention. His gaze snapped up to Jake.

"Huh, maybe I can get answers from the boy if you won't talk. I'm not willing to risk all my work here." He started to stand.

Panic ripped through Kyrael. The creature was going to try getting Jake to answer. That wasn't going to be pretty at the very best. At worst, he might force Serai out in the open before they were ready.

Flick wrung her hands and watched Ostanes walking toward Jake. Kyrael didn't need to hear her thoughts to know she didn't want to act out of turn and ruin anything.

But Jake was in very real trouble.

"There you are, Flick," Wade said, stepping into the room, Greyson following behind, a dubious expression on his face. "Greyson and I had some questions about the winter sports season. You promised yesterday we could ask you any questions we had." He stopped as if just realizing she was speaking with a teacher. "Oh. I'm sorry. Did I interrupt?"

"With impeccably horrible timing," Ostanes answered. "You boys would do better finding a different school guide. Ms. Felicity is a bad influence. I'm not sure why the office paired you with her for guidance." He nodded at the door for them to exit.

Greyson and Wade exchanged glances with each other and with Flick. Jake looked ready to pee himself. Sweat dripped across Flick's skin, and Kyrael clung to the pieces of their plan. Everything was falling apart. Where in God's name was Serai's unit?

Ostanes caught all this, his expression going dangerous. "That's it," Ostanes snarled. "This stinks worse than angel farts." He waved a hand at the door, and it slammed shut on its own. An orange glow surrounded both the window and doorframe. "Who are you working for?" he hissed at Flick. "Who are they? I've never seen them except in association with you. Present evidence of your master or meet mine."

Kyrael caught Jake's lips forming the silent word, "Okay," a moment before he threw a hand out to hold the others back. Jake's chin tipped up, all fear dissolved from his face, and Serai's voice rang through every word he spoke. "I'm the one guiding the girl at the moment. And you know as well as I do there's no way to meet your master. If he could be here, he wouldn't need you."

Ostanes hissed and shook his head in confusion. "Pieces I can't add together. Who are you?"

"You've sealed the whole building?" Serai demanded through Jake.

Ostanes growled at Jake. "I warded the whole property against the divine last weekend. I've grown tired of surprise visits by angels. If they kept popping in, they were going to notice something. So I ask again, who are you, and who do you serve?"

Jake crooked his fingers at Greyson and Wade, then held a hand, palm out in Flick's direction, ordering Kyrael to stay. The next moment, Serai stepped from Jake's body, head held high and commanding. She'd just been controlling Jake's body, so she had to feel exhausted. Kyrael admired her fortitude if nothing else.

Behind her, Adriel and Niciel stepped from their hosts, glittering in their armor.

"*What the fuck?*" Ostanes bellowed. "You can't possess humans without falling."

Serai raised her sword and leveled the point in his direction. "I assure you, we're not fallen. Submit, and I'll send you home swiftly and painlessly."

Crackling orange power swelled on Ostanes' hand. He threw this at Serai, but she knocked it away with her wing. Instead, the ball hit the window, and the glass melted, oozing down the orange barrier. Where the molten glass hit the wood frame, little flames licked up. Niciel flicked a finger at these, and the fire disappeared, black, charred spots left beneath the cooling glass.

"I'll take that to mean you're not making this easy for anyone," Serai said. Without lowering her sword, she directed Adriel and Niciel around Ostanes.

Ostanes flexed his right arm, and orange power shot

off like a shock wave when he extended it. It hit the classroom walls and disintegrated them in a shower of concrete dust.

"Niciel, shield," Serai commanded.

"*Give me control,*" Kyrael yelped to Flick. He had Flick's body under his power the next second, and he threw her at her friends, knocking them to the ground. "Down," he ordered.

A wave of angelic power ripped from Niciel, washing over them so hot Kyrael winced as Flick's scalp burned. But it was better than it could have been since Kyrael had gotten them all below the primary wave. The heat would dissipate as the power spread and insulated the school and its inhabitants from whatever the angels and the remala continued to throw around.

Unfortunately, it didn't help the students and staff outside the room when Ostanes exploded the walls. Bodies lay shredded, bleeding, and motionless in the areas. Kyrael used his power to calm the wave of nausea that threatened to bring up Flick's breakfast. Tears burned her eyes, and Kyrael blinked them back. He had to keep the four humans safe.

****

Greyson groaned and pulled himself out from under Flick. She'd moved so swiftly and accurately that Kyrael had to be in control, but thanks to the pair, Niciel's searing blast of power hadn't done any real damage to him. He glanced at the others, and they seemed fine as well.

"Where did they go?" he asked Flick.

But he didn't need her point to know. Following her gaze led him in the right direction. Ostanes had gone into the hall, trying to get away. Niciel, Adriel, and Serai moved like lightning, blocking his escape attempts and dodging the attacks he fired off. But somehow, the creature moved in a blur, keeping them all from gaining ground.

Serai's sword swung so fast Greyson couldn't follow where it started and where it missed in the silver streak. Ostanes ducked and shot off blast after blast. Niciel's shield caught and disbursed these in electrical pulses, which gave the shield walls the effect of an active thunderstorm. But outside his shield, the school didn't sustain any further damage.

Ostanes jumped to avoid Serai's next swing. At the same time, Adriel swept his scythe through, cutting off Ostanes' arm. Instead of blood, the hole sucked inward, drawing cowering small remala into the void. Their energy bubbled with his like watching wax melt in boiling water. Seconds later, a new arm swung a punch at Niciel on his way past.

Niciel caught the blow with his hand, using Ostanes' momentum to slam the creature to the ground. Ostanes let his body shatter, pieces skittering across the broken floor like a bloom of spiders. These crawled up the walls and ceiling, dropping onto the angels.

Flick gripped Greyson's arm, Kyrael speaking through her. "We can't let this go on. If he can break apart like that, all he has to do is get Niciel to drop the shield, and he's free to run in so many directions we'll never catch him."

Greyson nodded. "Got a plan?"

The shield across the ceiling bowed under someone's power, destroying the whole expanse, then repairing it as the shield righted itself.

Flick and Greyson paused to watch this, then Kyrael

said, with Flick's voice, "I have a plan. We need to keep him from moving so the others can land a fatal blow. I can use my electric weapon like a fence, but not with only Flick to run the current through. If the four of you link together, I can run the current through you all."

"You'd make us an electric cage?" Greyson mouthed, pausing mid-sentence to watch Serai swing her sword with one hand and douse a fire in a pile of rubble with the other.

"Can the four of you get around him?"

Ostanes dodged a kick from Adriel so quickly he almost seemed to teleport.

"I doubt it, but we'll try. I'll tell Wade. You tell Jake." Greyson leaned to whisper in Wade's ear. Wade didn't react until the very end.

"Kyrael wants us to contain that?" He pointed to Ostanes.

The creature had extended his arms without detaching them, and they wove around, pulling like gruesome putty, trying to keep the angels too far away to land a blow. Each time Adriel or Serai landed a blow, new remala were sucked in to repair the gap.

"There was a reason a whole unit of angels was supposed to take him on," Wade pointed out.

"And Mr. Ostanes' ward kept them out. I'm sure these guys only got in because we shielded them from the warding," Greyson countered. "We're all the help they've got."

Wade nodded. "We're never going to get the chance to explain to the other three, and they're keeping Ostanes as far from us as they can. I think we ought to try skirting the wall like we're aiming to get away. When Ostanes tries to run, we can dash out while all their attention is diverted. We can head him off and close around him if we time it right. The angels ought to be able to figure it out from there."

"Anticipating where he's going is a big unknown," Greyson said. "And if we draw his attention, we'll make their job way harder because he's likely to remember he can hurt us to hurt them."

"Got a better idea?" Wade sighed. "Look, while you were talking to Kyrael, I was watching, using the hunting Niciel and I have done as reference. His movements have a pattern to them. The angels have caught this, too, which is how they're keeping pace with him. But there's not enough of them to get ahead."

"Explain," Greyson said.

"Each time Ostanes tries to make a break for it, he shoots off some of his orange power. But he can't do it repeatedly. See how he has to spend time blocking in between?"

"Yeah."

"So. His orange power takes one angel to clean up and makes the other two dodge. They anticipate where he's going when he tries to run, but they can't dodge, beat him there, and attack all at once. So if we follow them to his destination, we might be able to close in around him. He won't be watching out for us. We just have to put ourselves in a place where his escape attempts will come close enough for us to utilize."

"Aren't you the strategist?" Greyson quipped. "Nice work." He waved the other two closer and outlined Wade's plan. When he finished, he added, "There's a partial wall to the left of where they've been fighting. Make it look like we're hiding there. The wall ought to carry Niciel's shield, so maybe the angels won't work so hard to keep him away from us if they think we've got the shield, plus Kyrael."

The others agreed, and they started their trek across the battlefield to the partially collapsed wall. Greyson had seen the initial carnage after the classroom exploded, but crawling through it turned his stomach inside out. They slipped through blood and concrete dust, which created a paste that coated his hands and knees. Most of the people who had been in the way lay still and silent. Even if they could have been saved, this extermination was taking too long. They weren't going to live until help came.

Others made Greyson sick. They groaned for help, gory injuries paining their voices. But if Greyson wanted any shot at assisting them, he had to help the angels defeat the contracted remala first.

They reached the wall after what seemed like an eternity of crawling through Hell. Greyson leaned back against the grated concrete, heaving for breath and sanity. He'd never imagined facing anything like this when he'd agreed to this job. They were in a real battle, one between Heaven and Hell, where human ideals of fair play didn't exist.

Wade peeked from around one side of the broken wall, holding tight to Jake's hand, ready to dash as soon as the fighting came close enough. Greyson took Flick's hand, and the two of them peeped out.

"How are you holding up?" he whispered.

"Flick's given me complete control until we contain the creature," Kyrael answered. "She's both disturbed and determined to end this before Ostanes destroys her whole school and the people she cares for."

Greyson focused on the fight, waiting for it to

wander back in their direction. Flick was a tough girl, not needing Kyrael to hold her together. Admiration swelled in his chest. He'd gotten with an incredible partner in more ways than one.

Ostanes threw another round of orange power at the wall. This time, it bounced off, shattering into a dozen smaller balls. They zipped about before exploding, so the shocks covered the entire area hemmed in by Niciel's shield.

The creature hurdled toward a doorway closer to Wade's side of the broken wall.

"Now," Wade shouted.

With Kyrael moving her, Flick ran impossibly fast, hauling Greyson along so his arm screamed in protest. She swung him around, and he whipped his other arm out just in time to grab ahold of Jake.

Raw positive energy rammed through his body, and the surrounding air electrified. Ostanes roared his frustration, caught in the middle of Kyrael's electric dome. Greyson's hands ached where he tried to hold onto Flick and Jake. But if he didn't hold, the dome would get a hole, and the stalemate would start again.

Without missing a microsecond, Adriel swung his scythe, aimed for Ostanes' neck. Greyson couldn't help the grin which spread on his face. They were finally done.

Then everything went wrong, and Greyson watched in horrified slow motion as Adriel's scythe ricocheted off a burst of evil energy Ostanes launched. The force of the swing kept the blade moving in a new direction—straight for Flick.

Serai dove between Flick and the scythe. The blade skimmed her wings, incinerating all the feathers on its way past. The two women landed in a heap, with Serai on top, still protecting Flick.

Ostanes used the distraction to bolt straight for the exit. But Adriel let out a scream of rage that caused even Niciel's shield to pucker. Faster than Greyson's eye could track, the angel streaked after Ostanes, burying his scythe in the creature's back. A millisecond later, Niciel severed Ostanes' head. Rather than bursting and disappearing like the smaller remalas, Ostanes exploded, spattering everything in a twenty-foot radius with a sickly green gore.

The stench of rotten flesh and decaying slime hit Greyson's nose a mere moment before searing pain. He glanced down and lost his breakfast, vomiting on the floor in front of him. Every spot Ostanes' sludge had touched already rotted. Gangrenous wounds opened on his body before his eyes, weeping thick yellow pus and foaming. The smell intensified, and his vision swam, his brain desperately clinging to control despite the overwhelming screams of his nerves. Beside him, Jake writhed on the floor in agony. Wade propped himself up on the wall, bone showing through rotten flesh all over his body.

Adriel grabbed Greyson just as black oblivion started to take him. Then relief washed over him. The contrast was so sharp it drove tears of sweet release from his eyes. His vision brightened, though still blurred. After another minute in the angel's arms, Greyson could finally stand himself back up.

He searched for the others. Niciel healed Wade, who looked normal again. Jake panted with his head between his knees, Kyrael's hand on his back. The saddest pair was Flick and Serai. Flick appeared fine, though dazed.

But Serai's wings were raw and naked, like chicken wings in the grocery store.

"Are you good?" Adriel murmured to Greyson.

"Much better. Thank you."

Adriel gave a short nod and rose, striding across to where Serai stood beside Flick. He grabbed the front of Serai's tunic at the neck and jerked her forward in one swift motion. His lips connected with hers, and their chests ran into each other. The moment their bodies touched, a blinding light took root at the spot, growing in size and intensity until Greyson had to use his hands to shield his eyes. A second later, a silent explosion rocked the building, and the light went out.

Greyson's mouth fell open, raw shock numbing his body. What the hell had happened? By the time the spots cleared from his eyes, Adriel and Serai stood glaring at one another like usual.

Kyrael had moved to put his hand over Flick's eyes. She swatted him away. "What are you doing? What was that?"

Niciel made a choking noise, then spoke, his voice stunned. "*That* was the equivalent of an angelic orgasm."

"*What?*" Greyson shrieked at the same time as Wade, Jake, and Flick.

"You could see Adriel and Serai?" Flick asked Jake.

"No. I mean, yes. The light flash I saw. I thought those two fought like cats and dogs?"

"They do." Niciel's voice still hadn't lost the stunned tone.

Flick repeated what Jake couldn't hear.

Adriel shrugged, nonchalant. "She saved Flick from dying by my blade. I would never have forgiven myself if I hurt Flick. Therefore, she saved me as well."

"Don't get used to it," Serai snapped, tipping her nose up. "The…the thing that just happened…don't get used to *that*. But you'd better get used to me saving your butt. If you're going to keep hunting contracted remalas, I'm going to be forced into saving you again, I'm sure."

He shot her a smoldering sideways glare. "I look forward to proving you wrong."

Wade cleared his throat. "Um, if you've had your moment, perhaps you could drop the shield and get help for those who were injured?"

Niciel snapped his fingers, and all traces of his barrier disappeared. Far off, sirens wailed.

"Are you going to fix my school?" Flick asked, pleading in her voice.

Adriel shook his head. "I'm sorry. Since there are fatalities, leaving them in a pristine hallway would cause confusion. Not to mention how many people would see the building miraculously repairing itself."

"But people used to see miracles long ago, right? Why not now?" she begged.

Adriel put a hand on Greyson's shoulder. "We should go. You don't belong here, and I don't want to cover up your presence when the inevitable investigation ensues." To Flick, he added, "Faith and proof are a different beast than they were in the era you are talking about. It isn't time for humanity at large to have proof of Heaven. I'll see you at your apartment when you get home."

## Chapter 22

Flick watched Adriel and Greyson vanish with a growing knot in her stomach. Niciel and Wade followed a moment later after giving her an encouraging wave. Despite having Jake, Kyrael, and Serai, deep loneliness chilled Flick.

Serai crossed her arms and surveyed the damage. "Given what we were up against, the collateral damage was minimal. Take what solace you can."

"What am I supposed to tell the rescuers?" Flick asked.

"All evidence is going to point to a gas line exploding. Tell them about whatever explosion you wish. They'll believe you."

"Speaking of explosions. Did you and Adriel really just have sex?" Flick blushed at her boldness to even ask, but her curiosity was killing her.

"It's not sex as humans define the act, but a fusing of our energy. On occasion, angelic passions warrant such a connection. The shock wave you're referring to is similar to nuclear fusion but without the harmful fallout." Her eyes narrowed, and she glared at Flick. "This is the last time you're ever to speak of *that* event. Adriel is—" She sucked in a quivering breath, and her nostrils flared.

"Understood," Flick agreed. Personally, she thought both Serai and Adriel wanted to do *that* a good deal more. They had such warped passion between them. What would it take to drive them together again? And why did they insist on torturing themselves and each other?

"I'm going to meet with my unit on the playing field and fill them in. Afterward, we'll do a deep purge of the grounds. As of tonight, the school property will be sanctified, and the blessing will last for years. You and your friends can attend in safety."

"Thank you. For everything, thank you so very much." Flick scrambled off the floor and hugged her savior. "I owe you my life, and I'll never forget. I promise to put my life to good use. I'll keep hunting, and maybe I'll have the pleasure of working with you again."

Serai plucked Flick off, a deep red blush gracing her cheeks. Despite her naked wings, Flick thought her more lovely at that moment than she'd ever seen her.

Serai twisted the end of her braid around her finger. "I guess I wouldn't mind working with you again. It seems Heaven isn't the only plane to host female warriors." She ducked her head as if all the emotional stuff weighed too much. "Later, human girl."

She vanished, and Jake stepped in beside Flick. "Want to fill me in?"

Flick told him everything he couldn't hear from Serai. By the time she finished, rescuers in their heavy gear and medics with bulky bags picked their way around the rubble toward them. Flick looked Jake over. His clothes were in tatters, and his body and face were smudged with oily black residue. His hair had been scorched in more than one spot. He looked like a survivor. Flick assumed she cut just as pathetic a figure.

Strong hands belonging to a medic checked her out.

At the same time, he peppered her with questions. The blur of healing had begun.

****

The extermination of the contracted remala happened on Thursday. Friday evening, Adriel paced Greyson's living room. Serai had promised to fill him in on the clean-up of the remala's work, but they still hadn't heard anything.

Greyson and Flick were in Greyson's bed, sound asleep. While the angels had fixed their physical wounds, their energy was depleted between the stress, the fight, and the damage Astaroth's ooze caused. They felt it as exhaustion, but Adriel knew their spirits were healing themselves.

He'd popped in to check on Jake but ended up leaving a note. The boy hadn't been altered in any way by hosting Serai. He'd be no more appealing to remalas than any other human. A human would have to contain remala energy to react with an angel's power.

The air behind him warmed with Serai's energy, and Adriel shivered. He wanted to bury himself in her energy and harmonize with it again. She was so maddeningly appealing. But even Gabriel couldn't order him to admit that out loud, so he paused for effect before turning to face her, keeping his expression cool.

"Took you long enough," he goaded.

She rolled her eyes and crossed her arms, knuckles white where she gripped her upper arms. "I have better things to do than play messenger to you. Be grateful I came in person. Use the moment to drink in my awesomeness because if I have my way, Gabriel will assign anyone else's unit to clean up your little team's messes. So it might be a while before you see me again."

"Hmph. I knew you couldn't handle what my team does." He tucked both hands behind his back, letting his body take on a cocky tilt. It would drive her up the wall. "It's okay to admit you need a century or two to recuperate before facing another contracted remala. But have no fear. My team will take out so many of the ripe remalas you'll be out of a job. The rest you need is coming right your way."

"Do you want to know the results of my unit's work or not?" she snapped. "Talk about resting on your laurels. You and your team packed up and left my unit to clean everything up. Do you realize that damned remala had infiltrated a local airline manufacturer? He'd screwed with all their planes, setting rot on internal components and all on a subtle time delay. In the next two years, those planes would have started dropping from the sky, one by one. Not one of the planes had the same rotten component nor the same schedule, so those humans could double-check all they wanted and still be hard-pressed to stop the carnage."

Adriel's stomach twisted. "I'm glad you stopped the disaster," he murmured.

"Yes, well," she sputtered. "It's my job, after all."

Adriel turned one honest and heated stare on her. "Until next time, then?"

"Right. Next time." She vanished, but not before he swore he saw his hunger returned in her gaze.

Before he had a chance to ponder this, Abrasael appeared in the living room, dropping to one knee and putting his hand on the floor in a bow. "Adriel the Executioner, Gabriel will be paying you a visit."

"When—"

On the last syllable of the word, Greyson's living

room filled with white light like a nuclear flash. This faded, and Gabriel stood in front of Adriel. The seraph shone too brightly on Earth to look at, even for another angel.

Adriel turned his face and bowed, greeting the exalted angel. "How can I serve you?"

"I believe congratulations are in order."

Adriel stayed in his bow. "It is my pleasure to serve God and Heaven. I ask for nothing more."

Gabriel chuckled. "I hear you got a little reward of your own, regardless. If I were a betting man, you and Serai are not a wager I ever would have risked. Would you like to work with her again in the future?"

"Will our duties cross paths in the future?" Adriel answered the question with a question to avoid the embarrassment of the truth.

He already wanted to shrivel up into an angel raisin. If Gabriel knew about him and Serai, the whole of Heaven knew. It could be eons before anyone else did something wild enough to divert attention away from them. Pairings between angels were a rarity on their own. Even a hint of a pairing between him and Serai… He'd dug himself a whole new notorious reputation.

"Your team caught a contracted remala. You stopped the demon's plans before they played out, and you exterminated the remala without the aid of an angelic warrior unit. That alone is impressive enough. But you went further and minimized human casualties. Only five perished. The others are being treated in human hospitals and are alive. God and Heaven are in complete agreement. Your team may become a permanent fixture with Heaven if they'd like."

Though his face was shrouded in his glory and

invisible to Adriel, he could hear the smile in Gabriel's voice. "As a reward for their service to Heaven, whenever your human partners decide to leave the team and live a normal life, they'll be assigned a guardian angel to accompany them until they pass. When you present the offer, assure them they never have to worry about remalas encroaching on their lives again."

Adriel dropped to his knees, touching his forehead to the floor in a grateful bow. "You're most generous. They'll be thrilled. Would you like me to wake them so you can tell them yourself?"

"No. They've been through enough. A meeting with a seraph can alter a human. We'll save the shock for another time when it's all they have to deal with."

"What about others? I'm sure with Raziel's blood results, you realize there must be others." Adriel raised his head off the floor, still averting his gaze from the light.

"Those who have entered adolescence or grown up with this ability will be assessed, and more teams like yours may be formed." Gabriel's following words carried enigma the way Mona Lisa smiled. "There's now an additional factor I can't account for." He turned to face the closed bedroom door. "A remala attack contaminated their blood in the womb. But for two decades, their bodies have been coping, blending that negative energy into the fabric of their DNA. When they produce a babe, a whole new factor enters the game."

"*When*?" Adriel yelped, spinning to face Gabriel despite the light. "What do you mean by when?" he called to the spot where Gabriel's glory lingered. But the seraph was gone.

## A word about the author...

Nikki Frank lives in the Pacific Northwest where she graduated from Western Washington University after studying English, Journalism, and Communications. Thanks to an insatiable appetite for tales filled with adventure, fantasy, and romance, Nikki crafts stories to satisfy those cravings, aiming for fast-paced stories that will transport the reader outside reality for a time. When she's not writing or reading, she enjoys working in her garden and exploring the globe with her husband and two children.

https://nikkifrankauthor.weebly.com/